NIGHT OF
THE SEVENTH
DARKNESS

By the same author

The Last Assassin
The Seventh Sanctuary
The Ninth Buddha
Brotherhood of the Tomb

NIGHT OF THE SEVENTH DARKNESS

Daniel Easterman

BCA

LONDON · NEW YORK · SYDNEY · TORONTO

This edition published 1991
by BCA by arrangement
with GraftonBooks

CN 9139

Printed and bound in Germany
by Mohndruck, Gütersloh

For Betty – who else?

ACKNOWLEDGEMENTS

So many people helped at different stages of this book, I hardly know where to begin. My agent, Jeffrey Simmons, and my editors in London and New York, Patricia Parkin and Ed Breslin, read, commented on, and discussed the manuscript at length – I cannot say how much their criticisms helped change the finished version for the better. Their first line of defence, my wife Beth, acted as critic-in-residence: a hard job, and worth three years of P. G. Wodehouse stories at bedtime.

I could not have done without Claudia Caruana's intelligent, informed and unstinting assistance with the research for New York. To Eddie Bell of Harper & Row, a million thanks for fixing up our trip to New York and helping it go so smoothly. Warm thanks too to Sergeant Raymond O'Donnell of the New York Police Department; Phil Petrie, Associate Director of Public Affairs, Kings County Hospital, Brooklyn; Jonathan Arden, MD, Deputy Chief Medical Examiner at Kings County; Mr Barrone of Barrone Funeral Homes, Brooklyn; and, most of all, to Richie Horowitz, our intrepid, entertaining and knowledgeable driver, who guided us through the best and worst of Brooklyn.

In England, thanks to Ian and Margaret Tarbit for their ideas on AIDS testing and post-mortems; Roderick Richards of Tracking Line; Elizabeth Murray; Tim Levitt for his naval knowledge; Fred and Christine Hardy for sharing their experiences of diving in the Caribbean.

A word of thanks also to all those whose publications I plundered for information about Haiti, above all Wade Davis, whose two intelligent and lively studies of the *zombi* are models of research and exposition.

PART ONE

The Circle Incomplete

Brooklyn

'Twinkle, twinkle little star,
How I wonder what you are . . .'

CHAPTER ONE

Fort Greene, Brooklyn
Friday, 18 September 199–
Late afternoon

The apartment smelled fusty. Angelina wrinkled her nose as she stepped into the hallway. Fusty. Or maybe something else. They'd only been away three months, and most of that time Filius had been there, Filius and maybe some friends of his. A girl maybe. Filius had said he didn't have a woman, but she found that hard to believe. He was good-looking, street-wise, and from the looks she sometimes found him giving her, Angelina didn't think he was gay.

'Home,' intoned Richard as he came in behind her, putting down two suitcases. The word was flat, almost meaningless: a narrow word in a narrow doorway. Angelina stood stock-still, letting it sink in. They were home, whatever that meant. Their next trip abroad wouldn't be for . . . how long? No telling. But what was that smell?

'You smell anything?' she asked, not turning round. Richard put his hands on her shoulders, pressing down a little. She disliked the pressure, the feel of his hands, hard, proprietorial.

'No.' He bent his face to her neck and sniffed. 'New perfume,' he whispered. 'Am I right?'

She'd bought the bottle of Fendi in Geneva on the flight back from Kinshasa. In the cab coming in from JFK, she'd applied a few dabs to strategic places, a little surreptitiously. For the three months they'd been in Zaïre she had studiously avoided perfumes. The heat turned them rancid on her skin. Or perhaps it had been her skin itself that made them grow sour.

'I don't mean that,' she said. Now she turned to face him. 'Don't

13

you notice anything else? Kind of fusty. Or is it "musty"? As though nobody had been here.' She shrugged. 'Maybe it's just the effect of being away. I'm not used to how our own apartment smells.'

Or maybe it was Africa, she thought. She never noticed smells so powerfully in Brooklyn. Flowers, fruit, people, the sweet smells of decay, the jungle bearing down, cloying and dangerous.

He sniffed the air again and looked at her, a sideways glance.

'It's your imagination. The apartment doesn't smell. Give it a day or two, you'll feel better. Get Africa out of your system.'

He carried the rest of the baggage into the hallway.

'Can you make some coffee, Angelina? I'm dead beat.'

Angelina made two cups of instant while Rick hauled suitcases to the bedroom and started unpacking. She found a jar of cookies that she had bought at Abraham & Straus on Fulton a week before leaving. They were still fit to-eat, so she put a few on a plate. Rick joined her in the kitchen. He did look tired, she thought. And not just physically.

The field trip had been a failure. Most of the time they'd been in Kisangani, then there had been the wasted weeks at Lokutu. Rick was fast turning into the sort of ethnologist who prefers working out of an air-conditioned office to sharing a tent with snakes and bugs. And he was turning her from his wife and assistant into his secretary and general dogsbody.

They drank without conversation, adjusting to the thoughts and sensations of return. School started in less than a week. The powers-that-be had decided to go back to a late fall start in order to pick up delayed registrations.

Rick had been on Long Island University's faculty for twenty years now, but he was still something of an outsider. Those of his colleagues who still lived in Fort Greene had apartments in the Towers building or the Hospital high-rise over on Willoughby; the rest had long ago moved out to Brooklyn Heights or Cobble Hill. But the Hammels stayed on in a decaying brownstone on Clermont Avenue, between Myrtle and Atlantic, stranded by a tide of upward mobility.

They had moved in ten years earlier. At first Rick had hoped that the brownstone revival would move in their direction. They had spent a lot of money on the property, then waited for things to change. They were still waiting. The paint on their door was peeling, their steps were blocked with garbage, and outside on the street young Haitian men and Puerto Rican girls with sad eyes dreamed of a sunshine only their parents remembered. And the girls wheeled babies in cheap buggies, and the babies kept their eyes shut in all seasons. In an unused nursery at the back of the apartment, white bunny rabbits hopped like ghosts across fields of dappled green.

Autumn was fumbling at the edges of the city. Crossing the river from Manhattan, it crept, unannounced and uninvited, past the old Navy Yard, all the way to Coney Island and the sea. Angelina looked out of the kitchen window onto a grey brick wall opposite. Brooklyn was a madness she had tried to escape, only to be dragged back, again and again, her hair in disarray, her eyes shining, softly wild, her mouth wide open in song or protest. What did Rick care?

She felt sure that summer would never come again, that, this year, winter's onset would be not simply inexorable, but permanent. She shivered and sipped her coffee and looked through unwashed glass at the fading autumn light.

After coffee, they finished unpacking, returning to the cheap dealboard closet clothes they never wore in New York, clothes they might never wear again. Angelina fingered them as she folded them away: light cotton frocks, a striped bikini, slacks she had taken for trips up country. She remembered the visit to Switzerland after her mother died, the distaste with which she had packed old clothes for charity. How suddenly the living became the dead, how death rubbed itself over their garments and their bedclothes, how it pervaded furniture and books. She lifted a pair of Rick's trousers. They felt to her touch like something a dead man had worn, second-hand, tainted. Quietly, she put them away on a wooden hanger, in a corner of the wardrobe, out of reach.

Rick was eager to make love. Here, in Brooklyn, he had come alive at once. That was why they stayed, why this apartment had become a chain for her. Brooklyn gave him life, as much as it took it from her. He took her to bed, urgent, roused, more vivid than she had known him at any time in Africa. She let him undress her, let him make his fumbling tour of her body, as though to reassure himself that she was still undamaged. Again the heavy touch of a proprietor.

Quietening him with a kiss, easing him with her lips but not her tongue, she masturbated him, slowly, without feeling, without remorse, with long-practised skill. And he came quickly, thoughtlessly, messing the sheets, Filius's sheets that she had forgotten to change.

He fell asleep almost straight away, naked, middle-aged, his thick back turned to her. She looked down at him with something of revulsion. He had become an unlovely thing in her eyes: his paunch, his flaccid, weeping penis, sunburned skin. On his square, heavy-browed head, the red hair was turning yellow. His lips were flushed, his cheeks stippled with blood. What did she love in him? Had she ever found anything to love in him at all? Truly?

She sat bolt upright, eyes fixed on the wall opposite, letting the room return in fragments to her consciousness as night came slowly into Brooklyn, autumnal, thick, heavy with misery. In Africa, the suddenness of night had always surprised and frightened her, the abrupt descent of the flecked sun, the instant presence of night in everything. But here the world spun less quickly, the earth crawled from light to darkness, there was time to put on armour against its coming.

She looked at herself in the mirror on the wall, the pale mulatto face, the frightened eyes, the heavy brows she had plucked as a girl. Letting the sheet fall from her breasts, she watched them in reflection, soft, becoming pendulous with age. Was forty-two old? Her hair still fell darkly on narrow shoulders, her waist had not yet thickened, she shaved her legs every second day religiously, and wore perfume at home. Why? she wondered. Did it make any difference? Had it ever made a difference?

Night came, and still she sat and listened as the city padded beyond her window, vast and predatory. Beside her, her husband's breath rasped, tearing at her ears. On a silent clock, green seconds flickered against the dark. She was in New York, not Africa. But outside another jungle sharpened its teeth beneath the same indifferent moon.

At eleven o'clock she got out of bed to fix something to eat. Rick was fast asleep. In the kitchen, she stumbled about in semi-darkness, her robe pulled tight against the chill air, opening and closing cupboards, rummaging through the freezer. She was reminded of midnigh raids as a child, the thrill of food eaten late, the taste of cold chicken. At least Filius had stocked the freezer as asked. Angelina had left him one hundred dollars for that purpose before leaving. If anything, he had overdone it. He must have made several trips to the Finast on Myrtle, where she knew he did all his shopping. The bottom drawers of the freezer were packed solid with heavy joints of meat.

She found a TV dinner higher up and slipped it into the microwave. In Africa, they had had a boy. He had cooked and cleaned and fetched for them, all for a pittance. To him she had been white, a white man's woman, as foreign as Rick. She had already forgotten his name. The alarm buzzed and she took the tinfoil tray from the oven, miraculously hot.

In the living room, she threw herself into a chair. Spooning rice and chicken into her mouth, she ate without savour. What was food these days anyway? The houseplants had not survived the summer. She had not expected them to, with or without Filius. They never did.

The smell again. Still fusty or musty, whatever. Fainter now, or more familiar perhaps. Not quite sweet, not quite sour, all around, yet nowhere in particular. For some reason she could not identify, it made her uneasy, as though, somewhere in her mind, she recognized it. A memory? An anticipation?

She swallowed the last spoonful of reconstituted chicken. Thank you, her stomach said, I really need junk food at my time of life. Back in the kitchen, she found a tub of butter pecan ice cream and a spoon.

Ice cream in hand, she went back to the living room and switched on the television. From channel to channel, she flicked without interest. Late-night talk shows, recycled situation comedies, rock videos, movies that had been old movies the day they were released. Canned laughter, canned applause, canned emotions. She switched off again.

Filius had promised to tape some films while they were away. In the rack were about a dozen, all clearly labelled in red marker in Filius's cramped Haitian hand. Channel 13 had screened a series of modern French movies over the summer. She scanned the labels: Zidi's *Les Ripoux* – he'd known she wanted that; Tavernier's *Coup de Torchon*, set in Africa – that could wait; *Diva*; *Subway*; *Betty Blue*. Yes, *Betty Blue* would be perfect.

She slipped the cassette into the machine and switched on. Images filled the screen. Béatrice Dalle and Jean-Hugues Anglade making love. Angelina relaxed. She snuggled down into her seat, deep into cushions, deep into the dark, anarchic world of Betty and Zorg. She knew how it would end, in madness and a quick death kicking against a lover's pity, but before that there was hope of a certain kind. The strains of travel washed away, Africa washed away, Rick and his sweat-streaked, porpoise-like body washed away. Sighing, she spooned cold ice cream into her mouth.

Abruptly, the film flickered and went grainy. A row of frames jumped, then the picture snowed up. Angelina leaned forward angrily. She had forgotten to tell Filius about the fault, forgotten to tell him to take the machine over to the electric shop on Fulton to have it repaired.

About two weeks before their departure, the VCR had started acting up. While recording, for as much as ten minutes at a time, it would slip out of 'record' into 'play', leaving gaps in the middle of tapes − stretches of flickering snow in the new ones, existing recordings in the old. Layers beneath layers, stripped away.

As she reached for the remote control, the snow on the screen began to clear. Slowly, the picture grew distinct again. It was not *Betty Blue*. That was curious. Angelina remembered that she had left blank tapes for Filius to use. He must have recorded something else on this one before taping *Betty Blue* on top of it.

There was no sound, just the faint hissing of the tape. The quality was poor, the lighting perfunctory. Huge shadows contrasted sharply with patches of brightness, hard and finely etched, like an exercise in Expressionism. Across the tiny screen, dark figures moved as though in slow motion, like turtles swimming in a green sea, like heavy fish in dim, stagnant waters, behind the glass of an aquarium, indifferent to the hand-held camera. No sound. The picture unsteady, darkness edged with light, light edged with darkness, grotesque figures moving, hesitating, still as stone.

Angelina watched transfixed. Her eyes would not leave the screen. In a long row, stretched through a half-circle, men and women sat upright in tall chairs. Out of grey shadows they seemed to watch her. Light crossed their faces, wavered, leached away again, but they did not move. Like statues, they sat absolutely still, their faces devoid of expression, drained of colour or animation. Some were black, some white, yet something in their unmoving faces transcended race. Something Angelina did not like.

Into the centre of the semicircle stepped a solitary figure, a man, naked to the waist, his dark skin glistening in the uncertain light. To his left, flames grew and shrank in a chafing dish set on a rough iron tripod. On his skin, sweat stood out like seed pearls, fine and translucent. Light fell on a shadow's edge. The man turned slowly to face the camera. It was Filius.

And not Filius. Angelina felt fine hairs like needles of ice rise against her neck. The familiar face was contorted and alien. Filius's lips were drawn back in a tight grimace, his nostrils flared, his eyes were wide and staring, red, possessed. She had seen such eyes before, in the faces of men and women ridden by the *loa*, at the height of *vodoun* ceremonies, their bodies suddenly empty, as suddenly possessed by gods.

Filius and not Filius. Man and not man. The figure turned and turned in a tight circle, dancing in silence, as though moving to music in his own head. He held an earthenware bowl hard against his chest. The light caught the surface of whatever it held, twinkling like a star every time he turned.

There was a crackling sound. The picture jumped and grew still again. The crackling faded and was replaced by duller sounds, each at first indistinguishable from the rest. Gradually, the sounds became clearer. Filius's breathing, harsh and uneven as he danced, a slow drumbeat like the pounding of a heart, unlike any *vodoun* drumbeat she had ever heard, an unknown voice speaking from the shadows. The words were indistinct at first, then with a terrible clarity they came to her, a Creole prayer for the dead that she had last heard in Port-au-Prince many years ago:

> *Prié pou' tou les morts*
> *pou' les morts 'bandonné nan gran bois*
> *pou' les morts 'bandonné nan gran dlo*
> *pou' les morts 'bandonné nan gran plaine*
> *pou' les morts tué pa' couteau*
> *pou' les morts tué pa' épée . . .*

> Pray for all the dead
> For the dead abandoned in the great wood
> For the dead abandoned in the great water
> For the dead abandoned in the great plain
> For the dead slain by knives
> For the dead slain by swords . . .

The dancer with the face of Filius stopped. The drum went on, steady, slightly offbeat, insistent. From somewhere there came a sound of sobbing, abruptly cut off. Filius raised the bowl in both hands and turned to face the silent figures watching from their seats. As he stepped towards them, the camera followed him, a pace at a time. Angelina knew somehow that the room on the screen was the room in which she sat.

pou' tou les morts, au nom de Mait' Cafou et de Legba;
pou' tou generation paternelle et maternelle . . .

For all the dead, in the name of Maître Carrefour and Legba;
For all the generations, paternal and maternal . . .

Filius dipped his hand into the bowl and drew it out again, stretching his fingers towards the first of the seated figures. His hand was red and wet with blood. Lightly, he traced the sign of the cross on the man's forehead. The figure did not move.

. . . ancêtre et ancetère, Afrique et Afrique;
au nom de Mait' Cafou, Legba, Baltaza, Miroi . . .

. . . ancestor and ancestress, African and African;
in the name of Maître Carrefour, Legba, Baltaza, Miroi . . .

None of the figures moved. The light fell more sharply on them now, as Filius moved from head to head, daubing crosses in thick strokes of blood. Angelina stared at the screen, her heart shivering, her bowels cold as snow. The light quivered. It glanced off the dancer's naked back, it lay on the cold, dry skin of the watching figures. No-one moved.

And at last Angelina understood why they did not move, why their eyes did not blink in the harsh light, why they let the blood run unhindered down their cheeks. She saw it clearly now: the formal clothing, the dry, matted hair, the ugly, blotched skin. None of the watching figures was alive.

The camera drew closer, drawn irresistibly to their ashen cheeks. Angelina bent forward aghast. Some must have been in the earth for at least two weeks, others perhaps only hours: the bloom of the mortician's art was still vivid on one woman's cheeks. Like grotesque wax dolls, like paper effigies, they sat immobile to receive the benediction of the cross. A Mass for the dead, with blood instead of wine.

The camera panned back to follow Filius. The drum ceased beating. Priest-like, Filius raised the bowl and poured out all the remaining blood in a thick crimson libation. But Angelina scarcely saw him; her eyes were fixed elsewhere. In one corner of the screen, indistinctly but unmistakably, the second figure from the right began to lift its head.

CHAPTER TWO

Sunday, 27 September

Rick seemed permanently tired. He had never seemed so tired to her before, so lacking in vitality. The vividness he had shown briefly after their return had already dissipated. Africa had sapped him, his work there had left him pale and enervated. The illness at Lokutu had left him without reserves. Or was it something else? Had the old worries come to the surface again? He never told her anything now. With sick familiarity, she watched him pass through the apartment every day, morose, ill-tempered, ill at ease.

He had watched the video with her and sneered it away, derisive and impatient with her fears. A prank, a game, chicken's blood and make-up – nothing to get on edge about. Look at the room, he said, look at the furniture. Nothing had been disturbed, there were no traces of blood.

But he seemed on edge himself. Angelina feared some sort of showdown, not just a tremor, but a convulsion that would tear them irrevocably apart. Like a sailor watching a darkening sky, she shivered, dreading a storm.

Over a week had passed. School had started and the first intimations of fall were everywhere. The leaves were growing yellow, the winds that sliced in off the river were colder every day. Angelina walked through half-empty streets waiting for winter, haunted by images of blood and the awkward, sullen postures of the living dead.

Old memories stirred in her, tales from her nursery in Port-au-Prince, *zombis* and *diabs* and *loups-garous*: the dead walking, impatient of the grave. She shivered in bed at night and told her rosary alone in the small hours like an adolescent waking out of childhood's long, uneasy dream. On the second day, she threw

22

away the meat in the freezer, packet after packet of it, pale meat larded with fat and speckled with frozen blood. Filius had still not shown up.

Rick drove to LIU each day and returned in the evenings frowning and unresponsive. She did not try to caress him; she saw no point: whatever his troubles were, he would not part with them lightly or share them for a kiss. But she knew something was wrong, something unseasonal that filled her mind and spirit with impotent dread.

In the mornings she painted, alone in the room she called her studio, tall, lifeless paintings in muted colours, thin and desolate renderings of images from her past. After lunch, she went for long walks to Fort Greene or Prospect Park; but however far she went, she could not shake off the sense of impending disaster that crept after her, rustling the fallen leaves that lay across her path.

The start of school usually saw Rick straining at the leash, eager for another year of lectures and seminars. He would start with his graduate students and work down to the latest batch of freshmen, outlining projects, refining timetables, imparting a sense of bonhomie to all and sundry, just to let them know what a swell guy he was. Each year, with a regularity that had always astonished her, he would come alive with the freshening winds and shortening days.

Alive for his students, at least. But towards her, with every year that passed, a little more remote. Not actively unpleasant – at least, not often – never violent. Just increasingly distant. When she talked to him, she sometimes felt like shouting, he seemed so far away. He had started to masturbate in private now, in the bathroom, furtively. To her dismay, she realized that she actually preferred it that way.

At least it was better than what the new school year usually brought. Each September, Rick looked forward to a fresh batch of co-eds, sifting them for the one or two he could always count on screwing by Thanksgiving.

He had never tried to keep his little affairs very secret, least of all from her. It had seemed a sort of bravado at first, a cry for help of sorts. Like a fool she had responded by loving him more, offering herself to him again and again until the truth had finally revealed all its hideous little teeth: that he did it to hurt her, that the more she made her body a reward for his infidelity, the more he enjoyed the pain he could inflict. So now she kept her body for herself and was hurt to realize that he did not seem to care. Or notice.

But this year he had not come alive at all. His step remained leaden, his cheeks pallid. He was forty-nine, angry, fragile, and devoid of grace. If he looked at himself in the bathroom mirror, he did not do so out of love.

She heard his key in the lock. It was already after eight. She guessed he had been drinking at La Belle Créole on Flatbush Avenue. He had started hanging out there about a year ago, drinking raw *clairin* and enjoying the buzz he got from being the only white man in a Haitian rum bar. He never got too drunk, of course; that was his forte, to drink and stay in control. To love and remain unmoved. He had loved her once. Hadn't he?

'Have you eaten?'

He shook his head.

'Do you want to eat?'

'If you've got anything. Have you got anything?' He put down his briefcase, a new one he had bought in June.

'I'll see.' She hesitated. He didn't seem too drunk. Still in control.

'Have you found Filius yet?' she asked.

'Not yet.' His eyes avoided her. He appeared, not merely tired, but edgy, as though the slightest push might set him off. His anger, when it came, was invariably cold. She feared the coldness more than blows: his careful, academic choice of words, his mannered tone, his pale, implacable eyes.

'What do you mean "not yet"? It's been a week, Rick. No-one you've spoken to can remember seeing him since early last month. I want to know what's going on. I want to know if this has anything to do with . . . that other trouble.' She didn't care if she pushed him over the edge tonight. Filius's disappearance had rattled her. In her belly, thin spiders of fear were crawling, warning her of danger. The last time any of their friends had seen Filius had been two days before Channel 13 transmitted *Betty Blue*.

'Nothing's going on. I saw Ti-Jouet at the Créole today. He says Filius was talking about going to Haiti. He still has relatives there. Ti-Jouet thinks he has a little *bien avec* down Jacmel way. A pretty girl, so they say. Seventeen and hot as a chilli pepper. He met her there last year on the field trip to Marigot. Ti-Jouet thinks she had a baby boy.' Rick paused and smiled. See, his little smile seemed to say, some Haitian women are able to have babies.

'That's where Filius has gone,' he continued. 'You'll see. He'll come back with his *maman petite*, get her in through Miami somehow, bring her up here by Christmas. You'll see.'

'I think we should bring in the police.'

'We've already been into that, Angelina. The subject's closed.' His left eyelid was flickering. A vein throbbed in his temple, dark, thick with blood. Tonight, she thought, he might just lose control for once.

'Not for me, it isn't. If you won't call the precinct station, I will.'

'You'll call nobody. Filius is in Haiti. Bring in the police and you'll just make trouble for him if he's trying to get his girl in through Florida.'

'What you mean is, it'll make trouble for you. That's what you mean, Rick, isn't it? Isn't it?' He knew what she meant. He wasn't dumb.

He snorted and turned away, heading for the bathroom. Angelina shrugged and sank into the nearest chair. What was the point of arguing? But she was right, she knew why Rick refused to bring in the police.

Half the Haitians in New York were illegal immigrants. They struggled over to Miami in old, leaking boats, having paid a lifetime's savings for their passage. A few drowned en route, others were rounded up on their arrival and sent to Krome Avenue Detention Center. The lucky ones made contact with friends and relatives and went underground as quickly as possible. Some stayed in Miami, the others headed north – those with a little money to Queens or Manhattan, the rest to Brooklyn.

They lived ten to a room in crumbling tenements of brick or trembled behind triple-locked doors in high-rise apartments. They took grey, menial jobs that paid a dollar an hour, sixteen hours a day, seven days a week, fifty-two weeks a year. Their streets were choked with filth, their neighbours were winos and junkies, their rooms were unheated, and they shared their food with rats and cockroaches.

It was better than Haiti. And nobody wanted trouble with the police.

Rick, on the other hand, didn't give a shit about who got sent back home and who stayed with the rats. Ten years ago, Angelina would have said he cared a lot. He was on committees for the rights of Haitian refugees; he kept his Congressman up late writing letters about the latest violation of the immigration laws; he collected money to send to would-be refugees from Jérémie and Cap-Haïtien. Ten years ago, she'd have said he did it all for love. Now she knew better. Now she knew he did it all for Rick. And he'd been doing it for Rick right from the start.

Haitians had been a godsend to him: a ready-made ethnic community on his doorstep, all his to poke and prod and label. He was the great white doctor and they were his patients. Since Baby Doc's accession in 1972 they had come to him in droves, and he had built a reputation on their broad, uncomplaining backs. But, like all reputations, it was as precarious as yesterday's goodwill. He walked the streets of Fort Greene, Flatbush or Bedford Stuyvesant with care – not out of fear of muggers, but out of nervousness that someone might see through him and walk on past on the other side.

Without his tame blacks, Rick was as good as dead. If his credibility went, just once, he knew he would never get it back again, not in a hundred years, not if he called on all the *loa* and all the ancestors in Guinea for their help. They confided in him because he was an honorary *neg'* beneath the skin of a *blanc*. But if he betrayed them, if he brought the police – or, worse still, the immigration men – into the nooks and crannies of their close-knit lives, they would quickly close ranks against him. And that, Angelina knew, might very well destroy him.

Unless, of course, something else destroyed him first. She thought she knew what that something else might be. And she thought Filius had become involved.

She heard Rick's feet drum down the passage once more. The front door slammed, shaking its single pane of glass. Silence filled the apartment again, dark and moody. Angelina leaned back in her chair and sighed. Maybe Rick was just jealous of Filius. Maybe he wished he too could have a seventeen-year-old as hot as a chilli pepper. A little *bien avec* who could give a man children as easily as sneezing. Who wanted to.

Jealous or not, it looked as though he had gone for the night. She would have to eat dinner alone. She stood up, feeling useless and lazy. Why not just microwave something straight from the freezer, eat it watching TV? The thought pulled her up with a jolt. The cassette was still in the VCR, but nothing could induce her to watch it again.

She wrinkled her nose. The strange smell was still hanging about, she was sure of it. Maybe she should do some cleaning. She decided to start in the morning.

Monday, 28 September
9 A.M.
Rick had not returned. Angelina lay flat on her back in bed, staring

26

at a patch of damp on the grey ceiling. Pale sunlight fell across her eyes like stale water, hard and grey through the interstices of irregularly slatted blinds. She remembered warm sunlight long ago, strong in the early mornings against her skin, long days at Cap-Haïtien, summers on Ibo Beach. And Tontons Macoutes in cheap dark glasses watching them, watching her father, waiting. Restless eyes behind dark lenses watching.

Breakfast was coffee, black without sugar. She sipped it slowly, feeling it creep inside her, hot and bitter, like her memories of Port-au-Prince, like her life here in Brooklyn. She emptied the cafetière. Rick did not return.

She started cleaning in the bedroom. First the bed, then the two closets, finally the carpet and paintwork. What began as a quick tidying operation rapidly grew into an all-out onslaught on years of dirt. She scrubbed and polished and vacuumed her way from room to room, as though the physical act of cleaning had become an exorcism. She was driving out ghosts, pale creatures in dark glasses, Baron-Samedi and Baron-la-Croix, Madame Brigitte and Marinette, all the *guédés*, all the spirits of the dead: her dead, Rick's dead, all the unborn children that shivered in the empty, angry spaces between them.

By noon, she had scoured both bedrooms and the bathroom. After a short lunch break, she decided to start on the living room. At first, all went smoothly. She was well into her stride by now, working to a fluent rhythm that turned each chore into an act of grace.

Filius had moved the furniture round a little, enough to irritate her. She liked things in their proper places. Bending, she pushed the sofa back against the wall. It was heavy and awkward, and she wondered why Filius had ever bothered moving it in the first place.

She paused for breath, sinking onto the sofa. As she did so, she sensed that something was wrong. Her eyes circled the room, nervously scanning the familiar for evidence of something out of key. A chair a little to the left of its accustomed position: but it wasn't that. Her Minton vase on the wrong side of the mantel. Not that. The Moroccan rug about two feet away from its usual place. No, not that. Or, at least . . .

It was at her feet. She had seen it as she moved the sofa. The old wine stain in the carpet had gone. It had been there for years, unlovely and ineradicable. The rug normally covered it.

On her knees now, she went carefully over the carpet. There was no sign that there had ever been a stain there. With an effort, she moved the sofa to the left, then to the right. Nothing. She picked up the rug. Nothing.

She crossed the room and moved one of the chairs. There should have been a stain here too, just to the left of the fireplace, where their old tabby cat Baron-Samedi had once peed profusely in protest at being locked into the room overnight. But there was nothing.

The more closely she looked, the more certain she became that this was not their carpet after all. Theirs had been a plain mushroom-coloured moquette that they had picked up cheap at John Mullins' furniture store on Myrtle Avenue six, maybe seven years ago. It had already been past its best. This one was the same colour, but not so badly worn.

Why would Filius want to replace their carpet? She pulled the sofa away from the wall again, leaving a wide area free at the back of the room. The carpet had been tacked down lightly along the skirting board. She pulled hard and it came up without resistance. She worked her way along the wall as far as the corner, then round the next side, pulling tacks out of the floorboards, easing the carpet loose.

Taking one corner of fabric in her hand, she pulled back, rolling it up to expose the floorboards underneath. Bare boards at first, and then . . .

She moved more slowly, feeling horror seep into her veins like poison. Images from a week before flashed through her brain in dull, ruinous succession. She heard the *petro* drums tapping in the night, saw blood in a warm stream pouring down against a jaundiced, nervous light.

The wooden floor was covered in a dark crimson stain. It started near the wall and spread in all directions, beneath the carpet. She rolled the moquette further back, uncovering foot after foot of reddened floorboard. The back of the carpet was blotched with red in places, where the fresh blood had soaked back up from saturated wood. As she exposed more floorboards, the fusty smell rose to her nostrils more strongly than ever.

That it was blood she did not for a moment doubt. She had seen it in the film: Filius with the bowl of blood, his dark libation to old, unspeakable gods. And she knew the smell – almost sweet, faintly cloying, insinuating itself between flesh and bone. She had smelt it before, rancid, profuse and all-pervading, deep in the underground cells of the old police headquarters in Port-au-Prince.

Someone had tampered with the floorboards. They had been torn up and nailed clumsily back in place. Fresh splinters showed like raw wounds through the stain. Bent nails betrayed an awkward haste.

She went to the kitchen and took a large screwdriver from the toolbox in the utility cupboard. Its flat blade wedged easily between two floorboards. She prised one up, nails creaking in protest, blood-soaked wood rough against her flesh, a fingernail tearing.

The stench that came flooding up was unsupportable. Angelina gagged and pressed one hand hard against her mouth. She rose and staggered to the window, flinging it open. The air that entered was tainted by nothing worse than traffic fumes and industrial waste. Behind her in the room, she sensed an older, richer pollution.

She found a scarf in a drawer and tied it round her mouth and nose before returning to the patch of reddened floor. Steeling herself, she thrust the screwdriver down hard into the narrow fissure between the next two planks. The nails groaned as they tore away from the joists. The hole in the floor became wider. They were on the ground floor here: underneath lay nothing but foundations.

Two years earlier, while installing a new gas fire, workmen had taken up some floorboards in this room. Angelina remembered a low, walled chamber, smaller than a cellar, about five feet deep and twenty square. Its floor had been covered in rubble, in which the workmen had found a broken clay pipe and two old newspapers dating from 1890.

There was insufficient light to see down through the hole she had made. She could feel her body trembling: she did not want to look. But she knew she had no choice.

The flashlight beneath the sink was next to useless, and there were no spare batteries. Then she remembered that Rick kept a Maglite beside the bed, which he sometimes used for reading at night. Small though it was, it had a powerful beam.

Maglite in hand, she knelt on the floor beside the gaping hole. The stench filled the room now, stale, corrupt and nauseating. She held her breath and twisted the flashlight's head to switch it on. A hard beam of white light stabbed down into the darkness.

At first all seemed a jumble, like the pieces of a half-assembled jigsaw. A mixture of colours, shapes and dull-edged madnesses resolved itself slowly into the lineaments of a nightmare. First a shoe, then a trouser-cuff, and finally a hand defined themselves against the trembling light, mere inches below the floorboards. The light swung this way and that, like a searchlight plucking bombers from an entangled sky. More hands, a decayed face, teeth jagged in a lipless grimace, naked limbs, clothed limbs, more faces, more hands, more feet, a tattered jumble-sale of death, bodies cast aside like abandoned dreams. Her hand lost its grip and the flashlight fell helplessly into the aperture.

As she stumbled to her feet, she felt acrid vomit rising in her chest. She staggered sideways, tearing the scarf away from her mouth. Again and again she threw up, until her stomach was empty. Crouched on all fours, she shivered, sobbing and retching uncontrollably. And all the time her brain screamed with the last image it had seen before she dropped the light: a face inches from hers, cheeks streaked with blood, eyes open and staring. Filius's cheeks, Filius's eyes, distorted but unmistakable.

Fumbling in the semi-darkness, she reached out a hand to touch his cheeks. His skin was cold, cold and dry as parchment. He did not move or utter a sound; but as her fingers found his lips, she felt a trace of breath, a faint and trembling thing, softer than the softest breeze, scarcely a thing at all. But it was a breath. Reason told her it could not be true: but she had felt cold air against her skin and she knew that either reason was lying or the truth was beyond any reason she had ever known.

CHAPTER THREE

Filius could not be reached. He was in a deep coma, a score of only three on the Glasgow scale. The police took him straight to the Cumberland Hospital in the Housing Projects, where he had to wait on a stretcher in emergency for almost two hours before being seen. Once admitted, he was put through a battery of tests. Dopamine and dobutamine were administered, a CT scan was ordered, and blood was sent for immediate checks.

By early evening he was still comatose. Heartbeat, respiration and body temperature were abnormally low. There were signs of uraemia and pulmonary oedema. His lips and extremities were cyanotic. Electrical potential in the brain was barely detectable. He was hanging to life by the thinnest of threads.

Angelina accompanied him to the hospital and remained by his side through the evening. His survival had become a sort of talisman for her. She talked to him in Creole, the way her old nurse had talked to her in the long summer nights back home. But he did not respond. The police let her stay in case he recovered consciousness enough to speak, knowing that, if he did, he might use Creole instead of English.

Just before midnight his vital signs began to fade. The doctor in charge ordered him put on a ventilator. He then went off duty. The orderly responsible for bringing the ventilator was called to emergency. By the time they got the machine to his room, Filius had been dead for twenty minutes.

The orderly pulled a sheet across his face, stark white with the name of the hospital stitched across the top. Angelina stayed a little longer, watching him in silence, waiting to help with the formalities of identification. She felt terribly alone. For the first time she realized that she too might die in Brooklyn.

They took her to the 88th Precinct station house, a dilapidated building on the corner of Classon and De Kalb, just down from the Emanuel Baptist Church. From outside, it looked like a fortress, guarded, protected, afraid. It was ugly and square, with a single round tower pointing like an accusing finger at the night sky. Angelina had never been there before, but its dirty red brick walls and grey stone windows felt familiar. Police stations had been part of her life once. She knew only too well their sounds and smells, their sudden, chilling silences.

She was tired, but every time she closed her eyes the show began again, the bizarre horror movie inside her head. Someone gave her a couple of tranquillizers, but they just made the images go fuzzy. She wanted to throw up, but her stomach was empty. The thought of food nauseated her. Somehow, she was aware that people were talking to her, aware that they wanted her attention; but she felt as though she had been encased in a block of ice, freezing and isolating her, preventing her from responding to the outside world.

A policeman in plain clothes who said his name was Lieutenant Abrams explained that they could not let her go home. The apartment had been sealed off; there were officers there now, removing bodies, sifting for fingerprints and bloodstains, taking photographs. She wasn't under arrest, but they wanted to question her as soon as possible. Did she have any relatives to go to? She shook her head. Friends? She shook her head again.

Abrams told the desk sergeant to fix her with a place to stay for the night. Desk sergeants are not social secretaries. The man on duty, Moskowitz, would not have called himself a racist; he just had a low opinion of black people. It did not matter to him what Angelina had just gone through, and he did not want to know. She looked like just another black hooker waiting for her man. He arranged for her to spend the night at the Regal, a cheap hotel on Myrtle Avenue.

The Regal was anything but. Most of its guests were cockroaches, the rest single-parent families on welfare. Social workers called it a halfway house. Halfway between squalor and poverty. Its long, echoing corridors were lit at exaggerated intervals by bare light bulbs trapped behind dusty wire cages. The green and white tiles that covered its public areas were cracked and smeared with dirt. It looked and smelled like a public toilet. It was the sort of place that would take a single mulatto woman in at one o'clock in the morning without asking questions.

Somebody called a police physician who was busy blood-testing drunks at the rear of the station. He accompanied her to the hotel and gave her an intramuscular shot of diazepam. In a matter of moments she felt as though she could have slept in the alley outside. Sleep came crashing in like waves against a coral reef.

And with sleep, nightmares. She could not be sure where one ended and the next began. Now she was in her father's police cell, listening to the Tontons whisper in the corridor; now she was suffocating, buried alive in a coffin made of splintered floorboards; and now they were raising her from the grave, men in cheap sunglasses, feeding her a paste of sweet potatoes, cane syrup and *concombre zombi*, baptizing her with oil before a cross of *sablier* wood.

But when she woke one dream stood out in memory: she had found herself walking in a dark, entangled jungle, between trees as tall as buildings, in ribbed and perpetual twilight. This was not Haiti, this was Africa, to which the spirits of all the dead returned. She could hear things grunt and slither in the shadows, but when she turned there was nothing to be seen but trees and creepers. She knew that she had been walking for weeks, but the rainforest had not come to an end. The further she marched, the denser it became. Rick was somewhere in front of her, out of sight; in their rear, Filius came creeping slowly on all fours, blind and deaf and dumb, his keen nose following their scent.

She came to a wall of roughly hewn stone blocks, so high she could not see its top. When she tried to walk round it, it seemed to go on for ever. At last she came to a tall golden door set deep within the stone. It felt heavy against her hand, but as she pushed, it fell slowly open. Stepping across the threshold, she came awake with a start and found herself in a strange bed, blinking at shadows on a strange ceiling.

Lieutenant Abrams was waiting for her downstairs in the lobby. He'd seen her apartment, smelt the odour of decay: he would have waited much longer.

'You want to talk here?' he asked.

She looked round at the damp, decaying tiles, the hard-backed chairs. A Puerto Rican woman passed, a howling baby in her arms, four older children clinging to her skirt.

'I was thinking more along the lines of the Waldorf Astoria,' said Angelina. 'I'm not being sarcastic. I just thought it might be to your taste.'

'I'm sorry. I've already bawled out Sergeant Moskowitz. He's more used to . . .' He stumbled to a halt, embarrassed.

'Call girls?'

'People in trouble.'

'I am in trouble.'

He nodded.

'Sorry. Yes, you are. Look, there's a diner across the street that serves real coffee.'

'What time is it?'

'Past twelve. You sleep well?'

'No. I had dreams. Can you tell me what's happening?'

'Relax. The doc gave you a shot. You had a bad time yesterday. How are you feeling now?'

'Numb. I . . . Does it have to be coffee?'

He shook his head.

'No. How about a milkshake?'

She smiled. Not a lot, but it counted as a smile.

'I was thinking more along the lines of a Jack Daniels.'

He returned her smile.

'I know, but the doctor . . .'

'Fuck the doctor.'

He pretended to be shocked.

'OK, lady, whatever you say. Jack Daniels it is. I know a place on De Kalb. My car's outside.'

He stood up, his eyes quietly fixed on her face. She'd been pretty once, still was in a faded kind of way. Pretty and sad. Her small mouth turned down at the corners, her eyes were like quiet windows across which an unseen hand had drawn pale shades. He liked her accent: a little like French, but with something added, something darker.

He wondered what sort of dreams she'd had. They didn't tell you how to handle dreams in police academy. He looked round at the tidy shabbiness of the halfway house. Nobody told you about them, but dreams were what mattered most to people in a place like this. Some dreams they needed just to stay alive; others they spent their whole lives running to get away from.

She followed him across the street to his car. A cold drizzle had been falling for some time, a constant shower falling from a slate-coloured sky. It had come out of the north-east, down from Long Island Sound. The streets were grey and dishonest and empty. Whichever way she looked, she saw nothing but the rain and the concrete. A starving cat scurried past looking for shelter.

She'd seen him watching her, guessed what he had been

thinking. He was thin, Jewish, too intellectual-looking for a cop. She thought he must be thirty-four, thirty-five. His jet-black hair was thinning at the temples, there was a sprinkling of stubble on his chin. He looked a little lost.

They drove slowly east along Myrtle Avenue, Abrams silent, unsure of her. She sat forward in her seat, staring blankly through the windscreen at the usual dreary streets. Tin cans and broken bottles, dog turds and old syringes: the rain soaked into a bent and crumpled universe of fear and loathing, block after block of hardened rage and love grown bitter and useless.

In a matter of hours, it had all grown cold and unfamiliar, and she realized, as though for the first time, how deeply she detested it. She turned her face away, looking for sunshine; but there was only the rain and the concrete and the addicts huddled in doorways outside the Kingsview methadone centre.

They turned right on Classon, past the precinct house, down to De Kalb. He pulled in on the next block and double-parked. She realized that he hadn't spoken since they'd got in the car.

CHAPTER FOUR

The bar was half Puerto Rican, half Italian. That was why they'd called it Murphy's. It was almost empty: a handful of graphics students from the Pratt Institute, an off-duty cop, a couple of black call girls in from Bed-Stuy for the afternoon shift, an old Sicilian talking quietly in rural Italian to the man behind the bar. Low lights, narrow booths with plastic leather seats, faded notices in Italian and Spanish, a sour whisky smell, the small ghosts of insignificant dreams. In baroque, rusted mirrors behind the bar refracted images of coloured bottles shimmered helplessly.

'You like this place?' she asked.

'No,' he answered. 'But it's quiet. No jukebox, no TV. We need to talk.'

She asked for a Jack Daniels. He brought a bottle and two glasses and set them on the table between them.

'How come a nice girl like you got started drinking this stuff?'

'I'm not a nice girl.'

'No?'

'No.'

They were in shadows, in their own booth, at the back of the bar. On the wall a dim bulb hid its light in a dusty shade. He poured her a full glass and half-filled his own. Her hand shook as she raised the glass to her mouth. It rattled jaggedly against her teeth. He said nothing, watched her press the glass hard against her lips, whisky spilling down her chin. Her eyes were bright with tears. There was rain in her hair.

'When did you last see your husband?' he asked.

'I don't understand . . .'

'You said you were married when we questioned you yesterday.'

'Did I? I suppose I did. I don't remember.'

'You said his name was Rick, that he taught at LIU.'

'That's right. He's an anthropologist. A big man, very important. He runs courses in Caribbean and African religions. Sometimes he screws his students.' She put the glass down. Somehow she'd managed to drink almost half. She noticed that he had not touched his.

Her eyes were wicked and lizard green, wide with tiny flecks of amber on the remotest edges of the pupils. The flecks vanished like dust in the least shadow. Hooded eyes, drugged with sleep: sleep out of which she had not awakened in over forty years. Sea-dark eyes, bereft, disenchanted, lonely, soaked with dreams. She fixed them on his without embarrassment, unblinking, pleading for some sort of vision transcending the simplicities of sight.

He looked at her with a sad expression.

'You said you had an argument two nights ago. Is that right?'

'An argument? Yes, I suppose. He walked out. He's done it before.'

'What about?' He hesitated. 'The argument: was it about one of his students?'

She lifted the glass, gulped at the drink, set it down again.

'No, I don't think so. I can't remember. We don't argue about that any longer. What's the point? I tell him I'm leaving, he says "Go home to Haiti". What sort of choice is that?' She looked at him. Why was she talking like this, parading her weaknesses in a cheap bar? 'I think . . . I think it was about Filius.'

'The man who died last night? The one in your apartment? Filius Narcisse.'

She winced. She didn't want to think about the apartment. At the bar, a student laughed uneasily. A Jamaican man came in and started talking with the call girls. Angelina felt goose pimples walk across her back.

'Yes,' she said. She wanted to get up and walk out, leave all this behind, forget anything had ever happened. 'We argued about Filius. He'd been missing. I wanted to call the police. Rick said "no".'

'Did he say why?'

She shrugged.

'Does it matter? He thought it might get some people into trouble.'

'What people?'

She hesitated, then shrugged. 'Haitians, poor people. He thought you'd make trouble for them if you started asking questions.'

'What sort of trouble?'

She shrugged again. 'Who knows?'

'Was he worried?'

'I don't know. Maybe. Yes. I think he was.' She knew he was. Why was the truth so hard to tell?

'What about?'

'He didn't tell me.' The lie came easily, like rage. She refilled the small glass almost to the brim. Her hand was steadier now.

'Had something happened?'

'Happened?' She felt frightened, trapped.

'Yes. You said something yesterday about a video. About this man Filius. You seemed afraid. You were ... incoherent.' He hesitated. 'Look, I understand. You were agitated.' He paused, toying with his glass. He had not drunk anything yet. 'Tell me about it. Tell me about the video.'

She explained as well as she could, her words stumbling and hesitant. He listened carefully, sensing the horror in her voice, seeing it in her eyes.

'What did you find?' she asked finally.

'Find?'

She held her breath. Her heart was making a racket, she was sure he could hear.

'In my apartment. In the living room.' *Beneath the floorboards*, that was what she meant. But she couldn't say it. Part of her still hoped it had all been a nightmare.

He hesitated.

'You know what we found. What you found.'

'How many?' she asked in a small, hesitant voice.

He took his time. 'I spoke with Doctor Taylor at the mortuary late this morning. Altogether, they brought in nine bodies. Four had died recently, within the past two months; the rest were much older. Taylor thinks they'd been taken from local cemeteries. Some were still in coffins.'

She could smell it even here, the stench of decay. It had followed her from Africa, it was here with her in the bar.

'Does Rick know? Have you told him?'

Abrams looked hard at her. He was feeling tired. He'd been up most of last night, taken a few hours' sleep, and been back at work since nine. Something told him this was going to be a bad case.

'Mrs Hammel, I have some bad news for you.'

She didn't seem to respond.

'Do you understand? Bad news about your husband.'

'About Rick?'

He nodded.

'He . . . His body was found early this morning. You were still asleep, we . . . didn't want to put you through another ordeal. We identified him from documents in his wallet. The pictures matched. Of course, you'll have to come to the mortuary later to make a formal identification; but not just yet.'

She said nothing at first, just stared at the table, at the glass of whisky. He hated this part of his job, the intimacy of bereavement that it forced on him.

'Where?'

'I'm sorry?'

'Where was he found?'

'In the park. Fort Greene, I mean, not Prospect. Under a tree near the monument. He'd been . . .' He paused. There was no easy way to say this. 'Someone killed him,' he said. 'A jogger found him early this morning. The body wasn't far from the path, there'd been no real attempt to conceal it. He . . .' Again he hesitated. He'd been there, seen the remains. 'His throat had been cut. And . . . his tongue had been ripped out.'

Someone flushed the toilet just behind their booth. A door slammed upstairs. A voice cried out plaintively in Spanish.

She looked up. He had expected tears or numbness, but not this. She was looking straight at him. She was staring into his eyes. And she was smiling.

CHAPTER FIVE

Rain fell all that day. In the streets, an unending downpour turned the world to water cradled in a curious dim light. The gutters were fat and swollen, choked with filth. Beneath leaden pavements the sewers boomed with a hollow, tormented ringing.

Angelina accompanied Reuben Abrams to the mortuary in Kings County Hospital. He wanted her to make the formal identification of Rick's body. They parked near the Trauma and Emergency entrance and walked through slanting rain to the mortuary. It lay on their right, up a short flight of steps.

There was no sign of death here, no reek of formaldehyde, just a plain lobby flanked by office doors. Reuben took Angelina through a door on the left marked 'Chief Medical Examiner'. A sign read 'Identification Hours 9.00 A.M. – 4.00 P.M.' Angelina wondered what happened to people who died outside office hours.

A door on the left was marked 'Brooklyn Homicide Police Personnel Only'. On the walls, posters offered advice to the newly bereaved. There were leaflets on a low wooden table. A clerk came out of one of the other offices and greeted Abrams with a casual familiarity that said they had both been through this before. He turned and glanced at Angelina, a small, sad-eyed man in spectacles.

'Mrs Hammel?'

She nodded. The clerk looked morosely at her.

'Will you step into my office, please?'

Her heart had begun to beat, triggered by the sterility of her surroundings, the absence of any real death in the air. This polite air was too thin for her to breathe.

At a cluttered desk, she was asked to sign a book, then requested to prove her identity. The clerk filled out a sheet headed 'Personal Identification of Body', three copies – one for the case file, one for the NYPD Missing Persons Bureau, one for the DA. She had never thought death could be this complicated.

'Mrs Hammel,' the clerk said, 'I'm going to show you a photograph of a man whose body was found this morning in Fort Greene Park. Take your time. If you can make a positive identification that it is indeed your husband, all you will have to do is sign this sheet. That will complete these formalities.'

She shook her head.

'No photograph,' she said. Her voice was firm, but her heart was shaking. 'I want to see him.'

'Mrs Hammel, I don't recommend . . .'

The lieutenant placed a hand on the clerk's arm. The clerk sighed.

'Very well,' he said. 'We have a room downstairs with a window through which you may view the remains. I'll ask them to prepare the body.'

Five long minutes later, they were ready. The clerk led Angelina to the viewing chamber. When she was seated, he drew a curtain aside. Beyond the narrow window, in a tiny, white-tiled chamber, beneath cold lights that buzzed and flickered fitfully, half her life lay naked on a stone slab.

Someone had combed Rick's hair back hard from his forehead. There were traces of dandruff on his temples. His chin was dark with stubble. They had covered his torso with a stiff white sheet and propped his head on a rubber pillow. He looked uncomfortable, even with his eyes closed. His lips were cut and bruised where his killer had struggled to remove the tongue. On one cheek a knife had left a ragged scar, its edges raw but bloodless.

He was pale and he was changed, but he was still Rick: the old Rick she had loved once, so long ago it hurt to remember, the Rick of recent years for whom she had lost all feeling. It made no difference now, no difference at all. She nodded her head once and made for the door.

Abrams took her by the elbow and guided her back to the offices upstairs. She leaned on him heavily. Her limbs felt like water. The sad-eyed man asked her to sign the identification form, indicating the spaces with a grimy fingernail. For the first time since her honeymoon, Angelina was conscious that the name she used was someone else's. As the official bent forward to retrieve the papers, she observed that he had the word 'God' tattooed on the back of his right hand and 'Jesus' on the left. He came round the desk and shook her hand, murmuring stale condolences in a stale voice. She noticed that he had bad breath.

At the door, he took her hand again and pressed something into it, a piece of folded paper. Outside in the lobby, she opened it out. It was a small pamphlet, heavy purple ink on pink paper. 'Eternal Life with the Lord Jesus'. She crumpled it into a ball and threw it down on the stark linoleum.

'Is he allowed to do that?' she asked. She felt the sort of anger that makes no sense and hurts because it has no meaning and no outlet.

He shrugged. 'It does no harm,' he said.

'But if you . . .'

'I don't think about it,' he answered sharply. He took her arm and led her outside. It was still raining.

She did not want to go to another bar. They stayed in the Ford and drove in silence through dizzy rain-drenched streets, like careless lovers without a bed, riding out the storm. He thought about her smile in the bar, when he told her her husband had been found in a park with his throat cut and his tongue ripped out. She looked tired: he was willing to take that as an excuse.

Darkness fell, quiet and drab. The rain still tumbled down, cold and tinged with sodden blue and golden lights. It fell in a steady cascade on the shining towers of downtown Manhattan, on bars and theatres and fashionable, grey-walled galleries, on glass and marble, perspex and bronze, lies and postures and simulacra. It fell without a thought on the dark tenements of Harlem, on the angry Babel towers of Brooklyn and the south Bronx, on the Housing Projects and the railroads, on wood and rust and broken glass, on more lies, more postures, more simulacra.

They drove uneasily through sparkling silver streets empty of people. The rain and lights struggled to make magic out of squalor; but nothing could dispel the darkness here. Their world was a harsh reality no wand could turn to fairyland. Rain drummed on the metal roof of the car and streamed across the blurred windscreen.

'Do you know who might have killed him?' Abrams asked. He looked straight ahead, not wanting to look at her.

She remained silent for a while, watching the raindrops settle and disperse. What would a Jewish policeman understand of the reasons for Rick's death?

'No,' she said. 'No-one hated him that much.'

'You think this was done out of hate?'

'No. I told you, no-one hated Rick that much. He must have run into someone, some crazy person.'

He reached out a hand and rubbed a hole in the mist on the screen.

'Some of the bodies we found in your apartment had been mutilated,' he said. 'Some had ears missing. Some had had their tongues torn out. Or cut out, it makes very little difference.'

She did not answer. They were driving west on Atlantic Avenue, beneath the dark elevated tracks of the Long Island Rail Road.

'Turn right on Portland,' she said.

He didn't need to ask where she wanted to go. Portland led straight down to Fort Greene Park.

'There's nothing there,' he said.

'I want to see.'

'It's dark. It's raining. There's nothing to see.' He had been off duty for two hours now. What was he doing, driving through the rain with this woman whose life had just been stripped bare? He should be looking for her husband's killer. Except that he was convinced she knew something: a name, a motive, an incident. And maybe something else, something he could not even guess at. He remembered her quiet smile in the bar.

She turned her face to him, and as she did so he saw her eyes reflected in the clouded windscreen. 'Please,' she said. The lights of a passing truck wiped her reflection from the glass. He turned the car.

The park had no gates to keep people out at night. A lot of winos and addicts spent the hours of darkness there, drinking Thunderbird or shooting up on heroin. Tonight it would be empty. Tonight the rain would keep things clean. For a little while.

They were already soaking by the time he found the path. He carried the flashlight that he always kept in the boot. His Browning .38 nestled softly against his ribs, snug in its little pancake holster.

'It was down here,' he said. 'Near the monument.'

A line of lights shone like dime-store haloes all along the path. Their fake promise of warmth in the darkness only served to make Reuben's sense of desolation sharper. He didn't want to be here.

They walked slowly down the path, Reuben in front, blinking hard against the rain, trying to form a pattern out of light and death and darkness. Angelina followed numbly, unsure of her reasons

43

for wanting to come here. Rick's death was still fresh, too fresh, like snow on a withered field. She still did not know how she should react. There would be a funeral, his parents would come down from Boston and his brother from Sag Harbor. There would be faculty and students; some of them would shed more tears than she. She was the withered field; for a few days, his death would make her white and gleaming. For a few days.

Reuben found the place at last, a tree set back about three yards from the path. The rain had erased all traces of that morning's work: footprints, trowel marks, plaster, the small holes in which measurement rods had been placed by the photographers.

'We found him here,' he said, playing the flashlight over the ground. It was coarse and sodden, clumps of trampled grass in a sea of mud.

Angelina felt a cold ripple of despair climb to her heart. She fought against it, breathing hard. She hadn't loved him, not for years; they'd had no future, not even in acts of betrayal. So why this wounding, this need to weep? Not for him, surely. For herself then. She had not wanted things to end this way. But it was better than nothing. Wasn't it?

'There's nothing here now,' he said. 'You see?'

She did not answer. She could see well enough: just mud and a scraping together of memories. By tomorrow there would be nothing at all. She thought she was crying, but when she reached a hand to her cheek, she found her face was wet with rain, not tears.

'Leave me alone,' she snapped, surprised by her own impatience. 'I need to think.'

He said nothing, just turned and handed the flashlight to her, then walked away without a word. The light stabbed like a thin blade through the thick curtain of rain, sweeping over the sodden ground. There should have been something else, she thought, something more significant than this. Rick would not have chosen to die in a place like this. It was too common, too anonymous.

She turned to go. As she did so, the beam fell on something at the very edge of vision. Crossing quickly to it, she stooped and reached out her hand. It was half-buried in the mud, but it lifted out easily. For more than a minute, she held it on the palm of her hand, letting the cold rain wash it clean. She knew what it was, of course. How could she not know? But she had not thought to find it here.

She looked round. Abrams was nowhere to be seen. He would

know nothing of her discovery: she knew it had been left there after the police had packed up and gone, left for her to stumble on. With a shudder, she slipped the object into the pocket of her coat.

CHAPTER SIX

In the car, she started shivering uncontrollably. Reuben switched the heater on to full and turned the car back out onto De Kalb.

'You'd better take me back to the hotel,' she said. 'I'm sorry about all this. Sorry I got you wet. You were right: there was nothing there.'

'I don't think that hotel's such a good idea. Not in your condition. You've had a tough day. The next few days may be even tougher.'

'Can I go back to my apartment yet?'

Reuben slipped across Fulton onto Flatbush Avenue. He shook his head.

'No way. The guys in Forensics are still taking it apart. I'm sorry. They'll put it back together again the way it was.' He paused. Nowhere went back the way it had been. 'Do you want to go there again anyway?'

She reached down and took off her shoes. They were full of water and her stockings were saturated. She thought she would never get dry again.

'No,' she murmured. 'Never.'

'Any friends? Relatives?'

She had friends, but no-one she wanted to be with right now. As for relatives . . . She shook her head.

He looked at her. Like a drowned rat, he thought. Then he glanced down at himself. Steam had started to rise from the leg of his trousers nearest the heater. He burst out laughing. She followed his eye, saw the steam, then glanced at herself. Water vapour rose from her as well. She threw her head back and shrieked with laughter. She had never laughed so hard before.

Her laughter rose in pitch, breathless, out of control, verging on hysteria. And as suddenly she was crying, her body convulsed, her chest heaving in pain. Reuben drew in to the kerb. He sat by helplessly, unable to comfort her. The car filled with vapour, like a steam room, no longer laughable. He reached over and switched off the heater.

Slowly, her tears subsided. Her self-control returned. She wiped her face, but it was futile, everything was wet.

'We'll go back to my place,' he said. He headed south towards West Flatbush. 'It's irregular, but what the hell? I have to spend time with you over the next few days anyway, so I may as well have you where I can keep an eye on you. Can you cook?'

She shrugged.

'So-so. What I do best is paint. I like to paint.'

'You like to paint? We'll save that for later. For the moment cooking would be fine. Even so-so cooking. Regard it as rent. Anything you need?'

'To cook with?'

'No, for yourself. All your stuff's still at your apartment.'

She shrugged.

'I could do with a shower. And a change of clothes.'

'I'll call by my sister's after I get changed myself. She's fat, but she used to be thin. About your size. She never throws anything. Lives in hope, I guess.'

He wondered why he was doing this, giving her such special attention. It wasn't that she had lost her husband: she was hardly the first attractive widow he had met in the course of his work. But she seemed so strangely alone, more alone than anyone he had ever met. And she had smiled that mysterious smile at him. Against his better judgement, he was in some measure captivated. He'd explain things to the captain tomorrow.

She felt strange, standing naked in his bathroom, her flesh covered in goose bumps. Her reflection multiplied in his mirrors, her thin body dark and glistening. All around her were Reuben's things: an electric razor, a single toothbrush much the worse for wear, a bottle of Clinique scruffing lotion, a line of male underwear drying above the bath. Nothing feminine, no evidence of a wife or a regular girlfriend. She wondered what she was doing, how she had come to be here. Why was he sticking so close to her? Didn't he have other things to do, other investigations that needed his time? Did he suspect her of complicity? Did he know something?

She took another towel from the cupboard above the central

heating tank and began to rub herself down for the second time. Nothing, she felt, would ever make her properly dry again. Her clothes lay in a wretched heap on the floor. She bent down to move them onto the radiator.

As she lifted her coat, the small wooden coffin fell from the pocket in which she had placed it. It was about five inches long by two wide and painted white. On each of its two sides and the bottom was the name of a different god belonging to the Congo rite. The lid bore Rick's name in small, badly formed black letters, next to a painting of Papa Nebo, the *vodoun* oracle of the dead. A hermaphrodite, he wore a white muslin skirt and above it a long-tailed frock coat. A black top hat was perched on his head and sunglasses framed his white-painted face.

This coffin was small. The next would be a little bigger. And the one after that bigger still. Last of all would be the real thing.

Angelina shuddered and prised the lid up, breaking a fingernail. As she had expected, the little box was filled with ashes: Rick's tongue, what was left of it.

Still trembling, she tipped the ashes into the toilet bowl. Breaking the coffin into tiny pieces, she wrapped the fragments in toilet tissue and tossed them on top of the ashes, then flushed it all away.

'Voodoo,' he said.

'I'm sorry?'

'Voodoo. What do you know about it?'

They were in his kitchen finishing the lamb curry Angelina had prepared. He'd had to stop her adding cream to the sauce: he still observed the law relating to kosher food. Nights like tonight, he wondered if it made any difference.

His parents had moved to Boro Park from Williamsburg in 1960, after the blacks and Puerto Ricans had started moving in. He'd been five years old, asthmatic, dressed in sidelocks and a knitted skullcap. All he remembered of the day of the move was how his uncle Avrum's hat had fallen off his head while he'd been helping Reuben's father lift a heavy cupboard into the van. Reuben had laughed heartily and been smacked.

Uncle Avrum had died a fortnight later, and Reuben had cried at the funeral, obscurely frightened that his laughter might somehow have sent the old man to the grave. But Uncle Avrum had not been old, just sick. And it had not been laughter that had killed him. Someone had uprooted him just one time too often.

In later years, Reuben had come to understand. Somewhere in himself he could still feel Uncle Avrum lurking, his huge fur hat tilted over his forehead, hugging the past to himself like a holy relic. Even after joining the force, even after his transfer to the 88th Precinct three years ago, Reuben had insisted on keeping his apartment in West Flatbush. It was fifteen blocks away from his parents' house in Boro Park, within walking distance of his childhood.

Near his parents' house, on 49th Street and 14th Avenue, was his old yeshiva, the Bais Yaakov. A couple of blocks the other way was the little basement synagogue where his father had first taken him to pray. None of his family lived further than fifteen minutes away. Out on the streets, blinking, he travelled in time.

When he went on duty, he became a cop. He acted hard-nosed, drank Budweiser, laughed at McMenemy's dirty jokes, worked shabbat when he had to. But those were just the things he did so they would let him be a policeman. At home he wore his kippa on the street and spent most shabbats at his parents' place.

Living two lives was difficult, but the alternative was worse. Every killing, every rape, every outrage against the flesh lacerated him inside. Some cops drank. Some beat their wives. His therapy was coming home to West Flatbush. Bringing Angelina back here with him was the first time he had compromised his personal code. He hoped he wouldn't have cause to regret it.

'Why do you want to know?'

'You know why. These killings, your husband's murder. There's some sort of voodoo connection, isn't there?'

She looked across the table at him. He'd taken her into his apartment, fed her, given her half a bottle of good wine. What did he want?

'Is there?' she asked in return.

'Listen,' he said. 'In this Goldener Medina of ours, there are thousands of cult murders a year. Do you find that hard to believe? So do I. But it happens to be true. Here in New York, we have some of the worst: Satanists, drug cultists, voodooists – every kind of weirdo. And some of them think human sacrifice is a cute sort of way to pass the time. You saw that video, you saw what was going on. So what can you tell me about voodoo?'

He was missing the point, but he didn't know it and she didn't feel up to putting him right.

'What makes you think the things you saw in that film had anything to do with voodoo?'

'I don't know. It looked . . .'

'Weird?'

'Well, of course.'

'And the people doing the dancing and so on were blacks.'

He nodded.

'So weird plus black plus murder plus some sort of religious ceremony equals voodoo?'

He began to feel uneasy.

'Not necessarily. There are a lot of black religions. There's Santeria, there's . . .'

'But you think this is voodoo.'

'Your husband spent a lot of time with the Haitian community. You're Haitian. The dead man, Filius, was Haitian.'

'In Haiti we call it *vodoun*.'

He shrugged.

'Same thing, surely.'

She put down her fork.

'No, Lieutenant. Not the same thing. Voodoo is Hollywood: zombies and pins in dolls and mumbo jumbo. *Vodoun* is the religion of most of the Haitian people.'

'I thought they were Catholics.'

'Catholicism is their church. *Vodoun* is their faith.'

'So you think these killings have nothing to do with . . . *vodoun*?'

She hesitated.

'I didn't say that. I just don't think the connection's that simple. If there is a connection.'

He paused and sipped at his glass. He felt out of his depth. For three years he'd been working in Fort Greene, and still the Haitians puzzled him.

'Are you a. . . ?'

'*Vodouniste*? No.' She shook her head. 'My parents . . . We were what people used to call the élite. Haiti may be the oldest black republic, but we mulattos have always stayed in charge. We have the money, the education, the links with France. We're more French than Haitian, more European than African. My family attended Mass every Sunday. We never felt a need to dance for God.'

'But your husband . . . You don't mind my asking?'

She closed her eyes for a moment, shutting out the new images Rick's name conjured up: a pale body on a slab, grey mud and grass, a small white coffin.

'No, that's OK. Rick was an expert on *vodoun* among other things. You can look up his books, read his papers. I don't think anybody killed him for that.'

'Maybe not. But I'd like to meet a few people, talk to them about what's been going on. Friends of your husband, friends of Filius. You can point me in the right direction. You can help me if you want to.'

Yes, she thought, *I can help. But helping you won't do any good. It's got to end here. With Filius, with Rick.* Her heart was shaking again. She felt sick. Sick and frightened.

'I can't help you,' she said. 'I don't know anything.' But she looked away when she said it, and for the first time he knew she was lying.

The telephone rang. He hesitated for a moment, looking at her, trying to decide whether she was playing games or simply frightened. Then he rose and went into the next room.

When he came back his face was troubled.

'It's to do with your friend Filius,' he said. 'Something funny's going on.' He paused and sat down. 'Some people came this morning to claim his body. Said they were relatives. They buried him this afternoon. I don't understand it. There should have been an autopsy.'

Angelina frowned.

'He had no relatives here,' she said. 'Did they give their names? The people who came for him.'

He shook his head.

'I don't know. I guess so. The hospital will have a record. But why have him buried so quickly? And how did they get round the autopsy?'

'It's the custom. Same in all tropical countries.'

He nodded.

'There's something else,' he said.

'Yes?'

'The lab report. Apparently there was some sort of mix-up and they went ahead with the report on the blood samples they took from him. There's something funny about them. Something out of the ordinary.' He hesitated. She was looking at him intently, as though she guessed what he was going to say. 'They want to dig him up again,' he said. 'The pathologist has just been in touch with the state's attorney to make an official request for an exhumation.'

51

CHAPTER SEVEN

Wednesday dawned pale and worthless, a tawdry day made shiny by yesterday's rain, the light sapped and drained, all vigour gone. For herself, Angelina had never known a day begin so flat. Literally, she did not know what to do with herself. Reuben had gone early to check on the aberrant lab report and help speed up the exhumation order.

True, there were things to be done about Rick's burial, but she had no stomach for them. At Reuben's suggestion, she had left it all to Rick's secretary at LIU. Mary-Jo was making all the arrangements: phoning round, placing notices in the papers, speaking with the undertakers. Angelina had not yet spoken with Rick's parents, did not want to. The secretary could take care of that as well.

She hauled herself wearily out of bed at ten. Her clothes were still a little damp, but better that than the bits and pieces Reuben's sister had lent her, all the wrong fit and grossly unattractive. She had formed an unlovely mental image of the sister: loud, lumpy – a round-faced Jewish matron with heavy breasts and ten kids, who used Avon cosmetics and shopped at Macy's once a month.

Reuben's apartment was filled with photographs: his grandparents in Hassidic dress, his parents, his brothers, his sister on her wedding day, aunts, uncles, cousins, nephews, nieces, the living and the dead. He had spoken about them the night before: 'These are my grandparents. I never met them, they died in Auschwitz. And this is Uncle Avrum: he died here in Brooklyn. The funny-looking woman is Aunt Rivke. And that's her boy Irving, my cousin: he's at the Yeshiva University.'

A litany of names, of faces, of memories. He never tired of reciting them: they were the most important thing in his life. They were his past. Without them, he was nothing, nowhere. They were the reason he had found her loneliness so hard to bear.

On a side table a little apart from the others were several coloured photographs of children. Angelina had picked one up.

'Who's this?' she had asked.

Reuben had faltered before replying.

'They're all photographs of my daughter Davita,' he said. 'She's ten years old. That's the most recent shot, the one with her and the horse; it was taken a month ago.'

The photograph showed a slim, dark-haired child with large eyes. She held the bridle of a small piebald pony in one hand, smiling against a shaft of sunlight.

'I didn't know you had children.'

'Just one, just Davita.'

'You're married?'

His voice sounded far away.

'Once,' he said. 'I was married once. There are no photographs. Excuse me . . .' And he had stood and gone to the kitchen to make more coffee.

Angelina picked up the photos and set them down again. They meant nothing to her, cracked, faded, crooked in their gilt and silver frames; but as she examined them a sudden wave of jealousy crept over her, so all-consuming she had to close her eyes and grit her teeth together hard to stop herself bursting into tears. The closeness of his family, the certainty of his ancestry — little matches that would set her alight if she let them touch her skin too closely.

She made breakfast and washed up. When that was done, she went to the bathroom and washed her face in soapy water. She needed toner, moisturizer, make-up. Maybe she would go shopping later. She washed her hair, using Reuben's shampoo, some cheap garbage he'd picked up in an all-night supermarket. It made her hair feel coarse. She couldn't find a hairdrier anywhere.

At ten past eleven she went back to the living room. The photographs stared at her from their heavy frames, each one a basilisk, its eyes boring into her flesh. She got up and turned them round, facing the wall. She tried to read, a detective story by someone called Robert B. Parker. Reuben had a row of them on one shelf. A serial murderer was killing black women in Boston. He left a red rose every time he killed. They were just words, she couldn't focus on them.

The photographs still watched her: their basilisk eyes could see through gold and silver. She put down the book and walked from room to room gathering them all together. They fitted into a large drawer in the kitchen.

In the living room Reuben kept tropical fish in a large tank. They swam together, back and forwards, back and forwards, their luminous colours the brightest thing in the room. Following Reuben's instructions, she tipped a little food into the tank and watched it descend in shining particles to the bottom. The fish were like her, she thought: denizens of the tropics doomed to swim for ever in a glass tank thousands of miles from home. She dreamed of sinking to the bottom of the tank and closing her eyes for ever. No-one would ever make her swim again.

At twelve o'clock she took some pastrami from the fridge and made herself a sandwich. She could not remember whether or not she had told the police about the parcels of meat Filius had left in her apartment. The sandwich felt heavy in her stomach. She left it unfinished.

At half past twelve she got up and took the photographs from the drawer. One by one, she removed them from their frames and laid them on the table top. Old photographs, the quick, the dead, the half-remembered. What right had they to stare at her? She found a pair of kitchen scissors in another drawer and started to cut the photographs into long strips, then the strips into smaller fragments. Losing her patience, she threw the scissors aside and began to tear the scraps with her fingers, shredding them into smaller and smaller pieces: Aunt Rivke and Uncle Avrum, cousin Irving and little Davita. When she had finished, Reuben's past lay in untidy pieces on the floor.

She went into the living room and found a bottle of Napoleon brandy in a cupboard. Sipping it slowly, she sat in silence, watching the little bright-tailed fish cruise back and forwards through their cramped universe. How many circuits of the tank made a lifetime? There was a valve near the bottom of the tank. She opened it and watched as the water began to drain out onto the carpet. The fish sank lower and lower in the tank, desperately swimming, fighting the unexpected current that was dragging them down. At last they lay on the pebbles, sand and weeds of the bottom, their luminous bodies writhing in a final struggle for breath.

At a quarter past one, she picked up the telephone and dialled a Brooklyn number. A familiar voice answered.

'Aubin, is that you? I must see you at once. Yes, right away. I'll come to your place. Wait for me.'

CHAPTER EIGHT

'Your Haitian was HIV positive.' Dr Pablo Rivera leaned back in his chair and gazed myopically at Reuben over the top of his spectacles. The doctor was in his mid-thirties, a delicate age in his profession – still young enough to care, experienced enough to know that what he did made precious little difference. Working in the Cumberland put him on the front line. He was fighting a war, but he was no longer sure exactly who the enemy was.

'You mean he had AIDS?' Reuben asked.

Rivera pushed his glasses back against his nose and shook his head.

'It isn't as simple as that,' he murmured.

They were in Rivera's office on the fourth floor of the hospital. Reuben felt ill at ease here. If he'd only known it, he and the doctor had a lot in common. They were both the children of immigrants who had chosen professions in which they could help other people. They had both started their careers as idealists. And they were both growing cynical and finding that it hurt.

The hospital served as a focus for both their discontents. Rivera was learning that medicine can do very little against poverty and ignorance. He vaccinated children and pumped their parents full of antibiotics: the old diseases went away and new ones took their place. And here in sterile corridors, behind walls of polished steel, Reuben saw the bruises and the knife wounds that mocked his every effort. Rivera stitched the wounds, Reuben apprehended the muggers, and all the while tomorrow's killers and tomorrow's victims sharpened their blades on a dozen high school play-grounds.

'You just said he had HIV.'

'I'll be more precise, Lieutenant. Mr Narcisse had antibodies to the HIV virus. He may have suffered AIDS symptoms, he may not.

If and when I can track down his medical records, I may know the answer to that. Not everyone with HIV goes on to develop AIDS. Not even all AIDS patients have HIV. And there are even some people – by no means all of them cranks – who don't agree that HIV is the cause of AIDS at all. That may not be received wisdom, but it is nonetheless possible to make out a very good case for it.

'However, the point at issue is not whether our friend had AIDS.'

Rivera leaned forward. Reuben noticed that he seemed tired. Most doctors liked to look tired; it made them feel good. But Rivera looked like the real thing.

'In due course I expect to obtain enough information on which to base a diagnosis. But whatever his symptoms, Mr Narcisse does not appear to have died of AIDS. I only mention his being HIV positive to explain how I came to get the lab report I telephoned about.'

The doctor paused. He almost managed a smile.

'Lieutenant . . . can I rely on your discretion?'

'Of course – provided the information you give me isn't material to this investigation.'

Rivera hesitated momentarily.

'No,' he said. 'It isn't material. The thing is this: quite early on in the whole AIDS crisis, people talked about what were termed "the four Hs". There were four social groups who seemed to be particularly prone to the disease. Each could be identified by a word beginning with the letter "H". Homosexuals were the best known. Then haemophiliacs and drug addicts using hypodermics. The fourth "H" stood for Haitians.

'One Haitian in every 20,000 suffers from AIDS. That's a high proportion. Haitians were one of the major "at-risk" groups in this country until their government kicked up a fuss and had the category abolished. Officially, I'm not supposed to treat Haitians differently to anyone else. In practice, I do.'

The doctor picked up a pack of cigarettes from his desk.

'Smoke?'

Reuben nodded and took a cigarette from the pack. Rivera lit it for him, then his own.

'Tell me, Lieutenant, where in this country do you suppose has the highest ratio of AIDS cases?'

Reuben blew a thin line of smoke through his lips.

'I don't know. San Francisco, I guess. Or maybe here in New York.'

'Wrong. It's a place called Belle Glade in Florida. What's Belle Glade got that other places don't? Rats is one. Bad sanitation's another. Slums. A very high tuberculosis rate. Malnutrition. And a predominantly Haitian population.

'The problem isn't that people are Haitians. It just happens that Haitian refugees are among the poorest people in this country. Haiti itself is the poorest country in the Western hemisphere. There's a link between poverty and AIDS, same as there's a link between heavy drug use or excessive sexual activity and AIDS. They all shoot your immune system to hell.'

Rivera stood and went to the window. His office looked directly onto the Ingersoll Houses section of the Fort Greene Housing Project. Most of his patients came from there. He himself had been born half a mile away, the son of Puerto Rican immigrants. With just a little less luck, he'd be down there now, struggling to survive on the street.

'A lot of the people we see in this hospital are Haitians. Officially, I'm not supposed to notice. Unofficially, I take a blood sample from each one and send it to the lab for analysis. They run a simple HIV test. It's a quick procedure nowadays, and I can find out in a couple of hours just what I might be dealing with. I ran a test on Filius Narcisse and, as I told you, he showed positive.'

He turned back to face Reuben.

'You may not like to hear this, Lieutenant, but that's why no autopsy was done. People don't like to carry out autopsies on cadavers with HIV. They're frightened they might get contaminated by the blood. So Mr Narcisse was put briefly on ice before being handed over to his next of kin for burial.'

'I don't think they were next of kin, Doctor. As far as I know, Mr Narcisse had no relatives outside Haiti.'

Rivera looked mildly surprised, but no more than that.

'I see. Well, whoever took the body, they seem to have been acceptable to the hospital administration. I don't interfere in that sort of thing. If there's been some sort of irregularity, take it up with them.'

The doctor paused and drew hard on his cigarette.

'Anyway, that wasn't the last we heard of the deceased. I took more than one blood sample from him before he died. For a while now, I've been sending HIV-positive samples to a friend of mine at College Hospital over on Atlantic Avenue. His name's Joe Spinelli. One of his hobbies is looking for HIV co-factors. He has access to a mass spectrometer using gas chromatography.'

Reuben stubbed out his cigarette.

'Meaning?'

'Meaning he looks for molecular structures to identify substances that might otherwise remain hidden. Things that won't show up in an ordinary blood test. He mixed a sample of Mr Narcisse's blood with ether. When the blood and ether separated again, he found traces of several unusual substances.'

'Such as?'

'I've made a list. You can take it with you. I'll be sending a copy to the coroner.'

'Just give me a rough idea. Was Narcisse using drugs?'

Rivera shrugged.

'Not these drugs. Joe identified a very large number of distinct chemical substances, very few of which would normally occur in any drug available on the street. The most likely source for some of them would be either the ingestion or subcutaneous insertion of a variety of herbs or animal products, probably including several species of insect, toads and fish.'

The doctor looked down at a sheet of paper on his desk.

'Let me see. Joe found traces of saponins, a large group of glucosides. In high doses, these can be extremely toxic. One variety, known as sapotoxins, used to be administered orally in parts of Africa as a kind of truth serum; in large amounts, they interfere with cellular respiration and lead to death. Joe doesn't think there were enough in this sample to indicate a lethal dosage.

'He also found varying amounts of tannins, acid resin, toxic dihydroxyphenylalanine, and a number of alkaloids, including prurieninine and prurienidine. These can all be found in a number of tropical plants, mainly climbing lianas of the Leguminosae family. In certain combinations they can act as psychoactive compounds which may lead to hallucinations.

'Here again, Joe doesn't think a toxic dose had been administered. The same applies to several other active chemicals from other plants and to most of those from animal products. With one exception.

'There were substantial amounts of tetrodotoxin in this man's blood. It's what we call a neurotoxin; in other words a poison that acts on the nervous system. Most neurotoxins are proteins, but tetrodotoxin is a nonprotein substance of enormous toxicity. To put it bluntly, it's one of the most poisonous substances known. It's sixty times stronger than strychnine, one thousand times more powerful than sodium cyanide. As little as 0.5 milligrams of pure tetrodotoxin will kill an adult human being. It does so by causing complete neuromuscular paralysis. Your man was poisoned, Lieutenant. The only thing that puzzles me is that he was alive when you found him.'

Rivera removed his spectacles. Without them his eyes looked weak and bloodshot. Reuben sensed that the doctor's tiredness was not merely physical. He recognized the look: he'd seen it often enough in his bathroom mirror.

'Lieutenant, if you want to know what happened to your Haitian, you're going to have to dig him up again. As soon as possible.'

CHAPTER NINE

Her meeting with Aubin had left Angelina ill at ease. For almost an hour afterwards, she walked without any conscious purpose down street after tarnished street. Her heels clipped the sidewalk as she strode along, a staccato beat like the tap-tapping of a *rada* drum. She shimmered through the streets, unaware of the music she made.

At about half past four she found herself at the bottom of Clermont Avenue, where her apartment was located. She had not meant to come here, not consciously; something had driven her, some compulsion she could not name. Looking up and down the street, she saw no-one she knew. There were no marked police vehicles anywhere in sight.

The apartment was sealed. Across the edge of the door and the frame, a black and white poster bore an official NYPD sign saying 'STOP: CRIME SCENE'. Angelina pulled the poster away and inserted her key in the lock. It turned without a sound.

Forensic had finished for the moment. She could see traces of their presence everywhere: dustings for fingerprints, light paste-board tags on objects, labels saying this or that item had been removed as evidence. Evidence of what? The living-room door was shut tight; she left it that way and headed for the bedroom.

In the closet she found a medium-sized suitcase and packed it with a selection of her better clothes. Two extra pairs of shoes. Fresh underwear. Something black for the funeral. She thought of taking black underwear: was that morbid? She didn't even glance at the bed.

Across the corridor in the bathroom she stuffed a large toilet bag full of expensive creams and lotions. Rick had never been mean about what she could buy for the bathroom. He liked her to look after herself, he used to say. That's all right, then, she used to tell him: who else is going to look after me?

Relics of Rick lay everywhere. His razor with tiny bristles lodged against the blade, a tube of shaving cream, dandruff shampoo, a pair of unwashed underpants draped unceremoniously over the laundry basket. She pretended to ignore them.

Looking up, she caught sight of herself in the mirror, the big mirror over the washtub. Sunken eyes, hollow cheeks, lank hair. She thought of crimson fish drowning in air, of desperate eyes rolling and growing still. Kicking, kicking, falling still. She looked in the mirror again. The harsh fluorescent light did nothing to soften the effect.

Her clothes were a mess. They needed to be dry-cleaned and pressed. Or maybe not. Maybe she would never wear them again. She undressed quickly, pants and bra as well, shivering. Her skin felt clammy. A swarm of goose pimples crawled across her arms and chest. She could do with another shower, a really hot shower.

The pilot on the gas boiler was still alight. She found a tube of body scrub in the cabinet. Stepping into the shower closet, she drew the curtain and set the temperature gauge to hot. As she turned the tap, water burst from the rose above her head, drenching her in freezing water that turned in a matter of seconds to steaming. She gasped, twisting round to let her back take most of the stinging cascade. As she grew accustomed to the heat, she closed her eyes and bent her head back, letting the water stream across her face. Slowly, she leaned backwards into the water, feeling hard needles on her breasts and belly. Her skin was tingling, the blood rising to the surface. She reached out for the body scrub.

Suddenly, she opened her eyes and blinked the streaming water away. She felt frightened without real reason, as though the apartment had suddenly come awake.

Behind the shower curtain, shadows loomed. The bathroom shuddered, indistinct behind a veil of steam and plastic. Water splashed on the curtain, drowning all sound. She felt her heart beat and reached for the edge of the plastic sheeting. As she drew it back, water sprinkled onto the floor. She blinked heavy drops out of her eyes and strained to see. The bathroom was filling with steam, the mirror already coated with an even film of mist.

She turned off the shower. The water stopped immediately, leaving a haunted silence behind. She stood at the threshold of the cubicle, listening. Behind her, water dripped on the tiles. Drip, drip, drip, like a leaking tap. She strained her ears for other sounds, for a hint of something moving in the apartment. Silence. And the cold dripping sound of water on cracked tiles.

Softly, she stepped out of the shower. A voice in her head kept telling her there was nothing wrong. What was she frightened of? She had heard nothing. But she knew what she was frightened of.

Her hand reached out for the bath towel draped over the rail. She wrapped it round her, tying it just above her breasts. Her bowels felt loose. It was nothing, she told herself. Behind her, water dripped like ice melting. She remembered her dream, the long walk through the jungle, the heavy moisture dropping from the leaves of giant trees. She knew what she was frightened of.

Heart in mouth, she opened the door. The passage outside was empty, full of its own silence. Familiar, yet suddenly alien. She had become a stranger here, in her own home. Something had driven her out and did not want her to return.

She crept on tiptoe to the bedroom. It was empty. Her heart hammered in her chest, she could not stop looking round. A voice in her head kept shouting, 'Get out, get out while there's still time!'

She grabbed a sweater and a pair of jeans and hauled them on. A pair of sneakers. That was all. She lifted the suitcase.

Suddenly, she realized why she had come to the apartment. The source of her inner prompting lay in Rick's study, if the police had not found it and taken it away. She put the suitcase down again.

Dressed, she felt less vulnerable than in the bathroom, naked. 'There's nothing out there,' she told herself. She'd seen the poster on the door, broken the seal herself. But they had other ways of entering. Yes, she thought, she knew what frightened her.

Soft as silk, she slipped into the passage. To her right, the living-room door sat impassive in its heavy frame. She had only to press down the handle, open the door, walk inside. They had all been taken away, the things beneath the floor, every last tooth and bone and scrap of skin. But that was not what frightened her.

She passed the living room, shivering involuntarily as she did so, and crept on down the passage to Rick's study. The door lay partly open. She took a deep breath and reached for the light switch. Bright yellow light filled the room. She hung back in the doorway, hesitating. It was vital that she retrieve what she had come for, yet the impulse to run was overwhelming. Blood pumped in her veins, thick and warm, like syrup.

The police had been through everything. That did not matter, of course: she was sure they had not known where to look or what to look for.

From the walls, the grim faces of African gods looked down. Beside them, Haitian oleographs of St George and St Patrick in gilded timber frames. A wooden crucifix bearing the image of a black Christ. A shelf of Congo figurines from Léogane – little fat dolls dressed in red and blue spangled satin. She felt their eyes on her, their scarcely restrained anger at her intrusion.

The desk had been rifled, and not by the police. Files, bundles of letters, pens, pencils, paperclips – a confusion of stationery – lay strewn across the floor. Drawers had been pulled out carelessly and their contents tipped out at random. Rick's three-hundred-dollar Italian lamp had been dropped and smashed. His two filing cabinets had been systematically scoured. Books had been ripped from the shelves along two walls, flicked through and tossed aside.

Section by section, she combed the filing cabinets. Xeroxes of estate accounts from Haiti dating from the late colonial period, all intact. All untouched, as she had expected. Copies of private letters from the same period and the reigns of Dessalines, Christophe and Pétion, complete but for one file. Whoever had done the searching had known what to look for.

In one corner stood a large wooden cabinet, its doors wide open, most of its contents strewn across the carpet. This had been the pride of Rick's collection: *livres de commerce* from 1735 through to 1788; several massive registers of revenues and expenditures known simply as *grands livres* from the French slaving houses of Montaudouin, Bouteiller, Michel and d'Havelooze; the *journaux* or indexes necessary to make sense of the great accounts; and several books of ships from traders in Nantes, Le Havre and La Rochelle, containing details of the slaving vessels themselves, the slaves embarked on them, deaths on board, routes travelled.

The cabinet was made from rosewood, a heavy, overornamented piece modelled on the Empire style. Rick had bought it ten years ago at a shop in the Heights. If the dealer had been telling the truth, it had been built by Phyfe during his late period in Partition Street – the modern Fulton. Prices for a late-Phyfe cabinet had been relatively low then, and Rick had bought it on impulse – one of the few impulses Angelina ever remembered him having.

The dealer had missed or forgotten to mention one detail, discovered years later by accident when moving the cabinet to its present position. If you pressed on an acanthus leaf on the entablature above the doors, a panel opened in the side. Angelina ran her fingers along the frieze, found the leaf and pushed. The panel swung back, revealing a large cavity.

From the cavity she removed a large notebook. She checked through it quickly; it did not appear to have been tampered with. She took a deep breath and started for the door. The gods on the walls watched impassively. All around, the apartment watched with them. She could sense it breathing, slow and steady, unhurried, waiting.

In the passage, the sensation grew. Insects crawled between her skin and flesh. She could not tear her eyes from the living-room door. She wanted to make a dash for the front door, out into the hall, into the street; but her feet were like a diver's feet, leaden, rooted, holding her fast in sightless depths. Inch by inch, she was moving towards the door of the living room. Her heart was beating so loudly now she thought the walls must shake. Her feet moved without volition, inch after inch, foot after fearful foot.

She could hear nothing but the sound of her own heart pounding, a *kata* drum, white sound against the darkness of night, opening the ceremony, opening the doorway to the gods. *Ouvri barrié pou mon, Legba* . . . The darkness cracking. *Ouvri barrié* . . .

She lifted her hand and pushed down the handle. Silently, the door swung open.

The room was bathed in a dark light. Angelina pressed the electric switch, but nothing happened. Slowly, her eyes adjusted to the fineness of the light, the grace of its absence.

On a chair, dark in the middle of the room, a figure was seated, half in, half out of shadows, indistinct features puddled by the half-light. Angelina stopped in the open doorway, tense, frightened, her eyes straining. She took a step forward. There was a sound and a movement to her right. Turning, she saw a second figure step out of the dim, unfocused shadows. The figure stopped and looked at her. Her breath came, sticky and irregular.

'You,' she whispered, her voice as soft as cream. Her head was spinning, the room was out of focus, her lungs were crammed full of the thick air. The figure stepped nearer. Angelina tried to turn, but the room began to tumble and her legs were like ice, melting.

CHAPTER TEN

It was dark by the time the exhumation order came through. The coroner's department had wanted to wait until morning. They liked to keep office hours wherever possible. 'The dead don't mind waiting,' said the clerk when Reuben called to collect the order. 'I do,' Reuben replied.

He wanted Filius out of the ground and he wanted him out now. Left too long, the blood in the cadaver would start to deteriorate. The police pathologist had explained that biodegradation of proteins in the enzymes would lead to the production of new enzymes and new proteins, and these in turn could break down any drugs still in Filius's system.

He had asked for further exhumation orders on the four recent bodies from the Hammel apartment. It had proved possible to identify them simply by circulating photographs to local morticians, and they had already been quietly returned to their graves.

That was when Reuben had first become aware that pressure was coming from somewhere to keep what Angelina Hammel had found beneath her floorboards under wraps.

The undertakers had all been cautioned not to breathe a word to relatives. To spare people's feelings, they'd been told; and that had seemed reasonable enough. But then one of the undertakers had started asking questions, awkward questions. Where had the bodies been found? Did the police have any idea who had dug them up? Were there any others?

At that point an official statement had materialized from nowhere like a piece of ectoplasm. There had been four bodies in all. The whole thing had been nothing more than a sick practical joke by some medical students from Long Island College Hospital. No need for relatives to be distressed unnecessarily. No need for promising medical careers to be nipped in the bud. Their dean had given the kids a hell of a dressing down. The bodies would be restored intact, the kids' families would pay for the new coffins and the burials; it would all be very discreet.

Reuben had stormed into Captain Connelly's office as soon as he saw the statement. 'What medical students?' he had asked. 'What families?' Connelly had just shrugged his broad shoulders and told Reuben to ignore the statement. 'It's to keep some people happy, Reuben. Be a nice guy, play along. It won't affect your investigation, I promise. This is public relations, is all.'

To make things worse, Doug Lamont had been sent down from the Press Office on Police Plaza. Full lieutenant at twenty-five. Whizz-kid, very smart, should have been in advertising. He lived in Manhattan, in TriBeCa. In a loft. Wore a suit by Issey Miyake, a shirt by Umberto Ginocchietti, Gucci shoes. Reuben remembered his Uncle Nathan's famous dictum: 'Never wear clothes you can't pronounce.'

Lamont and his designer outfit had been given instructions to field questions if and when they came. A couple of reporters from local papers had got wind of something, maybe from one of the morticians. One had come from the *Haïti Observateur*, which had offices over on the old Navy Yard site. Lamont had sent them away smiling, clutching a couple of juicy aggravated rape stories packed with 'privileged information', their heads spinning with a pious peroration about elderly widows who might have strokes if they heard that their nearest and dearest had been raised from dust before their time. To round things off, he'd fed them a liberal dose of 'you play ball with us, we'll play ball with you', hinting at goodies that might come their way.

Cub reporters, eager beavers who knew how to pronounce the names on designer labels, they had swallowed Lamont and his hundred-dollar smile like a plate of sushi, cold. Anybody could have done it. Why had Manhattan sent in Prince Charming?

None of the remaining bodies had been identified, nor were they likely to be, unless something came up on the dental remains. Reuben had put a new boy called Johnson onto the job of checking records for reports of graveyard vandalism. The bodies had gone on ice. And then the lab report on Filius had come in. Now they were lined up at the mortuary for a series of PMs that would continue through the night. Nothing complicated. They knew what they were looking for: traces of tetrodotoxin poisoning.

Reuben and his partner Danny Cohen drove due east on Fulton, before turning onto Jamaica Avenue, skirting the lower flank of the great complex of parks and cemeteries that links Brooklyn to Queens. Even in death, the people of New York preferred segregation to integration. High walls of stone and rusting fences kept Jews from Catholics, Puerto Ricans from Chinese. No doubt they went to fenced and bounded heavens.

'I hate this place,' said Danny. 'When I was a kid, my father used to bring me here. All those stone houses with "Cohen" above the door. I used to have nightmares. I thought "If you're a Cohen, they put you in one of those places". I thought they were little prisons.'

Just past Stony Road, they turned off into Cypress Hills. The cemetery was popular with Haitians, though as yet they had no separate plot there. It was non-denominational: here heathens mixed with believers, blacks with whites.

The rest of the exhumation team was already waiting at the cemetery office. Apart from Reuben and Danny, the team consisted of Steve Koreski from the state attorney's office; the pathologist who was going to perform the autopsy, a Lebanese doctor called Chamoun; the undertaker who had supervised the burial; and two long-haired gravediggers. To Reuben's surprise, Sally Peale was standing with the others. Sally was an old girlfriend, a sharp lawyer from New York City Hall's legal department.

'On time as usual, Reuben.' Sally was petite, blonde and as hard as nails. She and Reuben had seen a lot of each other once, about three years ago, on a very personal basis; but this was the first time they had met in a graveyard. For a moment, Reuben felt a familiar tug of attraction: Sally Peale was not someone you forgot in a hurry. With an effort, he smiled; they were still friends, still saw one another occasionally, still gave each other gifts at Christmas and Chanukah.

'What are you doing here, Sally? I didn't think City Hall had an interest in this.'

'Just keeping an eye on you, Reuben. How are you?'

'OK. You look fine.'

'I'm hungry. I'd planned a dinner for tonight.'

'Anybody I know?'

Sally sniffed.

'Would I know people you know? Give me a break, Reuben. Give Steve the authorization and let's get this guy out of the ground.'

Narcisse had been buried in the Parkside section of Cypress Hills, on the cemetery's eastern boundary, near the Memorial Abbey. The team drove slowly between tall, half-glimpsed trees. The lights of the cars picked out old Jewish graves on their right. A minute later they entered a vast area of Chinese burials, low stones topped by small rocks holding down scraps of paper.

They parked beside the Abbey and went the rest of the way on foot, walking in single file between low grey and pink headstones packed close together. The names were mostly Spanish. Nobody looked very important or rich.

The edges of the gravel path along which they made their way marked the sharpest of all boundaries. Their flashlights picked out names and dates, the stone figure of a tiny wounded angel, dim-coloured flowers beaten down by rain and wind. A new grave, partly boarded over, yawned like a fresh wound in the earth. Reuben gave it a wide berth, shuddering like someone in the presence of an omen.

Narcisse was buried behind the Abbey, not far from the Interborough Parkway. Looking north-west, Reuben could see the tall lights of Manhattan perfect against a low sky. At his feet, the fresh earth of the grave was barely visible beneath a heap of rain-drenched wreaths.

The diggers lifted two arc lamps from their truck, already parked nearby. They often worked at night, especially at this time of year. They switched on the lamps, ripping a swathe of light out of the darkness. Before starting work, they moved the flowers to one side. As they did so, a plastic-coated card detached itself from a large wreath and fluttered to the ground at Reuben's feet. He bent and picked it up.

'*Dormi pa'fumé, Filius,*' it read. There was no signature. Reuben slipped it into his pocket.

He had not noticed Sally come up beside him. She touched his arm gently, making him jump.

'Creepy business, huh?'

He nodded.

'Ever been at one of these before?' he asked. The sound of heavy spades slicing wet earth punctuated his words.

She nodded.

'Half a dozen. But not at night. What's so urgent about this one?'

He explained.

'I still think you could have left it till tomorrow,' she answered. 'Or maybe you just like the Burke and Hare stuff.' Behind her, the diggers bent to their task, mere silhouettes outlined against the harsh light. People stood around in little groups, whispering together or watching the digging in silence. Someone gave a nervous laugh.

'Speaking of Burke and Hare,' Sally continued. 'What's this story about cowboy medics at the College Hospital?'

He shrugged.

'PR,' he said.

'On whose instructions?'

'I thought maybe you could tell me.'

She shook her head. Her face was in shadow, but he could make out the whites of her eyes. It seemed like a memory. Perhaps it was.

'Look, Reuben, the way I heard it, you found, what was it? – nine dead people, none of them with any visible signs of violence. Somebody leaps to the conclusion that they've been dug up from local graveyards. Twenty-four hours later they've identified some of them and started putting them back into the ground. Believe me, that's quick work. So who wants these people buried?'

He shrugged, a vivid gesture borrowed from his father, who in turn had taken it from his father. It was a shrug with ancestry. 'I really don't know,' he said. 'Things have been moving fast ever since this case began. Somebody in high places wants to play things down.'

'You still have an investigation, don't you?'

'Yes, but that's mostly because of the man we're about to dig up here. I don't have evidence of foul play in any of the other bodies. The four that were reburied had already been given death certificates. All natural causes.'

The diggers were already up to their waists. The grave had not begun to settle, and the loose soil was easy to dislodge once they got below the level to which rain had sunk.

'What's going on, Reuben? Somebody's been asking questions at my office.'

'About this? Who?'

'I don't know. My boss passes them on to me, says they've been shunted down to him.'

'From inside your department?'

She shook her head.

'No. Maybe someone in the mayor's office. "Someone in administration", is how Jack put it. Don't quote me on this.'

'What sort of questions?'

'They want details. How many bodies, do we know their

identities, what's being done? Oh, yes, somebody seems interested in you as well. Jack asked me what I knew about you.'

'I hope you told him all the right things.'

She smiled. He remembered her smile from the past and as quickly shut the thought out of his mind. 'I said you were a *gonif*. What else should I tell him?'

'Does he speak Yiddish?'

'Who needs to speak Yiddish to recognize a *gonif*?' She paused, growing serious once more. 'What's so special about this case, Reuben?'

He did not answer at once. The diggers had struck the coffin and were starting to remove the last shovelfuls of dirt.

'I don't know, Sally. But I'd like to find out. Listen, if you hear anything, will you keep me informed?'

'Sure. Same goes for you.'

'Ask around, find out who's behind these questions. Will you do that?'

She nodded. They glanced at one another easily. It would take so little: a word, a touch . . .

'I think Dracula's about to come up,' Sally said, glancing down at the grave.

One of the gravediggers had come up out of the pit and was moving a winch into place over the hole. A strap was fitted through the four handles of the coffin, then attached to a line lowered from above. The second digger scrambled out and helped his partner operate the winch. Slowly, the coffin rose out of the earth, grinding gently against the sides of the hole on its way up, dislodging small clods of earth.

The world shrank to an oblong box, all eyes fixed on it. The entire scene seemed to Reuben suddenly ridiculous, like the denouement of some TV magic show, in which they raise the magician in his spangled casket, death-defying in straitjacket and chains. The winch jerked awkwardly, tilting the coffin. Something bumped heavily inside the box. The diggers went on winding.

Reuben helped the diggers manoeuvre the casket to one side. The brass nameplate was still shiny, scarcely dulled by its brief sojourn beneath the earth. The light shone like a curse, whitening the coffin. The undertaker stepped out of the little crowd holding a long screwdriver in his hand. He seemed nervous, his movements clumsy, magnified by the harsh light. Carefully, he worked his way round the coffin, loosening the screws.

The two diggers took the lid and slid it to one side. Reuben stepped closer, moving between the coffin and the light. A shadow fell across the interior. Reuben gestured and the gravediggers lifted the lid fully away. Reuben edged out of the light and looked down.

The coffin was empty. On the lace pillow where Filius Narcisse's head had recently rested lay a small white coffin covered in writing.

CHAPTER ELEVEN

She was splintered, fragmented, a prey to images of immaculate decay, walking half-blind down streets of lead and pitch as though the world would never end, as though she would walk for ever, unimpeded. Or as if the world had already ended and she had been left alone to lurch and stumble through the graves.

Her uncertain footsteps carried her, as they had on previous occasions of crisis, to the small Haitian church on Lafayette. The small white-painted building seemed to her less a beacon than a sepulchre, and at first she recoiled from it. The things she had witnessed over the past week, above all what she had just seen that afternoon, had brought her close to some kind of edge. She feared insanity, but more than that the possibility that a rational mind lay behind all this.

The church was dimly lit as it always was at this time of day, as though it simply waited to be animated. A red light burned at the little altar, cherry red, flickering slightly, the presence of Christ. Angelina crossed herself and genuflected awkwardly. She was not a pious woman, the slow movements of devotion made her clumsy. Above the altar, feebly lit and stained a dull crimson, the figure of a black Christ watched her slide into a pew and bow her head. Christ the slave, Christ the Maroon, Christ the bleeding redeemer of slaves. Could any of that be true?

She had been coming to St Pierre's for almost a year now, off and on. Rick's anger, Rick's indifference, Rick's heat, Rick's coldness – these had been the goads pricking her to a flawed devotion and an imperfect confession. Or was it simply that she was growing middle-aged and menopausal and in need of faith?

She was still trying to still her mind enough to pray when Father Antoine found her. He'd been expecting her ever since he heard of Rick's death. He knew, of course, that Rick had been a Protestant and would have no need of his services for the burial. But Angelina would need him, he had been sure of that.

The priest waited a long time beside her, watching in silence, waiting for her concentration to wander. But she was not concentrating, only distracted, as ill at ease with Christ as she had been earlier that day with Reuben and his memories. Finally, she turned and looked at Father Antoine.

'*Bonsoir, Angelina. Tout va bien?*'

She shook her head. Her eyes were huge, drained of expression.

'No,' said the priest, 'of course not. Forgive me.'

He sat down beside her, a big man, clumsy in his black cassock. His huge hands lay in his lap, useless for any act of consolation. Here, beneath the pain-filled eyes of his god, his priestliness forbade him to offer comfort in any medium but words.

'*Richard est mort.*'

'Yes, I know. Silbert told me yesterday. I've been expecting you. You should have come sooner.'

'I'm here now.'

'Yes,' he whispered. 'You're here now.'

'Father, I need to talk to you.'

He had never known her like this before. Troubled, yes; but never flat, never drained.

'Of course. We can talk here or . . .'

'No,' she said, her voice abrupt, cracking, 'not talk. Confess. I have things I want to confess. Please, Father, before it's too late.'

The big priest looked at her in confusion. In all the time she had been coming to his church, she had never once entered the confessional. Tonight she seemed shrunken, as though something were eroding her.

'We'll go over there,' he said, 'to the confessional. You'll find it easier.'

She followed him like a whipped dog, or like someone carrying a heavy weight, unable to set it down.

The small cubicle had been built awkwardly into the corner of the church, near the small chapel of St Michel. Little light entered it even when the church was fully illuminated. It was a dark place, intended for dark thoughts. Sins do not come out easily into daylight.

Angelina sat by the grille wondering why she had come here. What could the priest do? What could she say that would change anything?

'How long is it since your last confession?'

A shaft of light fell through the grille onto her lap, gilding her.

'Twenty years.'

The priest recited his formulae, she responded, then silence fell between them, heavy with the weight of so many unshriven sins. Where to begin? Where to end? Stammering, she said the first thing that came into her head. She had so little practice in this, her tongue would not cooperate in the betrayal of her heart. But slowly the words came, hesitant at first, then fluent, a stream of them pouring out, thick and delicious, almost choking her.

It took more than an hour, and when she had come to an end she was shivering and cold with sweat. In a shaking voice the priest pronounced the formulae of absolution. But she did not feel absolved. Nothing could absolve her. It was nothing she had done: actions can be blotted out by grace. It was what she knew. There is no grace for knowledge, no absolution for the things that lie in the mind, twittering.

Father Antoine was the first to leave the confessional. Angelina followed him, head bent, eyes on the floor.

'Is there anything I can do for you, Angelina? I want to help.'

'No, Father, nothing.'

'Have you spoken with anyone else about . . . these matters?'

She shook her head.

'It would be better not to. But I will be here any time you need me.'

'Thank you, Father.' She paused. 'I think I should go now.'

'Where are you staying? I may need to get in touch.'

'No, don't do that. It's all right, I'm with a friend.'

'At least let me know where you are.'

She gave him the address and he wrote it down in a small notebook he kept in his pocket. As he put the book away, she looked up at him.

'Does it matter that I don't really believe?'

How many times had he been asked that question?

He shook his head.

'I don't know, Angelina. The thing is to attend Mass and confess your sins. Leave the rest to God.'

'Is it really that simple?'

He looked away. On the altar, the red light flickered and went out. He fancied he had felt a draught.

She turned and walked away, down the aisle, out into the night.

Father Antoine stood for a little while in silence, his eyes fixed on the spot where the light had burned. He would replace the candle later.

He went through the side door that led into the rectory. No-one else was at home tonight. His legs felt heavy, he felt sick. In the study, he sat down, composing himself. Finally, he picked up the telephone and dialled. It rang for a long time before anyone answered.

'This is Father Antoine at St Pierre's. I have the information you asked for. But you must promise me that you will not harm the woman.'

A voice at the other end spoke calmly, reassuringly. Father Antoine took a deep breath.

It took only seconds to dictate her address, but it seemed like a lifetime to him. The light had gone out in the sanctuary. The church was in darkness.

'Listen,' he said when he had done. 'This is the last time you'll hear from me. Do you understand? I don't want to see you here again. Not here, not anywhere near me.'

There was no answer. The line had gone dead.

CHAPTER TWELVE

Reuben had given her a door key the night before. She let herself in with it, not knowing whether he was back or not. The passage was in darkness, but at its end she saw a light shining through the edges of the kitchen door.

She felt numb inside, without feelings. It was as though something dark and heavy was suffocating her: she longed for some fresh pain, some unfinished grief to tear her open and let her breathe again. She pushed the door gently and it swung open on a loose hinge.

He was sitting on the floor, on cold tiles, cross-legged among the mutilated fragments of his family and friends, sifting through a crazy jigsaw of smiles and faces, torn limbs and broken gestures, searching for something he could recognize. His hands were shaking. He was weeping silently.

She stood in the doorway and watched him, feeling neither guilt nor satisfaction. His fingers moved like the wings of unpatterned butterflies against dark petals, brushing his exploded past with tiny caresses, powder-soft. She almost wept for him.

He looked up at last and saw her watching, her features blurred behind a mist of tears. She said nothing. Her confession had left her mute and empty.

'Why?' he asked, knowing there was no answer.

She turned away from him. Blood was roaring in her head, tearing her silence to shreds. Like him, she wanted to knit things together again. She wanted to hear her own thoughts again. But there was only blood rushing in her brain and voices she did not recognize, calling her name from a great distance. She ran out of the apartment, back into the night.

The empty streets stretched in front of her like sewers, rank and uninhabited. It made no difference which way she went. She turned to the right and ran, blind and deaf, trying to drown out the voices in her head.

She had reached the corner of Coney Island and Cortelyou when she heard his footsteps tight behind her, hard against the pavement. There was neither breath nor will left in her; she was sapped and torn, unable to carry on. Her breath came in harsh gasps, a sharp pain riveted her side. She collapsed against the window of George's Restaurant, panting like a fox at bay. Inside, people were drinking coffee and eating the best cheesecake in Brooklyn. Bright American flags were pinned beside photographs of young men and women in a variety of uniforms. The inexhaustible immigrant longing for normality.

He came to her walking slowly. The tears on his cheeks had not yet dried. A woman passing glanced at them curiously, thinking them lovers in the heat of a quarrel. Angelina was shivering, gasping for breath. Her hair fell into her open eyes, long and angry. The woman watched for a moment, then walked on, indifferent. Everyone had troubles.

He touched her shoulder gently, but she winced and drew away, almost as though he had slapped her.

'What is it, Angelina? What are you frightened of? I won't hurt you. The photographs don't matter. I'm not angry, believe me. I'm hurt, but I'm not angry. I want to understand.'

She couldn't look at him, couldn't bear to see his eyes. All the time she was shaking. He touched her again and she felt something snap inside. Her hand went back and suddenly she was striking him, hard across the cheek, then again and again until she was pummelling him furiously with clenched fists, striking him anywhere and everywhere – his face, his arms, his chest, his stomach. And all the time she was silent, as though the rage had only her hands to express itself with.

He could scarcely control her. Her arms flailed, punching him, winding him. He did not want to hurt her, did not want her to hurt herself, but he had to stop her. Somehow, he managed to grab her arms, but she went on shaking, strained, convulsive, as though in the grip of a fit.

He shouted at her. 'Angelina, try to get control! Please, Angelina, stop this! You'll hurt yourself! There's nothing to be afraid of! I want to help you, Angelina. Please stop!' But she panted and spat and jerked her arms, trying to break free.

And then, as suddenly as it had started, her outburst stopped.

77

She went rigid, her whole body viciously tense. A moment later, she went limp, leaning against the window as though about to fall. He expected tears, and when they did not come, thought she might be beyond his help.

'It's all right,' she said. 'I'm all right, it's over now. I'm sorry I hit you. I'm sorry I tore your photographs.'

'That doesn't matter. Come back to the apartment.'

He tried to put his arm round her, thinking she might need some comfort, but she stepped away from the clumsiness of his gesture and walked ahead alone. He followed her back slowly, neither speaking, the silence round them tangible. Her breathing was still spasmodic and uneven, but the anger or the terror – he could not decide which it had been – seemed to have passed.

In the apartment, he sat her down with a glass of brandy and fixed a second for himself. She was still shaking visibly. At her first sip she shuddered. The roaring in her head had subsided until it was a faint murmur. The voices had become whispers, mercifully distant. She did not recognize them, but they knew her, knew her name, and she feared that, if they called insistently enough, she might go to them in the end.

'Feeling better?' he asked after some time.

She nodded. They were in the living room. He had cleared away the fish; the tank sat in the corner, dark and empty, the weeds on the bottom already starting to rot.

'Do you want to tell me what's been happening?'

She shook her head and held her glass out for more Armagnac. The taste brought back memories of home, of her last years in Paris. Her father had always sent to a friend in France for cases of Vieille Réserve cognac from the Charente. Dinner guests had lingered over it, saying no-one else in the whole of Haiti had such fine brandy. After his arrest, the Tontons had come to steal the last cases from the cellar. 'To impound it,' they had said, but it was stealing all the same. They had left nothing, but it had not mattered by then. No more guests ever came to dinner.

'I went to confession today,' she said.

'Really? And what did you confess?'

She hesitated.

'That's a secret between me and God.'

'And your priest.'

She nodded.

'Yes, my priest as well. But he won't tell you anything. They swear oaths, these priests. I thought you would know that.'

'Yes, I do know that. Half of the crimes in this city might be solved if that rule could be suspended for just one day.' He paused. 'I didn't think you were religious.'

'I can be when I need to.'

'Do you need to now?'

'I think so, yes.'

She changed the subject abruptly, telling him about the Vieille Réserve, then, without meaning to, about her father.

'Why was your father arrested?' he asked.

She shrugged. 'Why was anyone arrested in those days? The Tontons Macoutes killed innocent people just to make sure no-one felt safe. Father was a Minister under President Vincent and again under Lescot, back in the thirties and forties. Minister for Education on both occasions. When Lescot was overthrown in 1946, he left politics and concentrated on his rubber plantation near Jérémie. After Magloire came to power, he persuaded my father to take a seat in his cabinet, and when he was overthrown, my father went back to the plantation again. That was in 1956. Father was sixty. I was seven.

'The following year, Duvalier was elected, and before long the Tontons were hunting down members of the élite. Our family was high on their list: the Hypolite-Béliards are among the oldest of the *gens de couleur.*'

She smiled wanly.

'It's all colour in Haiti, you know. We've had light skins for longer than almost anyone, so we rank high in society.'

She shrugged and a frown crossed her face.

'Well, six months after Duvalier came to power, some men came to our plantation. They took father to Port-au-Prince. I never saw him again.'

She fell silent, gazing at the empty fish tank, at the empty glass in her hand. After her father's death in custody, her mother had been taken to a sanatorium in Switzerland. There was no diagnosis, no cure. Angelina was taken to see her once a year, but her mother never recognized her, never spoke. Outside her window in the long Swiss nights, heavy with the promise of snow, cold winds rose and fell against sharp mountainsides. Inside, on a table by her bed, there stood a photograph of a coral sea, dim in a silver frame.

As Duvalier's grip tightened on the country, the élite began to pack their bags and leave – some to Europe, some to the States. At sixteen, Angelina was sent to school in Paris. When things settled down a little a few years later, her aunt Classinia summoned her back to the family villa in Pétionville, high up in the hills above Port-au-Prince. She lived there with her aunt and a few servants, sipping the last of the good wine, watching the purple sun set across the bay, brushing her long black hair, and studying her face in a mirror of French glass brought to Haiti long ago from Nantes. At night she listened to the *tap-taps* negotiating the curves on the Pétionville Road.

'I wanted to be an artist,' she said. 'A painter. When I was in Paris, I studied a little. I had a teacher on the rue St Sulpice. He said I had talent. Back in Haiti, I painted every day; but Rick said I was wasting my time, that I could never become a serious artist there. He said I had to go to New York, that he would buy me a studio.'

'And did he?'

She shook her head.

'I had a room in my apartment that I called my studio, but it was too cramped and dark. I still paint a little, but only for myself. There were never any exhibitions or galleries.'

'Have you kept your paintings?'

She looked strangely at him, as though his questions had entered forbidden territory.

'There are some back in Haiti,' she said. 'And the ones from New York are in a storage depot in Bensonhurst. Nobody ever sees them. I don't know why I keep them – they just gather dust and cobwebs.'

'Could I see them?'

'You wouldn't like them.'

'How do you know?'

'I know,' she said, 'I know.'

Richard Hammel found her there on his first research trip to Haiti. She was twenty-four, he was thirty-one. He took her every afternoon for picnics to Kenscoff, and most evenings for dinner at the Oloffson. They danced disco at the Cercle Bellevue and merengues at a nameless club on the rue Poste Marchand. His research grant was almost depleted by the end of the first month. From time to time she accompanied him to a remote *houngfor* in the Artibonite valley, where they watched men and women become gods and goddesses. For two whole months she sparkled. For the first time in her life, she thought she was happy.

Up in the refined air of Pétionville, however, those of her

relatives who still remained in Haiti murmured their disapproval. Rick was American, far from wealthy and, worst of all, a man without ancestry. In their eyes that made him a thing beneath contempt. The Hypolite-Béliards inhabited a world of fine distinctions, a microcosm whose contours were determined by fine gradations of skin colouring – mulatto, marabou, griffon, black, white – and even subtler shades of taste and breeding. They spread rice powder on their faces, sipped absinthe at the Pigalle and ordered the latest novels from Paris. The marriage was forbidden.

Angelina married him anyway. The following day, her aunt disowned her publicly. Rick took her straight back to New York, to a small apartment in Brooklyn. Beyond its dirt-stained windows, nothing grew. No mountains, no forests, no coral seas. For a while she was happy and thought she was in love. And her clock ticked, and the slow threads unravelled in her wedding gown.

Later, she lay awake at night and listened to sounds that were not there. Sometimes she fell into bursts of fitful sleep and dreamed of a yellow dress she had worn as a little girl, when she was seven.

Angelina talked till it grew late. She had no photographs to show Reuben, only tattered memories. Sunsets and mirrors flickered in and out of sight; her words could not bind them, make them stay still. He wondered what she was hiding. And why.

It was well after midnight when he showed her to her room. She hardly remembered having slept in it the night before. As he started to close the door, she turned.

'Stay with me tonight, Reuben. I'd like you to. Please say you will.' Her eyes pleaded. Sunsets and mirrors. Dim shadows of a little girl.

'You're tired,' he whispered. 'We're both tired. Leave the light on if you're frightened. I'll be sleeping just down the passage.'

'Not for that,' she said, 'not for comfort.'

He paused. He understood. Her eyes had come alive.

'For what, then? We hardly know one another, Angelina. I'm not even supposed to have you here. If my superiors heard I'd been sleeping with you as well . . .' He spread his hands. 'Please, Angelina . . . Maybe if things were different . . .'

She closed her eyes and nodded. She did not want to see him. Sunsets and mirrors dazzled her. She did not see him close the door. She did not see him lean his head against it for a moment, then turn and walk away.

CHAPTER THIRTEEN

He looked at his clock. It was almost four A.M. Something had wakened him. He climbed out of bed and put on his robe. He could not remember when he had last felt so tired.

There was a light coming from the kitchen. Angelina sat there on the floor just as he had sat hours before. She had found a roll of scotch tape in a drawer and was busy pasting the pieces of his photographs together. He watched her pick and sort, joining edge to serrated edge, fragment to fragment, face to face.

When he came close she did not move, but went on with her sorting and sticking as though unaware of his presence. He looked at what she had done: completed squares and rectangles lay on the floor beside her, their edges uneven, the Sellotape crooked. Nothing matched. None of the pieces fitted together. The photographs she was building were as broken and diffuse as the debris through which she was sifting.

He reached down and put his hand gently on her shoulder. She looked up, not startled, not afraid.

'I was waiting for you,' she said. 'I've put your family back together again. Like Humpty Dumpty. Look.'

He lifted her carefully to her feet. She was dressed in the heavy nightgown his sister had sent. The clothes she had gone to her apartment to fetch were still there, in the suitcase.

The front of the nightgown lay open, exposing a little of her breasts. He reached out to close it, but his hand shook and he touched her cheek instead. She saw him look at her, felt her heart shake, her skin grow cold beneath the heavy fabric. He stroked her cheek with the hairs on the back of his hand. She kissed his fingers gently.

He could not resist her now. Smiling, she took his hand and moved it to her breast. As it slipped inside the gown, he drew her to himself and kissed her. Her lips tasted of salt, and he realized that tears were coursing down her face.

She bent back her head and he kissed her neck softly. His hand moved cautiously across her breast, brushing the nipple, tearing the breath from her. She leaned towards him and put her mouth against his mouth, kissing him hard, her tongue like a moth's wing fluttering against his lips and teeth.

Closing her eyes, she saw her own face in a rippling glass, Rick's face smiling, naked as winter, Rick's face bruised and pale on a bed of stainless steel, the sun sinking naked into a crimson sea, her mother naked and lifeless on a bed of silk. Frightened, she opened her eyes again. Reuben's face was close to her.

He helped her slip the nightgown over her shoulders, pulling her arms through the frilled, awkward sleeves. It fell heavily to the floor, leaving her cold and naked in his arms.

The room was spinning, she felt sick with need. He lowered his head and touched her breasts with open lips, turning her to water. Her legs could hold her no longer; she pulled him down, clutching him hard against her for fear that the world would tumble out of control.

She whimpered as his fingers touched her thighs, but his lips found hers and quieted her. She knew there was nothing pretty about sex, nothing shining in the body. Rick had taught her that. Rick and his cold hands and his moist skin. She expected nothing, wanted nothing. This was all there was or ever could be: a cold embrace, a moment of farce, a squirt of semen cold against her belly. She closed her eyes and saw Rick's face bloated in triumph.

They were naked and struggling now among the flotsam and jetsam of a hundred ruined photographs. The paper shards stuck to her skin, their edges biting her. She smelled vanilla and pepper, heard voices whispering, the wind among the rubber trees, felt Reuben enter her, cried out, cried out, opened her eyes, felt the world tilt and tilt again, heard her voice crying as he moved inside her, cried out and closed her eyes.

She wept for a long time afterwards, cradled in his arms. He had taken her to his bed and pulled the duvet over them like a tent. Her thighs were still smeared with blood. He could not understand how he had hurt her.

And then she stopped crying and explained, tearing the words bloodily from deep inside her, and he lay beside her in the darkness, wordless and wounded.

He fell asleep some time after that, exhausted, his arm still wrapped about her shoulders. Outside, a dark wind had come in from the sea and was blowing in tortured gasps across the sleeping city. A trashcan toppled with a crash and began to rock back and forwards on the sidewalk. Angelina lay awake, listening to it bang, one hand on Reuben's heart as it beat beside her. He did not waken.

He dreamed he was in a graveyard where the tombs were as high as skyscrapers and dogs ran back and forth in silent packs. A long line of people filed between the graves, he among them, long shovels across their shoulders, looking for a place to dig.

In a neglected corner of the necropolis, they fell on a tiny patch of freshly turned earth and set their spades to it. He dug like a madman, deeper and deeper, far into the earth. When he looked round at last, he found himself alone in the open grave, standing on a coffin, far away from everyone.

Somehow, he managed to squeeze himself into the grave beside the coffin and lift the heavy lid. He shone his light on the shrouded form inside. Angelina's face smiled up at him, unblemished, uncorrupted, unutterably beautiful. He bent to kiss her and her lips were warm. Slipping his hands behind her neck, he raised her to a sitting position. As he did so, he caught sight of her back. Underneath, she was a decomposing horror. Her bare skull showed through a tangled mess of matted hair. Where her flesh had been, maggots seethed in a stew of corruption. He dropped her and tried to climb back out of the grave. A moment later, he woke up screaming and found her beside him, smiling.

She soothed him, saying it was the wind that had frightened him, nothing more. They lay awake after that, speaking from time to time like old, familiar lovers who wake in the small hours. Finally, she told him what she had been afraid to tell him earlier.

'I went back to my old apartment today,' she whispered. 'The apartment where Rick and I used to live.'

'Yes, I know. What happened?'

She hesitated and reached out for him.

'I saw Filius Narcisse,' she said. 'He was sitting in our living room.'

'You saw him? You're sure?'

She pressed his hand tightly. All around them, the darkness crowded.

'I saw him,' she whispered. 'And I spoke to him.'

But she did not tell him who else had been there. He would not have understood. She did not yet understand perfectly herself.

CHAPTER FOURTEEN

'Dr Spinelli? This is Lieutenant Reuben Abrams. I called yesterday but you were out. I left a message with your secretary.'

There was a pause at the other end. Spinelli had just come on duty. He'd had a difficult night. His new girlfriend had just discovered Alex Comfort: they'd got as far as 'B' before he collapsed.

'Yes, Lieutenant. I got your message. You want to see me. What can I do to help you?'

Reuben explained what Rivera had told him, letting Spinelli fill in some of the jargon. He was sitting in the kitchen, drinking a cup of lukewarm coffee. Angelina was in bed, trying to sleep. Spinelli cut him off halfway through his explanation.

'Look, Lieutenant, I sent a report on this to Dr Rivera. If necessary, I'll testify in court that your victim died from tetrodotoxin poisoning. But that probably won't be necessary after the autopsy.'

'There isn't going to be an autopsy.'

'Why not?'

'We don't have a body.'

A long silence. When Spinelli spoke again, his tone had altered.

'The coffin was empty?'

'Yes. How did you know?'

Spinelli hesitated before replying.

'Lieutenant, if I'd had my wits about me, I could have warned you.'

'You knew this might happen?'

'No, Lieutenant. If I'd known I would have told you. I didn't tell you because I didn't use my imagination. This is only something I've read about, it never occurred to me that it could happen in New York.'

'And just what is it that you've read about?'

'Have you ever heard about zombies, Lieutenant?'

'Dr Spinelli, I don't want . . .'

'No, listen, Lieutenant. The man whose blood I tested was Haitian, right?'

'That's correct.'

Reuben heard Spinelli draw in his breath.

'I guessed that, Lieutenant. To be fair, I would have done so earlier if I'd taken the trouble to look at the man's name.' He paused. 'OK, listen to me carefully. Forget everything you've ever heard about zombies, every late-night movie you've ever seen, every comic you read as a child. What I'm talking about now is plain fact.

'Believe me, I feel every bit as awkward as you do using a word like "zombie". I'm a doctor, a scientist. So what I'm going to tell you is scientific fact. What the Haitians call "zombies" aren't supernatural beings – if I thought that, I wouldn't be talking to you, wasting your time. What they seem to be are people who have been put into a state of extreme narcosis, a coma more or less indistinguishable from death, declared dead, buried and then brought back to imperfect consciousness.'

'Is this just guesswork?' Reuben asked. 'Or have you proof?'

'Proof,' answered Spinelli. 'A close friend of mine is an ethno-biologist at Harvard. He studies plants and plant remedies in their cultural settings. Mainly, he looks for pharmaceutical applications for traditional herbal medicines. He's done a lot of work on hallucinogens among the Indian tribes in Brazil.

'A couple of years ago he heard I was interested in natural toxins. He introduced me to substances I'd never heard of. One of those was something called tetrodotoxin. The poison is a complex molecule occurring naturally in several species of marine fish, generally known as puffer fish or blowfish. The toxin can be found in their skin, liver, genital organs and intestines. As Dr Rivera explained to you, it's extraordinarily toxic.'

Spinelli stopped speaking. Reuben could hear him breathing gently, and in the background the sounds of a hospital going about its daily business.

'Lieutenant, have you ever heard about *fugu*?'

'Never.'

'It's Japanese for puffer fish. Over there, it's regarded as a sort of delicacy. All the best restaurants serve it. Thing is, it's potentially lethal, so only government-licensed chefs are allowed to prepare it. Mostly it's eaten as *sashimi*, raw flesh taken from the back muscles, which are nontoxic. Even so, people die every year from eating *fugu* that's been carelessly prepared. So why do you think anybody would want to take that sort of risk when they could enjoy a dish of prawns instead?'

'It must taste good.'

'On the contrary, I'm told it's nothing special. Taste doesn't come into it. What people are looking for is a legal drug experience. The idea isn't to get rid of all the toxin but to leave just enough so that the diner gets a feeling of mild euphoria. A little drunk, a little numb round the mouth, like you've just been to the dentist.

'So a lot of people get numb and feel a warm tingling. About one hundred a year die. What happens in between? There has to be an in between, right?'

There was the sound of a beeper going off.

'Just a moment, Lieutenant, someone's calling me.'

There was a brief pause while the doctor made a call on another line. Then his voice returned.

'Where was I?'

'In between numb and dead.'

'Right. Between numb and dead they go into a coma and – get this – they get taken to hospital and declared dead. All the time they're fully conscious. They can hear, their mental faculties are alert, they can even see if someone opens their eyes. But they can't move a muscle, not to speak, not even to twitch an eyelid. To all appearances, they are dead. Sometimes they end up being buried alive.

'In Haiti, they don't eat *fugu*, but they include puffer fish among the ingredients in a poison compound. A compound made by local sorcerers or *bokors* and popularly known as zombie poison. In other words, the stuff that turns people into zombies. The exact ingredients differ from place to place, but the poison always includes some sort of puffer. In other words, it contains tetro-dotoxin. If the amounts are right, the result is apparent death. That is stage one.

'Stage two is the burial, which usually takes place quickly. Stage three is exhumation, normally the same night. Stage four is the administration of an antidote containing *datura stramonium*. There's no evidence that *datura* or any of the other ingredients in the supposed antidote actually counteract the tetrodotoxin. But *datura* is extremely psychoactive. It produces a state of psychotic delirium, leading to confusion and amnesia. In Haiti, the popular name for *datura* is *concombre zombi* – the zombie's cucumber.'

Spinelli paused again. He stepped to the door. Reuben could hear him talking in a whisper to someone. A moment later he was back.

'Lieutenant, I've got to go. If you can come over to my office some time, I'll put together some materials for you. And I'll give you my friend's number.'

'Doctor, before you go: are you trying to tell me that you think Filius Narcisse has been turned into a zombie?'

'I'll let you make up your own mind about that, Lieutenant. I've just given you some basic facts. Weave what you like out of them. Let my secretary know if you plan to drop by. I'll try to make myself available.'

The line went dead. Reuben replaced his receiver and closed his eyes. What had started as a straightforward homicide case was rapidly turning into some sort of ghost hunt. He didn't believe in ghosts. Up until five minutes ago, he hadn't believed in zombies. An hour ago, Angelina had told him she had spoken to a man she had last seen declared dead in a hospital ward. Now a medical doctor was telling him she may not have been hallucinating.

· He picked up the phone again.

CHAPTER FIFTEEN

Danny Cohen arrived at 8.30 with two officers, O'Rourke and Grigorevitch. Reuben explained things while he shaved.

'You believe her?'

'I believe she saw something.'

'She could be reliving her original discovery, sublimating it by bringing her dead friend back to life. Sort of a transference thing.'

Cohen had been to college, had even majored in psychology. He had ideas.

'Listen, Danny, she's a smart lady. She's had a rough time, and maybe she's started seeing things, but I don't think so.'

'She says he really spoke to her?'

Reuben nodded. Angelina was still in bed.

'She tell you what he said? He didn't fill her in on the worlds beyond or anything, did he?'

'Cut it out, Danny. Something frightened her. You were there when we opened up that coffin last night. She knew nothing about that. So it's entirely plausible that somebody may have taken him back to the apartment. Some kind of joke maybe.'

'You tell her what we found?'

Reuben put down the razor and rinsed his face.

'What do you think, Danny? You think I enjoy telling a widow that I've just been exhuming one of her friends?' He was growing irritable at Danny's line of questioning.

'OK, OK. No need to get sore. So what did she say he told her?'

'She says he didn't know who he was, how he'd got there, who'd brought him there. He didn't recognize her, didn't respond to his own name. He was a sort of . . .'

'Zombie? Is that what you're telling me? You gonna put that in your report? C'mon, Reuben, wise up. She's been telling you too much about this voodoo crap.'

'Sit down, Danny.'

'What's to sit down? We've got to go. Save New York from the zombies!'

'Sit down and listen.'

There was nowhere for Danny to sit but the toilet. He lowered the lid and sat.

'After I telephoned you, Danny, I put a call through to somebody called Spinelli. Joe Spinelli. He's a consultant haematologist at Long Island College Hospital. I told you about him yesterday – he's the guy who found the tetrodotoxin in Narcisse's body.'

'Right, I remember.'

'OK. I told Spinelli what had happened, that Narcisse had gone missing, that somebody thought they'd seen him alive. I wanted a medical opinion. Some way it could have happened, something that would make sense in a report.'

'So what did he tell you? This tetrodotoxin gives you unearthly powers or something?'

'Don't get smart, Danny. Just sit there and let me tell you what he said.'

Reuben told him. The effect was gratifying. For the first time in the twenty years Reuben had known him, Danny Cohen was speechless. When he finally found speech again, his manner had changed dramatically.

'So you think he's still there? Just sitting there, waiting for somebody to come speak to him?'

'I don't know, Danny. I don't exactly have a lot of experience dealing with this sort of thing. Angelina mentioned that someone had taken the floorboards up again. Understandably, she didn't take the trouble to check on what was there.'

'You think there might be more?'

Reuben shrugged.

'More bodies? I hope not. One thing's troubling me, though. Angelina told me our seal was still on the door when she arrived. There's no back door to the apartment. So how did Narcisse get in? He may be a zombie, but he sure as hell didn't walk through the wall.'

'I think we should get over there. You ready?'

'Sure, let's go.'

Danny followed Reuben into the living room, where O'Rourke and Grigorevitch were waiting. As they left, Danny nodded in the direction of the guest bedroom.

' "Angelina", eh? Getting to know the natives, Reuben?'

'Leave it, Danny. The lady's a widow.' And until last night, she was a virgin as well, but let's not get into that. There were some things the Danny Cohens of this world could never understand.

At the apartment door, Danny turned to Reuben.

'Hey, I just realized what was wrong. What happened to your photographs, Reuben? The ones you had of Bubbie and everybody?'

Reuben did not reply.

Reuben went in first, followed closely by Danny. They'd known one another since they were kids together at the local Bais Yaakov yeshiva. Their first memory of one another was a fist fight outside school two days before Yom Kippur. Neither could now remember the provocation or the result, nor how they had become friends afterwards. They'd gone to high school together and only split up when Danny went to NYU. Then Danny had joined the force as well. For three years now, he had been assigned to Reuben's department, and for much of that period they had worked as partners.

Reuben felt the chill as soon as he stepped through the door. The seal had been broken, just as Angelina had said, and the door itself stood ajar. Danny came in his wake, whistling softly. The theme tune from *Ghostbusters*! Sometimes Reuben thought Danny had the sensitivity of a bag of potatoes.

'Kinda spooky, eh, Reuben? Cold too. Remember that bit in *The Exorcist* where the room freezes up?'

'Cut it out, Danny, this isn't funny.'

'It's just that I never had no dealings with the other side before.'

'You aren't going to have any now either. Listen, Danny.' Reuben turned and faced his friend. 'A joke's a joke, OK? But you know what we found in here last time. That wasn't funny, and this isn't going to be funny either.'

'But zombies, Reuben . . .'

'Leave off, Danny.'

Danny opened his mouth, took another look at Reuben's face, and closed it again. On second thoughts, maybe Reuben was right. Maybe this wasn't funny after all. And it *was* cold in here.

Officers O'Rourke and Grigorevitch were still standing on the landing. Neither man had been to the apartment before, but they'd heard plenty about it. O'Rourke crossed himself surreptitiously before venturing over the threshold. Grigorevitch was wishing he hadn't eaten such a hearty breakfast.

Reuben switched on the passage light. The door to the living room lay partly open, as Angelina had left it. Shadows crowded it. The chill seemed to emanate from there, or was that merely his imagination working overtime?

'Shut the door,' he ordered. 'I don't want the neighbours poking their noses in.'

'You think they're likely to?'

'Danny, people are creeps. Neighbours are creeps with windows. Your apartment smells, you have an argument with your girl-friend, they want to know what's going on. The people here know something big has been happening in apartment A. They just haven't been told what. But they're itching to know.'

'OK. So let's get this over with.'

Reuben took several steps towards the door. Suddenly he stopped and raised his hand. He sniffed cautiously.

'You smell something, Danny?'

Danny wrinkled his nose.

'No, I can't . . . Wait a minute.' He sniffed again. 'Oh, shit, Reuben. You don't think. . . ?'

Reuben went up to the door and pushed it open. The drapes had been drawn and the room was in darkness. Reuben put his hand round the jamb and found the light switch. He flicked it on. The room filled with a dull light. In the floor, boards had been ripped up, exposing a gaping hole. A cold draught came up from below. And with it a faint, sickly odour, unfamiliar and unsettling.

CHAPTER SIXTEEN

Angelina woke in a haze, as if on a morning of thunder. Her mind was fuddled and her senses awry. For fully half a minute she did not know where she was or how she had come to be there. Then memory flooded back in a torrent of disordered images: Rick, his mouth torn and ragged; their apartment defiled; Filius, sitting mindless and afraid in their rocking chair; Reuben's long fingers, fragile against her breast; fish floundering on a wet carpet; warm blood trickling down her thighs. She sat up dully, aching inside.

She was still naked beneath the warm sheets. With a sense of wonder, she ran her hands over her body, as though discovering it for the first time. Where had Reuben gone?

'Reuben!' she called. 'Reuben!' No answer. She got out of bed and found a grey kimono draped over a chair. It was on the big side, but she slipped it on, drawing the sleeves back.

The apartment was empty. She looked at her watch: 9.00 A.M. She realized that he must have gone to her apartment to check out the story about Filius. Of course, Filius had become a *zombi*, that was obvious.

She took coffee in the kitchen as before. The scraps of photograph still lay where they had left them earlier that morning. Traces of dried blood clung to them. She did not know whether to be happy or ashamed. How had Rick put it? 'I have a preference for non-penetrational sex.' Except for his co-eds, of course. He'd penetrated them often enough, or so he'd said.

After breakfast, she went back to her room to dress. Outside, the wind still howled, battering the day into submission. The streets were full of debris. A child ran, hooded and blind, in a staggered motion along the sidewalk. A car swerved to avoid a branch lying across the roadway. A thin dog shuffled past, sniffing desolately at piles of stinking garbage. A broken world, full of broken dreams.

Angelina wondered what was happening about the funeral. She should telephone Mary-Jo Quigley at LIU or ask Reuben for the name of the funeral director. Or maybe not. Maybe just let them get on with it and bury him somewhere, all his friends and relatives and co-eds. Somewhere decently out of sight.

First of all, though, she had to get herself some fresh clothes and toiletries. She should have asked Reuben to pick up the suitcase at her apartment. Maybe she could speak to him later about it. In the meantime, she could get some things downtown.

She called a cab. When it arrived fifteen minutes later, she ran straight out, slamming the door behind her. The wind struck her full in the face, and she bent her head down, fighting her way to the cab. She did not notice the man watching intently from a doorway on the other side of the street.

She got back to the apartment after eleven and dumped the shopping in her bedroom. Her bedroom, not his. She wasn't making any presumptions after a single night, and she didn't think he was either. A white Jewish policeman, for God's sake! Hadn't Rick been enough bad news for a lifetime?

She found a large plastic garbage bag and filled it with scraps of photograph from the kitchen floor and table. Once started, she went on to tidy the rest of the apartment. She'd heard about Jewish men, looking for women to play little mother. Reuben Abrams better not get any ideas.

When she finished, she made a decaff to drink with the jelly rolls she'd bought in town. Kids' food; but that was how she felt today: a little girl in a yellow dress. And a smell of vanilla and pepper in the air. Little Angelina on papa's knee, sitting so daintily, looking so demure, while the wind rustled the branches and ruffled her skirt. High in the air it went, high in the air.

At twelve the telephone rang.

'Yes, can I speak to Lieutenant Abrams?' A woman's voice, a Brooklyn accent. It sounded familiar.

'I'm sorry, he isn't here right now.'

'Oh. He isn't at the precinct either. The desk sergeant said he'd probably be home. OK, I'll ring back later.'

'Maybe I can take a message. Who is this?'

'OK, my name's Mary-Jo Quigley, I'm departmental secretary at . . . Just a moment. Is that you, Mrs Hammel?'

So . . . Little Miss Muffet, earning her curds and whey.

'Hello, Miss Quigley. I didn't recognize your voice.'

'I didn't know . . .' Embarrassed hesitancy. 'Are you under police protection or what?'

'Something like that. How are you, Miss Quigley?'

'I've been trying to get in touch with you. Nobody could tell me where you were. I didn't expect . . .'

'That's OK. I haven't much wanted to be around people right now.'

'I understand, Angelina. Can I call you Angelina? I can't say how sorry I am – about Professor Hammel. Animals, they should be garrotted. I mean it. The electric chair's too good for that type. They should be made to suffer.'

'What type is that, Miss Quigley?'

'You know. Degenerates. Blacks, Hispanics. I heard they mutilated him. That's gross. Animals, what else can you call them, people who can do that sort of thing? And such a sweet man, Professor Hammel. A saint. Nobody should die like that. But you don't need me to tell you. I was saying to . . .'

'Miss Quigley, I don't want to talk about this at present.'

'Oh, I'm sorry, I should be more sensitive. My psychosynthesist says I need to empathize more.' A pause. 'Listen, Angie, your parents-in-law are desperate to see you. They're staying in the Heights, at the St George. You like that place? Me, I hate it. Too big. Anyway, they'd like you to call them. The rest of the professor's family are coming in tomorrow to be at the cremation. Hey, Angie, you don't know what's happening, do you?'

'No, I don't know what's happening, Miss Quigley. Suppose you tell me.'

Mary-Jo obliged with the funeral details. Everybody would be there. There would be a service at the university chapel afterwards.

'Thanks for ringing, Miss Quigley. I'll tell the lieutenant you were looking for him. Perhaps he can ring you back.'

'It's no trouble. I can call again. It's just that the press have been hanging round. Him being a professor and everything: makes it kinda interesting. I was interviewed this morning for Channel 9. Don't you think Gary Douglas is the cutest? I . . .'

Little Miss Muffet was enjoying this. Angelina hung up.

She went to the bedroom and laid her purchases out on the bed. Using a nail clipper, she snipped off the labels. Two hundred dollars hadn't bought a lot; but she had to be careful about money now. Rich hadn't carried much life insurance.

In the bathroom, she stripped off the fat momma's things with a sense of relief. Reuben could take them back with a bunch of carnations. What had Jean Brodie called them in that movie? 'Serviceable flowers'. How very true. As long as she, Angelina, didn't have to make a courtesy call. He wouldn't expect her to meet his family, would he?

She looked at herself in the full-length mirror next to the door.

Who are you today, Angelina Hammel? Correction, Angelina Hypolite-Béliard. Double correction: Angelina Whoever-You-Like.

He'd liked her breasts, he'd caressed her legs and neck, he'd come all the way inside her. She couldn't believe it: as though it was the most natural thing in the world. She wondered if he'd want to do it again tonight. Maybe it wouldn't hurt so much this time.

Stepping into the shower, she turned the water on full. It was a better shower than the one she had at home, a proper cubicle with a glass door instead of a fiddling plastic curtain on a rail. Needles of hot water thundered against her skin. Steam filled the cubicle, delicious hot steam that bathed her lungs in warmth and misted the glass, shutting her off from everything in a tight little world of her own. Little Miss Muffet couldn't find her here. Filius the zombie couldn't find her here. Nobody could find her.

She shut off the water and picked the huge sponge up from the floor. She had bought a bottle of Clarins' Bain aux Plantes. A little luxury never did any harm. She poured a generous amount of the shower gel onto the sponge. Smiling, she leaned back and drew the wet sponge all down her front, across her breasts and over her belly.

And screamed and screamed and screamed. The sponge fell to the floor. And after it, the first drop of blood, then a trickle, then a stream. She staggered and fell against the door of the cubicle, smearing the glass with blood. Her feet went out from under her, kicking the sponge, dislodging one of the dozen razor blades with which it had been so lovingly stuffed.

CHAPTER SEVENTEEN

Reuben stood looking down into the opening, like a man on the edge of a vertiginous drop who knows that in a very little while the ground will crumble and he will plummet to the bottom.

O'Rourke had brought a large flashlight from the patrol car. He handed it to Reuben, relieved to watch the lieutenant go ahead of him. His hand shook visibly as he handed the light across. No-one wanted to go down there. No-one wanted to be first.

Reuben knelt on the edge and swung the light downwards in a series of gentle arcs, crisscrossing the empty, shadowed space. Crumbling bricks, old joists, earth that had been raked and sifted in the past few days without throwing up any clues. Cobwebs in the corners, miraculously intact. The darkness solid, sweet with death. But no bodies this time, not even a scrap of grave clothes.

On the side facing Reuben, bricks had been removed from the wall. Quite a lot of bricks. There was an opening big enough for a man to squeeze inside. Something crawled through Reuben's stomach: he knew he would be expected to go down there and climb through the aperture. There must be a tunnel, he thought: the hole in the wall was the source of the draught. And the fetid smell.

'I'm going down,' said Reuben. He was certain someone else had spoken, the words were in such contradiction of his state of mind. More than ever, he wanted to turn and leave this place.

'I'll come with you, Reuben.' Danny's voice sounded strange. The jocularity had been stripped away. In its place, Reuben sensed raw fear.

'OK. You'll have to crawl through after me.' Reuben hesitated. 'O'Rourke – you'll find another flashlight in my car. In the trunk. Would you get it for Detective Cohen, please?'

'Yes, sir. I'll get it at once.' O'Rourke would have done anything to get out of there. He took the keys Reuben offered him and turned to go.

'O'Rourke.'

'Yes, sir?'

'While you're fetching the flashlight, would you please call the precinct and tell them what we've found here? Tell them we may need some help.'

O'Rourke seemed to turn green.

'Do you expect to find . . . anything else down there, sir?'

Reuben paused, then nodded.

'Yes, Officer O'Rourke. That's exactly what I expect.'

O'Rourke turned and stumbled out of the room. Grigorevitch stayed behind. He was feeling queasier every minute.

No-one said anything at first. On the mantelpiece, a clock ticked tiredly. Reuben turned and caught sight of his own face, distorted in a cheap mirror. He looked away nervously. The clock went on ticking. Reuben noticed a fly, high up, circling. Then another, and another. Circling. Buzzing. Landing on the walls and ceiling. Without warning, the clock stopped ticking. In the sudden silence, the buzzing of flies was magnified.

O'Rourke took five minutes, but it seemed much longer. Danny did not thank him when he handed the flashlight over.

'Captain Connelly's in a meeting with the DA, sir. I left your message.'

'Thanks. Maybe you can call back later. We'll go down anyway. You stay here with Grigorevitch and keep your ears pricked. If one of us calls . . .' He had meant to go on to say, 'Come in after us', but the words died on his lips. 'Go for help right away,' he finished lamely. 'Understand?'

'Yes, sir.' O'Rourke hesitated. 'Good luck, sir.'

Reuben said nothing. He turned away, then back again. 'O'Rourke, did you ask what the DA was seeing Connelly about?'

'Desk sergeant said he thought it was to do with this case.' The policeman shrugged. 'But that could just be gossip, sir.'

Reuben nodded. Why should Connelly call in the DA at this stage of the case? They had no suspects, no definite line of enquiry. He gave a mental shrug and lowered himself through the opening in the floor. Danny followed a moment later.

The hole in the wall was ragged, about three feet in diameter, and set low down near the floor. Reuben knelt in front of it and shone the light inside.

'What can you see, Reuben?' Danny asked. Unconsciously, he had dropped his voice to a whisper.

'This is crazy,' Reuben answered. 'I can make out steps. Old steps roofed in with brick. They look even older than the foundation walls in here. Everything looks kind of mildewed. There are hundreds of old cobwebs. Some of the bricks are covered in moss. It looks a little damp.'

'Can you see anything else?'

Reuben shook his head.

'No. We'll have to go in.'

'Shouldn't we wait till Connelly gets here? Maybe bring in some Special Operations guys to handle it.'

'Danny, somebody's got to go in there. After last time, we know there could be survivors. I don't like it, but I've made up my mind and I'm trying not to think about it. You can stay here if you prefer.'

Danny bit his lip, shaking his head.

'I won't let you go in there alone, Reuben. I figure if you find some Ninja Turtles you'll just keep them to yourself.'

Reuben turned to his friend. He could sense his fear.

'What is it, Danny? What are you frightened of? Seriously.'

Danny shook his head again.

'It's OK, Reuben. It's just this place, it's giving me the creeps. Come on, let's see what's at the bottom of the steps.'

For a moment Reuben hesitated. Finally he nodded.

'Let's go.'

The steps went down about twenty feet before levelling out onto a flat surface. Stooping on the bottom step, Reuben shone his flashlight ahead. A narrow tunnel ran into the distance. Like the steps, it was lined with brick, cobwebbed, ancient, utterly without light.

The tunnel was narrow but large enough to allow a man through without undue difficulty. Reuben would have to stoop a little, but he would have no problem getting through. The ceiling was arched and rounded. The walls were cold to the touch. Reuben stepped inside and at once he felt the walls press in on him. God knew how old they were or how long it had been since anyone last crawled through here – assuming that the tunnel really had been intended as a passageway for human beings and was not just a branch of an old sewer or some sort of drainage channel for the Brooklyn–Battery Tunnel. The bricks could be loose, his passage might dislodge them, trapping him. He forced himself not to think about that.

Danny squeezed in after him. They would have to go in single file. Reuben set off slowly, swinging his flashlight into the pitch blackness. Behind him, he could hear Danny's muffled footsteps. From time to time, Danny's light would send shadows into the beam of Reuben's, weaving complex patterns among the crumbling bricks. They had no difficulty breathing: the air was malodorous, but fresh enough to breathe.

The tunnel seemed to slope downwards, but Reuben could not be sure. There were thick cobwebs in places: his hair and eyes were already streaked with them, and he could feel the legs of living spiders on his scalp and neck.

The powerful beam of the flashlight revealed only a short section of tunnel at a time: the passage was bending gently as it sank lower into the earth. They were already well out of sight of the opening through which they had entered, and Reuben wondered if anyone there would hear them if they called. Hemmed in by brick, choked by dusty cobwebs, he could scarcely believe that the apartment still existed. The world had shrunk to an impossibly narrow space, to bare bricks and the limits of his own body.

'You hear anything, Reuben?' Danny's voice sounded hoarse.
'Like what?'
'Don't know. Thought I heard something up ahead.'
Reuben swung his light back and forwards. Moss. Cobwebs. Nothing. He checked his gun, just to know it was there. Something scuttled across his path. A rat, sleek and rapid. It disappeared into the darkness. They kept on moving.

The sound of water dripping raised tiny echoes. There were patches of damp here and there on the walls and ceiling.

Without warning, a side tunnel opened on their right. Awkwardly, Reuben shone his flashlight into it. More ancient bricks, more shadows, more toneless echoes vanishing to nothing. Five minutes later, they passed a similar opening on their left. They were in some sort of labyrinth.

The air from the side tunnels felt fresher. Reuben was tempted to follow one in the hope that it might lead to a way out. But prudence suggested that it might be safer for the moment to remain in the main tunnel. They kept moving forwards. There were no more side tunnels. The passage stretched ahead of them without changing. Darkness like solid slabs of night, an old darkness, dank and threatening. Angry shadows, childhood phantoms, a beam of waving light, cutting, growing weak.

Suddenly, Danny hissed a warning.

'Stop, Reuben! Don't move!'

Reuben froze.

'What is it?'

'There's something behind me.' Danny's voice was tense. Reuben sensed that his friend was on the edge of panic. He should not have allowed him to come down here.

'Stay calm, Danny.'

'I heard something, Reuben. It came out of one of those tunnels back there.'

'You heard a rat, that's all.' Reuben could feel his own hair standing on end. Danny's fear was contagious.

'Not a rat, not down here. Listen, I heard it again.'

Reuben heard nothing. He turned awkwardly and shone his light on Danny. His friend was standing crouched with his back to him, staring back along the tunnel as though waiting for something to emerge from the blackness. Suddenly, Reuben heard it too, a scraping sound, low and directionless.

'Keep calm, Danny.'

But Danny was on edge, old fears of the dark intensified by his passage through the tunnel. By the time Reuben saw what he was doing, it was too late. Danny took out his gun and fired wildly into the darkness, again and again, until he had emptied the chamber of his pistol.

The shots died away, echo upon echo, leaving the darkness whole. There was a sound like rain dropping on dry leaves: the bullets must have dislodged pieces of brick. Danny's hand shook as he put the gun away. He knew he had acted stupidly. His flashlight was still pointed into the darkness behind. More fragments of brick skittered to the floor, followed by a small, intense silence.

'Reuben, I . . .'

As he spoke, another fall of tiny pieces began, turning in moments to a roar.

'Get out of there, Danny! The roof's caving in!'

Danny twisted back, as though by doing so he could recompose broken rock. The roar lifted in volume, drowning Reuben's voice. Reuben grabbed Danny's arm and pulled him along the passage. A cloud of dust rushed down the tunnel, enveloping and choking them. Reuben stumbled, picked himself up, ran on. Danny came behind, coughing, his lungs full of dirt.

The roaring ceased. Dust still filled the tunnel, hanging in the starkest of silences. There were small crashes, little rushes of broken rock, but the silence took inexorable charge, calming them, stilling their convulsions.

Reuben and Danny waited until the dust had settled, then crept back along the tunnel, ready to turn and run at the first sign of another collapse. The fall had been about fifty feet behind them. All around it, dust hung in a clumsy ochre cloud. They shone their flashlights on a mass of brick and soil and rock. The debris stretched to the ceiling and beyond, into a raw hole. Parts of the walls had collapsed on either side. There was no way past.

'What are we going to do, Reuben?'

Reuben played his light up and down the obstruction. It was solid enough, but patently unstable.

'I don't think we should waste time on this, Danny. We've no way of knowing how far back it goes. They'll know back in the apartment that something has happened and send somebody in to get us out. I'd rather not hang around here waiting – there could be another cave-in. Let's keep on going.'

Danny agreed. They had little choice. Reuben took the lead again and set off in the original direction.

'Keep close behind me, Danny. Switch off your flashlight – we don't know how long we're going to be down here.'

Danny switched off his light. All about him grew dark. The only light was Reuben's, several feet ahead.

'I'm sorry about what happened back there, Reuben. I must have panicked.'

'You were frightened, Danny. You were frightened before you came in here? What was it you were frightened of?'

There was a long silence. Reuben could hear Danny's breathing, tight behind him, his feet scraping on the coarse floor of the tunnel.

'It was a long time ago, Reuben,' he said at last. 'I used to have a dream. A nightmare. Before we met, when I was a little kid. The dream was full of tunnels, tunnels like this. I'd get into them somehow, and once I was in I realized something was chasing me.'

'Did you know who?'

'No. I don't think it was a person. But I knew it would kill me if it found me. I used to wake up screaming.'

'You're awake now, Danny.'

'No, Reuben, that's the really scary part. I'd wake up in my bed screaming, but nobody would come. I'd be all alone in my room and I'd be sweating and I'd call out, but nobody would come to help me. So I'd get up and open the door and . . . That's when I got really scared, because when I opened the door I'd be in the tunnel again, just like before, only this time I knew the thing that was chasing me was really close. And I'd run and run and turn a corner and . . . And then something happened and I really woke up. I can't remember what happened.'

'And this place reminds you of your dream?'

The silence stretched and stretched. Reuben stopped and turned, letting his light fall on his friend's face. The look of fear was real.

'This is my dream, Reuben,' Danny whispered. 'Don't you understand? That's why I panicked. It's my dream all over again. Only this time I'm not asleep.'

They walked on in silence. The air was already growing thick and stale. Whatever fresh air there had been had come from the two side tunnels.

And then, abruptly, the tunnel ended. There was a gentle bend followed by a slight rise that led directly to a brick wall. They could not go forward. And they could not go back.

They sat by the wall for what seemed a long time, saying nothing. The darkness pressed in on them. In a little while, Reuben's flashlight would run out. Danny's would give them another hour or two. Perhaps someone would come and rescue them by then. The darkness was very strong.

'You smell something, Reuben?'

Danny's voice sounded pale and lost.

'What have we been doing since we came in here?'

Danny wrinkled his nose and sniffed twice.

'It's not that, Reuben. Not the musty smell. It's something else.'

Reuben sniffed. Danny was right, there was something different.

'It's getting stronger, Reuben. It's familiar . . .' Danny took a deep breath. Slowly, the expression on his face changed. He seemed to go pale all at once, as though the blood had been drained from his cheeks.

'What is it, Danny?'

'Oh God, Reuben – I know what it is. It's gas. What I'm smelling is gas.'

CHAPTER EIGHTEEN

The gas was seeping slowly into the tunnel from a ruptured pipe at the cave-in. It crept, invisible and deadly, into the tight and silent spaces of the little world they had made, scarcely perceptible at first, but with every moment gaining a little strength. The air at the site of the cave-in was already hard to breathe. The broken pipe was out of reach.

Danny and Reuben tied handkerchiefs round their mouths and returned to the wall, knowing their lives were measured in minutes rather than hours. The gas would not take long to fill what little space there was.

Reuben shook his light up and down the surface of the wall that had cut off their progress.

'What do you think, Danny?'

Danny looked over Reuben's shoulder.

'Looks like it was put up quickly, not like the rest of the tunnel. The mortar's rough, crumbly in places. I think this is just a partition wall somebody put in here to seal the tunnel off. Could even lead to the outside.'

'Or the river.'

'That's outside. Anyway, I don't think that's a problem. The wall's old. If that was the river out there, it would have broken through a long time ago.'

Danny reached into a pocket and brought out a large penknife, the sort that has a blade for everything. It carried a spike, short but reasonably strong. Danny passed it to Reuben.

'Here, use this.'

Reuben started to work at the mortar between two bricks at shoulder level. It crumbled easily. Reuben worked quickly, coughing and wheezing as the gas grew thicker and more potent. Mortar came away in large pieces now, falling around his feet; when he had loosened enough of it, he borrowed Danny's empty revolver and swung it like a hammer hard against the cobwebbed brick, splintering it, dislodging it from the remaining mortar. The brick shattered and gave way, falling back into emptiness.

A hazy light was visible beyond the tiny opening. Reuben drew in a mouthful of unpoisoned air, musty but breathable.

'Give me your flashlight, Danny. Mine's too far gone.'

Reuben shone the light through the hole. Several yards away, he could make out what seemed to be a heavy metal grille, its bars pitted and rusted with age. The tunnel seemed to end after the grille, but Reuben could not see enough to tell what lay beyond. He had been holding his breath; sucking in air, he choked on gas and felt his head spin. He would have to enlarge the hole quickly.

Dislodging one brick made the rest easy. Reuben abandoned the gun in favour of his bare hands, pushing and pulling loosened bricks until they came away. One section of wall collapsed intact. It took only minutes to create a hole large enough to crawl through.

On the other side they found themselves in a short stretch of tunnel identical to the one in which they had already been. Using Danny's flashlight, they could see the grille properly now. It was a heavy gate, bolted on one side, the spaces between its bars woven with generations of spiders' webs.

Reuben swept the webs away from the middle section of the gate and shone the light through. Beyond lay a vast chamber, its walls and floor made entirely of brick. High up in the far wall, almost out of sight from where Reuben stood, a barred and broken window allowed a little air and a little light to creep in from outside.

The floor of the chamber was dotted with circular stone slabs like manhole covers. The slabs were pierced with holes and curiously smooth. The holes were about the size of large coins. It looked as though nothing in the chamber had been disturbed for a long time.

The bolt flew apart at a single kick, but it still took all Reuben's strength to move the gate even a couple of inches. The hinges had rusted fast. The effects of the gas were lessening rapidly now, but Reuben still felt giddy.

'Let me try.'

Danny squeezed past and took Reuben's place at the gate. He was better built than his friend and still worked out regularly at a gym on Fulton Street. The gate gave way. Not much, but enough.

The way was open. The chamber was waiting. For no particular reason, Reuben felt terribly afraid.

CHAPTER NINETEEN

Danny went in first, with Reuben close on his heels. They stood side by side, just past the entrance, nervously playing their flashlights back and forth along the walls of the tremendous room. Heavy brick, coarsely laid, bearded with tendrils of clinging cobweb, pitted and dark, its mortar gently crumbling. Reuben sensed the age of the place, the brooding presence of it, solid, confining, tomb-like. As far as they could judge, it was a large chamber, some hundred feet by as much again, perhaps twenty-five feet high. A heavy wooden door was set in the right-hand wall.

It was Danny who first noticed that the floor was slightly concave, sloping in from the four sides to a shallow centre. Along each of the sides ran a low gutter or channel, and from each corner in turn, four more gutters ran inward, converging at the centre, where the innermost of the numerous 'manhole covers' was situated, as if it were a hub at the heart of a wheel.

Closer inspection revealed that narrow channels had been cut into the brickwork throughout the concavity of the floor, leading from the four diagonal runnels to each of the manholes, about fifty in number, these last being distributed, it now appeared, in a series of concentric circles running out from the centre almost to the edge. The dimensions of the manholes were regular, each measuring approximately two feet in diameter.

Danny stepped onto the floor, for all the world like a dancer treading nervously onto an unfamiliar stage, waiting for music from the pit to stir him to performance pitch. But here there was only silence and the scrape of lonely feet on brick.

'This place gives me the creeps,' Danny whispered. 'What the hell do you think it is?'

'I don't know, Danny. I wish to God I did.'

'It's cold. Really cold. How far down you think we are, Reuben?'

Reuben shook his head.

'I can't say. The window's over twenty feet up.'

'We went down at least that far when we went in.' Danny paused and stepped towards the wall on his left. Reuben noticed that he deliberately avoided stepping on any of the manholes, picking his way between them like a child sidestepping cracks on the sidewalk.

'Reuben!' Danny's voice was still low, but the tension in it was marked. 'Over here, Reuben. Look at this.'

Reuben joined his friend, unconsciously picking the same path between the manholes. All along the left-hand wall ran a series of metal cages, each about the size of a filing cabinet laid on its side. They went closer and Danny shone his light inside. At the back of the first cage, beneath a pile of dust and cobwebs, he made out what looked like a pile of bones.

'You don't think. . . ?'

'It's some animal, Danny.'

'You want to take a look?'

Reuben shivered.

'Let's leave that to the guys from Forensics. Whatever it was, it's been down here a long time.'

Each of the cages held at least one pile similar to the first. Dust-covered feeding troughs lay against the cage fronts. Any food that might have been in them had long ago decayed to nothing.

Reuben made the next discovery.

Shining his flashlight upwards, he noted that the ceiling was made of stucco, badly crumbled in places. All around its edge ran a circle of what looked like rusted iron. He took it at first for ornamentation, yet thought it strange to find such a thing, however plain, in a chamber of such puritan aspect. And then the flashlight moved further over and picked out something bulky on the far side of the ceiling.

It was a kind of gantry. Its arm extended from the outer circle as far as the centre of the room, where it joined a smaller, inner circle, also of rusted metal. The circles, then, were not ornaments but rails for the gantry. From the inner tip of the arm hung a block and tackle fitted with a species of grappling hook, the purpose of which was immediately clear.

'Do you think it still works?' Danny's voice brought Reuben out of a brief reverie.

Reuben shrugged.

'Depends.'

'On what?'

'How old it is. How badly rusted. It could be put back in working order, sure. But for the moment . . .'

Danny stroked his light up and down the gantry arm.

'You thinking what I'm thinking?'

'That they used this thing to open and close the manholes?'

Danny nodded.

'You're probably right,' replied Reuben. 'It seems elaborate, but I can't think of any other purpose.'

'Lifting merchandise into the holes?'

'Maybe. Maybe.' Something about the arrangement made Reuben uneasy. The gantry had not been used for lifting sacks of flour, he was sure of that.

'Want to take a look inside one?' Danny's voice was hesitant.

'Not particularly.'

'No, me neither.' Danny gave a little shiver. Goose bumps ran all along his arms. He looked round uneasily. 'But something tells me we should. For our peace of mind.'

'How do you propose we do it?' Reuben asked. 'Those lids look as though they weigh a few pounds.'

Danny gave Reuben a withering look.

'You should work out more, Reuben. Come on, let's give it a try.'

Reuben nodded. He felt diminished, numb, unable to react any other way than mechanically. Deep inside, he felt a powerful urge to look over his shoulder. What had Danny heard in the tunnel, the scraping sound that had panicked him into firing? In spite of the room's great size, Reuben was feeling claustrophobic.

They chose the nearest manhole, having no reason to favour one over another. Reuben switched off his flashlight and Danny laid his on the ground, where it shed an oblique lozenge of pastel light along the floor. Facing each other, they hunkered down, settling into position carefully to avoid straining their backs. Slipping their fingers into the holes, they flexed their muscles and prepared to take the strain.

It was heavier than Danny had anticipated. Muscles bunched in their necks and shoulders, but the cover did no more than rock a fraction of an inch. Undaunted, Danny gave it everything he had.

'Come . . . on . . . Reuben . . . We . . . can . . . do . . . it,' he gasped.

Reuben closed his eyes. Lights danced and sparkled against a cloth of black; he felt as though his muscles would tear or his shoulder blades jump from their sockets. The slab lifted slowly, grating as they slid it onto the floor.

Panting, they rested. Reuben was the first to move. Picking up Danny's flashlight, he played it across the shadows inhabiting the pit. Dense cobwebs, a rustling of spiders' legs, something vague below. He used the flashlight to tear the webs to pieces. Nervously, he shone the light into the pit again. Spiders scuttling, disturbed and angry, dark legs shimmering. A handful of restless shadows. Steep walls of glazed brick, cracked and stained. On the bottom, another heap of bones, jumbled and grey. Old bones, brittle bones, long ago scoured clean of flesh by the legs of spiders. And on top of them a human skull, patches of dried flesh still clinging to the cheeks, strands of long, dirty hair straggling like seaweed across the bones beneath.

CHAPTER TWENTY

The strands of matted hair rippled like a fugue through Reuben's brain, repeating and repeating their stark, tangled message of decay. He shivered and moved away from the open pit, followed moments later by Danny.

The place was a graveyard of stone. God knew how many bones it contained or how long they had been here. Wherever they walked, the anonymous dead lay huddled underneath. No names were inscribed on the heavy slabs above their remains, no dates marked their births or commemorated their deaths.

Reuben reached the edge of the floor and looked back over the bone-pits. One thing disturbed him above all else: to bury the dead beneath stone slabs was not unusual; to leave them nameless was uncommon yet far from unprecedented. But why would anyone want to seal the graves with slabs like these, pierced with large holes, like the lids of boxes in which children carry their pet hamsters home?

Without realizing it, they had crossed to the foot of the steps, at the top of which the wooden door stood waiting. After their latest experience, neither man was eager to see what lay behind the door; but they both knew that, if there was a more straightforward way out than back down the tunnel, it could only lie through the door. And the gas, though much dissipated, was still streaming into the chamber.

Reuben climbed the steps while Danny remained at the bottom, lighting the way for him. Gingerly, Reuben touched the plain metal handle, steeling himself to turn it. The mechanism was stiff, but it put up little real resistance. Reuben braced his legs and pulled hard.

The door buckled at the top, then gave way all at once, moving outwards with a dark grinding sound. The odour of long-dead air filled Reuben's nostrils. The smell was stale and rotten, but it held a faint suggestion of something unexpected, a rich, complicated perfume that had been shut up in a confined space for centuries, faded yet lingering, attenuated to a thin, pale ghost, dark, drifting, pitiful.

The hinges locked and the door stuck halfway. Reuben stepped round the door and shone his flashlight into the opening. The entire doorway was veiled from top to bottom in a seamless cobweb. Reuben hesitated, as though the web were more of an obstruction than the door. Then, almost savagely, he tore it from side to side. The strands shrivelled and fell away, revealing nothing behind but an expanse of blackness into which no light penetrated. Whatever lay beyond the door, it was not daylight and it was not liberty.

Reuben prayed that this was not the entrance to yet another charnel house. What he saw next tore the prayer from his lips. Not horror, not terror, but a dream from which all horror and all terror had been surgically removed, leaving a small, insane rustling that betokens nightmare lurking in the interstices of sleep itself.

The door led into a second room, much smaller than the first, darker, heavier: a proper room made sinister by age. Beneath a low ceiling of lightly decorated gesso, dark wainscoted walls swallowed the yellow light from Reuben's hand torch. The floor was made of parquet covered in places by Persian carpets. There were traces of white sand where the wood had last been scrubbed – a practice that had died out in the nineteenth century. A mist of cobwebs flapped obscenely in the draught as the door swung open, then settled again, vast and brooding, a grey, dust-shrouded stillness that stifled the room.

The spiders had woven webs of time – wild, intricate puzzles in which to hold the years like mottled flies. Behind them, choked by shadows, the gilded spines of tall, leather-bound books paraded across shelves of dark wood. A globe of the world stood in a wooden support within the angle of the farthest corner, its oceans dry and faded, its cities fallen, its tall towers gutted and razed. A large spider walked on stilted legs through the dark heart of Africa, gaunt and black, striding across the world.

On the rear wall, in lieu of books, hung dusty portraits of men in eighteenth- and early nineteenth-century dress, iced with cobwebs, cracked and warped by long neglect. They stared at Reuben balefully, their hooded eyes cold and accusing. Each held in his hand what appeared to be a rod or sceptre of some kind, as though in imitation of a king or prince. But their clothing was dark and sober, and their stern features spoke, not of the softness of palaces, but of a life dedicated to higher things.

The wall on which the portraits hung was broken at its centre by a flight of some dozen stone steps leading directly to a low wooden door. On the door was painted in red a circle with rays streaming downwards, emblematic of the sun, and in the centre of the circle Reuben recognized the Hebrew words *yod, heth, waw, heth*: the divine name, Yahweh. Below the sun stood a lion holding an open book on which the Latin words *semper apertus* had been inscribed: For ever open.

At the centre of the room, facing the door, sat a high wooden desk shrouded in fantastic cobwebs that stretched from its surface to the floor, as though pinning it fast. It was on the desk above all that Reuben's nervous gaze lingered. Or, to be more precise, the thing that sat behind the desk.

It was the mummified corpse of a man, dressed in clothes that dated, like those in the portraits, from the late eighteenth or early nineteenth century: a drab Quaker-style cassimere coat over a black velvet waistcoat, a white muslin stock and cravat, nankeen breeches buttoned just below the knee. All much rotted now, yet still intact. The plain clothes of a scholar or a clergyman.

On the desk in front of the mummy, a large book lay open, coated in a thick layer of dust. But he could see none of it. His leather face was covered from chin to forehead by a great, circular web. And in the centre of the web a huge spider sat, many-legged, thin, quivering gently on its fine-spun cradle as it waited patiently for its prey.

The floor behind the desk was bare of carpet. Beneath a thin layer of dust, thick red-painted lines were dimly discernible. A large circle enclosed a five-pointed star, along the inner valleys of which ran two further concentric circles, about six inches apart. At the five points of the star stood tall candlesticks, still complete with yellow wax myrtle candles.

Reuben crossed behind the desk and bent down low over the pentacle. Brushing and blowing, he cleared a section of floor and stood up to see it more clearly. An inscription ran around the double inner circle. Reuben recognized several Hebrew letters and made out words that he guessed were Latin. Within the centre of the star numerous symbols were distributed according to no clear pattern. Some he recognized as astrological emblems, others as cabbalistic devices, but the rest were more obscure. They seemed almost African.

He stood up as Danny entered. Neither man spoke. Danny stood in the doorway, letting the scene sink in little by little.

'You OK, Reuben?'

'It's all right, I'm fine.'

'Is this for real?' he said in a hushed voice. But he knew it was real. He had seen it before: in his nightmare, years and years ago, huddled among damp sheets, screaming for the light. Deep down, Danny was frightened, very frightened. Deep down, Danny knew what happened at the end of the nightmare, what he had not told Reuben.

Danny stepped across to one of the bookcases. Brushing away the cobwebs, he pulled down a volume from the nearest shelf. It was a large book, folio size, bound in heavy calfskin, with large brass clasps. There was a small table nearby. Danny laid the book on it and opened the clasps. The pages were discoloured, but otherwise remarkably well preserved.

The title page was in heavy type. In the centre was a circular device made up of four concentric circles, forming a band in which were two sets of Hebrew and two sets of Greek letters. Inside the circle were various geometrical devices, more Hebrew letters, and rows of what appeared to be figures. At the foot of the circle were the French words: *Le Grand Pentacule*: The Great Pentacle.

As for the title, it too was in French: *Les Clavicules de Salomon. Traduit de l'Hébreux en Langue Latine Par le Rabin Abognazar et Mis en Langue Vulgaire par M. Barault Archevêque d'Arles*. At the foot of the page was a date: *M.DC.XXXIV: 1634*.

The book itself seemed to be some sort of treatise on ritual magic, complete with formulae for incantations, talismanic devices, diagrams, and drawings depicting magical rites.

Reuben joined Danny. Together they passed along the rows, pulling out books at random, examining each one in turn briefly, before returning it to the shelf. More volumes in French, several in Latin, with mysterious titles and curious inscriptions: *De Occulta Philosophia Libri Tres*; *De naturalium effectuum causis, sive de Incantationibus . . .*; *Staganographia, hoc est, ars per occultam scripturam animi sui voluntatem absentibus aperiendi certa . . .*; *Grimorium Verum*; *Lemegeton*; *Veterum Sophorum Sigilla et Imagines Magicae*; *De Septem Secundeis . . .*

114

In one row they found over forty volumes in English, German and Dutch. Near them were several books in Greek, almost a dozen in Hebrew, three in what Reuben took to be Arabic, and one in a script he did not recognize. The majority dated from the seventeenth and eighteenth centuries, having been published for the most part in Paris, Leiden, Cassel, Basle and Darmstadt. The most recent was a small half-folio in English, published in Boston in 1800 by Nathaniel Ackerknecht. Written by one Perseverance Hopkins, it was entitled *A Sober Warning to the Righteous, being an Account of the Recent Events at Nantucket*. It seemed to have been much read, and its margins were covered with notes in a fine, crabbed hand.

On a narrow table at the rear of the room, immediately beneath the brooding portraits, there lay a heap of cobwebbed papers, most of which, on close examination, proved to be letters. Strange letters, in a variety of languages, but mainly French and German, the texts interspersed with Hebrew and Latin quotations, strings of numerals, astrological and cabbalistic signs. Whole sections of some of the letters appeared to be in code. They came from all over Europe, including several from Mitau in Courland, and more than a few from Budapest, Riga, Brest, and other cities in the east.

Most interesting of all was a bundle of over forty letters in the same hand. They were in French and headed 'Cap Français'. The dates ran from 1762 to 1807, but the handwriting scarcely varied. Cap Français was, of course, the old name for Cap-Haïtien, the former northern capital of Haiti in the days when it was the French colony of St Domingue. The signature at the bottom of the letters was illegible.

The bundle was kept in a small box, separate from the other letters. At the bottom of the box was a flat gold object. In shape, it was a half-circle, about one foot in diameter, with a ragged long edge and smooth circumference, as though it had been broken from a larger disc. Its surface was covered in peculiar markings, all of them unfamiliar to Reuben. Something about it suggested that its origin, like that of the symbols on the floor, might possibly be African.

Reuben closed the box.

'Danny, just so there's no problem with Connelly later on, I'm letting you see that I'm taking these with me. I want to show the letters to Angelina. The half-disc as well.'

'I think we should get out of here,' said Danny. He made for the stairs.

'Just a minute,' Reuben called. All the time he had been in the room, his eyes had returned again and again to the seated figure at the desk. Something drew him in that direction.

He wanted to see the book, to look at the page the sorcerer in Quaker garb had been reading when he died. Cautiously, he approached the desk from the side. The mummy's hand rested on the page, thin and shrivelled, retracted like a claw. As Reuben moved it, he disturbed the body. The spider shivered and took fright, scuttling across its web and down behind, seeking cover in the empty socket of the sorcerer's right eye.

Reuben lifted the book, a hefty folio volume, and began to draw it away from the desk, as he did so tearing the webs that joined it to the mummy and the desk. A second large spider ran out from underneath. Reuben started, and the book slipped from his grasp, falling on the floor with a crash and closing. He picked it up, spluttering in the dense cloud of grey dust.

Reuben balanced the book on the edge of the desk and opened it again. The title-page read:

The Liber Arcanorum
or Ketab El Asrar
of Aben Pharagi Maroccanus Scriptor Nubianus
Rendered into the Englyshe Tongue
from the Latin Translation by Trithemius,
Done by an Englyshe Savant
And Most Lavishly Illustrated Throughout
With Drawinges Taken out of
The Original Texte,
From a Copy Found
In the Citie of Fayyum, Egypt
MDXLI

Slowly, Reuben began to leaf through the yellowed pages. On each left-hand page, the text of the Latin translation had been printed, facing the English version on the right. The main text consisted of short verses, which Reuben took to be spells, interspersed with lines of cabbalistic letters and talismanic devices written in Arabic:

لا إلٰه إلا الله هو والسلام ✸ سم ✸ ﻗﻮﺍ ﻫ ﺳ س ر س

He had only gone through about ten pages when the book,

which had lain unmoved for so long at a single place, snapped at the spine and fell open once more at its accustomed position. The page was taken up entirely with a woodcut illustration in the style of the sixteenth century. It took Reuben about half a minute to work out the subject and composition of the drawing. When he did so, he closed the book with a shudder and walked away from the desk.

The scene depicted was that of a graveyard, in which the events of the coming resurrection were graphically illustrated. The artist had transposed the scene from the supposed Egypt of the original, showing instead a European cemetery, dotted with the Virgins and crosses of the Christian faith. But this drawing bore no relation to the usual depictions of the resurrection, in which the dead rise up in radiant bodies of resurrected flesh, clad in white and filled with joy as they go to meet Jesus coming down from heaven.

Instead, the bodies of the newly arisen were putrid and rotten, clothed in the remnants of worm-eaten shrouds. On their decayed faces the artist had contrived to depict expressions of horror and extreme terror, while all around them was a mist-filled darkness within which strange shapes lurked.

But it was none of this that caused Reuben to close the book so hurriedly and with such loathing. It was the sight of the things that were licking and nibbling at the limbs and faces of the risen corpses, even where they stood trembling in their graves. They were a terrible shade of white, and their bodies, Reuben felt certain, would, if they moved, move in a most sickening way. One creature at the far left of the picture had turned its . . . face towards the reader with such an expression of hunger and triumph that nothing would ever erase its features from Reuben's memory.

CHAPTER TWENTY-ONE

The door at the top of the stairs had been locked from the inside, but the key had rusted fast. Danny smashed the lock with his foot, throwing the door back on broken hinges against the wall. Beyond lay a narrow wooden landing choked with dust. The walls were bare rock.

From the landing, a short flight of rickety wooden stairs began a winding ascent. They climbed slowly, numb, fearful of further horrors, conscious of the cracking and creaking of ancient wood beneath their feet. Whoever had built the subterranean vaults had taken a great deal of trouble to ensure their inaccessibility.

At the top of the stairs they came to a wooden trapdoor. Like the previous door, it opened onto darkness. Reuben's flashlight was virtually exhausted. Danny passed his up. In the stronger light, they saw another tunnel stretching ahead of them, narrower than the first and choked with thick cobwebs. Danny went first this time, breaking the webs with his arm and the flashlight, his eyes darting in and out of the darkness, watching for a sign of movement.

The tunnel ended in another flight of wooden steps, leading, like the first, to a trapdoor. Danny pushed it up and climbed through into the space beyond – a tiny, box-like chamber about three feet square. Someone had boxed the trapdoor in.

The wall was of bricks and mortar, very much like the one they had found in front of the grille. Like it, this one was much crumbled and weakened in places. Smashing a hole large enough for them to crawl through, they emerged into a long-abandoned cellar.

The building above was a warehouse in a state of total dilapidation, one of several in the Front Street area near the river that had been awaiting demolition for several years. They found the front door and stepped out into the late September sunshine, blinking away the darkness and the terrors of the night on a rubble-strewn street just north of the Brooklyn Bridge.

A reception committee was waiting at the Hammels' apartment. A team had been down in the tunnel for over two hours now, trying to dig through to Reuben and Danny, presumed dead or trapped. The zombie story had been related – with embellishments – to Captain Connelly, who had come close to having his long-awaited coronary. Danny had been taken off the case and assigned a new partner. Reuben had been suspended and was told to expect disciplinary action. IAD – the police Internal Affairs Department – had been notified. There was talk of an investigation.

'What the hell's going on?' Reuben demanded.

Nobody knew. Gisler, the lieutenant in charge, shrugged his shoulders and said it must be something to do with vampires. As he stormed out of the apartment, slamming the door, Reuben heard his laugh, loud and abrasive, behind him. Danny stayed behind to make a verbal report.

In the street, Reuben found a payphone. After half a dozen abortive attempts, he tracked down Sally Peale in an office somewhere in City Hall.

'I'm in some sort of trouble, Sally, but I don't know what it is.'

'Is this to do with the Hammel case?'

'What else?'

'Meet me downtown in half an hour, Reuben. There's a Chinese restaurant on Mott Street, number twenty. I'll see you there.'

'What's the name of the restaurant?'

'I just told you: number twenty. It's near the Chinese Museum. You'll find me on the ground floor.'

Chinatown was graceless, without vibrancy, a name more than a district. Reuben seldom went there. He disliked Chinese food, the abundant use of pork.

Sally was waiting at a table near the back, among shadows. She was dressed in an expensively-cut grey suit with a cream scarf round her neck, the perfect lawyer. He thought she looked beautiful. What had gone wrong between them?

'Sit down, Reuben.'

There was a blue and white teapot on the table in front of her, and two small china cups without handles.

'Have some tea, Reuben. It's *Pi Lo Chun*, green tea from Soochow. You'll enjoy it.'

'I'd prefer beer.'

She gave him a look which said, 'We've been through this before.' A waiter came past and she ordered beer.

Young girls in Chinese dresses wheeled *dim sum* from table to table on small, creaking trolleys, each with its own selection and labels in Chinese. Sally seemed to know or guess what was on each one. She pointed, ordering for them both, fat white dumplings and pale, wafer-wrapped delicacies. She knew their names in Cantonese. Reuben felt envious and awkward. He picked at his food, embarrassed to ask which if any of the little parcels contained pork.

'Would you prefer duck, Reuben?'

'I'm all right. This is fine.'

Sally lifted a *dim sum* parcel between two chopsticks and popped it into her open mouth. Her lips were sensual, the gesture erotic. Reuben felt a twinge of regret.

'What sort of trouble are you in, Reuben?'

He explained as best he could.

When he finished, she poured herself another tiny cup of tea. It was growing strong. She replaced the lid half on, half off the pot. A waiter came by and took the pot away. All around them Chinese voices rose and fell like chimes.

'Have you told anyone else about what you found?'

'Danny's making a report now.'

'But no-one else has spoken to you? No-one outside the force, I mean.'

He shook his head.

'The DA's office, is that what you mean?'

The waiter returned and replaced the pot, refilled with hot water. Steam drifted from the spout, languid and colourless.

'Something like that,' said Sally. She seemed distrait. A door slammed in the distance. In a kitchen out of sight, a steam jet hissed, desolate and old. On the wall above their heads, old samples of Chinese calligraphy hung fading, harbouring some sort of mystery. At a nearby table, two old men drank tea and smoked.

'Reuben, if anybody does come round asking questions, will you ring me?' She took a leaf from her filofax and scribbled digits on it. 'You can reach me on this number almost any time.'

Reuben glanced at it. It was not her home number or the

number he had just been using at City Hall. Without a word, he folded the paper and slipped it into his pocket.

'I have to go,' she said.

He hesitated.

'Are you seeing anybody?' he asked.

'Yes. Are you?'

She seemed unconcerned. But her eyes rested on him. He shook his head.

'I don't know,' he said.

'Be careful with the Hammel woman. I don't want you to be hurt, Reuben.'

'But you can't prevent it.'

She shook her head.

'No.' She ran her tongue along her lips.

'Are you in love with her?' she asked.

He looked away.

'I have to go too,' he said.

He called and called again, but the walls threw her name back at him and he knew she had gone. The silence bound him to her suddenly, revealing his need, his expectation, his disappointment. Yesterday, it would have been mere silence, today it was a wound, a blade of couch grass cutting an unprotected hand.

Closing the door, he looked at the other wounds he had brought home: cuts and bruises, trophies of stubborn curiosity. Those were the shallow wounds. Deeper still, he carried more permanent trophies, images of cobwebbed death that shuffled through his mind to find and occupy its fractured centre. Not even the tongue-lashing he had received from Connelly could wipe out that squalid archaeology of death.

His clothes were a mess. He went straight to the bedroom and stripped off his suit: it was only about ten weeks old, now it wasn't even fit for a welfare store. Feeling flat and despondent, he headed for the bathroom. Maybe a shower would perk him up.

Blood was spattered everywhere. Blood on the floor, blood on the towels, blood in the shower cubicle, like red paint smeared on glass and tiles. He panicked, running from room to room in search of her, finding nothing. Back in the bathroom, a closer examination revealed strips of gauze and lint, the empty drum from a roll of surgical tape he had kept in the cabinet. She must have been cut badly, then bandaged herself. How had it happened? She had been disturbed, but he could not believe she had tried to kill herself. This didn't look like attempted suicide.

He almost slipped on the sponge. It was just outside the shower, soaked in blood. He bent and picked it up, dropping it again when a blade sliced his finger. More carefully this time, he lifted it and took a closer look. The blades had been well concealed: just deep enough to stay hidden, just near enough to the surface to do their work efficiently.

Angelina had lost a lot of blood. She must be weak, could be lying unconscious somewhere. But where could she have gone? In her room, he found empty shopping bags. The clothes his sister had lent her were on the bed. She had bandaged herself, then dressed and left. Left without writing a note to tell him where she had been headed.

The telephone rang. Three times, then it stopped. A moment later, it began again. He ran to it, plucking it from the hook.

'Angelina?'

Silence. Then the sound of breathing on the other end, steady, slow. Someone listening.

'Who's there? Is that you, Angelina?'

The caller hung up. The promise of Angelina alive became the nervous burring of a call tone.

He saw Mary-Jo Quigley's name on the pad and called the university. Miss Quigley had not been trying to reach him. No, she hadn't seen Mrs Hammel, although she had spoken with her earlier. What time had that been? About twelve o'clock, she guessed. She'd told Mrs Hammel about the arrangements for the cremation. Wasn't it a shame they wanted to cremate him? It was sinful to burn a human body like that.

He thanked her and hung up. Maybe he was panicking too soon. The most likely thing was that she had bandaged herself well enough to get to hospital. The nearest was Kings County. Any cab driver would have taken her there.

Hospital reception had no record of a Mrs Hammel. The duty nurse didn't think any Haitian women had been admitted that afternoon.

He tried the Methodist Hospital and the Caledonian, west and south of Prospect Park. Nothing. The Maimonides Medical Center on 10th Avenue. Nothing. The church where she said she had gone to confession the day before. Nothing. The undertakers where Rick Hammel's body had been taken. Nothing. He put the phone down.

It rang five seconds later.

'Abrams.'

'That you, Lieutenant? Hell, I've been trying to get you for the past ten minutes.' A homicide squad sergeant, a man called Jesus Riley, the misnamed product of an Irish–Mexican alliance.

'I've been making some calls, Sergeant. What can I do for you?'

'Could you get over here as soon as possible, sir? There's been another homicide. Involves a lady by the name of . . .' He paused, as though consulting a record sheet. 'Yeah, the name's Angelina Hammel. The one whose husband was found in the park a couple of days ago.'

Reuben felt an almighty chill whistle through his flesh. His heart was empty. He felt nothing, he felt everything.

'She's dead?'

A heartbeat. How long a heartbeat is.

'No, sir. The lady's alive. She's been asking for you.'

'I don't understand. You said a homicide.'

'That's right, sir. Victim's a man by the name of . . . let me see . . . Aubin Mondesir. I guess I didn't say that right, sir. Mondesir was a friend of the lady's. So she says.'

'Who found him?'

'The Hammel woman. Says she found him dead, rang us straight away. She was there when the patrol car arrived.'

'How is she?'

Another heartbeat.

'Looks kind of rough. I asked if she wanted to see a doctor, but she said no. Then she mentioned your name. Said something about staying at your place. That right, sir?'

Reuben paused.

'Yes, Sergeant. That's right.'

'Just so I know, sir. I haven't put that into the report. I heard . . .' Riley hesitated.

'What did you hear, Riley?'

'Heard you had some trouble, sir. The captain got back about half an hour ago. Cohen was with him, says he wants to see you.'

'Connelly?'

'No, Cohen. You going to pick the lady up, sir?'

'I'll be down right away. Keep her out of trouble.' He paused. 'She isn't being held, is she?'

'No, sir. We'd like to question her later. But I thought you'd prefer to take care of that yourself. She isn't a suspect, if that's what you mean.'

'That's fine. Keep her there. Tell her I'll be there in fifteen minutes.'

She didn't speak. But her eyes told him a lot of things. Mostly, that she was frightened.

'You feeling OK?' A stupid question. Anyone could see she was ill.

She shook her head and looked at him. She wasn't smiling.

'Let's get out of here.'

He drove her straight to the Brooklyn Caledonian, used his police badge to jump the queue. She did not protest. On the way, he noticed that blood stains were beginning to spread across her blouse.

'I bought it this morning,' she said. 'It was brand new.'

She was crying as she spoke. But she wasn't crying for her blouse. And she wasn't crying for herself. She was crying for him. He had been inside her, he had taken Rick's place, her father's place; and without realizing it, he was becoming entangled in the nets of her existence. There was so much he did not know, so much he must never know. She didn't love him, that was impossible. But she wanted to go somewhere dark and private with him and pretend that she did.

He still found it hard to accept that she had still been a virgin – a virgin with experience, maybe, but as untouched as a thirteen-year-old. Could that be a motive for murder? Between cold sheets, cold actions shiver against the flesh.

He imagined the hell of that, the daily misery of such a marriage. The self-mockery, self-doubt, self-hatred. Understandable if she had sought an end. She was still hiding something, he was sure of that. Just what had she been confessing to her priest yesterday evening? Information relating to Rick's death? Knowledge of her own complicity? He prayed not. He thought he was falling softly and unwillingly in love with her.

Her cuts needed sutures. The doctor treated her like he treated any black woman with razor cuts: he stitched her up, but he made her feel that it was all a waste of his precious time. She had to ask for something to kill the pain. His curt instructions to the nurse implied that she should be hardened to this sort of thing. Didn't it happen often enough? Didn't nigger women expect to be slashed by their men? Wasn't endurance of the knife a sign of bravery in Africa, weren't scarification and cicatrization tokens of maturity?

124

She said nothing, felt nothing. In a way, the doctor was right. She wore her cicatrices on the inside. But they were marks of shame, not pride.

The drive home took place in silence. Darkness thickened in familiar streets. The wind had gone, leaving the city flat and desolate. Behind lighted windows, behind slatted blinds and pleated curtains, the figures of men and women moved in slow motion, executing a measured dance of death, smiling and holding hands, bowing and turning, clothed and naked, washed and soiled, twirling, dipping, menace and grace, finger to finger, palm to palm, without music, swaying, eyes closed, eyes open, breast to breast, lip to silent lip, engulfed by shadows in a mindless minuet. The car moved slowly past the windows, past open doors, past dim stairways. Reuben watched the patterns of the night ripple across Angelina's face, turned his eyes away and watched the road uncoil. And turned again and saw serrated shadows etched against her eyes.

CHAPTER TWENTY-TWO

'Who did it?'

She turned away, hunched in her chair, eyes closed, an empty glass in her hand.

'Who cut you like that? Who put the razors in the sponge?'

'I don't know.'

'I think you do. They followed you here. They know you.'

She hesitated. Her eyes opened, unfocused, sad, accusing.

'Not me. They don't know me – they knew Rick. Can I have some more?'

She held out the glass in silence while he filled it.

'They followed you here, dammit. What were the razors for anyway? Some sort of warning? Was that it?'

She stared at him, tongue frozen, eyes wide apart. Her head moved up, then down. Yes, she nodded, yes.

'What about? What are they warning you about?'

'I don't know,' she said. And filled her mouth with whisky.

'You must know, or they wouldn't waste their time.'

She hesitated, swallowing.

'Perhaps they're making a mistake.'

He turned aside in disgust.

'How can I help you if you won't tell me the truth?'

'I don't want you to help me. I didn't ask for your help.'

'You need it, dammit! Look at you.'

He stood abruptly, slamming his own glass onto a side table, fighting down a sudden anger that was mixed with fear. Storming into the kitchen, he turned on the tap and splashed his face with water before filling a glass. A minute passed, then he heard her come and stand behind him.

'They're dangerous people,' she said. 'I don't want you involved.'

126

He turned to face her.

'I am involved,' he said. 'I'm a policeman, this is my job.'

'I don't want the police mixed up in this.'

'You don't have any choice. Your husband's been murdered. Your friend Filius was poisoned. Somebody planted a sponge full of razor blades in my bathroom. My bathroom, in my apartment. They broke into a police officer's home. Whether you like it or not, the police are mixed up in this. And in case you hadn't noticed, I thought I had gotten myself more than a little involved with you this morning. Or maybe you've forgotten that already.'

She winced.

'No,' she whispered, 'I haven't forgotten.'

'Good,' he said. 'Because I haven't forgotten either.'

For a split second a current of tenderness ran between them. Then he remembered that he was still angry.

'Why did you go to see this man Aubin? The one you found dead this afternoon.'

She sat down at the table. If only she could sleep. If only he would give her a little peace, allow her to think this thing through.

'Aubin is . . . was a *vodouniste*, a *houngan*. I went to him for help.'

'You said you didn't want help.'

She looked down at the floor.

'Not your help,' she said. 'Not ordinary help. Aubin understood. Aubin knew how to help. He knew these people, knew their methods. Someone had arranged for an *expédition de morts* against Rick. And another against me. They'd paid a *bokor* for a *pouin chaud*.'

'I don't understand.'

'No,' she said. 'You don't, do you? That's the point I'm trying to make. You're a *blanc*. You can fuck me, but you can't get inside my skin, you can't dance with me.'

Reuben paused before speaking.

'Angelina,' he began. 'We could both play this game. I could confuse you with a mouthful of Yiddish catchwords, tell you you're a *schwartze* bitch, and give you a lecture on racial purity Jewish-style. But I'm not going to do that because I don't think like that and I don't believe you think like that either.'

'How the fuck do you know what I think?'

'OK, let's suppose I'm wrong. You're a very cool black lady and a honky Jew like me can't get within a million miles of you. So precisely where does that get you? The answer is, in very deep trouble. Because I don't think you can handle this thing yourself and I don't think you've got anybody else to turn to.' He made eye contact with her. 'But from the way things look, you need help and you need it fast.

'Let's agree that there are kinds of help I can't give you, the kind you expected from your friend Aubin. That doesn't mean you don't need the sort of help I can offer. Chances are, you need it even more. I don't know what an *expédition de morts* is. But my bet is it doesn't hurt half as much as a spongeful of razor blades. So why don't you just sit back and tell me what you know? When you've finished, we can have something to eat and a bottle of French wine I just happen to have tucked away in my fridge. After that, who knows? We might watch the *Late Show*. We might play Monopoly. We might go to bed.'

She sat very still, her eyes on him, seeing him and yet not seeing him. When she spoke, her voice seemed to come from far away. If she listened very hard, she could hear a white heron crease its wings in flight.

'Twelve years ago,' she started, 'Rick and I were in Haiti. He was doing research in the north of the island, based in Cap-Haïtien. His topic was the role of *vodoun* in the revolution of 1791. He used to make regular visits to Bois Caiman, just south of the town, where the *vodoun* ceremony was held that sparked off the uprising.

'One day somebody suggested that he should pay a visit to an old plantation house not far from Bois Caiman, a place called Petite-Rivière. Most of the French manor houses in that area were burned down during the revolution, but Petite-Rivière survived. Rick had been told there were still papers at the house dating from before the revolution.

'We went together, it was a hot day in summer.' For some reason she seemed to remember everything about that day – the weather, what she wore, what they ate, the shapes their shadows made against the walls, the rasping of crickets in the brown fields. She had been naked beneath her dress, it had clung to her like a damp rag.

'We took the road through Plaine du Nord and Gallois, then turned west into the hills. Petite-Rivière is completely isolated. I think that's why it survived the uprising. Our Jeep had difficulty keeping to the track. We arrived mid-morning. There was red lichen on the walls. I felt clammy, angry at Rick for dragging me out there. But he wanted my help looking through any documents we might find: my French was always better than his.'

She hesitated, as though haunted by a defect of language. Someone walked across the floor above, a man's feet, heavy and deliberate. She thought of the swooping beauty of orioles, of orange and shadek trees throwing shadows on burnt grass, of the hedge of *sablier* that had circled the house like a fence of knives, its thorns cruel and sharp.

'Petite-Rivière wasn't much of a place. What Boukman and his rebels had failed to do, time and the climate had done instead. It had originally belonged to a branch of the Pays de Bourjolly family, French colonists from La Rochelle. At the time of the revolution, the owner was Jean-Claude de Bourjolly, who was, among other things, the local agent for Riedy and Thurninger, the largest of the Nantes slaving houses. According to contemporary historians, de Bourjolly managed to escape the massacres and somehow or other get himself out of Haiti to America.

'The present owners were poor mulattos who grew sisal for sale to an American company in Le Cap. They claimed to be descendants of the first black family to own Petite-Rivière after the Bourjollys fled. Perhaps, perhaps not. In Haiti, everyone looks for some descent. We are all *ti Guinée*, children of Africa, but we are desperate for roots. To be black is not enough, to speak *langage* is not enough, we must have names, we must become a people of pedigrees.'

She hesitated, thinking of her own twisted roots, of the rank soil in which they had grown.

'They lived in old rooms from which the grace had long since been ripped away. No water, no electricity, just shadows of the past. Someone's past, anyone's past, it did them just as well. There were two old men outside on a long verandah playing *dames*, watching the world slide away a little further every sunset. They paid us no attention.

'Rick and I found the papers crammed into a large metal trunk in an attic full of dried coffee and mouse droppings. They were surprisingly well preserved – somehow the trunk had kept out damp and spores and mould. Their condition was far from perfect, of course, but most of them were surprisingly legible.

'We spent all that day reading through them and sorting them roughly into piles. A little girl watched us – I think she was the youngest child of the family, about eight or nine years old. She was pretty but quite deformed – her head hung at an angle, tilted against her shoulders, as though the neck had been broken, almost as if she had been hanged. Every time I looked up, she was watching from the corner. Just watching, saying nothing. I tried to talk to her, but she would never reply.'

Angelina fell silent, looking past Reuben at a memory, her fingers twisting unconsciously on her lap. The child had died soon afterwards, Rick's contact had mentioned the fact casually in a letter. For months Angelina had been haunted by an image of the little girl laid out on the long deal table where she and Rick had spread the letters, crumpled in a thin white dress, her neck still twisted, her virginity torn by a superstitious parent using a thick wooden stick, to ensure she did not become a *diablesse* after they buried her. Innocence is an open gate for whatever foulness seeks to walk into our garden.

'Rick offered the family money for the trunk and its contents. They took fifty dollars – American dollars, not gourdes – and felt sure they had made a bargain. I suppose they had: what use were old scraps of paper to them? They couldn't even read.'

She remembered leaving in the crumbling dark, the doomed child watching from the door, speechless, perhaps already stricken with whatever was to kill her, the wrong turns, the plunging track, headlights tangled in green and monstrous leaves, the scent of *vétiver* in the tainted, clammy darkness. A *kata* drum had played for miles until it too faded and they were wrapped in silence. Far away, across a broad nameless ravine, lights had flickered in a long line like fireflies along an unseen path. The people of the hills walking to the *houngfor* to become gods.

Looking back, she wondered if there had been any omens that night, anything that might have hinted at what was to come, but nothing came to mind. She looked hard at Reuben, at his hands and eyes and face. What, she wondered, would he look like when they had finished with him? Would they let her look? Would they let her touch him? Would they let her kiss him while he died?

CHAPTER TWENTY-THREE

'Most of the papers dated from Bourjolly's time. There were letters from *armateurs* – slaving houses – in France, letters from friends in St Domingue and elsewhere in the French Antilles, bills of lading, copies of several *rôles d'armement* giving details of ships and their crews, minutes of the Assemblé provinciale for the northern sector of the island, even some pages from a *grimoire* . . .'

'A *grimoire*?'

'A book of magic spells. They're still quite popular in Haiti. *Le Petit Albert* sells very well in shops on the rue Poste Marchand. They're used in *vodoun* ceremonies.'

'I see. Go on.'

She hesitated now, the clarity of memory growing blurred by a presentiment of more immediate truths.

'It took weeks to sort and read through everything. We worked together on the papers – Rick's French wasn't up to the eighteenth-century style. But he did the hard work – the historical research, tying together random facts, making a pattern out of mere odds and ends. And he found a pattern, a very coherent pattern, one that grew a lot sharper over the next few years.'

She paused briefly, then hurried on.

'Bourjolly had got himself mixed up in something very peculiar. *Une affaire très étrange et effrayante*, that's how he described it in a letter to one of his friends in La Rochelle.'

'When was this?'

She shrugged.

'Seventeen seventy-five, seventy-six. We never knew for sure. Most of what we did find out was pure guesswork. Rick trawled libraries in France and Haiti. He spent two summers locked away in the National Archives behind the cathedral in Port-au-Prince. His eighteenth-century French got rather good. He combed second-hand bookstores in Paris, went to manuscript auctions in the Hôtel Drouot, spent a fortune. By the end, he was an expert on the French–Haitian slave trade.'

He sensed her reluctance to come to the point.

'You haven't told me what it was that Bourjolly got mixed up in.'

She shivered slightly, as though a thin wind had sought her out and found her alone in his room. Crossing her arms about her chest, she leaned her chin on the back of one hand, her eyes on the floor.

She closed her eyes briefly, opened them again. 'Something . . .' – she looked straight at him – 'something came ashore on a slave ship. It had come from Africa – something . . . or someone.'

'I'm not sure I . . .'

She ignored him, all thoughts concentrated on events two centuries old.

'He was afraid. Afraid but fascinated. Whatever – or whoever – it was, it changed his life. In his first notes, he makes only passing reference to it, but with time his letters and journals – what we could find of them – become the work of a man obsessed.'

She looked past him at the wall. It started crumbling and she looked away. Stupid wall, why couldn't it stay still? She had to concentrate, had to keep her mind on the here and now. Or else the world, the whole world would start to crumble.

'Rick never really understood,' she went on. 'But I knew almost at once what it was that Bourjolly found. What it was that had come from Africa.'

She hesitated for a moment, then continued.

'There was a city,' she said. 'A city deep in a forest, the Ituri rainforest in what used to be the Congo. They call it Zaïre now.' She smiled to herself. This was like a fairy story, one of the stories her father used to tell her in the days before he was taken away from her. He would seat her on his lap and smile at her and stroke her hair with his big hands, and when she had settled down he would tell her stories. In bed in the long evenings, he had read to her from the *Thousand and One Nights*, the French translation by Galland. But this was no fairy story. This was true.

'The city was called Tali-Niangara, but Arab traders from the north referred to it as Madīnat al-Suhhār – the City of Sorcerers. Tali-Niangara was built of stone, and they say its walls were almost as high as the highest trees, and its gates were fashioned of wood and iron, and sheathed in the purest gold. That may be a fable, but it is true that the inhabitants of Tali-Niangara were sorcerers.'

'How do you know all this?' he asked.

'My father told me when I was very small. Stories had been passed down, stories from the old days, from the Kongo slaves. They said that at the heart of Tali-Niangara stood a citadel where the gods lived and where they talked with men. The people of the city had no need of an army. Their weapon was the simplest of all: fear. Outside the gates, the people of the forest, and beyond them the villagers who lived on the edge of the forest, and further still the people who inhabited the banks of the Congo River lived in a state of terror. They sent tribute to Tali-Niangara every year, after the rains: cattle and grain, leather and cloth and spices, much gold and silver, *nkisi* and slaves. And every year they sent young men and young girls for the gods of Tali-Niangara, none of whom they ever saw again.'

'Why was that? Why would people just accept such a state of affairs? What were they afraid of?'

'You are a Jew,' she said, 'not an African. It would be hard for you to understand. The gods lived in Tali-Niangara. They gave power over life and death to the sorcerers of the city. The people on the fringes lived in fear of that. If they did not send the tribute, their crops would fail, the game would disappear, their cattle would die, their children would grow sick and die. Better to lose a few than all. The lords of Tali-Niangara had little need of walls or armies.'

She sat silent for a while, stilling her heart. Was her own fear the same fear or something more rational? She could not tell.

'For centuries nothing changed,' she went on, telling the story as her father had told it, as her grandfather and grandmother had told it before that. 'The rainforest grew and spread in all directions, the river carved a deeper channel to the sea, the people of Tali-Niangara danced and sang and offered tribute to their greedy gods. This is how the story was told to me. The priests wrote books in Tifinagh, a script brought to them from the deserts to the far north by traders. They wrote the words of their gods on thin plates of beaten gold. That was the only purpose of their civilization: to write down the oracles of the gods and pass them down from generation to generation, each one adding to the work of the one before. It is said that the citadel of Tali-Niangara contained a library of over ten thousand golden books.

'And it is said that the priests made a circle of gold on which they inscribed words of great power and a diagram of the city, and gave it to their kings to wear as a token of their right to rule, and their power over the lives and deaths of all in the city and beyond.'

She looked up.

'This is how the story was told to me, Reuben. By my father, when I was very young.' She closed her eyes. 'For centuries nothing changed. And then, one day in early spring, a band of men with skin the colour of milk appeared at the gates of Tali-Niangara, men with swords and cannon and muskets, men who did not fear the gods or the priests who served them. They gained admission to the city and were offered hospitality by the king and his counsellors. In secret, spells were uttered against them, but they had no effect. Curses were written down, but they remained unharmed.'

For a month the strangers remained, eating, drinking, resting. Finally, on a dark night, they killed the king and his bodyguard, looted the citadel, taking many of the golden books, and took captive fifty of the city's finest young men, including seven priests. Morning found them deep in the forest, laden with gold and in charge of a slave coffle of the best quality.

The coffle moved slowly, urged on by whips, but at a pace dictated by the trees and undergrowth through which they passed. The slavers were not unduly harsh towards their captives – each slave represented an investment of time and money that had yet to be recouped. No-one wanted his share to die before they reached the Indies.

But the forest was hostile. The slavers had to reach the river and make it back to its mouth before their ship set sail without them. And the gods of Tali-Niangara had begun to take a slow but sure revenge.

One by one the slavers perished, some by simple accident, two from snakebites, but most from fever. They began to leave behind unnecessary baggage, and at last the gold objects, all save a few, that they had brought so far. There were fatalities among the slaves as well, but far fewer than among their masters. By the time the coffle reached the banks of the Congo, there were only five white men left alive and thirty blacks. Four of the blacks were priests.

Back on board the slave ship, the survivors' story excited much interest, as did the remaining golden artefacts they displayed in private to the captain and his first officers. A larger expedition, properly equipped, might bring home untold wealth in precious metal and handsome slaves. The ship set sail a week later. They were not yet fully slaved, but were eager to reach the Indies and get home to Liverpool.

The crew was badly outnumbered, but terror of the open sea and conditions on the slave decks kept the cargo passive for the first weeks of the long journey. All the time, however, the four priests were plotting, first with their fellow-exiles from Tali-Niangara, then with picked individuals from among the other slaves. The days went by without much happening. There were deaths among the slaves, mainly from flux. Two of the crew succumbed to fever. Below decks the stench grew unbearable.

The mutiny began as they entered the Caribbean. It was late at night. Most of the crew were sleeping. Despite their weapons, despite their greater fitness, despite their knowledge of the ship, the sailors were quickly overpowered. During the next week, the survivors were tortured. They were not alone. Once in control, the men of Tali-Niangara treated everyone else as their vassals; whether they were white or black made no difference.

Only two white men were spared. One was the ship's pilot, a man called Bellamy. The other was a French slaving agent who had been taken aboard the ship after the loss of his own vessel off the African coast. His name was Jean-Claude de Bourjolly, the man whose papers Angelina and Rick found at Petite-Rivière.

'We discovered much information about the voyage in Bourjolly's letters,' continued Angelina. 'Things my father had never known, things that had never been recorded. Bourjolly had some knowledge of African languages and had long been fascinated by the religious and magical practices of the blacks he had met in Haiti. He had helped the men of Tali-Niangara take control of the ship.

'Now he advised the leaders of the mutiny that it was in their interest to abandon ship and seek refuge among the maroons, escaped slaves scattered through the mountains of Haiti. The longboat was large enough to hold all the survivors from Tali-Niangara and a few slaves they had kept to serve them, together with Bourjolly and Bellamy, without whom they knew they would be lost.

'Before getting into the longboat, the priests discovered the gold circle that had belonged to their king and other pieces of looted gold concealed in a chest in the captain's cabin.

'They broke the great circle in two and took one half on board the longboat, to remain with them in exile. The other half was left on board the ship in the great chest, together with the gold *nkisi* and the books of the gods that had been brought from Tali-Niangara.

135

'The senior priest remained on board with them. He would pray for a dark wind from the west to take the ship and blow it all the way back to Africa, to the mouth of the Congo, along the river to the shores of the great forest. He would return to Tali-Niangara to speak with the gods in the high citadel. The men of Tali-Niangara would build canoes and return for their brothers in the west. The circle would be reunited. There would be a new king. And the gods of Tali-Niangara would take their revenge. That would be the beginning of the Night of the Seventh Darkness. The night of the resurrection of all the dead.'

Angelina stopped speaking. She had shut her eyes, blotting out the present. In her mind, she could see the priest, his slavery thrown off, standing alone at the prow of the little ship, dreaming of a forest he would never see again. She wondered what had happened to him in the end. Had the ship sunk or been captured by another vessel? Rick had spent years trying to find out. And almost as many in a vain search for Tali-Niangara itself. Tali-Niangara and its fabulous library of golden books.

'Is that all you know?' asked Reuben after a while.

Angelina opened her eyes.

'I'm sorry,' she said. 'I was drifting.'

'Is that all you know?'

She shook her head.

'Not quite. There's a little more. Bourjolly and Bellamy came ashore with the slaves, somewhere in the north of Haiti. It's said that Bourjolly had the pilot murdered once he had served his purpose. I don't know what sort of story Bourjolly concocted to explain his rescue, but he returned to Petite-Rivière soon after that and continued with his former business.

'However, he remained in contact somehow with the slaves from Tali-Niangara. In time, they realized that no help was going to arrive from the city, that they would never return to Africa. Within a few years, Bourjolly succeeded in finding places on his estate for all of them. He forged papers of origin for them. The ship on which they had come was never found. They were all treated well at Petite-Rivière. Bourjolly found them wives from among the Congolese slaves that arrived at Cap Français. They settled and had families, including the priests. There was no rule of celibacy for them to obey.'

'Why? Why did Bourjolly do all this? He was a slave trader himself, you said. An agent for a slaving house in France.'

Angelina nodded.

'He wanted knowledge,' she whispered.

'Knowledge? Knowledge of what?'

'Of whatever the gods of Tali-Niangara had taught their priests. The spells, the prayers, the words of power. Bourjolly wanted to be a magician, you see. He had studied the black arts in Europe. But by the age of forty he had gotten nowhere. In Africa, he had heard tales of Tali-Niangara, the Madīnat al-Suhhār. With the help of the men he had rescued, he thought to find the answers to all his unanswered questions, to obtain access to the most ancient mysteries.

'He believed Tali-Niangara had received its knowledge from Egypt, the fountain of all wisdom. He was a Frenchman of his period. In those days in Paris, philosophers believed that Egypt had been the source of the *prisca sapienta*, the original wisdom that the ancient Greeks had lost. So he gave his slaves their lives, security, food, women. In return all he sought from them was knowledge of forbidden things. It must have seemed a fair exchange.'

She fell silent. Reuben looked at her.

'Did he get what he wanted?' he asked.

She looked up. Her eyes were like white opals, steady and watery pale.

'Yes,' she answered. 'He was given knowledge. Knowledge and power. And the hope of immortality.'

CHAPTER TWENTY-FOUR

Reuben got up and crossed to the window, intending to draw the curtains. He glanced out into the rain-exhausted street. Inexplicably, dry leaves lay sharp and crisp beneath the washed-out mantle of a sodium lamp. Traces of Angelina's voice floated on the stillness like a broken rose in water, scattered petals drifting down a dark, tormented current. In his mind, a dim pattern was beginning to form, inchoate as yet, unchannelled, its dark edges lit by the stuttering dawn of an uncertain understanding.

'I don't understand,' he said. 'All of this happened in the eighteenth century. This is the 1990s.'

She looked up, a quizzical glance, and hugged herself more tightly.

'Is it?' she asked.

'Here it is,' he answered. 'In this room it is.' He glanced at the calendar on the wall, a grid of days and weeks held firmly in the here and now.

'But outside?' she insisted. 'It could be any time. Years and dates don't matter to these people. They had no calendars until the slave ships came. Time is all the same to them: past, present, future – it's all one thing, all one substance.'

'What people? You talked before about "dangerous people". What did you mean?' He turned his back on the window, on the night.

'About a year ago,' she said, 'someone got in touch with Rick. He didn't tell me who it was, not at first. But he was frightened, from the beginning he was frightened.

'He'd been writing to people, speaking to people for over five years and nothing had ever happened. Librarians, booksellers, other academics, experts on African and French colonial history, scholars of *vodoun*. They were all as puzzled as we were by what

Rick had found. One of them must have shown some of Rick's papers to a friend. Or that friend to another friend, we could never find out. But the phone call came, then the first visit.'

Angelina paused. Her hands were shaking now.

'Before leaving Haiti,' she went on, 'Bourjolly founded a religion. He called it Le Septième Ordre, the Seventh Order. He believed there had been six secret orders through history who had been chosen to guard the occult truth: the Pythagorean Brotherhood, the Egyptian followers of Hermes Trismegistos, the Templar Knights, the Rosicrucians, the Freemasons and the French Prieuré de Sion. His brotherhood was to be the Seventh Order: the last and the greatest.

'He modelled it partly on European magical orders and partly on African secret societies like the Bizango. It taught a mixture of western occultism and African sorcery. And it prophesied the resurrection of all things when the true king came to sit again on the throne of Tali-Niangara. The Night of the Seventh Darkness.'

An inexplicable look passed over Angelina's face. Reuben could not say quite what it was, whether dream or fear or memory or all three combined. A moment later it had gone.

'His first followers were his own slaves,' she went on. 'They converted others. And he converted most of his own family and several friends in Haiti and France. When the revolution came and the whites were driven from Haiti, the fraternity was led by the priests of Tali-Niangara. It still exists. It is still powerful.'

'And they are here, you say? Here in New York?'

'They have members here,' she said. 'Not Haitians – Americans. There are cells in France and several of the former French colonies in Africa. Elsewhere perhaps, I don't know.'

She held her hands tight together to stop them from shaking. Her voice felt rough, hard to control.

'They visited Rick,' she said, 'and suggested that he drop his research. He was frightened, but not badly enough to be scared off something so important to him. He just dropped what he'd been doing and changed the course of his investigations. What he discovered next really did frighten him.'

She shivered again, more visibly this time.

'Are you cold?'

She shook her head.

'Let me finish,' she said. 'Rick made enquiries. He asked one of his graduate students to help him, the man you found in our apartment, Filius Narcisse. After the revolution in Haiti, Bourjolly came to the United States. He arrived in Florida and made his way north as far as New England, where he lived in Nantucket for a while. Something unpleasant seems to have taken place, and he was forced to flee.'

Reuben looked curiously at her. He suddenly remembered the book he had found in the underground chamber: A Sober Warning to the Righteous, being an *Account of the Recent Events at Nantucket*. Written nine years after the Haitian revolution.

'From Nantucket he headed for New York, where he settled on this side of the river. He bought a farmhouse just outside the village of Brooklyn-Ferry, and a warehouse on Front Street.'

Reuben felt a deep chill settle in his bones. He was beginning to understand what he had seen earlier that day.

'The apartment building Rick and I lived in, the one on Clermont Street, was built on the site of Bourjolly's farmhouse. We were living west of the park before that. About eight years ago, Rick found some old deeds. The farmhouse was there until the 1840s. Brooklyn was growing, and they needed the land to build on. Bourjolly was dead by then, but he had a son, Pierre. Pierre built a row of houses over the farm. He lived for years in the house our apartment was in.

'Rick became obsessed by the idea of living in that house. He'd inherited some money, and he made an offer to the people living in our apartment, a Puerto Rican family. Rick paid them a good price and they sold out.'

'When did Bourjolly die?' asked Rick.

She shrugged.

'I don't know. Nobody knows. It's not recorded. Rick spent a lot of time looking; he even tramped round old graveyards for weeks on end, searching for a gravestone. But he drew a blank. It's as if the old man just disappeared. Maybe there was another scandal brewing; maybe someone forced him out of Brooklyn, just like he was forced out of Nantucket.'

Reuben pursed his lips.

'No,' he said. 'I don't think so.' He stopped. 'I'll explain in a moment. But you were telling me about the things Filius found out.'

'Well,' continued Angelina, 'it seems that even before he arrived in this country, Bourjolly had been building up a network of contacts, people interested in occultism and magic like he was.

They included some eminent people. With their help, he gathered a small following here. That may have had something to do with what happened at Nantucket. Some of his followers went on to become prominent figures in the new republic – lawyers, academics, clergymen, politicians. There was a vogue for secret societies and cults then. The Swedenborgians had just founded an American church at Baltimore. The Freemasons were well established: George Washington had been initiated in 1752.

'By the early nineteenth century, the Seventh Order had become more than just an intellectual pastime for influential Americans: it was itself a major path to influence. It grew more secretive, not less. Members were sworn to loyalty on pain of death, and by all accounts the threat of punishment wasn't a bluff.

'Membership was by invitation only. Those who accepted the invitation had to commit a serious crime: theft, rape, incest, arson, sacrilege – but above all murder. The heads of the society retained full details of the crime together with a written confession in the hand of the aspirant. That kept people quiet, very quiet indeed.

'During the nineteenth century, the American branch had no contact with the group in Haiti, though they did preserve links with Paris. They kept their power and influence, and the order became extremely wealthy. The pattern of membership has changed. There are still judges, senators and government officials. But now the order also includes several industrialists, a couple of media tycoons, property developers, stockbrokers . . . and a number of people connected with organized crime.'

She paused and her eyes lifted and grew large, and he caught sight of her eyes and the pain in them and the small lights that shifted across their borders, and he knew she was telling the truth at last and that in telling it she was risking everything. Not just her life, but everything. And in the moment he understood that, he grew afraid as well.

'Rick knew about this? He and Filius found all this out?'

She nodded. A marionette without fear or pain. Empty.

'Why didn't they come to us or the FBI?'

She tried to look away, but he held her gaze.

'He wanted . . .' Her voice was reed-like, thin. 'He thought he could join them, at least get them to divulge information he could use. At the very least he would have a book that would crown his career, alter our understanding of Haitian history. But I think he expected more than that. These were men with power, men with influence. Rick was ambitious. He talked once about his chances of becoming a presidential adviser on Caribbean affairs. He tried to play with them. They don't like that. They don't like being played with.'

'And you. Are you playing with them as well? Is that what the warning was about?'

Her eyes wandered.

'Look at me, Angelina. Is that what they were warning you about? To stop playing games with them?'

She shook her head, an imperceptible movement.

'They're looking for something. Something they think Rick had. Something they want very badly.'

'A file? Evidence?'

She shook her head again.

'They have most of his files. They came yesterday or the day before, took everything they could. But they missed something, the one thing they really wanted.'

'What was that?'

'Rick's notebook,' she said. 'He showed it to Filius once, about a year ago. When I saw Filius yesterday, he admitted that he had told the order about it before they poisoned him. He used the notebook as a means of getting into the order.'

'Filius was a member?'

She shook her head.

'No, but he wanted to be. The ceremony recorded on the video tape was to have been the first of several. It involved . . .' She hesitated. 'I think Filius killed someone. That was the blood he had in the bowl. The whole thing had been recorded to provide a hold over Filius, something even better than a signed confession.'

'So what happened?'

She shrugged.

'They couldn't find the notebook. Filius wasn't to know. Rick had a safe hiding place. I found it yesterday and took it to the nearest branch of the Banco di Ponce. I left it in a safe-deposit box.'

'So they turned Filius into a zombie.'

She seemed to wince, then nodded.

'A *zombi*, yes, if you like. Dead for a while, then brought back to life by means of an antidote. It was a secret Bourjolly's slaves brought from Tali-Niangara. How to kill a man without killing him.'

'But they really killed Rick.'

She nodded.

'Yes. When Filius failed them, they waited for Rick to return from our trip to Zaïre. They wanted to take him by surprise, but the video alerted him. That was a mistake, I think. The video. Someone left it for Rick to see, to frighten him. But Rick always thought he could outsmart other people. Even then he thought he could keep one step ahead. I don't know what he did or what he told them. Maybe he tried to make a deal. Whatever he tried, it didn't work. They killed him. And now they're putting pressure on me.'

'But they don't want to kill you because you know about the notebook.'

'That's right; but they may be frightened I'll hand it over to the police. They know I went back to the apartment.'

'What's in the notebook?'

'The things I just told you about, with details of names and dates and so on, stuff Rick had been able to dig up. He had evidence that could have proved highly uncomfortable for them. I don't think he could have destroyed them, but he could have caused them considerable inconvenience.'

'Is that all?'

'No. Rick kept records of all his research on the ship that brought Bourjolly and the slaves from Tali-Niangara to Haiti. He came very close to discovering the ship's name, maybe even locating the wreck . . .'

'There's a wreck?'

Angelina shook her head. Her hair fell softly across her forehead, tumbling over her eyes. She brushed it back.

'I don't know. Rick was sure the ship could not have sailed far. If it wasn't found drifting and brought to harbour, it must have gone down.'

'Why is the wreck so important?'

'Because it contains half of the golden disc. For the Night of the Seventh Darkness. Without it the king will not return.'

'Do they have the other half?' He did not tell her yet what he had found.

She shook her head. This time her hair did not move. Reuben wanted it to move, to see her brush it away again with that easy gesture.

'Rick thought Bourjolly kept it. It must have disappeared with him. I know Rick had ideas about where it might be. Something to do with the apartment building. Maybe he thought Bourjolly had buried it on his farm somewhere.'

'He wasn't entirely wrong.'

'What do you mean?'

Reuben stood and went into the living room. He came back carrying the box he had removed from the underground chamber. From it he took the bundle of letters and passed them to Angelina.

She looked through them silently, one at a time, her fingers delicate against the fragile paper. One entire page crumbled as she held it. Paper and ink and the unfractured past. She read for a long time. Finally, she looked up.

'These are all addressed to Bourjolly,' she said. 'They're from a mulatto in Cap Français, an educated man, a clerk. He seems to have been Bourjolly's chief link with the order in Haiti. Where did you find them?'

Briefly he told her. He was no longer in any doubt that the mummified remains had been those of Bourjolly himself.

Finally, he lifted the golden semicircle from the box and handed it to her. It was shrill and flat and hard, and all across it lines of incised writing walked like peculiar insects.

Angelina ran her fingers gently across it.

'This writing is in Tifinagh script,' she whispered. 'It must be genuine.' She looked up.

'They will kill you,' she said. 'They will do anything to lay their hands on this.'

'I know,' said Reuben. 'I know.' And he took the gold half-moon and laid it in the box and closed it without a sound.

The telephone rang, loud and shrill like beaten gold. Angelina jumped. Reuben picked up the receiver. He listened briefly, said, 'I'll be there', and replaced the receiver carefully. He sat for a moment staring at the phone, then looked at Angelina.

'Captain Connelly wants to see me. He's sending a patrol car over to pick me up. Won't say what it's about. But he sounded on edge.'

He picked up the receiver again and punched in a number from memory. Danny answered right away. He sounded ill-tempered and in no mood to do anyone a favour, but Reuben leaned on him until he gave in.

'Get here quickly, Danny. And, Danny . . .'

'Yeah?'

'Bring your gun.' Reuben put the receiver down.

Angelina was waiting in the living room. She seemed nervous, overwrought.

'I have to go,' Reuben said. 'Connelly's given me no choice. He says it's important. I don't want you here alone, so I've asked my partner Danny to come over. He should be here in about fifteen minutes if he doesn't hang about. Use the entryphone. His name's Danny Cohen, he's about six four, well-built, early thirties. You'll like him. Don't let anybody else in. If he asks what's going on, tell him.'

'I don't want you to go, Reuben.'

'It's OK. I won't be long. I promise. Danny will take care of you. Trust me.'

CHAPTER TWENTY-FIVE

Listen. What can you hear? First, the sound of your own breathing. Then blood pumping in and out of your heart. And if you listen very, very carefully, you can hear the blood in your head, like a river in flood. They are the only sounds that matter: when they fall silent, when you hear nothing, there is only death.

He took a deep breath in the darkness and let it out again. Two more for good measure. His heart was racing, out of control. He felt light-headed, sick and apprehensive. With the return of full consciousness had come a vast, unending fear. The fear was like a blanket, wrapping him, smothering him and, like a child beneath tight bedclothes, he kicked and struggled, only to find it tighten about him.

He had been in unspeakable darkness. He had watched helplessly as they declared him dead, listened terrified to the nails slamming into the lid of his coffin, to the clods of wet earth dropping heavily into his grave until there was no sound anywhere, no breath, no bloodstream, not even a beating heart. Worst of all was knowing. Knowing they would return, knowing they would free him from the grave only to take him somewhere more terrible. When the sound of spades had sliced through the darkness, and been followed by a dreadful scraping of metal against wood, he had been beside himself with fear.

They had lifted him from the coffin and fed him a sickly paste of sweet potato, cane syrup and *concombre zombi*. On the following morning, they had given him a second dose, then left him alone. Consciousness had returned, but with it a terrible madness induced by the psychoactive agents in the *concombre*. Half-crazy, he had lain in darkness on a bitterly hard floor, while his inner demons raged and trumpeted. They had come for him before noon and taken him by car to another place.

He had escaped through long tunnels smelling of damp and rooms filled with bones and things without shape or colour. He had found himself at last in an empty room, familiar yet strange, like the woman who had spoken to him there. And the man, the man who had frightened her so much. Now, of course, he could remember: the woman had been Angelina, the room had been the one in her apartment where it had all started, the blood and the hungry silences. He could not remember who the man had been. In the end they had brought him back here and put him in the darkness behind a heavy, bolted door.

Someone struck a match, and a yellow flame spurted in the darkness. In an instant it grew calm. An unseen hand placed it against a candle wick, stroking it gently, coaxing it into life.

Sing, said a voice and another voice sang, lifting the words higher and higher until they touched the ceiling and hung in tiny, suspended clusters. He could make out the dim figures of two men, one tall, one of medium height. Their backs were to him. They were dressed in red and black, in long embroidered robes that touched the floor. The tall man was half-singing, half-intoning a hymn.

His companion lit a second candle. Flame in proper measure, light in fluctuation. Indistinct, a low altar trembled in front of him. A third candle grew flame and a fourth. The song went on and on, weaving out of the abraded silence dark patterns of love and terror.

On the broad surface of the altar, images of the *loa* stood flanked by brightly coloured oleographs. Small pots covered in variously patterned cloths, *govis* holding the *loa* and spirits of the dead. On a large plate, a goat's skull with brown candles in each eye-socket, beads draped across its horns. A jawless human skull grown thick with accumulations of candle grease. A copy of *Le Petit Albert*, festooned in strings of red and purple beads, coated with dust, untouched, untouchable.

The men turned to face him, both singing now.

. . . *odâ owèdo mêmê odâ misn wèdo, diêké, Damballah-wèdo têgi nêg ak-â-syel* . . .

A large wooden cross stood to the left of the altar, dressed in multicoloured cloths and bound with thick ropes. At its foot bottles, some wrapped in sacking, some clear: *clairin*, whisky, vermouth and brandy. On the right of the altar stood the *madoule*, the sacred coffin of the Bizango societies.

The sight of the coffin awakened a hive of memories. They buzzed in his head, stinging without pity.

147

Who is your mother?
La Veuve, la madoule. The widow. The sacred coffin.
Who is your father?
I have no father. I am an animal.
Who is your wife?
I am married to the grave.
Who is your son?
I have no children. The dead do not give birth.

He remembered the questions, his answers. Standing naked before the altar, his eyes blinking in the candlelight, painful after what seemed an age in pitch darkness, he called it all to mind. The questions. The answers. And the price.

The singing stopped. He stood frozen to the spot, as though the poison was still working in his system. Expressionless, the men advanced until they were inches from him. The tall man spoke.

'Filius Narcisse?'

He nodded, too frightened to frame a reply.

'Who is your mother?'

He shook his head, unable to reply. The question was repeated.

'Who is your mother?'

The answer came out of the past, in a voice cracked by thirst and fear.

'La Veuve.'

'Who is your father?'

'I have no father. I am an animal.'

Without warning, the men stepped to either side of him and grasped him by the arms. He did not resist. They pulled him and he came, legs like jelly, trembling as they dragged him across the floor.

In the side wall of the *bagui* was set a low, narrow doorway on which a *vévé* had been painted in red. The doorway opened and he was half-marched, half-dragged into a small circular chamber bare of either furniture or ornament. Walls and floor and ceiling had been painted in white. From the high, arched ceiling hung a single bulb, its pale light bouncing off the stark white walls, bringing tears of sudden pain to his dark-adjusted eyes.

The room was filled with a low-pitched, inarticulate sound that rose and fell in harsh, irregular cadences, now breaking, now resuming, slipping through his veins like ice. The sound came from underneath the floor, rising disjointedly out of rows of small holes pierced in what looked like circular manhole covers. It was less a babble of incoherent voices than a steady, muted moan, a plangent cry of despair.

He would have thought these the voices of animals, of things without souls, were it not that he knew them to be human. To have been human once.

One of the manhole covers had been raised and slid aside. The opening was just wide enough to permit a man to pass through.

As though at an inaudible signal the tall man spun him round while his companion slipped a rope and harness over his head and round his shoulders. He cried out for help, knowing none would come. At the sound of his alarm, some of the whining voices rose in pitch, like echoes of his own. There were no words. They had forgotten language along with their humanity. In time, he knew, he would understand their gibberings perfectly. He wondered if they talked with one another in the long, long darkness.

The men hauled him struggling to the edge of the hole. As he reached it, he went suddenly limp, all fight sucked from him by the sheer horror of his position. The tall man bent and whispered in his ears, words in a long-dead language, the last words in a human voice he would ever hear. He cried out as his feet were kicked from under him and they began to lower him into the narrow pit.

The rough stone sides grazed his hips and shoulders as he sank lower and lower on the end of the gently turning rope. Five feet, eleven feet, deeper and deeper, the circle of light above growing smaller by the second.

At fifteen feet he struck the cold hard surface of the floor and felt his legs give way. Except that the shaft into which he had been lowered was not wide enough to permit him even to crouch. His knees cracked against the side, his buttocks rested on unyielding stone.

Half-standing, half-crouching, he sobbed uncontrollably. An imperceptible tug on a thin cord released the harness. It fell away and was hauled up rapidly out of sight on the end of the rope. His last contact with the world above, his severed umbilical cord.

Some, he had once been told, lasted ten years, twenty years. One, it was said, had gone on as long as forty: bent, misshapen, blind, no longer remotely human. He could not understand why they did not simply stop eating the food that came every second day. Crippled, insane, in constant pain, they went on living. That was the horror, that they could not turn their backs on life.

There was a grating sound high above. The pierced slab was pushed back over the hole, clanging into place with a note of utter finality. For a moment that seemed a lifetime the howling stopped.

A deep, unearthly silence fell on the chamber, filled with the echo of stone ringing against stone. Soft footsteps moved away. A door opened and closed. Someone laughed. Someone sobbed.

The light remained lit. So you could just see, out of reach, nineteen tiny holes like pinpricks in the everlasting blackness. A reminder of the light. Like stars, he thought. Like tiny, twinkling stars.

CHAPTER TWENTY-SIX

The patrolman was a stranger to Reuben, hard-jawed and tight-lipped. He did not speak during their long journey, other than to introduce himself. When Reuben asked where they were going, he shrugged and said, 'I'm taking you to Captain Connelly like I've been told,' before turning his eyes back to the road.

'I haven't seen you at the precinct,' Reuben said. 'You've just been transferred?'

The man said nothing.

They drove in silence through streets without memory. Brooklyn was in a state of perpetual flux. The old Yiddish stores of Reuben's childhood now had Caribbean and Spanish names; synagogues had been turned into churches with names like the Trinity Holiness Church of America; familiar faces had become the faces of strangers. The car was warm but uncomfortable. Reuben gazed through the windscreen; the heavy glass made everything seem far away, like a city seen through water. Outside, night clung to the streets for warmth.

They headed east through Queens and Nassau County, out of the city into the semi-rural parts of Long Island. Reuben dozed briefly, woke to find himself being driven through a great darkness, the only lights those of the car. The long beam pulled a crystal world out of nothing: a chalk-white road, pale hedges, dark trees with the stain of winter on their leaves. A farmhouse flashed into view and was gone at once, white painted gables flat against the dark. A small windmill turned gently in a sea breeze. A horse stood in a silent field, pawing the tangled grass.

They arrived at a gabled house set far back from the road among trees and heavy shrubbery. The style was colonial, the fabric modern. Light shone from a single window in a cupola stark against a dark-grained sky. The first and second floors were dark. The house was like a ship adrift in the night.

The patrolman led Reuben inside, still wordless and sullen. He seemed familiar with the layout. A switch to the right of the door lit a long hallway and a white-banistered staircase.

'Go on up,' the patrolman said. 'You're expected.'

The stairs led directly to the third floor. A long carpeted corridor took Reuben past closed doors to an opening out of which light streamed almost to his feet. His heart was out of step, his breath thick in his nostrils. The house felt cold. There was a tinge of damp on the air. Somewhere, a heavy clock was ticking, neither slow nor fast. The open doorway drew Reuben in. Behind it stood a spiral stairway that led upward into a lighted space.

Reuben climbed the stairs slowly, one at a time. He came out into the cupola, a large area over which a glass dome stretched. The air was warm and humid. It was as though Reuben had stepped into a tropical greenhouse on a sharp winter's night. Luscious plants grew everywhere in abundance. Palms and vines and astonishing red flowers made a world in miniature. Brightly coloured orchids flourished in pots of sphagnum moss, secluded among masses of thick foliage.

Captain Connelly was seated in a wicker chair to Reuben's left, his heavy frame wedged into it like a man's hand in a woman's glove; he was nervous, diminished, not really present. As Reuben entered, the captain made no gesture of welcome or recognition. There were sweat stains on his chest and beneath his armpits. Tiny beads of perspiration covered his forehead.

Some distance away from Connelly, his back to the room, a dim figure stood gazing through the window into the darkness beyond.

Reuben approached Connelly. The captain watched him sharply, but said nothing. The second man turned. He was a handsome man in his early fifties, clean-shaven, his grey hair cut close to his head. A wide forehead sloped down to thick eyebrows and a sharp nose. A thin scar ran down his right cheek, white and sharp as a razor blade. He spoke gently, in a softly pitched voice that suggested a tight nervous energy wrapped up inside. Energy, strength, violence perhaps. The most indirect of violence, the best controlled.

'Have you ever noticed, Lieutenant, how dark it can grow even a few miles from the greatest city? There is more darkness in the universe than light. One day it will extinguish everything.'

'Who are you?' Reuben demanded. 'What do you want?'

'To talk. Nothing more.' The stranger paused. He gestured

towards a wicker seat like the one in which Connelly was sitting. 'Please, Lieutenant, take a seat. This won't take long.'

Reuben sat reluctantly. The stranger took a chair facing him. On the edge of vision, a fluorescent light flickered. There were no stars in the sky above the glass dome.

'Your captain and I,' the stranger began, 'have been holding a long and interesting conversation. Have we not, Captain?'

Connelly said nothing. It was as though he had been hypnotized. He watched and listened, but he was not present.

'We have been talking about the Hammel case. Someone will have told you already that you have been suspended. On considering your case, however, we have overruled that decision and given you another assignment instead. You will be given details tomorrow. Please do not waste your own time or anyone else's trying to take the Hammel investigation any further. You will find no answers. There are no answers. The case has been closed. Permanently.'

'Who are you?' Reuben asked for the second time. The stranger looked at him oddly, as though the question made little sense.

'That scarcely matters, Lieutenant. I've brought you here tonight as a matter of courtesy. Please don't abuse it. Be assured that I speak with the highest authority. Anything I say has been sanctioned at very high levels. You are under instructions not to mention this meeting or to reveal its contents to anyone. Do you understand?'

'On whose authority?'

'I already told you – the highest. Do I have to spell it out? This is a matter of national security. It's no longer police business.'

'What are you?' Reuben asked. 'FBI?'

'I'm not at liberty to divulge that. Your captain can vouch for me. If you like, you can call me Smith. Will that make you happy?'

'Smith' folded his hands on his lap. He was in control of things and he knew it.

'Lieutenant, I advise you not to cross me. I have complete jurisdiction in this matter. I require your cooperation: your full cooperation.'

'And if I refuse?'

'Then I shall have you arrested for obstructing my enquiries. I warn you, Lieutenant, this is a matter of the utmost gravity. You would do well not to withhold any information I may seek nor to try to fob me off with false or deliberately misleading statements.

153

But we're wasting time. I'm sure you understand exactly what I want from you. And that I know how to get it. Now, I'd like you to tell me what you found today. What you found in the tunnel.'

Reuben hesitated. It made no sense for the FBI to be involved. Did they know about the order's connection to organized crime? If not, why not come out and say so? And why shut down the investigation?

'I'm putting it all in my report . . . Mr Smith.'

Smith shook his head.

'There will be no report, Lieutenant. Do you understand? I only want a verbal statement from you tonight. Just to set my own mind at rest.'

Reuben knew there was nothing he could do. Smith had the whip hand, whether he was from the FBI or another agency. Carefully, Reuben explained to Smith what he and Danny had found. But he said nothing about the letters or the gold half-circle. He hoped Danny had kept quiet about them as well.

'What will happen now?' he asked when he had finished.

'Happen?'

'To the things in the tunnel. The books and everything.'

Smith leaned back in his chair.

'Nothing,' he said. 'Nothing will happen to them. They will remain where they are. The tunnels are a health hazard. I would not be surprised if either you or Mr Cohen has contracted an unpleasant disease. The city authorities have already given instructions to seal the tunnels off. Eventually, they will be filled in.'

Smith's hands were by his side, fleshy hands that rested softly on the arms of the wicker chair, the right hand just slightly out of sight. Behind him, dark green leaves arched against the night. The fluorescent tube flickered like the aura at the start of a migraine.

'Let us pass on, Lieutenant. I want to know what the Hammel woman has told you. I am informed that she has been living with you for a few days now. You have been very charitable. But she must have told you something of interest by now.'

'I don't think we talked about anything that would interest you.'

Smith's voice underwent a subtle but perceptible change. The urbanity slipped away and was replaced by menace. The menace was almost tangible, something you could reach out and touch, like a knife.

'I assure you, Lieutenant Abrams, that anything you and Mrs Hammel may have talked about is of consuming interest to me.'

Reuben got out of the chair.

'I'd like to leave,' he said.

'That would not be advisable, Lieutenant. Please sit down.' The man who called himself Smith made no move. It was all in the voice.

'Are you threatening me?' asked Reuben.

'I don't know,' said Smith. 'Do you feel threatened?'

'Yes, I feel threatened.'

'Good. Very good. That is exactly how I want you to feel. Please sit down.'

Smith turned to Connelly. 'Captain, perhaps you would like to show the lieutenant the items you so kindly brought with you.'

Connelly looked up, like someone woken from a bad dream. He nodded and bent down to lift a briefcase sitting beside his chair. From it he took a large, thick envelope. He passed it to Reuben.

Reuben opened the envelope and slipped out its contents onto his lap. There were around twenty photographs, large colour prints. They showed children, both girls and boys, ranging in age from about five to thirteen. The children were all naked or partly clothed, their bodies arranged in what might pass in certain minds for erotic poses. Reuben recognized the photographs.

About a year earlier, he had found them in an apartment where a homicide had taken place. The investigation had led to the uncovering of a ring of paedophiles throughout Brooklyn Heights. There had been arrests. Most of the cases had yet to come to court. The photographs had not yet been used in evidence.

'Unpleasant, aren't they?' said Smith. 'It seems they were found in your private locker at the 88th Precinct. Fortunately for you, they were handed to Captain Connelly here, who has not yet passed them on either to Vice or Internal Affairs. I'm sure you appreciate just how difficult life could become for you, Lieutenant, if he were to do so.'

So that was it, thought Reuben. A crude but effective piece of blackmail. They could plant more photographs anywhere they liked: in Reuben's desk, in his apartment, maybe even in his security box at the bank. He had handled a lot of obscene material on that case: there would be no shortage of photographs bearing his fingerprints.

Reuben stood. He looked down at Connelly, then at Smith.

'I want someone to drive me home.'

'The patrol car is waiting for you downstairs.'

Reuben turned and headed for the stairs.

'Take care, Lieutenant.' Smith's voice was dark, tired, almost seductive. Behind him, heat rose from the little jungle. 'Think about what I've just said. Think very hard. And, Lieutenant . . .'

Reuben turned. Both men were watching him.

'Watch your back.'

CHAPTER TWENTY-SEVEN

'Trust me.' The two most dangerous words in the language. Any language. But Angelina trusted nobody, not even herself.

When Reuben went, he left behind a silence as frightening as a protracted scream. The silence howled at her until she pressed her hands over her ears and locked it in, deep down, away from the night outside.

Danny arrived ten minutes later, a little on edge. He had been planning on spending the evening alone, to take the edge off his sorrows with a few drinks. Babysitting Reuben's new girlfriend had not been on the agenda. The first half-hour passed awkwardly. Angelina was petulant, frightened, ill at ease, and Danny had come to her sullen and perplexed. Connelly's lecture had done its work inside him. Danny didn't mind that Reuben was keeping the woman in his apartment, nor that he wanted him to look after her. He had done half a dozen personal protection jobs in the past. That was the problem: he knew just how boring they could be.

They talked of this and that. Danny found a large bottle of Glenfiddich in the drinks cabinet and poured two generous glasses. He wasn't on duty, after all.

He wondered just how much Angelina knew about what was going on, how much of that day's business Reuben had revealed to her, if anything. Apart from Connelly, he'd spoken about it to no-one himself. It still haunted him: the long tunnel, the room with the pits and the cages, the sleeping library with its blind and cobwebbed guardian.

The evening wore on. The level in the whisky bottle went down, most of it via Danny's glass. Angelina told him about the razors and how she thought they had come to be there. The rooms were quiet, very quiet, tense, still full of Reuben's abandoned silence. No conversation helped. She talked about Rick in careful sentences that were somewhere between grief and celebration. Danny scarcely responded. He seemed to be somewhere else, thinking or dreaming or floating in a place fast between.

It grew cold. Angelina lit the gas fire. Little yellow flames flickered and cast an artificial cosiness across the dim room. She wondered when she had last seen sunshine, real sunshine.

'Reuben had a lot of photographs,' said Danny. 'Photographs of his family. He always had them, every apartment he ever lived in. Did he tell you what he did with them?'

Angelina looked at the bobbing flames, at the reflections they made in the brass surround. She saw her own face reflected, its mute image warped by metal and flame.

'They're gone,' she said. 'Reuben threw them out. He'd had enough of them.'

Danny looked blankly at her, sensing the deceit, yet unable to articulate it.

'Reuben would never do that,' he said. 'He loves his family. They mean everything to him.'

'I know.' She spoke gently, her words filled by the hissing of the fire. Nothing but rain and mist, and in the summer heat without light. 'But it happened.'

Danny looked at her, at the firelight in her hair, saying nothing. He thought Reuben would find her beautiful. Such things happened. Perhaps she was beautiful, he didn't know. He did not ask much of a woman himself. But Reuben was different.

'Have you slept with Reuben?' he asked, astonished by his own effrontery.

'Yes,' she said.

He looked at her again. Yes, he thought, Reuben would know how to touch a woman like this, how to talk to her.

She leaned towards him.

'Tell me about Reuben,' she said. 'He told me you were his best friend. That you've known him for a long time.'

Danny nodded. He watched a lock of hair fall quietly across her eyes, watched her hand brush it back. The firelight glided across her skin, turning it to copper. Reuben would find her mysterious and cold and beautiful, Reuben would know how to break down her reserves.

'Reuben is the loneliest man I know,' he said. 'He has his family, he has friends, he's almost never alone. But he's as lonely as somebody living on the moon. He's lonely and he's perplexed, only he won't admit it to himself.'

158

'Perplexed? About what?'

Danny shrugged.

'About life, I think. No, that's wrong. About goodness.'

'I don't understand.'

'Reuben was brought up to believe in goodness, in the power of virtue. His parents are strict. Not Hassids, but observant. They told him God is good, that the universe is pervaded with goodness. In spite of everything, in spite of the Holocaust. Worse than that, in some way *because* of the Holocaust. That's what they used to tell him.'

He paused, looking at her skin, watching the firelight transform it. She seemed to glow from within.

'But Reuben can't find that goodness, so he worries and gets upset. He thinks God is part evil, that maybe there is no God. But his childhood was filled with God. He can't get rid of God without getting rid of his childhood, and he can't get rid of his childhood without getting rid of his parents, and he loves his parents. So he's perplexed. And everywhere he looks he sees evil instead of the goodness he was brought up to expect.'

'Because of his job? Because he's a policeman?'

Danny shook his head. He sipped more whisky. It had started to taste sour in his mouth.

'Not because of that. Because of who he is. The job doesn't help; but Reuben would find fault with God even if he was a rabbi. Which he isn't.'

'Is that what makes him lonely?'

Danny hesitated then nodded.

'Yes,' he said. 'I'd never thought of that, but I think that's it. The universe isn't full enough for him. He tries to fill it with people or memories or something, but what he really wants is goodness. Not love or harmony or peace. Just goodness.'

'What about women? Does he have anyone?'

Her heart beat awkwardly, in forlorn cadences. His loneliness drew her to him like a blind moth through endless darkness.

'He has you.'

'Only last night. I slept with him once. He doesn't have me.'

'He has nobody else.'

'And before?'

There was a long silence. The cold outside pressed densely against the windowpane. When Danny spoke, his voice had altered.

'Reuben was married once. Did he tell you that?'

She nodded.

'His wife was called Devorah. She was more beautiful than anything you can imagine. They were childhood sweethearts. They grew up together on the same street, spent all their time together. She was just nineteen when they got married. Reuben was twenty-one.'

Danny fell silent, listening to voices from the past.

'They were happy?'

He looked up and nodded.

'Yes,' he said. 'Very happy. I've never seen people so happy. It lasted four years.'

'What happened?'

Again the silence.

'You can tell me,' she said.

'There was an accident,' Danny said. 'They were on holiday with their daughter Davita at a Jewish summer camp in Massachusetts, in the Berkshire Mountains. The camp's really a small settlement of summer cottages on a lakeside. Devorah and Reuben went swimming one morning very early. There's a current in the middle of the lake. Devorah wasn't a good swimmer. She knew about the current, but that morning for some reason she was careless. Reuben lost sight of her, then saw her struggling. He did what he could, but he couldn't save her. He's never forgiven himself.'

Danny looked away. There were tears in his eyes. He had known Devorah a long time too.

'And their daughter?'

'Davita? She lives with Devorah's parents. Reuben couldn't cope alone, so they adopted her. He visits as often as he can. They're in Canada, a place called Hamilton, just south of Toronto. They moved away from here after the accident.'

Danny fell silent again. He wondered what Reuben had done with his photographs of Davita. Angelina said nothing. She stood and went to the window.

The street was empty. Empty and altered. Without people, streets change, lose meaning. But she was not deceived. They were out there. In luxury apartments, in offices of glass, in lobbies of polished marble, in long, sleek cars, in indoor gardens splendid with vines, at the tops of spiral staircases, their feet poised to descend, in tunnels of deepest night, in graveyards speckled with shadows. Out there. Waiting.

160

CHAPTER TWENTY-EIGHT

Angelina woke with a start, surfacing from a dream of scars and ruined beauty. The wind had risen again, tumbling into the night-slumbering streets like a drunk, howling, clattering, spilling pockets of dark rain like cheap wine on stained and broken sidewalks. She lay in bed and listened to its roaring, and something told her it had not been the wind that had woken her. The clock beside her bed said 1.15. Reuben should have been back ages ago.

For a matter of seconds the wind dropped and a silence full of suppressed rage filled the night. It was like the moment when, between the *rada* and the *petro* drums, in the thin space between love and lust, a silence shivers among the gods. She knew something was wrong. The wind cried out again, breathless, hunting, in search of peace.

She pulled back the bedclothes and stood trembling in the darkness, naked, cold and blind. A cotton robe lay at the foot of the bed. Groping, she found it and slipped it on. Her hand hovered for a moment over the light switch, but she thought twice and pulled it away.

In the passage nothing moved. Danny had stayed on in the living room after she went to bed. She wanted to call his name, but fear held her back. They were here, she was sure of it. Here with her in the private spaces of her darkness. She moved slowly, holding her breath. The wind was muffled now, but other sounds came to her finely attuned ears: a creaking joist, wood panelling cracking in the cold, the apartment stretching and relaxing in the spaces of the night. She had to get to Danny at all costs.

The door to the living room was outlined by thin white lines of light. She moved towards it on bare feet, as though in slow motion, every muscle tense, every hair on end, like threads pulled taut against the bright straining edge of a razor blade. The door seemed

161

miles away, small and unreachable. In her ears, the silence hissed like steam, making her flinch.

An age later, she finally reached the door. If only she had brought a weapon with her, a stick, a shoe, anything to defend herself with. Her breath was thick and clumsy, choking her, her heart was being strangled by a giant hand. Shaking, she reached for the handle and opened the door. Light flooded into the passage, drowning her.

She thought she screamed, but the voice that cried out was inside her, ringing in vast, empty silences. She could not give physical voice to her fear.

Danny was still in the chair where Angelina had left him. Death must have been rapid. The wire had cut deeply into his neck, slicing through his windpipe as easily as a sharp blade.

A footstep sounded on the floor behind her. She spun round, stifling a cry. A tall man stepped out of the kitchen. He held a heavy gun in one hand, a long silencer attached to the barrel.

'You don't listen, Mrs Hammel,' he said. 'We send you warnings, but you don't listen. We told you to go home to Haiti, to forget all this, but you stay here and mock us.' His voice was steady, his breathing soft and calm. She looked into his eyes for comfort, but there was none. He spoke of Haiti, of going home; but she knew there could be no homecoming for her now, no journey back over dark waters, only a winter's night in Brooklyn and the wind heavy between stone buildings and her executioner towering over her with sadness in his eyes.

'Lieutenant Abrams can't help you now,' he said. 'You're on your own. You know what I want. I won't harm you if you tell me where it is.'

She realized that he had taken Danny for Reuben. A small mistake, but she clung to it the way a man about to hang clings to the buoyancy of air.

He was moving towards her now, slowly, with deliberation in his step, conscious of his strength, keyed-up, alert. His height alone intimidated her.

She moved backwards into the room, shaking with fear, her eyes fixed on his face, desperate for time, desperate for Reuben to return. And in that moment the thought hit her like a slap across the face: what if Reuben had already returned? What if he was lying dead in another room?

She panicked and turned, twisting away from him like a trapped animal. As she did so, her eye caught the half-empty bottle of Glenfiddich sitting where Danny had left it earlier. Without pausing to think, she snatched it up by the neck and smashed it hard against the edge of the table. Whisky and broken glass fell together onto the carpet.

She raised the long bottleneck with its jagged edge, slashing the air, warning him off. Terror would give her the courage to cut him, she knew that.

'Stay back!' she shouted. 'Stay back or I'll hurt you.'

The man only smiled and moved warily into the room. He was confident in his strength, scornful of her ability to harm him; but down on the streets he had seen more than once what broken glass could do, even in a frightened man's hand. He could shoot her, of course, but he preferred not to take the risk that involved. If she died, they might never find what they were looking for. He slipped the gun back into its holster.

He was only feet away now, forcing her round the room like a dog driving a sheep, moving her into a corner. She stumbled against a low stool, caught herself, and slashed out wildly with the broken bottle. The man swayed as he pulled back, losing balance momentarily. Taking her chance, she lunged forward, jabbing at his face. The glass tore his cheek, just below the left eye, gouging a line of flesh away, opening the cheek to the bone.

Blood sprayed out onto the carpet. The stranger staggered, crying out; but as Angelina drew back her hand to strike again, he grabbed her wrist and pulled her arm down forcibly, jarring it, jerking the broken bottle out of her grasp. Then he was on her, his weight bearing her down, pressing her to the floor. Ignoring the pain of his wound, he grabbed her with both hands around her neck, squeezing hard. Blood poured from his wound, hot against her eyes and in her open mouth.

She flailed out in sheer terror, crying, spitting, her hands pummelling his chest. He held tight, pressing harder and harder, his fingers like steel bands. Her blows started to weaken, they became less and less precise, now they were mere taps, now nothing. And a great blackness blossomed in her head, shot with flashes of light, and there was pain, and no breath, and nothing, and nothing, and nothing.

He let her head fall back to the floor with a heavy thud. Her face and neck were drenched with blood. Shaking, he stood and looked down at her.

'Now,' he whispered, gritting his teeth against the pain, 'now we can begin.'

CHAPTER TWENTY-NINE

Reuben drew up to the kerb and shut off his engine. Instantly, the night filled with the roaring of wind. He switched off his lights and looked out into the darkness. Thin clouds scudded nervously across a watery, frightened moon. He rested his head against the steering wheel. The plastic felt cool but devoid of comfort. He felt drained. Not just tired, but dry, emptied of self. His limbs felt heavy, as though embedded in concrete. His head throbbed with pain.

He had been brought back almost two hours earlier by a different driver in an unmarked car, a black Lincoln with Washington numberplates, and dropped outside his apartment. The second driver had been no more communicative than the first. Dark fields, then bright lights on the Long Island Expressway back to Brooklyn.

Reuben had watched the Lincoln drive out of sight, then taken his own car and driven straight to the precinct. Kruger had been on the desk. That at least was a bonus – Pete Kruger wasn't the sort to run to Connelly with tales about late-night visits.

Reuben had gone down to archives, in the hope of finding something to make sense of what was happening. An hour later he sat staring at a blank wall while fine goose pimples crept along his spine and cold sweat bathed the palms of his hands. There were no files. Nothing related to the case. No exhumation records. No files on organized crime investigations with Haitian links. Nothing on Richard Hammel. Nothing on Filius Narcisse. Nothing on Aubin Mondesir.

Afterwards, he had telephoned Sally, using the number she had given him. There had been no reply.

He sat in the car, staring through the windscreen at a street as empty as himself. Higher up, the branches of angry trees attacked the darkness, lashing out madly, tearing the night to shreds. He felt cold and sick and hungry. All he wanted to do was sleep.

With an effort, he dragged himself from the car. In an instant, he was just another piece of debris, pummelled by the storm. He locked the car door and turned towards his apartment building. As he did so he glanced up.

Something was wrong. His sluggish brain struggled to interpret the warning that his tired eyes had registered. He stood, leaning against the car, looking up at his apartment, fighting the tiredness.

Suddenly he understood. There was no light in the living room. No light, but there should have been. Danny hated drawn curtains. If he was in there they would be wide open and light would be streaming from the window. It was after one thirty, but there was no way Danny would have gone to bed. And if he was sitting up watching Angelina, the most logical place for him to be was in the living room. With the curtains open. Reuben slipped a hand inside his coat and drew his .38.

He stopped at the foot of the stairs to remove his shoes. Inwardly, he cursed himself for having left Angelina so long, for having allowed her to remain at an address her attackers knew about. Holding his breath, he began to move up the stairs one at a time, his back pressed against the wall, his gun aimed upwards along the stairwell. Nothing was moving. There were no sounds.

His door was at the end of the first-floor corridor. Halfway there, he saw that it was lying open a fraction. Behind it, a light was burning in the passage. The corridor was cold, deserted. He felt his hands grow clammy with sweat. His mouth was dry. Blood moved in his veins like muddy water, sluggish and afraid.

At the door he spread himself against the wall and listened. At first he heard nothing, then out of the silence he plucked a small, wavering sound. A voice. A man's voice, low, insistent. Not Danny's voice. Slowly, he pushed the door open.

He swung into the opening, his gun ready, fear and anger charging him, wiping out his tiredness. The empty passage stretched away for ever, familiar, unfamiliar. He stepped inside, his unshod feet silent on the soft hall carpet.

The living-room door was wide open. From it, he could hear the man's voice, louder now.

'It will not be painful,' said the voice. 'You will feel nothing at first. After a while you will begin to feel dizzy. Your limbs will seem light, there will be a sensation of numbness in the tongue. Soon after, you will start vomiting. You will grow cold, extremely cold. The numbness will move to other parts of your body. Paralysis will follow. What happens next will depend on how exactly I have measured the dose. You may become comatose. You will be buried alive. Or you may die. But it will take a long time, and you will be fully conscious right to the end.

'However, it is your choice. If you choose differently, you can avoid any harm coming to you. It is entirely up to you.'

There was no reply.

Reuben felt as though something primitive had crept into his blood. He was a hunter stalking prey. Robert de Niro on a mountaintop, high above a swirling mist in autumn. Elation filled his emptiness. Filled him and contaminated him at the same time. He crept to the door and inched his head round.

They were off to the left, behind the door. The man had his back to Reuben. Angelina was strapped to a chair, staring straight ahead. On a low table beside the chair sat a large hypodermic syringe and beside it a bottle filled with a dark-coloured fluid.

Reuben took a careful step through the door. As he did so, he noticed something on the floor near the chair in which Angelina was sitting. A man's body sprawled on the carpet, the throat sliced half through by a wire. Reuben closed his eyes tightly and clutched the door for support. A great beast lifted its head and bellowed, shaggy and misshapen across abandoned hillsides. Reuben opened his eyes. Danny was still there. In his heart, like a terrible weight, Reuben could feel the beginnings of a lifetime's pain.

His instinct, his yearning was to pull the trigger, but he could not risk hitting Angelina. And he wanted the man alive. The roar of the wind masked his entry to the room. He moved to the right, away from the door, in case there should be a second man in the apartment.

'Put your hands very slowly behind your head,' said Reuben. 'Take one step backwards, then turn and face me. If I see anything resembling a weapon in your hand, I will blow your head all round this room.' He spoke quietly, using words he had used before, going by the book, watching his prisoner for the first sign of trouble. But his hand was shaking and his head was roaring like the wind. *Not Danny*, it screamed. Danny can't be dead! But Danny was lying rigid on the floor and the man with his back to Reuben had killed him, and Reuben hoped he would give him an excuse to blow him away.

The man fell silent and lowered his hands to his sides.

'Put your hands behind your head and turn round like I told

you. I would rather shoot you than let you live, so be very, very careful.'

Slowly, deliberately, the man turned. His face was pale. There were traces of blood in his eyebrows and on his neck. A large plaster had been stuck over one cheek.

'Whoever you are, mister, you're making the biggest mistake of your life,' he said. 'Now, take my advice. Put the gun down, back off, and go on back to wherever you came from.'

'Undo the straps. Let her out of the chair.'

'You're making . . .'

Reuben fired once over the man's head. Very close.

'OK, OK. Keep cool.' The man turned and stepped behind the chair. He unbuckled the leather straps. They fell to the floor. The man straightened, and as he did so his hand moved swiftly, and he came up twisting and firing.

He was good, but not good enough. Reuben's first bullet took him in the right shoulder.

The stranger staggered, thrown off balance by the bullet's impact. The gun flew from his hand across the floor. His face showed momentary signs of pain, then grew calm again. He kept on coming.

Reuben fired again. The second bullet took the man in the stomach, low down. Again he staggered. Deep in his throat a low roaring sound began. Suddenly, he moved, taking Reuben completely by surprise, throwing himself onto his assailant. Reuben staggered back, firing twice, missing both times.

Before he could regain his balance, Reuben was knocked sideways by his assailant's flailing arm. In an attempt to recover, he sidestepped towards the coffee table. Slipping awkwardly, his stockinged foot landed heavily on a shard of broken glass. He cried out and fell, the gun flying from his hand, crashing into the wall out of reach. A second lump of glass caught him in the small of the back, near his right kidney. He cried again, lurching forward onto his stomach, trying to get away from the glass.

Twisting to reach the piece of bottle embedded in his back, Reuben saw the stranger halt and turn. He began to pull the shard away, struggling to get to his knees, but the man was on him, bearing him down, using his weight to pin him against the floor. The room started to spin. The pain in his back was tearing at him, wrenching him into unconsciousness, filling him with itself, like thousands of tiny glass splinters.

From an inside pocket, the stranger drew out a long, sharp-bladed knife. He drew back his right hand, aiming the knife at Reuben's head. Desperately, Reuben found the strength to twist aside. The knife caught him on the temple, a glancing blow that took a chunk of hair and flesh with it. The man raised the knife a second time.

Reuben brought his knee up hard into the man's groin. He grunted and doubled up, dropping the knife. Reuben repeated the blow, then turned hard, throwing his assailant off. With an effort, he dragged himself aside.

The tall man was rallying already. Reuben found the lump of glass and pulled it free. It had pierced through his overcoat, deep into his flesh. He could feel blood soaking into his clothes.

He staggered to his feet, looking for his gun. The stranger was up again, knife in hand. A searing pain went through Reuben's right foot as he pressed down on it. He stumbled, allowing his attacker to catch him and bring him down again.

Reuben had his opponent's arm this time. The man's face was pressed down against his, his breath in his nostrils, his eyes wide open, full of rage. Rage and something else. Triumph? Ecstasy? Loneliness? Duty? He held the knife with powerful fingers, forcing it down nearer and nearer Reuben's throat.

They had rolled near to the chair on which Angelina was still sitting, unable to move. The knife was inches away now. Reuben's left hand touched something hard and cold. Taking it in his fingers, he lifted it. It was the hypodermic. It had been knocked to the floor during the struggle.

Reuben arched his back, struggling to bring his left hand round. The point of the knife was against his throat now, his right arm was weakening. In his head, bright lights exploded and a dull pounding echoed like thunder.

He twisted sideways another couple of inches and pushed up hard with the hypodermic. The point took the man full in his right eye. There was a faint popping sound as it burst its way into the ball. Reuben let go of the syringe. It hung slightly askew, still embedded in the eyeball. The stranger screamed aloud, both his eyes wide open in surprise and horror. The knife dropped as he clutched with both hands at his eye.

Reuben rolled away. He was groggy and his gun was still out of reach and he thought he was going to throw up. The stranger writhed in agony, blood-reddened fingers fumbling at his face. The hypodermic had fallen to the floor.

Reuben crawled towards the spot where he had last seen the .38. It was only feet away, but it felt like miles. He reached it at last, and as he did so the nausea rushed over him in waves. He threw up, felt the room heave, smelt vomit in his nostrils, sensed searing pains in his back and foot. He lurched forward, fumbling for the gun. The floor came towards him, rushing fast like a train, and hit him hard. There was nothing after that.

CHAPTER THIRTY

The night stood still. After hours of madness, the wind had dropped. Like a butcher's knife passing over bone, it had scraped the sky clean, leaving a broken web of tangled stars, fever-bright and naked in a perfect winter blackness. As suddenly as it had come, the gale had spent its force. Now a charged and violent stillness brooded over the city. The wind had scoured it too, but it remained dirty and wretched. No falling stars dropped into its wounded streets, no fire from heaven came to burn its dross away.

They lay like spent lovers on Reuben's bed, not sleeping, not talking, just listening to the night pass by. It would be day soon, but not for them. Before long, there would be light. But not for them. They were in constant darkness now.

The stranger had gone, taken his wounds and staggered out bloody into the last of the storm. The chair in which Angelina had been strapped stood empty. Danny lay where he had fallen in the lounge, unseeing eyes staring at the ceiling. He could wait.

Angelina lay in Reuben's arms like a child stripped of innocence and greed. She felt dead inside and old, and she knew you were one or the other, but it didn't matter. The struggle with Danny's killer had left her bruised, but otherwise unhurt. Unhurt on the surface, where it meant nothing. Reuben held her, but she knew that in his mind he was holding Danny, holding his own childhood before it slipped away from him for ever. He was further than ever from the goodness he sought, trapped in the middle of life without dreams or reasons or beauty. She leaned back against him helplessly and felt his unquiet breath touch her neck.

'We have to leave here.' His voice was a whisper in the darkness. She went on gazing into space, saying nothing, wanting nothing.

'They know where we are,' he said. 'Once the man who was

here makes it back to his friends they'll come looking for us. We have to get out.'

A long silence followed. She felt his breath on her skin, calm and unfamiliar, a tiny, fragile thing on a night of storms.

'He came last year,' she said. 'Several times. He was the man who visited Rick after the first phone call.'

'Did he tell you where he came from, who sent him?'

She shook her head.

'He had some sort of official card. An ID card. I never saw it, Rick told me. As if he belonged to a government agency.'

'Did Rick ever say which agency? Did he have suspicions?'

'No,' she answered. 'The card didn't say.'

'But Rick believed he was from the government?'

In the darkness she nodded unseen, long strands of her tumbled hair brushing lightly against his cheek, strands of her life tangling with his.

'Do you think he could be responsible for the killings? Filius, Rick, maybe your friend Aubin?'

He had to listen hard for her reply.

'Yes,' she whispered, very sweet and gentle. He kissed her on the neck. Her skin tasted faintly of blood. He closed his lips and rolled away.

'We have to leave here,' he said.

One of Uncle Shmuel's more celebrated sayings was: 'Winter is for penguins.' He had never seen a penguin in his life, outside Prospect Park Zoo. For that matter, he hadn't seen very many winters either. Not since leaving Europe anyway. Every September he and his wife Rivke packed half a dozen suitcases with summer-weight clothes and boxes from Steingass's Deli, locked up their apartment in Boro Park, and took an Eastern Air Lines 727 direct to Miami. They had been going there since 1954. This year was no exception.

Reuben's cousin Dora was puzzled when he asked for the key, but she knew better than to ask questions from family. Especially when 'family' means a police lieutenant who once saw you kissing Hymie Kornblum in the back of a Ford and has never forgotten. She gave him the key and a promise that she would mention it to no-one. Reuben guessed he would have two or three days clear before it proved too much for her to keep bottled up. Maybe a day longer before Smith or one of his boys came knocking at the door. Or shooting their way in.

'How's Danny, Reuben? I haven't seen him in weeks. Is he still seeing that little blonde? What was her name? Tanya? Sonia?'

'Dora, please don't ask me about Danny tonight. I'm sorry, I can't explain.'

The blood drained from Dora's face.

'Is something wrong, Reuben? Has something happened to Danny?'

He needed to speak to someone. But not now.

'Danny's dead, Dora. But I can't talk about it yet. It's something I can't deal with. Not yet. I'll come round in a couple of days. I'll tell you everything then.'

She looked at him as though he had struck her a heavy blow. Her eyes were beginning to well with tears. He looked round. Angelina was waiting in the car out on the street. It was dawn. He turned and walked slowly away. Later, much later, like a memory, he heard Dora close the door.

He called the precinct from the apartment. Pete Kruger was still on the desk. He took the news about Danny hard. Reuben gave him a detailed description of the killer.

'Who is this guy, Lieutenant? We got a file on him?'

'He works for a government agency. I'm willing to guarantee you won't find so much as a parking ticket listed in his name. He killed Danny in mistake for me, but I think he would have killed him anyway.'

'Homicide will want to talk to you, Lieutenant.'

'Not now. Tell them I called in sick. There are things I have to do. I'll be in touch in a couple of days.'

'The captain won't like this.'

'I don't expect him to.' Reuben paused. 'Tell them to look after Danny.'

'I'll see to it. Lieutenant, before you go, I've got a message for you from Maguire. Do you want me to read it to you?'

Sam Maguire was with Homicide. He'd been put onto the Mondesir case.

'Go ahead.'

'He says to tell you that this guy Aubin Mondesir,' – he pronounced the first name as Awbin – 'the one they found yesterday . . .'

'I know who you mean.'

'Seems Mondesir was into narcotics. A pusher. Not major league or nothing, but doing all right. Dealt in smack, coke, some crack.

Maguire thinks maybe he crossed some of his friends or somebody wanted to move in on his territory. He's going to be with Narcotics this morning. Wants you to ring him.'

'Thanks, Pete. Tell him I'll be in touch. But not yet. I need some time for this other thing. Tell Sam he's probably right. Mondesir got in with the wrong people.'

He hung up and stood for a long time just staring at the telephone. Inside, he was crying, but there were no tears in his eyes.

Angelina had gone to bed. He found her sleeping there. Sleep seemed like a good idea. He couldn't remember when he had last felt such deep tiredness, such agony of mind. His wounds were hurting badly, but a handful of painkillers would take care of that. He found some in the bathroom, then joined Angelina in the bedroom. Shmuel and Rivke had twin beds. Reuben was asleep even before he hit the mattress.

It was well past noon when he struggled back to consciousness. He was aching in several places and his wounds were stinging. His head felt as though it had been packed with lead shot and shaken. At first he did not remember the night before or what had happened to Danny. When he did, the memory came with a freshness that was all but unbearable. He lay stunned, breathing heavily, waiting for his mind to catch up with the pain.

Angelina was already up. There was an indentation where she had been lying on the other bed. She would be in the kitchen. He doubted if his aunt and uncle would have left any fresh food, but there might be cookies and coffee. Reuben rolled himself stiffly off the bed and staggered into the kitchen.

Angelina was not there. There was no sign of anybody having made food or drink. He went to the bathroom. The door was wide open. Angelina was not inside.

'Angelina! Where are you, Angelina?' His voice echoed dully in the empty apartment, dying away among dust sheets and polythene bags. He felt fear stab through him like a long, polished needle.

Room after room he hunted for her. She was nowhere.

He found the note pinned to the rear of the front door. 'Reuben – I need to sort things out. I need time and I need space. Please don't try to find me. I have your phone number here in case something comes up, but I'd rather not have to use it. I'm grateful that you looked after me. I'm grateful that you loved me. And I'm sorry about your friend Danny. Be good. Whatever that means.'

It doesn't mean anything, he thought. *Doesn't mean anything at all.*

CHAPTER THIRTY-ONE

He tried to contact Sally again. There was still no answer. He rang her number at City Hall and was told she was not there. When he gave his name, he was told to hold on. Half a minute later, the person at the other end said Sally had left a message for him. It consisted of a name and an address: Dr Nigel Greenwood, Kent Hall, Columbia University. That was all. Reuben thanked the speaker and hung up.

The switchboard at Columbia put him through to Greenwood's extension. The voice that answered was English, the accent straight out of *Brideshead Revisited*.

'Ah, yes, Miss Peale spoke to me about you last night. She said you had made certain discoveries that would interest me, and she thought I might in turn be of some assistance to you. I have a double class in a few minutes, but I'm free after that. Why don't you come out to Columbia? Say in about two hours' time. You'll find Kent Hall behind the entrance opposite West 16th Street. Just go up the steps in front of the library on your left. Kent Hall's just past there on your right. You can't miss it. My name's on the board downstairs, beside the lift. I'll be waiting for you.'

Reuben took the Bourjolly letters and the half-circle of African gold and packed them in a box. He took a cab to downtown Manhattan, paid the subscription for a safe deposit vault, and left the box there.

Getting to Columbia took a while. Central Park was closed to traffic. Broadway was choked. The lift at Kent Hall was out of order. He found Greenwood at last in a small office on the fourth floor. The room was nineteenth century, wood-lined, crammed with books and papers. Greenwood filled the rest of it perfectly. Reuben wondered if the university selected its faculty on the basis of how they looked in what was to be their natural habitat. The Englishman wore a tweed jacket, mustard waistcoat, brown cords and a paisley-pattern bow tie. He was in his forties, balding, slightly fat. There was a strong smell of pipe smoke over everything.

They shook hands and Reuben sat on the opposite side of the desk, peering at Greenwood through the gaps between piles of precariously balanced books, many of them old leather-bound volumes. The covers were foxed and stained, a little like their owner.

'Do you know Miss Peale well?' asked Greenwood.

'We're ... good friends,' Reuben replied. 'We've worked together on several cases.'

'Same here. She brings her problem cases to me, I help out when I can.'

'You teach law?'

Greenwood smiled and shook his head.

'No. Nor anything remotely like it, I'm afraid. I'm a medievalist with a specialization in the Latin translations of Eastern texts. By "Eastern" I mean "Middle Eastern" – mainly Hebrew and Arabic. I had a research post at the Warburg Institute in London up until six years ago; then a professorship came up here and I leapt at it. Things aren't what they were in England, certainly not in the universities. Death by a thousand cuts. Professorships are like gold dust; and a field like mine is always among the first to go. "Can you make any money out of it?" they ask. "Does it have industrial applications?" I have to answer, no. Why on earth should it? They would have asked Socrates or Plato the same question. Given them the sack, I shouldn't wonder. So I came here: the barbarians aren't quite as much in evidence. So, what can I do for you?'

'I'm not sure, Professor. Latin texts?' Reuben looked round the room. Books in Latin. Books in Hebrew. Books in what he took to be Arabic. It seemed familiar.

'Well, the texts are raw material,' said Greenwood. 'I actually write on the history, sociology, and social psychology of occultism: things like magic, witchcraft, astrology. You may not take such matters seriously. Personally, I do not. That is to say, I do not believe in them. I would not, for example, consult an astrologer about what I should do tomorrow or next year. But people in past centuries did believe, and their beliefs shaped their actions. Hence the importance of studying those beliefs. And there are still plenty of people who believe in such matters today. New York has tens of thousands of occultists of one kind or another.'

'And Sally brought her legal problems to you? I don't understand.'

Greenwood leaned forward in his chair. He needed a haircut. Two haircuts.

'Well, not legal problems exactly. There is rather more to Miss Peale than I think you realize.'

'Really?'

'Yes, really. A good deal more. But I think that is for her to explain. She told me you had made . . . certain discoveries.'

Reuben nodded. He explained as best he could what he and Danny had found in the tunnel and the chambers beyond.

'Do you remember the titles of any of the books you saw?' Greenwood asked.

'Only a few. There was one in French. *Clavicles* I think it was. Translated from Hebrew.'

'Yes. That would be the *Clavicles of Solomon*, the Key of Solomon the King. There aren't many printed copies around, though I've seen plenty of manuscripts. It's the most important of the *grimoires*, the textbooks used by magicians in Europe. Supposed to have been written by King Solomon himself. Nonsense, of course; but there are several books of magic ascribed to him in tradition. Did you know he was supposed to have been a magician?'

Reuben nodded.

'Yes, some of the midrash . . .'

'Ah, yes, of course. You are a Jew. I forgot. There are numerous Biblical traditions. Many of them passed into Islam, and through Arabic texts into Latin. Well, did you find any other books?'

Reuben recited the names of the few he could remember. Greenwood nodded at each one, as at the names of old friends. But at the last he looked up, startled.

'Say that again.'

'*A Sober Warning to the Righteous*,' repeated Reuben. 'It was an account of some events at Nantucket around 1800.'

The professor remained silent. His face had clouded. He seemed uneasy for the first time since Reuben had entered the room.

'That is a very rare book,' he said at last. 'Only a few copies were ever printed, and even fewer survived. I think most of them were burned. But I've seen one in the library at Yale.' He paused. 'The events it describes are most unpleasant. To find it in a library such as you have described I find . . . unsettling.'

'I think it may be connected to other matters,' said Reuben.

'Indeed? And what matters might they be?'

Carefully, avoiding any temptation to dramatize or embellish his narrative, Reuben related to the professor the details he had learnt from Angelina about Bourjolly and the Seventh Order. It took a long time. When he finished, Greenwood sat staring across the desk, motionless, his face pale, almost ashen.

'You say there were letters.'

'Yes, a lot of letters. I took the ones that had come from Haiti. I've still got them.'

'But you say there were others. From Mitau, Budapest and Riga.'

'Among other places, yes.'

'I see. Perhaps, Lieutenant, it is better you did not carry them away.' Greenwood pushed away his chair and stood. He walked to the window and looked out. Below him, students walked to classes in the fading light of an autumn afternoon.

'Lieutenant, tell me, do you know what has become of those tunnels, the chambers you discovered? Are your people exploring them?'

Reuben shook his head.

'I don't think so, not unless they're pulling the wool over my eyes. I was told they'd been sealed off. I think they plan to have them filled in.'

The Englishman nodded. He turned away from the window.

'Perhaps that is for the best. Yes, even at the cost of such a library, that might be for the best. But I think they will have taken the books first. And the other things as well . . .'

'Sally thought you could help me.'

'Yes, perhaps I can. But I need time. I would like to see the letters you took from Bourjolly's library. And I would very much like to speak to Mrs Hammel.'

'I'm afraid I don't know where she is. She left this morning. I think she plans to disappear.'

A look of concern crossed Greenwood's face.

'I'm sorry to hear that. Try to find her, Lieutenant. For both your sakes, it is imperative that you find her. I can't help you any further at the moment. Contact me tomorrow. Here, this is my home number: you can ring me there. I will expect to hear from you. Now I suggest you go and try to find Mrs Hammel. As a matter of extreme urgency.'

CHAPTER THIRTY-TWO

Reuben returned to the apartment about six. As far as he could tell, no-one had followed him and no-one had the building under surveillance. Angelina had not come back. He went first to a corner store and bought some groceries. He was not hungry, but he knew he had to eat. Back in the apartment, he ate cold food without enjoyment. After that he renewed the dressings on his wounds.

At eight he rang his parents to tell them about Danny. They'd heard the news already from Danny's brother. His mother told him they had been worried about him all day. Some men from the police department had been round that afternoon asking questions. Reuben's mother thought their names were Quirk and Maguire. They wanted Reuben to get in touch.

His mother wanted to know where he was, and for the first time in his life he lied to her. 'I'm in New Jersey,' he said. He was growing anxious about his cousin Dora and when she would tell people his whereabouts. Two days was optimistic. He gave her twenty-four hours at most.

'Are you in trouble, Reuben?' His mother's voice was brittle with worry. He felt eight years old again, without the stout scaffolding of innocence.

'A kind of trouble, Mother.'

'Is it . . . Is it to do with what happened to Danny?' A dumb question, but she had to ask it.

'I loved Danny, Mother. He was like a brother.'

'Reuben, I have to meet his mother. I have to speak with her. Her son was found dead in your apartment. You are missing. The police are asking about you. What am I to say?'

'Tell her what I just told you. Tell her Danny and I were working together on a case and someone killed him. Tell her I know who the killer is. I'll find him, Mother, I promise.'

'In New Jersey? You'll find him in New Jersey and bring him back?' Her voice seemed infinitely sad to him, like music he had once known and now knew no longer.

'No, Mother,' he whispered. 'I won't bring him back. I'll kill him.'

The phone call came just before eleven. 'Can I speak to Lieutenant Abrams?' A woman's voice, a little hoarse and breathless. A dingy sort of voice, it sounded as though it hadn't been washed in weeks. Not Angelina's voice, but a similar accent.

'I'm Abrams. Who's speaking?'

'Is not important. You got a pen and paper?'

'Unh-huh.'

'So, write down this address: 497 Gibson Street, Bedford Stuyvesant. Apartment nineteen. You got that?'

'Yes, I've got it. What do you want me to do?'

'I got a friend of yours here. She in trouble, bad trouble, say she want you come fetch her. Right away.'

'What sort of trouble?'

'Bad trouble, *m'sieu*. She need your help. She need it bad. Better come right away.'

'Let me speak to her.'

There was a stillness, then the voice returned.

'Wait.'

He waited. It seemed a long time, but it could not have been more than three or four minutes. When Angelina came to the phone, her voice was scarcely recognizable.

'Reu . . . Reuben?'

'Is that you, Angelina? What's happened?'

Another stillness, as though she had gone away again.

'I'm . . . I'm . . . Reuben . . . get me . . . I need . . . Help me . . .'

Her voice tailed off, indistinct, the words half-formed. She sounded drunk. Drunk or . . . high. Christ, he'd been stupid! Aubin Mondesir had been a pusher. Not major league, but getting there. Angelina had gone to see him yesterday to score; but she'd got nothing because he was dead. All that stuff about his being a voodoo priest and giving her some sort of spiritual sustenance had been pure bullshit.

'Angelina, what have you taken? How much? Have you OD'ed?'

But Angelina did not answer. The other woman came on the phone again.

'Like I say, she need your help. You got the address. You want to help, you better make it quick.'

The line went dead. The silence that followed was not golden. What is?

CHAPTER THIRTY-THREE

There are theologians who say that hell is not a place, but a state of mind. They are wrong. Hell is Gibson Street.

Reuben drove slowly with extinguished lights, watching grey shadows mingle on each side. The walls of tall, eroded houses loomed from the darkness like silent mausoleums. They had been polished and elegant once, full of life and comfort at Thanksgiving and Christmas. Now they huddled together in the squalid gloom, in and out of season, tattered and grimy, all comfort gone. It was as though someone had come down with a greasy rag and rubbed all their brightness away.

In places, braziers burned on the open sidewalks, throwing red sparks out upon the glistening air. Huddled around them, bent against the cold, small groups of fallen angels folded uneasy wings against the sharp, unwelcoming night.

Dark, haggard figures scuttled in and out of half-lit doorways. From dim and curtained windows, behind panes of cracked and twisted glass, hidden eyes stared and slowly blinked, seeing nothing. Snatches of broken music surged out of nowhere – harsh, brittle, full of measured despair. The wind took it and snapped it in two, like glass.

Reuben passed a ruin that had once been an apartment house. It had been neglected, then abused, then stripped, then abandoned, then gutted, and finally left to rot. There was a hole in one wall, about six inches square. Graffiti danced all round it. Arrows pointed inwards from the rim towards the centre. It looked like a significant hole. It was.

Reuben knew what the hole was for: you stood on the street side and put your hand through the opening, clutching as many dollars and dimes as you'd been able to scrape up during a day's hustling. A hidden dealer would take your thin wad and replace it with an even smaller packet holding a sixteenth or less of H. The anonymity was pure, the heroin anything but.

Reuben watched a couple of shivering angels shuffle past, drowning in a narcotic dream. Drugs could not make them rich. Drugs could not take away their hunger or their cold or their despair. But drugs could make them numb. Numbness was good. Numbness was better than sleep. Numbness was God enthroned in a paradise of lies.

The street had a darkness all of its own, as though God had created it especially. None of the streetlamps worked. The last one had been smashed two years ago, and nobody had ever come to replace it. The residents preferred it that way.

Number 497 was one of the reasons. It was a Renaissance Revival brownstone, five storeys high. Tall and black and gutted with shadows. Most of its windows had been boarded up, the ornamental iron balustrade that had once climbed the steps was long gone, the brickwork was crumbling. Words like 'Renaissance' and 'Revival' sounded like sick jokes in Bedford Stuyvesant.

Reuben parked the car directly opposite. He got out and locked it, watching out of the corners of his eyes for signs of movement. A kid was watching him from the steps of a house two doors down. Ten years old, maybe less. Reuben motioned to him, calling him over. The boy stared at him for a while, hesitating. Reuben motioned again.

Casually, the boy detached himself from the railing against which he had been leaning. He knew the language of the street better than he knew English. He came towards Reuben, a swagger in his step. He wasn't a child. Childhood was short-lived round here: kids moved into adulthood as soon as they could steal purses or hot-wire cars or run dope or pimp for their sisters. Some could do all of those things and worse by the age of six.

The kid stopped several feet away, swaying lightly on the balls of his feet. He knew Reuben was a cop: the white face was enough. Civilians didn't come round here unless they were desperate or lost, and Reuben did not look either of those.

'Yeah?'

Reuben took a ten-dollar bill from his pocket.

'This is yours,' he said. 'I want you to look after my car, see nobody touches it. If it's still OK when I come out, you get two more. That a deal?'

The boy looked at the note, then at Reuben, then back at the note again.

'Twenty now, thirty after,' he said.

Reuben shook his head.

'I'm not here to bargain, son. Take it or leave it. But if I come out and find so much as a scratch on this machine, I'm coming back with some friends and you are going to wish you'd taken the money.'

'I got friends, too, mister.'

'You've got shit. Don't fool with me, son. You take the money, you look after the car, you watch me drive away from here with a smile on my face, and you wake up in the morning thirty dollars richer. Not to mention the value of my friendship. Bring in your friends and all you've got is big trouble.'

Reuben still found it bizarre to be talking like this with a child. But they learned their English from TV and their manners from the street. Chances were the kid was already a prostitute and the star of a dozen paedophile movies. Santa Claus and the Tooth Fairy didn't figure in his vocabulary.

The boy hesitated a moment longer, then he held out his hand.

'Make it forty and you've got a deal.'

Reuben shook his head again.

'Thirty-five. Ten now, the rest after. I won't be long. Think of it as getting rich quick.'

The child pursed his lips and spat on the ground.

'You better not be long, mister. I got things to do.'

Reuben handed over the ten.

'Remember,' he said. 'Even a single scratch and you'll see me again.'

'Wouldn't want that, mister. Wouldn't want to see you again, ever.'

Reuben turned to go.

'Hey, mister. Where you goin'?'

Reuben pointed.

The kid shook his head slowly.

'That's a shooting gallery, mister. If you got a friend in there, he's not worth bringing out.'

The street door lay partly open, held ajar by a battered shopping trolley. The sign on the side said it had come from Finast. Reuben pushed it aside and stepped through. A sharp wind followed him, blowing dust and trash and pieces of old newspaper into the narrow hallway.

A 'shooting gallery' was a place where they lined addicts up in a room and cranked them up one after the other. The same spike for fifty or more in a row before it started to get blunt.

The lobby was desolate, lit dully by a single dust-shrouded bulb. Smells of stale beer and fresh urine hung listless on the battered air. On the left, a dim stairwell stumbled through half-lit landings to heights of absolute darkness. Spray-can graffiti held the crumbling plaster of the walls together, bright blues and greens and yellows on a base of dull brown paint: a roster of forgotten names, proclamations of love and hate, a hooker's number, gang slogans in misspelled French, a phallus and testicles, a woman with her legs spread. Art in the service of desperation.

A man was leaning at the foot of the stairs, arms crossed, back gently arched against the loosened balustrade, face masked behind creased shadows. He wore a cheap navy suit and imitation Gucci loafers, the little bridles on their aprons tarnished already by the first salt rains of autumn.

Reuben knew why he was there. This was a guard post on tribal territory, and he was the watcher. It was war in the streets out there: American blacks against West Indians, Jamaicans against Haitians, blacks against Hispanics. This was gangland. And Reuben belonged to all the wrong gangs.

The man came forward, a couple of steps, like a gigolo advancing at a dance. His face was still in shadows. He knew the shadows well, how to come and go in them. Reuben caught a glimpse of golden earring, a narrow cheekbone grazed momentarily by light, a small hand in a tight leather glove, the fingers bright with golden rings.

'You lookin' for someone, *blanc*?' The question was spoken slowly and deliberately.

Reuben shook his head.

'I don't want trouble. Someone rang me, told me to come down here. Apartment nineteen. Maybe you know about it.'

The man sauntered forward into a patch of yellow light. In his mid-twenties, he was handsome, pomaded, self-controlled. A smell of cheap perfume clung to him, a thin veil over an underlying odour of sweat. He moved like a man who did not expect to live to thirty. Didn't expect to. Didn't much want to.

'You want coke, *blanc*? Crack? Maybe you in the wrong place. Very bad for you here; very dangerous.'

'Someone phoned me. A friend of mine needs help. A Haitian, Angelina Hammel. Apartment nineteen.'

The man eyed him like a pest control agent surveying a roach. The look made Reuben tense. He was being sized up. Reuben had brought cash, all he had taken from his own apartment: nearly five hundred dollars. A man could get himself killed for a lot less. Down here, they killed people for a pair of sneakers or a baseball jacket.

'I don't want coke, I don't want crack, and I don't want trouble. I'll be out of here in five minutes. You won't even smell me.'

'I smell you already. You smell like a cop to me.'

Reuben had to decide quickly whether to tough it out or try to play it soft. The lookout scared him. Not because he was tough, but because he was not. Men like him were straw: they would burn in a very little flame. But like straw everywhere, they liked to hurt sometimes, just to show that, given the chance, they too could be flint.

'That's none of your business. This is private. I said I'm not looking for trouble. But if you give me any it won't be private any longer.'

Time to make his move. Reuben started for the stairs, intending to brush past the lookout. As he did so there was a flash and the man was holding a long knife inches away from Reuben's face.

Upstairs someone coughed, a long, racking cough that spluttered out into breathlessness. A door slammed. Music came, rapping to a steady beat. Down in the hallway, everything was quiet. Reuben could hear himself breathing, a primitive, alien sound.

The man held the knife close to Reuben's throat. The long blade shimmered heraldically, smooth, well-oiled, razor-sharp. Reuben took a step back, his eye tight on the blade. The man moved forward, keeping the knife in place. He was poised, easy, entranced by the shining of his own blade. He had done this before.

Abruptly, Reuben sidestepped and spun, rolling out of the blade's reach. The man slashed thin air, twisted and slashed again, catching Reuben's shoulder. Reuben moved in, trying to get close. The younger man turned and lunged: a fencer's movement, but without a fencer's grace or a fencer's strength. Reuben sidestepped easily and brought his hand down sharply on the thin forearm. Bone snapped with an audible crack. Numb fingers dropped the unblooded knife to the floor. The man bent double, whimpering.

'Next time,' said Reuben, 'pick on someone your own size.'

CHAPTER THIRTY-FOUR

Apartment nineteen had long ago ceased to be an apartment in any meaningful sense of the term. Its battered and scorched front door had been strengthened so many times with steel plates, mortice locks and bolts that it resembled more than anything the gate of a medieval fortress.

On either side of the door, a ghetto artist had employed considerable skill to paint two garish figures, like Chinese deities guarding the entrance to a Buddhist temple. The name of each figure had been printed in crude red letters underneath. On the left stood 'Baron H', a skeletal god of heroin, with a pale soapy skin and tiny pupils set in dreaming eyes. From a scrawny neck hung a necklace of spent syringes, and from his open mouth and nostrils wreathes of drug-heavy smoke coiled towards the ceiling.

His counterpart was 'L'Impératrice C', a tall woman dressed in a white muslin dress under a man's black frock-coat. She wore a shiny top hat like the *vodoun* god, Baron-Samedi, her nostrils were red and dilated, and blood dripped from her long fingernails. Her face had been daubed a chalky white. In one hand she held a bottle of rum, in the other a gravedigger's long-handled shovel. Heroin and Cocaine, the guardian deities of the new Hades.

Reuben banged on the door and went on banging until someone came.

'All right, all right! I coming!' came a testy voice. An eye appeared behind the small glass peephole, then vanished. Heavy bolts clanked noisily back. The door opened about six inches, taut against heavy chains. Reuben could see no-one. A bitter smell of heroin smoke wafted through the narrow opening.

'*Oui?* What you want?'

'I've come for Angelina Hammel.'

There was a pause, then the door closed. A rattling sound as the chains were drawn through hasps, a muttered oath, and the door re-opened. The space behind was thick with shadows, the air tight, almost unbreathable. Dotted among the shadows, small purple lights danced gently at floor level. The apartment resembled a field hospital in France around 1916. Large holes had been smashed through all the walls, as though heavy artillery had bombarded them. One room led into the next. And over everything a pall of grey smoke hung like mist over trenches of the dead and dying.

On low beds, on ancient sofas, on the bare floor, the damned were scattered carelessly about, as though in slumber. Some moved in their stupor, some lay still, while all about them coils of soporific smoke tumbled in a slow and measured dance. Here, in the inner sanctum of its faith, the dragon moved as incense, warm and rich and comforting.

Reuben coughed. Beside him stood an old black woman, bent and gnarled as a withered tree. She pushed home the bolts in the door and shuffled her hunched frame round to look at him. Her teeth were gone, her eyes half blind with cataracts, her hair a few tufts on a naked skull.

'Angelina? You want see Angelina?'

Reuben nodded. Her voice was stretched and hoarse, yet somehow beautiful, as though it was all that remained of a once-aching loveliness.

The crone murmured something unintelligible, then turned and walked away, beckoning. Reuben followed. On his left, one thin man bent over another, injecting him carefully in the back of his leg, the needle seeking a vein not yet collapsed. Further on, a large-eyed woman sat on her haunches, her hand idly stroking the neck and shoulders of a man lying rigid on a sheet of dirty foam rubber.

A bleak compassion ran softly through the smoke and chilly air. Love was not wholly absent in hell. Not wholly absent, not wholly present. No god offered salvation on the strength of it. A shot of heroin was a shot of heroin, however lovingly administered.

Angelina was lying on her back, legs bent high against her chest, eyes open, staring without animation at a web of shadows high up on the ceiling. Her face was relaxed and blank, as though a thin and subtle blade had separated it from pain and memory. No blood, no mess, no stitches: a very perfect surgery. But the wound would heal and the skin would close and the pain would return, fiercer than before.

'What happened?'

The little woman stared uncomprehendingly at him. He bent down. Angelina's breathing was shallow but regular. On the floor near her lay an empty syringe. Her sleeve had been rolled up. Someone had introduced her to the joys of mainlining. Or had she already played that game a little? He wondered who had telephoned him. It had not been the old woman. Something was wrong, but he could not even guess what it was.

From the apartment upstairs a dull sound drew his attention. Not loud, not wholly soft, as elegant and jagged as ice floating on swollen rivers to the sea in spring, a drum was beating, its rhythms hard and clear on the drugged air. Above their heads, the gods were gathering. Not the gods of this place, but the old gods, strong, persistent, angry against the accumulating darkness of a new world and a new age.

The brittle tapping of the tiny *kata* drum was joined by the slower throb of the *ségond*, pulsed and rhythmical, calling the gods to dance. In the steady, naked air the low throbbing hung over them, heavy and drifting as snow.

Angelina stirred, as though something deep within her had been awakened by the drumbeats. Her lips trembled, opening a fraction, breath coming in fragments.

'Africa . . .' she whispered. He bent down to hear her. Her voice had a thinness he had only heard before in the dying. 'Africa is coming . . .' she said. And he looked round and felt it in the air, dense, tangible, creeping through centuries and across seas into the broken harbour of the drug-saturated room.

Her lips grew quiet, her eyes flickered and grew still. Reuben straightened.

'I want to move her,' he said. 'Can you help me carry her down? I have a car outside.'

The old woman broke into a grin.

'We take her together,' she said. 'We go ride in car together.'

Together they managed to get Angelina through the door and onto the landing. Taking her down the stairs would be more difficult. Reuben slipped her arm round his neck while the old woman kept her legs clear of the floor. Step by jarring step, flight by flight they eased her down until they came to the last landing. Reuben looked down. Two men were waiting for him at the foot of the stairs.

He turned to the old woman, obscurely hoping she had the

power to help. But she was already gone, haring back up the stairs with what little breath remained in her. He turned back and looked down again. They were still waiting.

CHAPTER THIRTY-FIVE

Somehow he didn't think these were friends of the gigolo whose arm he had broken, come to repay him in kind. They weren't dressed like anybody's friends. He could tell by their eyes that they meant business and that they were unaccustomed to making mistakes. Now he understood what had felt wrong: the whole thing had been some sort of set-up.

He helped Angelina down the last flight. She whimpered once, speaking broken words in a language utterly strange to him. He told her all was well, that they would be home soon. But they had no home to go to, and all was not well.

They waited while he laid his burden down. One was white, one black. They were impassive, one on either side of the door, like gods guarding the route out of the Underworld. Reuben felt his .38 against his ribs, a dismal, aching weight.

The white man wore a cashmere overcoat, dark burgundy, unbuttoned. His hair was swept back and lightly oiled. On his feet he wore expensive brogues, English shoes with a high shine. He was smoking a long cigarette between tight, unsmiling lips. As Reuben came nearer, he took it firmly between the index finger and thumb of his right hand, removed it from his mouth, and let it fall. A line of smoke fanned through his lips and lay for a moment like a thin veil over his long smooth face. He crushed the cigarette beneath his foot with a small, circular motion.

Reuben could smell the corrupted stench of raw urine. It filled his nostrils with an acidic, lonely odour, the underlying perfume of the ghetto.

'You're a long way from home, cop.' The white man spoke, tense, irritated words. The accent was Florida, the manner cosmopolitan. He was a white man who had spent a long time with blacks. In a different place and time, with different friends, he might have been a civil rights worker or an anthropologist. He would think black and talk black, but his skin would always betray him.

'You get lost, maybe? You come here looking for something soft and white down among the nigras? Looks like you found something soft and black instead.'

'The lady's sick. I'm taking her home.'

The man shook his head.

'The lady is wanted elsewhere. And you are not wanted at all.'

'In that case, I'd like you to let me past. But the woman comes with me.'

The Floridan turned to his friend.

'What do you think, Augustin? Is this man talking what I think he is talking?'

The black man returned his partner's gaze. He was oiled and sleek and well-muscled, dressed in a white wool suit. His little shaven head caught beads of reflected light and turned them all at once to gold.

'Shit,' he said. 'He talking shit.' The accent was Haitian, via Miami.

'That's what I thought.' The white man turned to Reuben. 'You met a friend of Augustin's last night, a man called Kominsky. Kominsky is hurt bad. He has bullet wounds. He is blinded in one eye.'

'His right eye,' Augustin said.

'He will never see again with that eye,' murmured the white man. 'He is hurt in body and he is hurt in soul.'

'Hurt in soul,' repeated Augustin. 'He like you to suffer.' Augustin ran a thin hand over his shining crown, as though reassuring himself of its smoothness. 'He ask me to see to it when I leave the hospital. So you got to suffer.'

Augustin slipped a hand into his inside pocket and withdrew it holding an ivory-handled flick knife. He pressed a button and a thin blade glistened in the pale light.

Reuben moved his hand towards his jacket. As he did so, he heard in quick succession two cold, deliberate clicks as more knives were opened. Out of the shadows at the rear of the ground-floor hallway, two dark figures emerged. The street door opened and a fifth man entered. The latest arrival turned and secured a thick chain across the door. The way out was barred.

Reuben felt beads of sweat sting his forehead. He drew his

revolver. Nervously, he watched them circle round, five moths caught in the trammels of his light, uncertain where to commit their wings. Their silence unnerved him. He imagined that they sang to one another in the empty reaches of the night, when the city grew silent, like deep-plunged whales booming in the darkness of Nantucket Sound, violent lullabies to ease them quietly to sleep in the dark, unpainted nursery of the ghetto. Their eyes were huge and hungry, beyond pity or appeal.

Reuben drew back the hammer of his gun and drew a bead on the white man, whom he took to be the group's leader. As he did so, he felt a sudden edge of cold steel against his throat. A voice whispered in his ear, 'Throw down the gun.'

Up until that moment, everything had seemed to move in slow motion. In less than a second, it all speeded up again, so fast it went out of control.

The man with his knife at Reuben's throat had come inches too close. Reuben leaned into the blade, letting his assailant tilt a fraction further to the right, tipping him just to the edge of imbalance. Unconsciously, the man brought his right foot forward three inches to compensate. Reuben let his arm go limp and held the gun down, as though about to drop it as ordered. Instead he fired into the man's instep.

The crack of the gun was followed instantly by a scream of pain and the clatter of a knife hitting the floor. Reuben slammed back and sideways, throwing his would-be assassin to the ground. He got off another shot, winging one of the two men who had emerged from the hallway. The figures in front of him scattered, fanning out. The white man drew an automatic pistol, aimed quickly and professionally, and fired twice, narrowly missing Reuben's shoulder.

There was a sudden splintering of glass followed by a much louder sound, like a controlled explosion. The street door lifted off its hinges and crashed backwards, careering into the wall, gouging out chunks of raw plaster before tilting back on the chain and swinging half into the street.

Through the gaping hole where the door had been, three men entered the hallway. Two were dressed in what looked like the uniform of a SWAT team, black Kevlar vests and peaked caps. They carried suppressed MP5 sub-machine guns without stocks. The third was the man who called himself Smith. He was dressed in a light-blue suit and carried no weapon of any description. In the street outside, a blue light flashed, jewelling the night.

Three of the men with knives turned and broke away. They did not go far. From the rear of the passage, two more figures with sub-machine guns made an appearance. There was an abrupt, nervous silence, broken moments later by the clatter of steel blades hitting the ground.

Smith walked up to the white man who had been the leader of the group. He raised a hand and struck him hard across the cheek. The man staggered but stood his ground. Smith was the first to speak.

'This was unauthorized,' he said. The other man hung his head. 'However great the provocation, nothing is done without authorization. You know the penalty.'

'He blinded Kominsky. He shot him and put out his eye. Kominsky wanted him dealt with.'

'An eye for an eye? Is that it? Kominsky makes a mess of things, so you have to go one better? This is an operation, do you understand? Not a game, not a picnic, not some personal vendetta.'

Smith turned to one of the SWAT team — if SWAT team it was.

'Take them outside,' he said. 'Drive them back to headquarters. I'll deal with them later.'

Soon he was left alone with Reuben and Angelina. He held out a hand to Reuben.

'Your gun, Lieutenant, please.'

'I don't think you have the right to ask me for it.'

Smith looked impatient.

'You are not a policeman any longer, Lieutenant. You are a murder suspect. Things have worked out better than I might have hoped when I last spoke with you. You can either hand me the gun or try to shoot your way out. Now . . .' He paused and stretched his hand nearer to Reuben. 'The gun, please.'

Reuben hesitated a moment longer, then handed the gun to Smith.

'Thank you, Lieutenant. That was a wise decision. Come with me.'

CHAPTER THIRTY-SIX

They call Brooklyn 'the borough of churches and cemeteries'. You pray, you die, you go to heaven. Heaven isn't Brooklyn, of course. Heaven isn't any place people actually live. Church is the nearest some people get, which isn't saying much.

Strictly speaking, the place to which Reuben had been brought was not a church any longer. It was just a derelict shell waiting for the bulldozers to arrive and put it out of its misery. A priest with tired eyes had come and taken the relics away from beneath the altar, together with the grains of frankincense that had been deposited with them, bones and blood and dried flesh. The altar stone was gone, the sanctuary lamp extinguished, the murmuring of benedictions hushed. Nothing remained but a faint echo of holiness – a spire without bells, walls without statues, windows without images, broken and boarded and sad.

Reuben sat on what had been the altar table, shivering in a stiff draught that blew through a door at the back. The only light came from a dozen or so gas-fired lamps that had been set up before his arrival. Smith had gone an hour ago, leaving him with two heavy types who had been waiting outside on Gibson Street. They resolutely refused to answer any of Reuben's questions or to be drawn on where Smith had got to.

Reuben had been bundled into another Lincoln, blindfolded and driven to the church in silence. Angelina and he had been separated. He did not know where they had taken her. Once, trying to get some sort of explanation from Smith, he had been punched hard in the solar plexus and told to keep quiet. He lost all sense of time and direction. They had travelled a long way, but Reuben had a feeling they were still in Brooklyn, that the car had gone in circles to its destination.

The doors at the front of the church opened and Smith entered, accompanied by two more heavyweights. With them came a much thinner man whom they were pushing in front of them. The fourth man stumbled and picked himself up awkwardly. He appeared to be handcuffed and in pain. As the small group drew nearer, Reuben recognized Smith's prisoner as the man who had killed Danny, the one he had heard called 'Kominsky'. Kominsky looked rough. He wore thick bandages over the right side of his face. He was wearing pyjamas and had slippers on his feet. Someone had taken him straight from a hospital bed. He looked at Reuben uncomprehendingly. Still bunched together, the small group came within ten feet of the altar and stopped.

Smith detached himself from his companions and came softly towards Reuben. Reuben slid off the stone table. The older man gazed at Reuben detachedly. There was no feeling in his eyes, no more than if he were an entomologist and Reuben a moth pinned to a specimen board. Reuben's mother would have recognized the look. She had been through the camps, she had seen men and women with that look many times. It still lingered in unsuspected corners of her life, even now in old age. Reuben sensed it vividly, as though her recognition had been passed in blood to his own eyes and heart. He sensed it and shivered involuntarily as Smith came close.

'There used to be angels here,' Smith said. His voice sounded far away. 'In the windows, with red and purple wings, like terrible butterflies. And just up there, on either side of the altar, two plaster angels leaning over us at Mass, golden, with their hands stretched out.'

He paused and turned slowly, scanning the desolate walls and shadowed ceiling, searching in vain for something no-one else could see.

'I was a child here once,' he said. 'My father used to bring me to this church for Mass, after my First Communion. Once a week and on holy days. I became an altar boy. They dressed me in white and gave me a censer to carry. I thought I was pure at heart. We all did. Pure like Jesus. Pure like Father Tirali.' He paused, looking high up at thick shadows above the transept. 'How quickly we learned the truth.'

He looked back at Reuben, his eyes empty.

'What about you?' he asked. 'Did you have angels? Little gold angels to watch you lose your purity? Or are you still pure at heart, Lieutenant? You come of an angelic breed, do you not?'

'The place my father took me to had no images. Not even angels.'

Smith raised his eyebrows.

'No? How sad. Angels are very beautiful.'

'What have you done with Angelina?'

'How like a Jew to change the subject. What makes you think I have done anything with her?'

'She needs help. Medical help. If she goes into a coma, she may die.'

Smith took a step closer. His breath laid a faint cloud on the chill air.

'She's safe, Lieutenant, perfectly safe. The question is, are you?'

Reuben looked round, at the church, at the powerfully built men in padded suits, at the thin man trying not to show his fear.

'I think it's time you gave me an explanation, Smith. You've no authority to hold me here. You don't even have a charge.'

'No? I think the charge is very clear. You are suspected of murdering your former partner, Danny Cohen. There is a warrant out for your arrest. You were picked up tonight in an apartment house known to be used by dope peddlers. You were in the company of a coke user and several known dealers. And you were in possession of a briefcase containing ten pounds of one-hundred-per-cent pure Colombian *perica*. Wholesale value around two hundred thousand dollars. A lot more if it ever hit the streets.'

Smith folded his arms across his chest. He looked long at Reuben, as though measuring him for his next words.

'You're a dangerous man, Lieutenant,' he said. 'You know too much. And too little. My superiors want to silence you. There are different ways of achieving that, of course. Simple ways. And more complicated, such as the one I have chosen. The reason for my taking the difficult option is that I need to present you with a choice of your own. My superiors want more than just a promise that you will keep your nose out of their affairs. They want all the information you have succeeded in gathering, they want any files Mrs Hammel brought to you from her apartment, they want a certain notebook, and they want whatever it was you took from the underground chamber yesterday.'

'What would I get for giving you all that?'

Smith shrugged.

'To walk out of here without a stain on your character. Tomorrow morning you may go to your precinct house as usual. No-one will arrest you. No-one will even know about this evening's little incident. On the contrary, you will find a letter on your desk from the police commissioner notifying you of a significant promotion.'

'And if I tell you to go to hell?'

'You go there with me. You will be found guilty of Danny Cohen's murder. It will be proved that he uncovered your involvement with narcotics peddling. You will be sentenced. There will be no need to use those photographs I showed you. Perhaps I can use them for someone else. Mrs Hammel possibly.'

'I know who killed Danny. With half a chance I can prove it. I only have to open my mouth in court.'

'Yes,' said Smith. 'Perhaps you can.' He half-turned his head and snapped his fingers peremptorily. The men behind him stepped forward, pulling Kominsky forward.

'You are, I think, destined to be Mr Kominsky's nemesis,' said Smith. 'You have already wounded him very badly. And you have cost him the sight of one eye. And here he is, and here are you.'

Smith gestured to one of the heavies. The man pushed Kominsky to his knees. The wounded man looked frightened. Not angry, not vengeful, just frightened. He shivered uncontrollably.

Smith had not taken his eyes off Reuben. He held out his hand and the man on his right handed him a pistol, a Browning 9mm Hi-Power autoloader. Smith took it with the nonchalance of a man who had held one often enough not to think about it any longer. He held the gun out to Reuben.

'It is loaded,' he said. 'I make you Kominsky's executioner. He would have had his friends kill you tonight. Your life for his eye. Last night he killed a friend of yours in mistake for you. Your friend's life for yours. Now you can make amends. Kominsky's life for your friend's.'

Reuben took the gun. Smith's bodyguards had levelled their own weapons on him. He knew he would not have a chance to point the pistol at anyone but Kominsky. Kominsky looked at him, his single eye eloquent with terror. Reuben lifted the gun. It felt heavier than any gun he had ever raised before. He thought of Danny lying on the floor with his throat sliced open. Of Angelina strapped to the chair next to him. He held the gun to Kominsky's head. If he shut his eyes it would be just like target practice. Fire, reload; fire, reload. He shut his eyes. An eye for an eye, a life for a life. 'I'll kill him, Mother,' he had said. His finger pressed against the trigger.

He opened his eyes and dropped the gun. Smith was watching him, unperturbed.

'I take it that you decline my offer, Lieutenant.'

Reuben said nothing. His hand was shaking. Smith picked up the gun. With unaffected casualness, he pressed the barrel against the nape of Kominsky's neck. Kominsky was shaking like a leaf. Reuben looked into Smith's eyes.

'Last night,' said Smith to Reuben, 'and tonight again perhaps, you may have thought that the difference between yourself and Mr Kominsky was that between love and hate. Or love and indifference. Perhaps that is so. But since then things have become simpler. You still have a chance between life and death. You made that choice just now. But Kominsky made his choice last night when he failed in his mission.'

Smith pulled the trigger and blew a hole the size of a fist through the back of Kominsky's head. A violent shudder went through the ravaged body, blood threw itself in pulses through the desanctified air. Reuben shut his eyes. Kominsky's body slumped lifelessly to the ground. The sound of the explosion echoed again and again through the abandoned church.

Smith handed the gun back to his associate.

'You have until tomorrow morning, Lieutenant Abrams. Five A.M. I will see you then.'

He turned and started to walk away. Reuben opened his eyes and watched him go. In mid-stride Smith paused and turned his head.

'I'm very sorry, Lieutenant. I forgot to mention how very well your mother looks. What age is she now? Seventy? She looks very well. I'm sure she and your father will both live to a ripe old age. Don't you think so?'

And he turned and walked away and there was no sound, no sound at all, and on the floor where priests and acolytes had walked, blood flowed like a bitter memory of wine.

CHAPTER THIRTY-SEVEN

Reuben looked at his watch. Two-fifteen, less than three hours before Smith was due to return. They had put him in a small room that had once been the sacristy and was now filled with rubble and a smell of damp. In one corner, a broken plaster statue raised its hand in a pointless gesture of benediction. He had a chair, a light and plenty of time in which to think. The single door was locked from the outside, the window with its clumsy board of plywood lay out of reach, even when he stood on the chair.

Smith held almost all the cards. To be precise, he had Angelina and Reuben's parents, not to mention a stiffening corpse lying unshriven in a side chapel next door. The corpse may not have been much of an asset, but it said Smith could be every bit as ruthless as he seemed. Reuben, on the other hand, had a notebook, a gold half-circle, and a story about a boat that had once sailed from Africa. The problem was knowing just how important all that was to Smith and why. Reuben could try stalling, but there was every chance that to do so would cost his mother, his father and Angelina their lives.

The simple solution seemed to be to tell Smith all he knew, tell him where the semicircle and the notebook had been hidden, and turn up in the morning to collect his letter from the commissioner. Unfortunately, nothing Reuben had seen of Smith made him think he could trust him. He could tell Smith everything and Smith might still kill them all. Smith was not an independent agent. He was answerable to men more powerful than himself. What he had done to Kominsky, they, no doubt, would do as readily to him. Angelina and Reuben knew too much to be left in circulation.

At two-thirty, one of the heavies made his rounds. A different one looked in every half-hour, checked that everything was normal, and locked the door again. Each one in turn refused to be drawn into conversation, even to the extent of answering the simplest of questions.

He was hungry and cold and desperately in need of sleep, but there was no food and no heat, and true sleep would not come. Once or twice he dozed in the chair only to waken with an aching neck and the barbed hooks of nightmare still embedded in his brain. His wounded foot and back hurt badly. And he knew there was no way out.

At four o'clock he asked for a cup of coffee or tea – anything that might warm him and keep him alert. The guard merely shrugged and left. Nothing came. Outside, a siren wailed in the distance, grinding the stillness into little bits. They were in the city all right. But where?

He didn't notice the scraping noise at first. It came from high up, at the window. He turned and glanced up. At first he noticed nothing. The lamp shed a very limited light, and most of the board covering the window was hidden in shadows. Then, just as he was about to turn away, his eye caught a movement at the bottom corner of the window, on the left-hand side. The nails were being pushed back out of the windowframe. There was no glass, and Reuben felt the tiniest shiver as a faint draught edged through the tiny opening. There was a rattling sound and he caught sight of something dropping from the bottom of the window onto the floor. The board fell back into position. He heard a sound outside, as though someone had jumped lightly to the ground. Then silence, heavier than ever.

The door opened and the previous guard entered. He was carrying an MP5K, the stockless miniature version of the standard MP5. It was a fraction over one foot long, less than half the length of an MP5A2, and weighed only 4.4 pounds. But the bullets it fired went just as fast and did just as much damage.

'I thought I heard something. What are you up to?'

Reuben's brain raced. He glanced down at the floor in front of him. Near his right foot was a piece of broken stone, part of the building waste with which the room was filled. He drew his foot back and kicked it hard. It landed in a pile of rubble with a muted rattling sound.

'Just kicking about. If you brought me some coffee I'd have something better to do.'

The guard glanced round the room. For a moment Reuben thought he would notice the small gap in the window-board, but it

202

was too well shadowed from where he stood. He shrugged and went out again. Reuben heard the key turn dutifully in the lock.

He got up and walked softly over to the spot just below the window where the object must have fallen. It was obvious enough if you were looking for it: a small metal tube about three inches long, taped at one end. He picked it up and peeled away the tape.

A loose roll of bond paper dropped into his open hand. There was a typed message on one side, produced on a manual machine with dropped 'e's:

Reuben – Remember the chimp with the funny walk at the Bronx Zoo? The one we saw the day after we first met? OK, that's just so you know this note is genuine. Hide the tube and destroy this paper as soon as you've finished reading it. The man you call Smith is holding your parents hostage at their apartment. Mrs Hammel has been taken to a private hospital, where she'll be safe for the next twenty-four hours. Concentrate on your parents and yourself. Agree to Smith's demands, but insist on seeing your parents before handing anything over. Once you've been taken to their apartment, tell him the things he wants are kept in a concealed safe in your own place. Insist again that your parents accompany you there. A loaded gun has been placed in the second drawer down on the right-hand side of your desk. The rest is up to you. If you succeed in getting out, ring the number I gave you. It will be manned permanently for the next seventy-two hours. I can arrange safe custody for your parents and help you find Mrs Hammel. In return I need your cooperation. Please take care. Sally.

Reuben held his breath. The room seemed to shift, as though its moorings had come adrift. He closed his eyes, fighting a sensation of dizziness and nausea. When he opened them again, the sacristy was unchanged. The dust and rubble lay all around as before. The statue gazed dispassionately at him, sinless and without pain. There was a sound of feet outside. Quickly, he shredded the message, slipped it back into the tube and pushed the whole thing through a hole in the back of the statue's head.

CHAPTER THIRTY-EIGHT

Smith was precise in his timing. They brought Reuben out to him at one minute past five. A fine tracery of dawn light was creeping nervously through a broken window high above the nave. The body of the church was raw and stained. The morning was empty of purpose. There seemed no possibility of warmth or comfort anywhere.

Reuben put his conditions quietly and without apparent emotion, hoping his nervousness did not show. Smith was fragrant and detached, almost withdrawn; he had slept well, bathed and perfumed himself before leaving for the church. To the casual eye he looked like an accountant or a computer salesman setting out to work, pale-eyed and tightly buttoned and ready to earn another day's worth of pension. Like an accountant or a salesman, he seemed bored by the proceedings, as though last night's brief violence had emptied him of rage and hope together. At his feet, a pool of antique red quivered across the dust as the unsteady light found a surviving pane of vivid scarlet glass.

He agreed readily to Reuben's conditions, as though they had in some measure been expected. Reuben sensed that Smith possessed that curious instinct of the successful criminal, an intuitive ability to distinguish between violence for an end and violence without purpose. Being tough is no good if you do not know when to bend. A moment's hesitation, then he shrugged his shoulders and nodded.

Abruptly he indicated to his men that it was time to leave. They extinguished the lamps, performing in their fashion a second ritual of deconsecration. Kominsky's bloodied body they left on the altar steps, an offering of sorts. A trace of Smith's expensive perfume lingered in the unheated air, completing the sacrament with incense.

* * *

Everything went as planned. Reuben's parents were tired and frightened, but unharmed. They had long ago learned to master their fears, trained by a stiffer lash than any Smith could wield. His mother wore a copper-coloured woollen dress and a pepper shawl. Her hair was pinned back as always in a tight bun. No make-up, no jewels. Just an old woman who had looked death in the face too often for it to matter one time more. She smiled nervously at Reuben, then looked away. Reuben saw her as if for the first time.

His father sat beside her, holding her hand, saying nothing. Reuben had forgotten how fragile the old man had grown, how tightly his mottled skin was stretched over wasted muscle and brittle bone.

'They come with me,' Reuben said, daring to press his demands now they had come this far. 'I hand the papers over to you, you and your people leave. That's it. Two old people: it's nothing to you.'

Smith shook his head this time.

'They're alive. You've seen them. What more do you want?'

'I want them to stay alive. You can have what you want, all of it. But I must have them. Your exhibition last night did nothing to make me trust you.'

'It was not intended to. The very opposite. But if it keeps you happy and saves time, I see no reason to be difficult. Where are the papers?'

Reuben hesitated just long enough to make it seem real.

'At my apartment.'

'You're lying. My people have been through that place with tweezers. There's nothing there.'

'I didn't leave them in a drawer for you or anyone else to find. They're there, believe me. What the hell would I have to gain by lying?'

Smith pressed his lips together.

'I don't know. But you've got plenty to lose. If I don't have those papers in my hand in the next half-hour, I will personally cut your mother's throat over your kitchen sink.'

That was when Reuben decided to kill him.

The apartment was cordoned off just as Angelina's had been. Using his own key, Reuben let everyone in – his parents, Smith and two of Smith's subordinates. The others had gone off duty. It had been a hard night.

Up to this point, Reuben had given almost no thought to what might happen once he found the gun. The first problem was his parents: he did not want them anywhere within the line of fire, assuming that there was going to be some shooting. The second was how to take care of three trained combatants in the confines of a small apartment with just one gun and no back-up. The gun – if it was there at all – would give him an edge for about three seconds. And after that?

He turned to Smith.

'My parents should be lying down. You've kept them awake all night. Look at my mother. She's tired and she's frightened. My father too. They can wait in my bedroom while we get this thing sorted out.'

Smith glanced at the elderly couple.

'Take his mother into the bedroom. Keep an eye on her. The father can stay with us.'

Reuben did not try to argue. At all costs he had to prevent Smith suspecting anything. One of the bodyguards took his mother into the bedroom. At least both problems were now somewhat reduced.

The study was neither light nor dark, but suspended in a sort of twilight. Someone had closed the blind – Reuben normally kept it open – allowing only a pale, insignificant light to filter through.

Smith entered first and switched on the overhead light. More than tweezers had been used on the room. There was little actual mess – good searchers are systematic, not clumsy – but it was evident that not an inch had been spared the attention of expert hands and eyes. Even the wallpaper had been peeled away in places.

Reuben crossed to where Smith was standing. His father followed, then the man guarding him. The old man closed the door and stood leaning against the jamb. He seemed near to collapse. His face was grey and sickly. Reuben looked at him, but there was no expression in the old eyes.

'The papers are in a floor safe,' said Reuben, improvising at every step. He wanted to kiss his father, tell him he loved him. Frailty kept them apart. It had always done so. First, the frailty of childhood, then that of youth, and now the final frailty of age. 'I keep the key in my desk.'

Smith glanced round at his companion.

'Parker?'

'It's OK, sir,' the man said. 'We did a good job on this room. The desk is clean.' He meant there was no gun in any of the drawers. Reuben hoped he was wrong.

'Did you find a key?'

Parker shrugged. He had broad shoulders. When he shrugged a lot of muscles rippled beneath his tweed jacket. On his left shoulder, under the jacket, he carried a pistol in a holster. He still held his Uzi in his right hand, casual but not off guard.

'No way of knowing, sir. Curtis did the desk. He's good on desks. Does a thorough job.'

'He won't have found it,' Reuben interrupted. 'I keep it taped in the back of a drawer. Out of easy reach.'

'Curtis is good,' Parker repeated. It was heartwarming to hear the team spirit at work.

'I'll check it, for God's sake.' Reuben made for the desk, trying to retain some sort of initiative. The last thing he wanted was for Smith or his gunman to put his hand into the drawer in search of a non-existent key and bring it out holding a pistol. If there was a pistol.

Reuben reached the desk. Smith was watching him closely. What if the message had been some sort of hoax? What if Curtis had been in here *after* the gun was deposited, what if the desk really *was* clean? Better not think. Try to look cool. Reuben opened the second drawer down as instructed and slipped his hand inside.

It lay there waiting, hard and sleek and as cold as Smith's heart. He knew it at once: a Heckler and Koch P7. He had used one before for target practice. The heavy butt with the squeeze cocker in front identified it at once. Someone had used forethought: with a four-inch barrel, the gun was easy to conceal and manoeuvre. The butt felt unusually thick. Reuben guessed it was loaded with the thirteen-round magazine rather than the standard eight. He fumbled, getting his fingers round the awkward butt. In a rage, his heart hammered deep inside his chest. He felt sick.

'Something wrong, Lieutenant?' Smith took a step forward.

'The key's gone. Your thugs have made a pig's breakfast of this place.'

Smith edged closer. Reuben kept on making fumbling gestures. He felt remote. His hand moved in a dream.

'Let me look.'

Reuben glanced up. His father was still by the door. Parker stood near him, too close for safety.

Smith was by his side now. Like a man on the edge of a hurtling precipice, Reuben cast everything away and jumped into the void, swinging the gun up and round in a single action, grabbing Smith by the neck with his free hand, ramming the gun hard against his temple, ruffling his neatly combed hair.

He felt Smith stiffen, not in fear but readiness.

'Tell Parker to put his gun down. He has about two seconds.'

Reuben tried to keep his voice calm. But inside a storm had taken hold of him.

Parker hesitated. Smith nodded. The big man dropped the Uzi. At the same instant, he reached out for Reuben's father, pulling him in front of himself as a shield. A moment later, he drew his pistol and held it to the old man's head. Stalemate.

Reuben hit Smith hard on the side of the head, knocking him to the floor. Smith groaned and tried to get to his knees, but failed to make it. Reuben threw himself behind the desk.

Whatever he may have become since, Parker had been trained in hostage rescue, not terrorism. He dumped his shield and went into a low crouch, shooting through the desk at the spot he thought Reuben had reached, his pistol pumping out a series of heavy-duty Glaser bullets that ripped the veneer and woodchip to shreds. Reuben just made it behind a metal filing cabinet. Parker's next three rounds ricocheted blindly off steel. Reuben stood and got off two rounds. They took Parker full in the belly, ripping the stomach wall apart and throwing him back against the wall. Whoever had loaded the gun must have used high-velocity ammunition.

A heavy foot kicked the door open, throwing Reuben's father sideways to the floor. A moment later, the second guard rolled into the room, ducking, twisting, and rising smoothly into a crouch. His Uzi lifted, seeking a target. Reuben shot him in the face at close range. The silence that followed was very pure.

CHAPTER THIRTY-NINE

'Papa, are you all right?' Reuben bent down and lifted his father to a sitting position. The old man was shaken, but seemingly unhurt.

'Yes,' he wheezed. 'I'm all right. See to your mother, Reuben. See she's not hurt.'

Reuben helped the old man to a chair. Hurriedly, he picked up the fallen guns. Parker and his partner were no further threat. Smith was out cold. Carrying the gun, Reuben dashed to the bedroom. His mother was crouching on the bed, her back against the wall, praying in a quiet voice. She looked up in fear that turned to relief when she recognized her son.

'I heard gunshots, Reuben. Is your father safe?'

Reuben nodded.

'He's fine.'

'I want to see him.'

'He's sitting down in my study. I don't want to take you in there. Two men are dead.'

'I've seen people dead before this, Reuben. Two more won't hurt me.'

'Wait. I'll bring Papa to you.' Reuben dropped most of the guns, retaining only the P7 for his own use. He returned to the study.

His father was sitting where Reuben had left him. Smith was on his feet. In one hand he held a pocket radio transceiver. In the other he grasped a steel knife with a bevelled point and a razor edge. On the floor lay strips of tape that must have been used to secure the knife to his calf. He held it with the blade pressed deep inside Reuben's father's mouth. The old man was spluttering, scarcely able to breathe.

Smith neither paused nor turned as Reuben appeared in the doorway.

'Abrams has just come back,' he said softly, speaking into the handset. 'I'll deal with him first. Get here as quickly as you can. And tell unit six to hurry.'

Releasing the switch, Smith returned the handset to his pocket. He kept his eyes on Reuben's father.

'Toss the gun gently in my direction, Abrams,' he said. 'Very gently.' His voice was calm and controlled. He did not seem to be under any pressure.

'I'll kill you anyway, Smith. Let him go.'

Reuben saw the imperceptible movement of Smith's hand as he pressed the tip of the knife into the soft area behind his father's palate. Drops of bright blood mingled with saliva appeared on the old man's lips. He was gagging for breath. His thin hands gripped the edges of the chair like twigs. Reuben capitulated and tossed the gun towards Smith. It landed by his feet.

As the gun hit the floor, Smith pressed forward and up simultaneously. The knife was made of high-carbon steel. It could pierce a steel drum without bending or snapping. The old man's head was paper to it. The thrust lifted Reuben's father from the floor. Smith held him like a fish on a gaff, while blood exploded from his open mouth. The old man lurched, twisted and went limp. A length of steel protruded from the top of his skull.

Reuben cried out and ran towards Smith. Smith's hand was drenched with blood. He let go of the knife, dropping the dead man with it and, stooping, snatched the gun from the floor.

Reuben was only feet away. He saw the barrel hesitate, then rise. All reason gone, he flung himself backwards, crashing heavily against the door jamb. Smith fired twice, hot bullets hacking plaster from the wall mere inches from Reuben's head.

Numb, Reuben rolled through the door, twisting as he tumbled, staggering to his feet. A bullet whistled through the doorway half a second after him. He found his balance and turned to see his mother outside the bedroom. Their eyes met.

Reuben grabbed her and pulled her towards the front door. Behind him, he heard feet at the study door. There was an occasional table beside the front door, bearing a glass vase. Reuben picked up the vase, turned and hurled it full at Smith as he came through the door. It caught him hard in the chest, knocking him off balance and winding him.

'Run, Mother! Run!'

Half-carrying, half-dragging, Reuben pulled his mother along the passage to the head of the stairs. They were halfway down the first flight when he heard Smith crash through the apartment door. His mother was light, but she had begun to panic, and Reuben found it hard to manhandle her down the stairs.

'Avrumel!' she shouted. 'Avrumel!' His father's name. She had heard the shooting and seen the blood. 'Avrumel!' she went on shouting, in a frenzy now, fear and grief mingling. There were tears on Reuben's face as he dragged her away, bright tears turning his father's blood to water.

Smith was hard behind them. His feet sounded heavy on the stairs, pounding like hammers. They reached the street door. Smith was perhaps a flight behind. Reuben pushed his mother through the door. 'Run!' he shouted. 'Keep running!'

Smith appeared at the top of the stairs. He got off two quick shots, barely an inch too high. Reuben followed his mother through the door. He caught her at the kerb. There was nowhere left to run.

Passers-by looked round as they heard the shooting and the sound of running feet. From near at hand a siren wailed, coming rapidly closer: someone had called the cops.

Suddenly, out of nowhere, a black sedan came skidding towards them. A man wearing a balaclava was leaning out of the passenger window, aiming a pistol in their direction. Reuben threw his mother to the ground, covering her with his body, and at the same moment Smith came out of the street door. The car screamed to a halt, bumping along the kerb. There were loud screams. People ran for cover. The siren altered in pitch as a police car rounded the corner half a block away.

Smith hesitated. Reuben got his mother to her feet and pulled her behind a parked Volvo 760. A moment later, the windows of the car shattered as the gunman in the pursuit vehicle got out and started firing in their direction. He was carrying an ugly-looking Franchi SPAS twelve-gauge shotgun, pumping a shell into the chamber, firing, pumping, reloading with a fresh magazine every eight rounds, pumping and firing again as though he was out hunting ducks.

There was a squeal of tyres as the police cruiser slammed on its brakes. A uniformed policeman in the passenger seat leaned through the side window, pointing a large handgun at the sedan. The gunman turned, aimed and fired twice, shattering the cruiser's windscreen. A second later, he went down, his throat torn away by a .357 Magnum bullet.

Someone threw open the rear door of the cruiser, shouting at Reuben and his mother. 'Hurry up! Get in!'

Smith ran forward, trying to get behind the Volvo. The figure in the back seat of the cruiser fired at him, forcing him back. A second sedan came at full speed from the direction of the park. The police marksman was out of the car now, aiming across the roof of the Volvo to give covering fire to Reuben and his mother. They scrambled across the street, Reuben pulling the old woman. She was rigid with fear, unable to act for herself any longer.

Reuben pushed her onto the back seat.

'Get her out of here!' he shouted. 'I want Smith!'

'Leave him.' A man's voice, sharp and uncompromising.

'He killed my father.'

The second sedan screeched to a stop. Two more gunmen were already piling out of it, firing indiscriminately.

'Later. We've got to get out of here.'

There was the sound of another siren. Reuben hesitated a fraction longer, then tumbled into the cruiser, pressing his mother down against the seat. A battery of machine-gun bullets burst through the rear window, climbing and exiting through the roof. The driver was already in gear and moving off at speed.

The car lurched round the corner and picked up speed. There was no siren now, just the roar of the engine and the squeal of tyres on the blacktop as they twisted through the traffic. Cars pulled in to the right to make way.

Reuben straightened and helped his mother to sit up. She felt heavy.

'It's OK, Mama. We made it.'

Silence. He caught sight of the face of the man beside her. He looked down at his mother, at her eyes. They had not made it after all.

CHAPTER FORTY

Babylon is tinted glass. Tinted glass and tinted lives. And in the dark thoroughfares, broken glass and broken dreams. There are hanging gardens on towers of bronze, and whores walk lightly on streets full of steam and stars, while high above them, on thrones of painted cedarwood, pale princes in the latest fashions watch them pass.

The car with black-tinted windows drove north-west towards the towers of Manhattan, passing over Brooklyn Bridge. The Hudson ran underneath, watercold, riverbright, bladed with liquid steel. To Reuben's right, the sprawling edifice of the Watchtower building held silent vigil over the world of the unchosen. There would be no resurrection today.

The police cruiser had not been a police cruiser. That was all anyone had been willing to tell him. They had abandoned it in a private garage on Eastern Parkway and transferred to the present car, a Chevrolet. Another vehicle, a long black car without windows in the rear, had collected his mother's body. She had seemed too small for it, for the foolish length of it. They had laid her on a stretcher and wheeled her out into the open air briefly before shutting her inside, as though for ever. There had been no rush. Reuben had watched the car head out into the street and mingle with the morning traffic along the Parkway, sunlight twinkling on its wing mirrors.

They were on the South Street Viaduct now, heading into town. Reuben was numb. He did not speak to the man beside him, the one who had risked his life snatching him out from under a hail of gunfire. The man had said his name was Jensen.

Reuben wondered where Smith was now, what he was doing. Reuben could see his hand, Smith's hand, the blood laced about it, his father's blood. He could hear echoes in his head, the sound of a

213

knife in his father's skull. Behind a wire-mesh fence on the right, kids were playing basketball. The whole world seemed to be going on as though nothing had happened.

They turned left onto East 34th Street. A few blocks further west, the car drew up outside a newly built tower of bottle-green glass. Its name was displayed in gold letters above a shimmering entrance: Izumo Taisha Tower. The letters spelled out the name in Japanese and English both. It meant nothing to Reuben.

Jensen led Reuben through a crowded lobby to two rows of elevator doors, six to each row, facing one another. Wind roared through the elevator shafts. A soft bell chimed and on their left doors opened. Some people stepped out, but only Reuben and Jensen entered. Jensen produced a key from his pocket and inserted it into a security lock on the console. The lift began to rise.

They went up in the elevator together, towards the clouds, in silence. Bright yellow numbers shimmered as they climbed. The silence grew. The numbers vanished and were replaced by Reuben's mother's face, by its arrested vehemence. Her face and his father's face blurred and became one. Reuben shook his head. The numbers stopped at the ninety-ninth floor, but the lift went on climbing. At last the bell chimed and the doors opened.

Emptiness as far as the eye could see, shut off by walls of tinted glass. An uncarpeted floor of raw concrete. Items of building equipment. No walls, no partitions. The row of elevator shafts provided the only breaks in the monotony.

Far away, near a high window, several figures were standing. Jensen motioned to Reuben that he should walk that way. As he did so, most of the figures detached themselves from the window and came towards him. Three men, all in their mid-thirties, shook Reuben's hand and introduced themselves. He forgot their names at once. He had no space for any but the simplest of names, Smith. His eyes remained on the last figure, the one who had remained at the window, gazing out. When he was only a few paces away, he stopped.

'Hello, Reuben,' Sally said in a lost voice, a voice little more than a whisper. 'I'm sorry,' she said. 'I can't tell you how sorry I am.' And he sensed the anguish in her voice, and the regret and the anger, and he said nothing. Nothing at all.

'Come here, Reuben. Here to the window.'

He still said nothing, but stepped up to the window beside her.

'Look out there, Reuben,' Sally whispered. 'What do you see?'

He looked out and saw low clouds drifting about the highest buildings – Pan Am, Chrysler, American Brands. There were no people anywhere. From this height, they were not even visible as specks. Only his father and his mother adrift in the lifeless air, reflections without substance.

'New York,' said Reuben.

Sally shook her head.

'No,' she said. 'Not New York. Babylon. Babylon the Great, the Mother of Harlots and Abominations of the Earth.'

He did not ask what she was talking about; he thought he knew. The clouds moved sluggishly, painfully, breaking and re-forming as they passed through the city. Pale sunlight filtered through them to the streets below, starved of warmth or meaning. His parents were dead.

Sally turned.

'I am truly sorry,' she repeated. Awkwardly, she reached for him and drew him towards her, embracing him gently. He endured the embrace for a moment, then pulled away. He could not bear to be touched. He was still in shock, still numb with bereavement. Sally let her arms fall to her sides. It was cold in the vast, unheated space.

'Let's sit down, Reuben,' she said. 'We have to talk.'

Someone had arranged plastic chairs in a circle at the centre of the floor. The four men were already seated. Reuben followed Sally and was offered a place. Sally took the remaining seat, facing him. She was dressed simply, in a burgundy skirt and sweater. She wore little earrings in the shape of crocodiles. Her eyes were unreadable.

'Reuben,' she began, 'I know you want to be alone, but there isn't time. I also know you must have questions, but I must ask you to be patient. I may not have answers to all of them, others it may not be possible for me to answer now, some maybe never. You will just have to accept that.

'The matters I am about to divulge are highly classified. They're among the most sensitive items of information currently on record in the United States. Not even the president has been informed of them. Nor is he likely to be, unless . . .' She hesitated. 'Unless circumstances force our hand.'

Reuben interrupted.

'Who are you, Sally? Why are you doing this? Why are you killing all these people?'

Sally shivered and leaned forward in her seat.

215

'Please, Reuben, let me talk. Let me explain. After that you may ask any questions you wish.'

Reuben nodded. The empty space in which he sat was nothing compared to the great gulf that had opened inside him. His father was standing by the window looking out at the emptiness. He would not turn his head.

'First of all,' Sally said, 'let me introduce the others properly.' She said their names and they stood, one by one, and shook Reuben's hand: Chris Leach, a former psychology professor, tall, wiry, pensive; Curtis Kolstoe, a lawyer like Sally, plump, with large brown eyes and a penetrating stare; Hastings Donovan, an ex-cop, red-headed, well-built, reserved; and Emeric Jensen, a former theology teacher from Dartmouth College.

'Emeric,' said Sally, 'maybe you'd better explain a bit about us.'

Jensen raised his eyebrows. He was blond, about thirty-five, delicately built, and somewhat shy.

'Why do you always pick on me?' he asked.

'You used to teach theology,' Sally answered. 'This is your punishment.'

Reuben sensed something between Sally and Jensen that was not professional rapport and was not friendship. He shrugged inwardly. What did a little thing like that matter now?

Jensen leaned forward with his elbows on his knees and his chin resting on clasped hands. Reuben imagined this was how he had started seminars back in his teaching days.

'The five of us are part of a larger team based in Washington,' he began. 'Our official title, when we use it, is CSA. That stands for the Cult Surveillance Agency. I know that sounds a little weird, but I can assure you we aren't weird at all. We're a regular government agency set up six years ago as part of a collaboration exercise between the FBI, CIA and National Security Agency. The CIA has been getting edgy about fundamentalist sects for years, ever since Rios Montt made himself president of Guatemala back in – when was it?'

'Eighty-two,' Kolstoe said.

'Back in eighty-two. You may recall that episode. Montt belonged to an American sect called the Church of the Complete Word. When he became president, they had no more than eight hundred members in the country; but immediately afterwards money started coming in from all over the place. All the diehard fundamentalists were going to make Guatemala safe from com-

216

munism and godlessness. If he'd lasted long enough, the Church of the Complete Word would have run the country.

'Rios Montt was only the tip of an iceberg. There was Khomeini in Iran, of course. Just before he was deposed, Marcos was made head of the Transcendental Meditation organization in the Philippines. The Moonies are deeply involved in financing anti-communist movements in several Latin American countries.

'During the eighties, religion became a major political force again, and it doesn't seem to matter whether the people involved are traditionalists or not. The FBI started getting interested around the time of the Jonestown massacre in Guyana. Here in the States, cult members frequently mess with the federal authorities. They kidnap somebody, move him or her across state lines; maybe a deprogrammer sticks his head in, takes the kid back to Kentucky or Oregon. All federal offences. I don't have to tell you about cult-based murders.

'All this was getting too complicated for one agency, especially since most of these cult groups are international. So a presidential committee was set up in 1987 to recommend what sort of action should be taken. The result was the CSA. At which point I hand you back to Miss Peale.'

Sally did not move at first. She seemed to be marshalling difficult thoughts, weighing what could not be weighed, balancing what could not be balanced. Reuben thought she looked tired. Tired and sad. He thought she looked more sad than tired. As though a great weight lay on her.

'Reuben,' she said hesitantly, 'I know you're tired. I know you've been through a lot and you'd like to have time to yourself and a chance to sleep. But I want you to listen to what we have to tell you first. Then you can sleep or do whatever you feel you have to do.

'The problem is that things are starting to move faster than I anticipated. What happened last night and this morning took me completely by surprise. We didn't know that Kominsky would send his friends after you, that they would set you and Mrs Hammel up like that. Or that Smith would take advantage of the situation. It might have been days before he found you. By then we'd have been in a position to take him out.'

She paused, uncertain how to go on.

'Suppose you tell me exactly what's going on,' said Reuben suddenly. His voice was quiet, but it was inflected with anger. After what had happened, after such a nightmare, to be sitting so calmly in a green silence above the city talking of problems and advantages, as though analysing a game of chess. 'My best friend was killed two nights ago, I saw my father knifed and my mother shot this morning, and you behave as though this is all in a day's work. Just who the hell do you think you people are?'

Sally stood up, agitated. She wanted to hold Reuben, reassure him, comfort him. But this was neither the time nor the place.

'Just try to keep cool, Reuben. It won't help if you get angry. You can't do anything, you can't bring anybody back; but you can sure as hell make certain that Smith and his bosses don't do the same thing to anybody else. Now, do you want me to go on?'

Reuben nodded.

'I'm sorry,' he said.

'OK, listen carefully. I was transferred to work with the CSA two years ago. I'd already been working for the FBI for ten years, the past five of them as an undercover agent in City Hall. There's no need to go into what I did there, but you can probably make some intelligent guesses. Two years ago my boss called me to his office and introduced me to Emeric and Curtis.

'They'd been working for about six months on a major investigation, and a lot of trails seemed to lead to City Hall. The investigation involved a religious cult with a membership recruited exclusively from the upper ranks of society. I think you know what cult I mean.'

She took a deep breath.

'At first it seemed like a regular investigation, just a little more bizarre than usual. Then it started to get complicated. We began to put more people on it, and the complications grew worse. A year ago we found some clues that led to Washington. High up in Washington. Smith will have suggested as much to you. He was not lying.'

'Who is he? He said he represented "the highest authority". What did he mean?'

Sally frowned and looked at her colleagues. Leach shook his head. She turned back to Reuben.

'I'm sorry, Reuben, but I can't reveal that. All I can tell you is that the Seventh Order has infiltrated several government agencies over the years.'

'He said "the highest authority",' protested Reuben. He was angry. What right had these people to keep him in the dark? 'Did

218

he mean the president? Is that what you're afraid to say? I have to know.'

Chris Leach interrupted.

'Lieutenant, I understand your frustration. But this is a national security issue. We want your help, but you don't have clearance for this information.'

'Then get it. If you want me to help you, I need to know what's going on. Who Smith is, who his bosses are, how high this thing really goes. Otherwise, you can all go screw yourselves.'

Reuben was shaking now. Images of blood made patterns behind his eyes. He leaped to his feet and headed for the elevator. Sally came after him, reaching for his arm. He pushed her away violently. He would find Smith himself. Find him and send him to hell without anyone's help.

He pressed the button for the elevator. Nothing happened. He stabbed repeatedly at the button, and still the elevator did not come. He slumped against the wall, sobbing. Images of blood. Photographs torn and bloody on his kitchen floor. A spider striding across a continent of blood.

CHAPTER FORTY-ONE

Sally held him for a long time while he wept. She had loved him a little, but not enough. There had been gaps in Reuben's life, raw holes that no-one could fill. Now they had grown in a matter of days to unimaginable proportions. She doubted if he would ever find peace again.

She wanted him now for selfish reasons. National security, the public good, even the saving of human lives were mere clichés. Sally wanted Reuben because he could help her achieve her ends. All the time she held him she thought of nothing but means and ends. There was a little pity in her somewhere, and a little love, and a lot of sadness, but they rattled brokenly inside her own emptiness.

Hastings Donovan, the red-headed cop, came over with a bottle of bourbon and two glasses. When Reuben had recovered enough to drink, Donovan sent Sally away and sat with him, plying him with whisky. He talked at random about his experiences on the force. He'd been with the vice squad for eleven years, seen too much, felt too much. This wasn't much better, but it was enough to keep him sane.

Kolstoe, the lawyer, drew up a chair.

'I've been in touch with Washington,' he said. 'They've given a go-ahead for you to have a full security clearance. I know you feel bad, and I know this isn't the best time; but I think we should do some more talking. Some real talking. Are you up to that?'

Reuben nodded, still numb, still shaking.

'I'm OK,' he murmured. 'I'm ready.'

They formed a semicircle once more. Kolstoe took up where Sally had left off.

'Smith's real name,' he said, 'is Forbes. Warren Forbes.' Sunlight came through one of the windows, falling green and golden across

220

his face and down onto the dusty floor. 'He is a senior official in the CIA's Directorate of Operations. Since the age of nineteen, he has been a fully initiated member of the Seventh Order. His father was a member before him. He was in Vietnam and Cambodia, had a complicated career there, became a CIA operative.

'Forbes is only one of several members of the Order who have risen to important positions within the US intelligence community over the past twenty years or so. We know the names of some of them, others we just suspect. We know that there is a group run by Forbes within the CIA. Forbes is in charge, but he receives his own instructions from the central committee of the Order. Or so we think. We don't really know. Most of the time we're going on informed guesswork.

'For several years now, there has been a renegade movement within the Directorate of Operations, made up of men who aren't happy with the way the country's foreign policy is being directed, who are dissatisfied with how the country itself is being run. Forbes is a key force in this movement. Over the years he has arranged for other malcontents to be initiated into the Seventh Order. It's given him a hold over them, allowed him to steer their overall policy in directions favourable to the Order. The Order has its own ideas about how this country should be run and how we should handle our foreign affairs. Broadly speaking, its ideas are right-wing and extremist.'

Reuben raised a hand to interrupt the lawyer.

'You're telling me you've managed to pull all this together in the past couple of years?'

Kolstoe nodded.

'CSA has more resources than you might guess. We managed to infiltrate Forbes's group within the Directorate. Up until two months ago, we had a fairly steady flow of information. Then it dried up suddenly, and we haven't had any contact from our mole since then.

'In spite of that, we still continue to monitor the Order, and we know that something major is being planned. The Hammel business panicked some of them and let us get a little closer. It brought Forbes to New York. It made them lean on some people a little too heavily. They're in danger of blowing their cover. We think Forbes knows that and wants to act now, before it's too late.'

'Why are you telling me all this?'

Sally broke in.

'Because we need your help, Reuben. Angelina Hammel knows more than she's telling you. She isn't a member of the Order, and what she said about being in danger from them was true. They want her husband's notebook, they want to find the ship that brought the Order to Haiti. We think they're planning something on the island as a preliminary to a series of political manoeuvres in the Caribbean and Latin America. For some reason the boat is important. Angelina knows something. She has a brother who is chief of the Haitian secret police. We think he visited her here in New York a few days ago, then went back to Haiti.'

Sally breathed in hard.

'Reuben, I want you to persuade her to go to Haiti with you. She trusts you, she has already confided in you. She knows the country very well, much better than she pretends. Let her use the notebook, find whatever it is the Order is looking for, bring them out into the open.'

Reuben shook his head.

'This is crazy. We don't even know where Angelina is.'

'Yes, we do. I said so in my note. Forbes had her taken to a hospital in Westchester County, a place called St Vincent's. She's being kept there under surveillance, but we can get her out. She'll need a few days to recover from the overdose, but if all goes well you could leave for Port-au-Prince in four days' time.'

'Tell me what I get out of this.'

'Forbes is still at large, Reuben. We want you to help put him behind bars. For a very long time.'

Reuben got to his feet.

'I don't want him behind bars,' he said.

Nobody said anything. Reuben walked to the nearest window. It was smeared with putty, white fingerprints against the glass. They were so high here the world did not seem to matter.

'We aren't particular.' Jensen, the theologian, had spoken. 'Prison is only one option. No-one would object if you found other ways of dealing with Mr Forbes. He is not of critical importance. It's the people behind him we are really after.'

'And Angelina? What happens to her?'

'Nothing. She has done nothing that we know of, nothing criminal. It's for you to decide.'

Reuben watched sunlight fall on a small white cloud.

'I will have to attend my parents' funeral,' he said. His voice sounded far away to him.

'That isn't possible, Reuben,' said Sally. 'You know it can't be done. Forbes has men out looking for you. Your own people have a warrant out for your arrest. The funeral is the obvious place for them to look. I'm sorry, but it's out of the question.'

'I'm the eldest son, I have to recite the kaddish.'

'It's out of the question, Reuben.'

There was a long, awkward silence. What they were asking was very hard.

'I will at least have to see Devorah's parents to explain. And Davita. I will have to spend time with her. You will not deny me that.' He turned and looked directly at Sally.

She nodded.

'Very well, Reuben. But you can't go to their house. Let me arrange it.'

The cloud broke and he saw a great precipice all the way to the ground. For some reason he remembered a story from the Christian gospels, about how Satan had taken Jesus to a high place and tempted him. Reuben looked out on nothingness. There were no angels there to catch him if he fell.

PART TWO

The Circle Full Again

Haiti

'Lavender blue, dilly dilly, lavender green
When I am king, dilly dilly, you shall be queen.'

CHAPTER FORTY-TWO

Moments of arrival, moments of departure. And sometimes, between them, moments of grace – perhaps as few as two or three in a single lifetime. Even if someone should be blessed with more than that, the moments will be stretched out so finely and with such vast distances between, that nothing will fill the waiting. Not dreams, not hopes, not lies. No, thought Reuben, not even lies.

The late-afternoon Haiti Air flight for Port-au-Prince had left La Guardia at 16.05 and was due to land at half past eight. Reuben had been provided with money and a new identity backed up by watertight documentation. He was travelling as Dr Myron Phelps, with papers showing that he was going to Haiti on a Fulbright award in order to complete work left unfinished by his late colleague, Dr Richard Hammel. He was accompanied by Dr Hammel's widow, Angelina. At the airport, nobody had waved goodbye.

The plane dipped and rose again as it entered a pocket of turbulence. Angelina stared straight ahead, suspended in her own thoughts, if she had any. The doctors at St Vincent's had saved her life, but they had not given back her soul. Taking her from the hospital had been simplicity itself. Sally had brought all the necessary documentation, Emeric Jensen had been introduced as Professor Hammel, and no-one had remembered a recent murder victim of the same name. Why should they? In New York, like anywhere else, killers get the headlines, victims are numbers on the back page. They had taken Angelina out together, one on either side, holding her arms like old and valued friends. She had known neither of them. It had not mattered.

The next day had been difficult for Reuben. While Angelina rested in a Manhattan hotel room, he travelled on his new passport into Canada. Sally had arranged for Devorah's parents and Davita to stay in a hotel in Port Rowan on the shores of Lake Erie.

Telling Davita about her grandparents' deaths was harder than he could have imagined. She had loved them extravagantly. He spent two days with her, walking, explaining, nursing her grief with his own grief. He had not told her about Danny. Danny was well, he told her when she asked.

On the evening of his return to New York, he had contacted Nigel Greenwood. The Englishman had sounded frightened. He had hung up on Reuben.

The following day, he and Angelina had gone to her bank and to the safe deposit vault in order to recover the things they had locked away. Reuben had decided to take everything to Haiti.

Another round of turbulence, worse this time. Angelina glanced through the window. Out in the darkness a small green light flashed on the wingtip, the very extremity of flight. An hour ago, she had watched the sun set behind the Appalachians, green and purple, a monstrous sign. The sea moved far beneath them, rich with waves.

The 737 lurched again. A wild crackling attacked the intercom, then the pilot's voice came over clearly, announcing that he was taking them up to avoid an electric storm ahead. A stewardess asked everyone in French and English to return to their seats and fasten their belts. The pitch of the engine changed and there was a marked tilt as the little jet lifted.

Glancing round the cabin, Reuben felt conspicuous. He was almost the only white passenger on board. Two rows in front of him there sat an American couple in early middle age. Reuben wondered what their business was. Nobody went to Haiti for tourism now, and very few for trade. Duvalier and his Tontons Macoutes had done a lot in their day to dampen enthusiasm for the place, and the regimes since then – with a little help from AIDS – had only reinforced the general impression of abject poverty, danger and insecurity.

The plane levelled out. Angelina glanced through the window again. She felt a vague presentiment, an onset of darkness. The wingtip moved solidly through nothingness. Not far below, black thunderclouds flashed into view as lightning washed across their backs. There was no sound.

She was deeply conscious of her own mortality tonight, fine threads drawn taut, easily snapped, as thin as spiders' webs between weaving and dawn. Between her teeth and tongue, she could taste the moments; they glided like ice across the ridges of her inner mouth. Moments were all she had, all anybody had, the last as delicate as the first. Beneath her, clouds exploded silently in flames and returned to darkness. She felt flimsy and trembling, upheld by air. It was warm in the cabin. Haiti was down there, waiting.

'Why are you angry with me?' she asked.

Reuben looked round. She had hardly spoken until now.

'Angry?' he said. 'I'm not angry.'

'Yes,' she replied. 'You are angry. Is it the cocaine?'

He did not reply at first. Looking past her, through the dark window, he saw sheet lightning dapple fin and cloud.

'Not the cocaine,' he answered grudgingly. 'The deception. On top of Danny's death. My parents' deaths. Your silence, your games.'

'All that?' she said. The plane seemed for a moment to drop, weightless, uncontrolled, then it gathered strength and pulled the air around itself once more. Angelina breathed deeply. She was not afraid, but fear touched her edges, like a thin tickle in the throat that may become a cough in time.

'You think too highly of yourself,' she said, 'to feel my deceit so . . . intimately. We hardly know one another. You're nothing to me, just a man I've shared a bed with.'

She regretted the words once she had uttered them.

'I'm sorry. That sounded flippant. But you must understand: yours would be the least of my betrayals. The cocaine was there before you, I saw no reason for you to be involved.'

'I was involved.'

'But not because you slept with me. That was another involvement. You confuse things when you talk like this. I'm several people, you can't own all of me. Perhaps not any of me.'

'I don't want to own you. What good would that do?'

She watched the green light beckon. As far back as she could remember, she had been owned by men. Different currencies, different rates of exchange, but the same caresses, the same infidelities.

'Did you bring cocaine with you?' he asked.

She nodded.

'Sally gave me a quarter-kilo. Enough to keep me out of trouble. I don't have a big habit. Maybe I can sell some: we may need money.'

'I've got money.' The CSA was taking care of everything. 'Are you mainlining?'

She shook her head.

'Not regularly. Three, four times in the past month or so. I still snort. Reuben, I've only been using coke for eighteen months.'

'But you need it. You've got a need.'

She seemed ready to deny it, but in her hesitation recognized the truth.

'Yes,' she whispered. 'I'm not an addict, but I need it sometimes. This week I needed it. Rick, Filius, all of that. You.'

'Rick started you, didn't he?'

She nodded.

'It was one of his compensations, like clothes or perfume. Coke was the best, the nearest thing to sex.'

'I don't approve,' he said.

She looked out again. The storm was massing everywhere beneath them, like a city.

'No,' she whispered. 'I know. You thought I was exotic at first, a tropical fruit the gods had dropped in your unpolluted lap. Danny could have his blondes, but you had something better, you had me, a black widow who'd never been laid.'

He tried to look away, but she held him with her eyes.

'I opened my legs and you came crawling in and you thought I would be grateful . . .'

'Please, Angelina, let's not . . .'

'One early-morning screw and you thought you had it made. Then you found out I'm a dope fiend, the sort you read about in your Sunday paper, and you remembered all the times your momma warned you about us – the bad girls that nice boys don't date, the bad black girls Jewish boys shouldn't be seen with, and you knew in your heart of hearts that all you ever wanted was your precious Devorah . . .'

'Stop this, Angelina, stop it now. I don't want you talking about Devorah.'

'Why not? Is she some sort of saint? You never talked about her, you didn't even have photographs of her in your apartment. What was wrong? Was she so different from the rest of us?'

He lifted his hand as though to strike her, then let it fall. He could feel her anger, like an open flame close to him.

'No,' he said, his own anger falling away from him. 'She was just like the rest of us. Two days before the accident, I found out she was seeing somebody else.' He paused. Angelina was the first person he had ever told this to. Not even Danny had known. 'I let her drown,' he said. 'I didn't try to save her.'

CHAPTER FORTY-THREE

There was a sudden, heavy lurch. The plane seemed to tumble sideways. The lights flickered and went out. For what seemed an eternity, they swooped through darkness, finally levelling out in a buffeting of angry winds. The lights blinked twice then stayed on. There was a crackling as the Tannoy came to life. The pilot's voice came through again, less sharply this time.

'Ladies and gentlemen, I'm sorry to have to tell you that, owing to the bad weather we've been having, we are being forced to divert to Jacmel. Transport will be arranged from Jacmel to Port-au-Prince or, for those who prefer, there will be overnight accommodation. Our estimated time of arrival at Jacmel is 2100 hours. Since there may still be some rough weather up ahead, I would ask you all to remain seated and to keep your safety belts secured.'

It was dark and wet and driven with wind at Jacmel. The airport was deserted, unprepared for an incoming flight of any description, least of all an international one. Soon after the plane taxied to a halt, a military Jeep drew alongside, carrying four armed soldiers and an officer. The soldiers took up positions on the tarmac, faintly visible from the plane. The officer looked things over before returning to the terminal.

No-one was allowed to leave the plane, not even the aircrew. Two hundred yards away, in the small terminal building, a single yellow light was the only sign of life. It seemed impossibly remote. The storm had passed, and in the cabin it was growing uncomfortably hot. No-one complained. They had all been here before, if not in Jacmel itself, in a place very like it.

As the waiting lengthened, Angelina grew sleepy and unreachable. Reuben covered her with his jacket and left her in a light doze.

He wanted to go outside, out of the stifling cabin, into the waiting night. Inside the cabin, little pools of light illuminated groups of passengers, some chatting, some sitting passively. Most seemed nervous, landing so far away from the capital. Rumours of the behaviour of Jacmel customs officials were circulating, causing disquiet.

Passing along the aisle to stretch his legs, Reuben was hailed by the American man two rows along. He was a tall man with swept-back hair and a small ginger moustache, neatly trimmed. Aged maybe forty-five, conservatively dressed, bright-eyed and bushy-tailed. Not military, Reuben thought, not quite a businessman, certainly not a tourist. The broad, open face exuded something – not innocence exactly, certainly not naïveté. Desperation, perhaps.

'Hi! The name's Doug. Doug Hooper. This is my wife, Jean.'

Reuben glanced down at the tiny woman in the window seat. She'd been bought in a Woolworth's somewhere in the Midwest – downtown Kalamazoo or a shopping precinct outside Indianapolis. Doug had bought her with coupons probably, she'd been just what he wanted, and every day he kept her squeaky clean, almost as good as new. Reuben noticed that she was wearing a Holly Hobby dress; it had probably been part of a batch she'd bought in the early seventies. It was in great shape.

'Reu . . . Myron Phelps. Pleased to meet you.'

'Why don't you take a seat, Myron? Looks like we're going to be stuck in here for a little while.'

There was plenty of room: the flight had been half-empty. Reuben saw no escape. Reluctantly, he slipped in beside them.

'You with that lovely black woman back there?' Jean Hooper asked. She had big eyes and bunchy little eyebrows that went up and down independently when she talked. Her voice was startlingly pleasant.

'I . . . Oh, yes,' Reuben stammered. 'Sure, she's with me.'

'We couldn't help noticing you both together. You make such a handsome couple.' Doug's voice was coarser than his wife's, but he'd been working on it. 'She your wife?'

Reuben got some saliva moving in the back of his mouth. He shook his head.

'No,' he said. 'She's . . . a widow. Her husband died recently. He was a colleague of mine at LIU. We're travelling to Haiti together to finish up some of his work there.'

The Hoopers' faces moved simultaneously into what Reuben took to be their bereavement-counselling posture.

'I am so sorry to hear of your friend's death,' said Doug. 'You must tell his widow that we will pray for her. And her husband. Souls in the Abha Kingdom need our prayers for their progress.'

Reuben frowned.

'In the where?'

'The Abha Kingdom,' interposed Mrs Hooper. 'It's Arabic for the Most Glorious Kingdom, the realms beyond.'

Reuben took a deep breath. He should have guessed: missionaries. Military organization, business acumen and Holly Hobby dresses. And not even regular missionaries, but devotees of some obscure cult.

Reuben half-rose. Doug put a gentle hand on his arm.

'Don't worry, Myron. We're not trying to convert you. Our faith forbids proselytization. We just like to share the good news with everyone God sends our way. We're Baha'is, members of the Baha'i Faith.'

'Missionaries,' said Reuben. 'You're missionaries.'

They looked hurt, as though he had said the wrong thing. Doug pursed his lips a little and tried to smile; Jean performed a half-circle with her eyebrows.

'Not missionaries,' she said. 'We don't have missionaries in our faith, no more than we have clergy. Doug and I are pioneers. That's our name for those who leave their homes to bring the cause of God to other lands. Not missionaries, Myron: pioneers, just like the old settlers. There's a difference.'

Reuben nodded. He was sure there was. It was just that he couldn't see it.

'You've got some sort of centre here?'

Doug nodded.

'Been here some time. But it's hard for the native believers. They've got so little money, so little education. They need outside help, for a time at least. Jean taught high school back home, French and English; I had a little engineering company. We never had a call to pioneer before, but back in April we were visiting our temple in Wilmette, out near Chicago. That was when we got the call. I sold up, Jean packed her job in, and we bought a little shop in Port-au-Prince.'

Reuben looked at them, first one, then the other. They had that air of aggressive sanity only the professionally religious acquire.

'You bought a shop in Haiti?'

'Yep.' Doug laughed, a loud, nervous laugh that brought glances from round the cabin. 'Sounds crazy, doesn't it? Well, we don't care. It's our sacrifice.'

'What sort of shop?'

'A bookshop,' said Jean. 'We're going to sell a range of books – educational, religious, uplifting. Books on world peace, world unity, the brotherhood of man.'

'You believe in that, do you? The brotherhood of man?'

'Well, of course. It's the essence of our faith. The founder of our faith, Baha'u'llah, came to earth with the mission of unifying mankind. It won't happen all at once, but the day will come.'

'Do you have permission?'

'I'm sorry?'

'Permission to sell books? I've heard the government is . . . a little strict on the subject of publications.'

Doug Hooper frowned.

'No, sir, I don't think that will be a problem. We have nothing pornographic, nothing subversive. Just uplifting books on universal peace and world harmony. We have a friend in the government, General Valris. He was Minister of Culture until a few months back. We were in touch with him before he got moved into his present position. He's Minister of Defence now. Jean and I thought we'd have to make contact with the new Minister of Culture, but no, the general said "Come right ahead". He's enthusiastic. It seems ironic, doesn't it, a general helping the cause of peace? But nothing happens by accident in the cause of God. These people like the Baha'is, they know they can depend on us, on our loyalty. We are loyal to the government of any country we may live in.'

'Even dictatorships?'

Hooper gave Reuben a disapproving look.

'That's not for us to judge, sir. We don't involve ourselves in politics. Our mission is to bring unity, not to add to divisions.'

Reuben managed to stand.

'I wish you both luck,' he said. He paused. 'You do understand that there's no-one in Haiti who can help you if you get into any trouble? No embassy, not even a consulate. You'll be on your own.'

Jean Hooper smilingly shook her head.

'No, sir,' she whispered. 'Not alone. Baha'u'llah will be with us

237

every step of the way. He's with us in here now. He's all the embassy we'll ever need.'

'I'm glad to hear that,' replied Reuben. He was in the aisle now, moving away.

'Come and look us up,' Doug Hooper said. 'We'll be living behind the shop at first, just till we get settled in. It's in the rue des Casernes, not far from the National Palace. Just call in, you'll be very welcome.'

The intercom cleared its throat. All conversation ceased, as though someone had flicked a switch. A moment later, a stewardess's voice jabbered into life, distorted by interference.

'Mesdames et Messieurs. Ladies and Gentlemen, we have just received official confirmation that all passengers are to disembark at Jacmel. Coaches will be waiting to take you and your luggage to Port-au-Prince, where immigration and customs formalities may be completed. On disembarkation, all passengers are requested to surrender their passports pending transit to Port-au-Prince, where they will be returned for inspection. Will passengers holding non-Haitian passports please retain their entry cards?

'On behalf of Captain Forestal and his crew, I wish to thank you for having flown with us. We trust you have had an enjoyable journey and look forward to welcoming you aboard Haiti Air again very soon.'

In the silence that followed, somebody opened the door. Steps had been wheeled up to the fuselage. From outside, the sound of crickets came whirring close, a languid, empty sound. No-one seemed eager to leave the security of the plane.

CHAPTER FORTY-FOUR

Angelina sensed the mood of the other passengers as soon as Reuben wakened her.

'They're frightened,' she said.

'What about?' Reuben was busy lifting down his hand luggage from the rack.

'About being here in Jacmel, instead of Port-au-Prince. They feel out in the open, vulnerable.'

'Are we in any danger?'

She shrugged.

'*Qui sait?*'

Stepping through the open door and down the steps, Reuben felt exposed. Trying to smuggle a gun into Haiti had been considered and turned down as too risky. Jensen had promised to get one to him in a day or two through a contact known only by the codename Macandal, after an eighteenth-century slave leader. Until then Reuben would have to go unarmed. The political situation was volatile, the army and secret police had become a law unto themselves. Packing a gun might bring trouble; but trouble might come anyway.

He saw the Hoopers go ahead of him into the large wooden shed that served as the main terminal building, their self-confidence wrapping them round like a blanket. In a way he envied them.

There was an air of chaos in the terminal. Soldiers with guns stood at each entrance, casual but alert. At two trestle tables, a pair of corporals were collecting passports and shepherding people to different parts of the shed. People had started to argue, there was sporadic pushing and shoving.

Reuben sensed right away that the chaos was more apparent than real. On a small platform towards the top end of the shed, the officer who had come out to the plane was watching proceedings very carefully. He wore tight-fitting battle fatigues and a soft green beret complete with silver cap badge. Beside him stood a thin-faced man in civilian clothes, a beige suit and an open-necked white shirt. He wore black sunglasses. The shades were a cliché, the expression on the mouth beneath anything but. On the wall behind the pair hung a coloured lithograph of President Cicéron, dressed in military uniform. A large white fan turned languidly in the middle of the ceiling, slicing the heat like bacon.

They were separating people according to a system whose logic was not immediately obvious to Reuben. It was his turn to approach the table. The soldier said nothing, just reached out a hand for his passport. Reuben was on edge, hoping the CSA boffins had done their job properly; but the corporal barely glanced at the photograph. He added the passport to a small heap and nodded at Reuben. '*Là-bas!*' he said in French. 'Over there.' Reuben was expected to join a small group of people that included the Hoopers and three men who looked Hispanic, possibly Dominicans.

The corporal looked at Angelina, then at her US passport, then sharply back at her again. He snapped something in Creole and she murmured an indistinct reply. Wordlessly, he jerked his head back, despatching her to a different queue to the one in which Reuben was standing.

Reuben took a step forward. Angelina shook her head in warning. Reuben ignored her.

'*La femme de mon collègue,*' he protested, using schoolboy French. '*Avec moi.*' The soldier ignored him. Reuben went right up to the table and put a hand on the man's shoulder. A few feet away one of the armed soldiers drew back the bolt on his rifle and pointed it meaningfully at Reuben.

'Go back, Reuben,' said Angelina. 'I'll be all right.' She had used his real name consciously. The fictitious Myron Phelps, she thought, was fragile, he would force her to indiscretions. But calling him Reuben had solidified him for her. He was coming close; she thought she wanted him again.

Without warning, a commotion broke out nearby. The man in sunglasses caught sight of someone in the crowd. He whispered to the officer, then turned and pointed. There was no attempt to conceal the gesture. The officer nodded to two of his men. At that moment, the target – a young man in his late twenties wearing a blue T-shirt and jeans – saw that he had been spotted. He tried to break away, but was headed off by a second man in civilian clothes, carrying a small pistol. One of the soldiers moved in to help. The man struggled briefly, then slumped and let himself be dragged towards the little platform. A woman screamed and was held back forcibly by friends.

The man in sunglasses stepped down from the platform. He made no effort, showed no emotion. His hands were in his pockets, his eyes hidden. With an economical gesture, he motioned the soldier away. This was police business, he was in charge. Above him, in the ceiling, the fan moved sluggishly in a futile circle. The policeman looked his prisoner up and down. He asked a couple of questions but received no answers. The prisoner was agitated, he kept moving from foot to foot. People pretended not to see, made efforts not to look. A woman was crying. The queues were moving again.

A third policeman arrived from nowhere. He was older than the others and wore a blue suit and an old, battered cap.

'Tonton,' whispered Angelina. 'There are still some left.'

The second and third policemen held the prisoner hard by the arms. He did not strain against them. The man in sunglasses repeated his questions, or perhaps he had thought of new ones. His prisoner either would not or could not reply.

Sunglasses slipped a hand into his jacket pocket and removed it holding a small white object. A golf ball. He tossed it into the air three or four times, then made a fist round it. Calmly, he slammed the fist into the prisoner's solar plexus. The man tried to double up, but his captors held him hard, ready for the follow-up. The next punch was harder, much harder. The man choked. They held him firmly. The third punch ruptured something. There was a tearing sound and saliva flecked with blood appeared at the captive's mouth. Sunglasses drew back his fist for another swing.

At that moment, there was a shout. Reuben looked round and saw Doug Hooper striding towards the platform, all arms and legs and indignation.

'Jesus!' whispered Angelina. 'He'll get himself killed.'

Hooper had worked himself up. A soldier tried to stop him but was unceremoniously pushed out of the way. Moments later, the American was at the platform. The two assistant cops had let go of their quarry, who was on his knees, choking and gasping and spitting blood. Hooper put a hand on the man's shoulder and addressed himself to the policeman in sunglasses.

'Just who the hell do you think you are, mister?' he shouted.

'You can't just go punching up on people like that. I'm sure as hell going to report this when I get to the capital.'

The man in beige looked round, first at his assistants, then at the officer on the platform. They exchanged puzzled glances. Hooper took a step closer to the policeman.

'Hey, you,' he called. 'Look at me when I'm speaking to you, goddammit. I want your name and some sort of explanation. I'm a personal friend of General Valris.'

'Keep your nose out of things that don't concern you, *blanc*.'

Reuben looked round. Jean Hooper was standing about six feet away from him, praying intently.

'Is there any Remover of Difficulties save God,' she murmured. 'Say: Praised be God. He . . .'

'Mrs Hooper.' Reuben caught her shoulder. 'Mrs Hooper, I think you should go over there and bring your husband back before there's trouble. I don't think he knows what he's getting into.'

For a moment Jean Hooper seemed not to recognize Reuben. There was a blankness about her gaze that troubled him. Then her eyes changed and she was with him again.

'Don't worry, Mr Phelps. He's quite safe. You'll see.' She wasn't smug or overconfident or anything, Reuben decided; she was just plain unable to see the reality of what was happening. Or maybe the reality she saw was a different reality. It didn't make any difference, though: Doug Hooper was still going to get hurt.

It didn't take long. The man in sunglasses didn't lose his temper. Nobody lost his temper but the tall American. He stepped up close to the policeman and grabbed his lapel. The policeman clicked two fingers together. One of his assistants borrowed a rifle from a nearby soldier, stepped up to Hooper, and rammed the butt hard into his face. The American went down without a sound. His cheek had been opened to the bone and he was bleeding.

Jean Hooper fainted. Angelina ran across to her, unnoticed by the soldier at the table. The man in sunglasses looked round, caught sight of the little group, and strode across.

'*Vous êtes avec l'Américain?*'

Angelina got to her feet and explained.

'No, he was on the plane with us, that's all. This is his wife. They've never been in Haiti before, they don't understand yet.'

'Understand?'

'Respect. They don't have respect.'

The policeman nodded. Reuben noticed that he had bad teeth.

'Take him away,' sunglasses said, 'before he gets hurt. When he comes round, explain to him. Explain about respect.'

CHAPTER FORTY-FIVE

The coaches left five minutes later. 'Coaches' was a misnomer: all anyone could lay hands on at such short notice were two *tap-taps*, ancient trucks transformed by paint and tin and wooden panelling into a cross between a railway carriage and a vast communal taxi. Gaudy paintings and portentous slogans gave them a mad, fairground air. One bore the legend *'Celui qui dort dans la paresse se réveillera dans la misère'* all along the top edge. 'He who goes to sleep in idleness shall awaken in misery.'

In the rush, Reuben managed to keep Angelina with him. They helped Jean Hooper pull her husband on board and made room for him on one of the two wooden benches that ran down the sides of the *tap-tap*.

Hooper's wound was bleeding heavily, but there was no hope of proper attention before they reached Port-au-Prince. An elderly Haitian woman clucked round the unconscious man for several minutes, went away, and finally returned with some sort of poultice that she laid on the wound. Hooper moaned and struggled briefly, but did not recover consciousness. The woman explained to Angelina that she always travelled with a bag of herbs in case of illness. The poultice contained *cadavre gâté*, aloe vera, comfrey, borage, clubmoss, and several other items Angelina did not recognize. These would effectively staunch the bleeding until a doctor could put in sutures, but even the old woman admitted it was a makeshift job. Reuben hoped Hooper would stay out cold until then; but he thought it unlikely.

'He must see a *dokte feuilles* when he gets to Port-au-Prince,' she said, giving the name of a good man to Angelina. Angelina made a note of the name, but she knew Hooper would never go there. Like all missionaries, he was willing to give but unable to take. That would be his downfall.

Jean Hooper was strangely useless, as though the shock of the incident had wrecked something fragile and lonely in her, something her faith could not quite restore. Or something it did not even recognize. She sat on the bench beside her husband, near but not quite touching him, a small green-backed prayerbook in one hand, reading baroque invocations in a singsong voice that seemed oddly detached from both her and her surroundings.

Two soldiers were assigned to the coach, one to guard each end. Technically, the passengers were still in transit and had to be watched until they had completed immigration formalities. The soldiers seemed bored. They ignored the passengers and were in their turn ignored. On their laps they carried French F-11 carbines. The guns were only .22 rimfires, but in the confined space of a *tap-tap* they could make their presence felt.

The *tap-tap* was uncomfortable, but it made solid progress along the road north. For some reason the new highway direct to Léogane was closed, and they were forced to take the old river valley route via Trouin and Carrefour Fauché.

The darkness was not absolute. With the passage of the storm, a large moon had taken possession of the sky, its edges rimmed with gold. The road was a patchwork of mud and rain-filled potholes. No other traffic passed, no-one walked or rode in either direction. It was as though they had fallen off the edge of the world into an emptiness of rain and moonlight. The *tap-tap* bumped and ground its way along in first and second gear, its vestigial suspension useless against the jolts and shudderings of the road. Sometimes, when the *tap-tap* found an easy patch and the roar of the engine lightened, a humming of frogs and crickets drifted across the open fields.

Small hamlets stumbled past, mere clumps of thatched *cailles* clinging precariously to the sides of the little highway. Doors and windows were firmly closed. No-one came out to watch them pass. In Haiti, only the *sans poel* – members of the Bizango secret societies – and the police move at night.

They followed the stream bed as far as Trouin, fording its swollen waters again and again as they struggled along in low gear. At Trouin, the driver turned left at the church and began the slow descent to the northern coast. Behind them trundled the second *tap-tap*, carrying the remaining passengers. The whereabouts of the luggage was an impenetrable mystery. Most of the passengers had given their own up for lost.

The narrow road turned and twisted spasmodically, as though the dim headlights were carving it at every moment from the darkness. Once, a small cemetery appeared out of nowhere, low whitewashed tombs behind a crumpled hedge of *médicinier*. There was no glass in any of the windows, and a cool breeze swept through the coach, refreshing at first, then chilling. Out of the darkness, the perfume of night-scented flowers came to them, ironic and heavy.

At Carrefour Fauché they turned right onto the main peninsula road. It was nearing midnight. Somewhere between Fauché and Dufort, they lost the second *tap-tap*. Reuben remembered seeing its lights when they made the turn onto the wider road. Five minutes later, it was no longer there. Even on a long straight stretch it did not reappear. Reuben mentioned the disappearance to Angelina, who spoke in turn to one of the soldiers. He told her to shut up and sit down.

Doug Hooper was regaining consciousness. For a moment his eyes flickered open, and Reuben thought he saw in them a flash of cold anger. Then the pain washed over him and his eyes closed involuntarily. The *tap-tap* lurched heavily, throwing Hooper hard against the side. He let out a groan, wordless, distressed. His wife increased her efforts to invoke a reluctant God. The old woman rummaged in her bag and brought out a small blue bottle with a cork stopper. Taking Hooper's head in one arm, she contrived to open his mouth, unstopper the bottle, and administer a few drops of a dull brown liquid. Hooper spluttered once, then grew limp.

Angelina asked the woman what she had given Hooper. She merely shrugged and slipped the bottle back into her bag. Some remedies you don't talk about. But whatever it was, it had an immediate effect. Hooper was unconscious again in moments.

They went through Léogane. The road was better here, asphalted most of the way. A roadsign read 'Port-au-Prince 30 km'. They would be there soon. Nobody had told them whether they were being taken into the city or out to the airport. Probably the latter. No-one was going to get much sleep tonight.

The *tap-tap* had just crossed the first of the two bridges over the Monance River when the driver caught sight of a roadblock up ahead. Two police Jeeps were slewed across the road. A uniformed policeman stood in the middle of the highway swinging a red lamp from side to side. The *tap-tap* driver pulled on his brakes and came to a halt several feet from the first Jeep.

246

'What's going on?' he asked.

The policeman ignored him. The door of the nearest Jeep opened and a man stepped down. As he crossed the headlights, making for the front door of the *tap-tap*, Reuben caught a glimpse of his face, all-seeing eyes hidden by dark sunglasses. It was the secret policeman from the airport, the one who had ordered Doug Hooper to be struck. Obviously, the main Jacmel–Léogane road was not as impassable as they had been given to believe.

The man in the beige suit climbed into the *tap-tap*, followed by a younger policeman in uniform. The atmosphere was tense. At a signal from the constable, the driver shut off the engine. A massive silence filled the vehicle. In the distance an owl called twice.

The secret policeman looked slowly up and down the coach. His eyes did not rest on either Doug or Jean Hooper. It was as though he had forgotten that incident. Jean had fallen silent, mouthing her prayers – if they were prayers – behind tight lips. The policeman reached inside his beige jacket and drew out two small books, American passports. He opened first one, then the other.

'Phelps,' he said. 'Professor Myron Phelps and Madame Angelina Hammel.' He looked up. 'Will you please identify yourselves?' He spoke in English with an American accent.

The question was a formality: their photographs were in the passports. Reuben stood up.

'What do you want?'

'You will please accompany me.'

'Where to?'

The man said nothing in reply. He replaced the passports in his pocket, turned and went back down the steps. They could hear his feet on the blacktop as he walked back to the Jeep. Then a door slamming. Then silence. And finally the waiting night.

CHAPTER FORTY-SIX

They were driven at speed towards Port-au-Prince, the night thickening around them, a first whiff of pollution crowding the sea air. Their Jeep travelled in front, carrying them and the men in Tonton Macoute uniform from the airport. The man in beige followed in the second car, driven by the younger policeman.

Shortly after Thor, they turned off to the right, heading into the hills above the capital. Close to the city, the countryside was no longer deserted. Cars and *camionettes* blundered past them, honking loudly up and down precipitous hills. On the verges, mules piled high with sacks and bundles of firewood waddled in awkward convoys. Along one side of the road, all heading in the same direction, a crocodile of peasant women passed, their heads heavy with fruit and vegetables that would be on sale by dawn in the city's Marché de Fer. Everyone they passed, whether behind a wheel or on foot, pretended not to see them. A rusting sign read 'Pétionville'.

'I used to live near here,' Angelina whispered to Reuben. 'Up in the hills, away from the crowds, away from the dirt. It hadn't changed much when I last visited. The rich still have their villas and their clubs. The poor still live in Port-au-Prince.' As though in confirmation of her words, a shaft of bright moonlight plucked out a white villa perched above a rise, an elaborately twisted balcony facing the sea, a driveway choked with poinsettias, frangipani and flamboyants. In a high window framed with bougainvillea, a solitary light kept vigil behind pale shutters. Reuben glanced at Angelina as if seeing her for the first time.

Moments later, the Jeep swept noisily into an elegant, cypress-lined square. There was a small Catholic church on one corner. Facing it, the Hotel Choucoune was still alive with merrymakers. A handful of expensive cars sat on the gravel outside, guarded by a mournful-looking man in a battered cap. They passed the hotel and drew up alongside a smaller building whose function would have been evident even without the sign reading 'Garde d'Haïti' above the door. The second Jeep parked beside them and the man in beige stepped out.

They were ushered inside. The door led precipitately into a square lobby that narrowed at the rear into a long, empty corridor. Naked bulbs hung just above head height, each carving out a narrow jurisdiction. On several of them hung old fly-papers, thick with the bodies of dead insects. Dead flies, dead air, dead lives. On the walls were pinned rows of *affiches*, all bearing the texts of government declarations: Laws and bylaws, extracts from the penal code, *décrets, règlements, avis, ordonnances de police.* The black letters stuck to the posters like yet more flies. The edges of the *affiches* were brittle and curled.

A wooden chair and wooden table rested by one wall, under a photograph of President Cicéron. There had been other photographs on that spot before: the marks of vanished nails were still visible in the unrepaired plaster, like the stigmata of small, unnecessary crucifixions. Nearby, a slogan had been painted in bold letters, strong orange against pale blue: *Continuerons la révolution contre la tyrannie, le despotisme et le Duvalierisme.*

No-one sat at the table. No-one leaned against the wall. The entrance had a deserted, crumbling, expectant air. From somewhere nearby, a faint hum of machinery played lullabies to the night, unoiled, bitter, unappealing. The man in the beige suit directed them with a dirty fingernail to the corridor at the rear. As they entered it, the sound of the machine faded and was lost. No lullabies tonight.

Here, the mountain coolness that made Pétionville so popular with the rich and powerful became a rheumatic, clinging chilliness. Reuben had expected cries or screams, the clichés of a police state; but nothing untoward broke the silence. Nothing but the sound of their feet, echoing and hollow on the blistered concrete.

At the end of the corridor, a black metal staircase led up to the next floor. Where it debouched onto a small landing, they turned left down a side corridor that led with the inevitability of a dream to a single steel-rimmed door. The door bore no name, just a number: AP7. Beneath the number, earlier figures had been solicitously painted out. And beneath that?

The man in the beige suit knocked. Here, he was not king,

perhaps not even a prince. But he kept his sunglasses in place. A man needs his illusions. A voice called out, '*Entrez*', and they went in.

It was not, Reuben decided when he thought it over later, a remarkable room. All the harder, then, to understand why it so unsettled him. Perhaps he had carried with him from New York visions of blood-smeared walls. Perhaps he had expected bright lights and hunted faces shining with sweat. It was not like that at all. It was plain and quiet, a mundane room in a tree-lined suburb. The windows were shuttered, blank. The walls were salmon-pink, meticulously bare. In one corner a birdcage hung, white, rococo, carpeted with seeds. In its centre, on a wooden swing, a summer tanager perched, its rose-red plumage smooth and unruffled, its little black eyes, keen and sultry, watching them enter.

On a plain metal desk a simple reading lamp cast a soft glow on the features of the room's other inhabitant. He was a man of medium height, a mulatto, aged about forty, refined rather than good-looking, sad-eyed, heavy-lidded, spent. He wore a plain white linen shirt and a dark green tie of Chinese silk, perfectly knotted. Pressed under other circumstances to describe him, Reuben might have guessed his trade to be that of poet or musician. There was a wounded intensity about him, a fervour or a tentativeness that suggested inspiration or pain much internalized.

In his hand he held a fountain pen, poised above a sheet of paper. He had just been writing or was about to write. The indeterminacy seemed deliberate, part of a game he played, a gesture with no purpose other than to keep others guessing. There was nothing else on the desk, just the lamp and the sheet of paper. Reuben looked quickly round. The whole room was naked. A birdcage for ornament, a desk to write on, a chair on which to sit. And in one corner, a second chair, heavier than the first, bolted to the floor.

'Thank you, Captain Loubert,' said the man behind the desk. 'That's all for now. Leave the passports and go.'

The man in beige took the passports from his pocket and left them on the desk. The door closed behind him. The silence that remained was palpable, charged. For the first time all evening, Angelina seemed genuinely on edge.

'My apologies,' said the man behind the desk, speaking easily in barely accented English. 'They tell me you had a difficult flight, that your plane was diverted. And now you have been dragged here to see me, miles out of your way, through that terrible Haitian countryside.'

He stood and came out from behind the desk. His chair grated unpleasantly across the floor. In one hand he held the passports.

'How are you, Angelina?' he asked. He smiled, a broad, uninhibited smile, without depth. He moved towards her, but kept a little distance. Angelina remained silent, her eyes fixed on the floor.

'Why didn't you write? Why didn't you tell me you were coming? I could have met you at the airport, saved you a lot of trouble. You don't want trouble, do you?' He moved closer, put the palm of one hand against Angelina's cheek. She seemed upset by his nearness. Upset, but not afraid.

'There was no time,' she said. 'It was a last-minute decision.'

The man looked hard at her.

'Evidently,' he said. His hand dropped and he faced Reuben.

'I am sorry,' he said. 'I have not introduced myself. Major Bellegarde, Chief of Security for this *département*. My jurisdiction covers Port-au-Prince and the surrounding region. And you . . .' He glanced down at Reuben's passport. 'You are Professor Myron Phelps. A friend of Rick's.' Bellegarde held out his hand. Reuben took it. Then shook hands with a restrained formality that seemed out of place.

'I have the honour to be Angelina's brother,' Bellegarde continued. 'Rick's brother-in-law. I confess I never knew him well, but I am nevertheless distraught to hear of his death. And under such terrible circumstances. One hears such dreadful things of New York. Are they any nearer to finding his killer?'

Reuben shrugged.

'I couldn't say. I've heard that the police may be closing the case for lack of evidence.'

'But that is absurd!' Bellegarde regarded his sister intently. '*Ma pauvre* Angelina, a widow at such an early age. I grieve for you.'

The major turned abruptly and went back to his seat. He still had not apologized for the absence of chairs.

'What do you want with us, Max?' asked Angelina. She seemed little affected by his frivolous show of compassion.

'To see you, that is all. To satisfy my curiosity. To remind you that Haiti is not always . . . a safe place. *N'est-ce pas?*'

He spread the passports on the top of his desk, a little like a croupier preparing the table for a game of cards.

'You understand, do you not, that in the event of trouble, you cannot have diplomatic representation?'

'We are not expecting trouble,' Angelina said. It was a game in which no-one could speak the truth.

'Of course not. But trouble sometimes comes, whether one wants it or not. That is its nature.' He paused and pushed the passports towards the extremity of the desk, as though inviting them to come to him in order to collect them. 'You understand my function here? We are no longer Tontons Macoutes. We are the Bureau de la Sécurité Nationale. People are not afraid of us as they were of the Tontons. They come to us in moments of trouble. It is our duty to prevent trouble, trouble of any description. You do understand, don't you?'

'Is that why one of your men had an American citizen assaulted with a rifle butt at Jacmel airport this evening?' Reuben had been storing up anger about the incident, unable to vent it until now.

Bellegarde did not flinch.

'The incident has been noted. Mr Hooper will not be charged. But he must learn to be careful. I understand he has certain religious affiliations, that he is dedicated to a philosophy of obedience to the state. We expect great things of a man with such a philosophy. He in turn may have expectations here. But first he has to learn where such obedience begins.' Bellegarde paused. The tanager sang and fell silent. Its wings had grown weak with long captivity.

'And you, Professor,' the major continued. 'What is the purpose of your visit here? I take it that you have a purpose, that you are not here merely for a bout of nostalgia.'

'Myron is here to continue Rick's research,' said Angelina, a little too hastily.

'Yes, of course, Rick's research,' Bellegarde echoed. 'African influences on early Haitian culture.' He smiled deprecatingly. 'Our records are surprisingly complete. We throw nothing away. Not even from the old days.' He paused and turned his attention to Reuben.

'Forgive me, Professor, but is it not term-time? Shouldn't you be at – where is it? – Long Island University, dispensing lore and wisdom? The summer is the time for research, surely?'

'I'm on a sabbatical,' answered Reuben. Too glib, he thought. Too ready with the right reply.

'I see. Yes, of course, a sabbatical.'

'There are plans to publish Rick's last book, the one he was working on when he was killed. There may even be a *festschrift*, a memorial volume.' Reuben hurried on. He was being imprudent, spending all his explanations in one go, but the room impelled him, the charge in it, the nakedness. 'I decided to come here to tie up all the loose ends. Rick left plenty of leads.'

Bellegarde smiled. It seemed an honest enough smile, unforced.

'Leads. You talk like a policeman, Professor. You must find time to visit me, I'd like to chat about your leads. The dark continent, the new world, all of that. You will keep in touch, won't you?'

'Well, of course. Naturally.'

'No, it's not natural at all, Professor. It would be natural to avoid this place as much as possible. But I insist on our chats. *Nos petites causettes*. It is not the American way, I know, but I will force a certain intimacy on you. Angelina knows me very well, of course. She has no need of chats or intimacy, do you, Angelina?'

Angelina shook her head gently, pathetically.

'But you, Professor, I want to keep a fatherly eye on you. I want to be sure you are safe. Angelina too, of course. A brotherly eye. You would not credit it, but I have heard rumours of her death.' Bellegarde's eye caught Angelina's, a malicious capture. He did not smile. 'Unfounded rumours clearly: witness your presence here tonight. You are not a ghost, are you, Angelina? Or one of our notorious *zombis*? A *zombi cadavre* perhaps, or a *zombi astral*.' He hesitated. 'No, I don't think you are any of those. You seem as alive as ever to me. But rumours make me nervous. They are a sort of neurosis, a malady that threatens the very basis of society. Here in Haiti we take rumours very seriously. My job is their elimination.'

Bellegarde stood. He turned to face Reuben once more.

'Take my advice, Professor. Keep me informed of your activities. The climate at this time of year can be very unhealthy for foreigners.'

He took the passports from the desk and handed them to Reuben and Angelina.

'Here,' he said. 'You should keep these safe. Perhaps you would be better with a passport from one of the Bizango societies. That will allow you to walk freely by night, wherever you choose to go. The *sans poel* walk where they wish. But then you know all about Bizango.'

Neither Reuben nor Angelina said anything. In the cage, the tanager watched and listened.

253

'I do not know where you intend to stay for the duration of your visit, but I would appreciate it immensely if you would keep me notified. A telephone call will do: the phones are working very well these days. Our beloved president places a premium on efficiency. A new Haiti is emerging. You will see.

'For tonight, I recommend you stay at the Choucoune opposite. Mention my name: they will give you a preferential rate. Your luggage has been taken there already. Everything is in order.' He glanced meaningfully at Angelina. 'Nothing has been disturbed. You have my word for that.'

Reuben nodded.

'Thank you,' he mumbled. He felt foolish. Bellegarde seemed not even to notice him.

'Angelina,' said the major. 'I would like you to have something, a reminder of this reunion. Here.' He went to the cage and opened the door. The tanager flapped its wings and hopped along the bar. Bellegarde whistled and slipped his hand towards the little bird. He caught it expertly in a single motion. It scarcely fluttered as he took it. He held it out to Angelina. 'It's yours,' he said. 'The hotel will find a cage for you to keep it in. It has no name. You can call it anything you like.'

She took the bird from him, flinching slightly as it wriggled in her cupped hand. Bellegarde smiled and opened the door.

As they made to go, Reuben glanced down at the floor, where something had caught his eye. On the wooden floor, near the doorjamb, there were traces of blood. And beside the blood, like a tiny piece of ivory, a human tooth. Reuben looked up. Bellegarde took his hand and shook it. The light from the corridor fell across his body, casting a long shadow back across the floor, onto the second chair, the chair bolted to the floor.

The man in the beige suit was waiting to take them out again. He went ahead of them, back down the stairs, along the narrow corridor, into the sleeping lobby. Not a word passed between them. Outside, fairy lights were still shining on the hotel. It was like a passing ship, white and appalling in the night.

Angelina opened her hands. She had crushed the tiny bird to death. Its black eyes stared at her, seeing nothing. She dropped it quietly to the ground. The air was cold. She shivered as they walked to the hotel.

CHAPTER FORTY-SEVEN

Far below, the sea hummed and shimmered in a haze of morning heat. It was as if there had never been a storm, would never be a storm again. Far away, draped in mist and white cloud, the Île de la Gonâve marked the start of the deep waters of the western bay. Northward, beyond the Cul-de-Sac plain, green and blue mountains touched a copper sky. And beyond the mountains, yet more mountains, like an obsession, darkening as it gained in strength.

The taxi gave a jolt as it struck a pothole. A moment later and they were out of the sunshine, drumming in steep shadows past a row of tattered wooden houses, their gingerbread eaves and latticed shutters twisted and broken, their gaudy paintwork stained and peeling. The little Peugeot rounded a sharp bend, almost throwing off the cases precariously balanced on its roof-rack. It was nearly noon.

Angelina had been tempted to stay in Pétionville. She had felt herself cocooned in the hotel. Cocooned and seduced. Clean white sheets, cool air, crisp linen on her breakfast table, hot chocolate *à la française*. She had taken her time over breakfast, thinking of the insurance money that might soon be coming her way, of how many nights of clean sheets it would buy.

Then Reuben had come and punctured her idyll. He had spent a sleepless night, harried by queer dreams and little nightmares. Bellegarde knew everything, he had known before their arrival, he had been expecting them. Was it perfidy or chance or a simple comedy of errors? More than ever Reuben felt like a pawn in someone else's deadly game. Should he tell Angelina that he knew Bellegarde had been in New York, that brother and sister had met there?

'We have to leave,' he said. 'Bellegarde's on to us, he's stringing us along. The best thing we can do is keep out of his way.' He had come to her room after finishing breakfast in his. They were sitting outside on her balcony, looking down into the hotel courtyard.

'You can't do that,' she murmured, biting into a chocolate brioche.

'Why not?'

'You'll see,' she said. A thin line of melted chocolate trickled across her chin. She licked it away lazily.

'Why didn't you tell me about him? Why didn't you warn me?'

'What good would that have done? He was bound to learn of our arrival sooner or later. It was just a question of when.'

'You said . . . You implied your family had been pushed out of politics after your father, after his arrest. How come your brother is head of the secret police in Port-au-Prince?'

She shrugged.

'Oh, Maxeldwan is much more than that,' she said. 'He's not just Chef de Sécurité for the capital, you know. That's just his official title. Actually, Max runs the whole thing. He reports directly to the president.'

'You haven't answered my question.' Reuben was ill at ease. Her manner had changed again since coming here, during the ride to Pétionville. She seemed to be slipping back into something he could not define, a style, a mannerism . . .

'You forget that wheels come full circle here,' she said. 'Max didn't like life in the wilderness, he wanted influence, he regarded it as his birthright. So he changed his name to Bellegarde – my mother's name. Then he made the right friends and waited for Duvalier to go. Duvalier went, Max's friends found their destinies, and Max was given his own little fiefdom.'

With deft fingers she broke a croissant in half and spread butter and jam on it. Carefully, she poured herself another cup from the silver *chocolatière*.

'He knows who I am,' said Reuben.

'Oh, I don't think so. You're nobody. Max is not omniscient.'

'He knows I'm a policeman. He hinted at it. "You talk like a policeman, Professor," that's what he said.'

Angelina smiled, as though indulging him.

'But he's right. You do talk like a policeman. You are a policeman. Nothing sinister in his guessing.'

'Yes, Angelina, there is. Bellegarde knows something is going on. He knows I'm in this country under a false name, on a false passport. He could have me arrested for that alone.'

'That wouldn't be Max's way. He'd never act hastily. Softly, softly, catchee monkey, that's his method. He'll have us watched, see what we're up to. And now . . .' She laid her knife down. 'Suppose you tell me exactly what it is we're supposed to be doing here.'

Reuben looked at her, astonished.

'You mean you don't know? Didn't Sally fill you in? She told me you understood the dangers, that you'd volunteered to come with me, show me the ropes.'

Angelina nodded.

'She told me a little. But I was still half-drugged on Sunday. I'm only really coming round now. Sally told me she was working for the government, that you had agreed to work for them as well. She told me you're in trouble, that they've called off the investigation into Rick's murder, and that the only way for you to clear your name is to break into the group here. And she told me I'd be in greater danger if I stayed in New York. Well? Is any of that true?'

He explained in as much detail as he could. Angelina listened intently, watching the sun shift in the courtyard and tiny birds dart in and out of tall, elegant trees. When he finished she remained silent for a while, her face a mask. Sunlight touched her. His fingers grazed her hand and moved away again.

'Watch out for Max,' she said at last. 'He'll watch and wait and let you think you have a long, long rope. But in the end he'll hurt you. And kill you if it pleases him.'

Her chocolate had grown cold. Tiny crumbs lay on her lap like gold. She shivered and was silent for a very long time.

The slums were worse than anything Reuben had imagined. Angelina had insisted that the driver take them that way, she wanted Reuben to see, wanted him to get Haiti in perspective. This was what she had been brought up to avoid, what her brother Max worked so hard to perpetuate.

The first thing Reuben noticed was the heat, the second was the stench. People lived here like dogs, like vermin, in their own excrement, in a world of garbage, among open sewers, beside the rotting carcasses of dead animals. Their homes were cardboard boxes, plastic bags, pieces of beaten tin. They lasted a night, two nights, sometimes as much as a week, and then the rains came and hammered them, or a high wind rose out of the sea and blew them away, or fire broke out and burned them down. The shanty town was a thing of wind and air, constantly shifting, growing, falling, combining, recombining.

Last night's storm had wrought havoc. People scurried through mud and foul-smelling refuse, retrieving scraps of sacking, burlap and nylon, tin cans, broken sticks. Brooklyn was bad. Gibson Street was bad. But compared to this, life there was luxury. Reuben closed his window, shutting out the stench and the sounds. But he could not shut out the faces.

They drove on into the city, through narrow streets packed with cars and *tap-taps*, pack animals and two-wheeled carts pulled by wheezing men and narrow-chested boys, a frantic explosion of legs and wheels, where nothing mattered so much as getting through at speed. Reuben kept his eyes closed most of the way. Angelina directed the driver to a quiet street near the Catholic cathedral, just off the rue Bonne Foi. The street seemed to have no name. Angelina did not give it one.

They stopped outside a two-storey wooden house, painted bright pink with blue shutters. Worn steps led up to a glass-paned door. Angelina pulled a bell while Reuben waited at the foot of the steps with the luggage. People passed, staring uninhibitedly at him. A few children called out bravely, ''*allo, blanc!*' and ran away giggling. Footsteps sounded inside the house. A young girl in a white dress opened the door and peered out. Angelina whispered a few words to her and she disappeared.

Seconds later, the doorway was filled with a tumult of noise and colour. Angelina was swallowed up by a huge woman who seemed to be made of yard upon yard of bright printed cotton. The two women embraced, held one another at arm's length, and embraced again. And all at once Angelina was weeping uncontrollably, cradled in the other woman's vast bosom like a wounded child.

Still weeping, Angelina was led inside, leaving Reuben stranded at the foot of the steps. The door had been left wide open. He waited a minute longer, then just picked up the cases and carried them inside.

Angelina was not hard to find. She had been taken to the rear of the house, to a large kitchen redolent with herbs and spices, where she sat on a low, stiff-backed chair surrounded by the huge woman and a cluster of others, all of lesser bulk. Everyone ignored Reuben.

Bit by bit, Angelina's tears subsided. Someone brought a bottle of *clairin*, someone else started singing in a low voice. Finally,

Angelina glanced up and caught sight of Reuben standing awkwardly in the doorway, hot and ill at ease. She smiled and beckoned to him.

'Reuben, I'm sorry, I've been very rude. Let me introduce you.' She stood up and took the large woman's hand in hers.

'Reuben, this is Mama Vijina. Vijina is a *mambo*, what you would call a voodoo priestess. Rick and I always stayed here when we were in Haiti. She taught him what he knew about *vodoun*, introduced him to the *mystères*. I've just told her that he's dead. Vijina liked Rick. She was one of the few people who did. I think she understood him. Or something.'

Vijina was, Reuben guessed, in her mid-fifties, maybe a little older. Her body was a triumph of the flesh, hidden in a voluminous cotton robe printed with vibrant colours in an abstract pattern. On her head she wore a matching scarf, tied in the traditional manner. And between the two lay her face.

Reuben found himself unable to look away from her face, to disengage his eyes from her eyes. It was an ordinary face raised by some inner alchemy to another level. Or perhaps an extraordinary face toned down and made bearable for ordinary mortals. The more he looked, the less he understood. He sensed serenity and at the same moment anger; unbridled lust hand in hand with absolute purity; vision and blindness, pride and humility, age and infancy – a mass of contradictions and no contradiction at all. He looked away at last, as though he had been released, and caught Angelina's eye.

'You'll see,' she said. 'You'll see. Rick didn't understand at first either.'

Angelina turned and spoke quietly to Vijina in Creole. Reuben heard his name and once, he thought, that of Max Bellegarde. There were other introductions. No-one spoke English.

'This is Locadi,' said Angelina, pressing forward the young girl in white who had opened the door. She seemed about sixteen, pretty but shy. 'Locadi is a *hounsi*, one of Mama Vijina's novices. She'll look after us. I'm told she speaks a little French, she'll understand if you speak slowly.'

Half an hour later, food was brought: some fried plantain, red beans, aubergine, plenty of rice. During the meal, Reuben watched Angelina. Since arriving at Mama Vijina's she had undergone another transformation. The spoilt brat of Pétionville had vanished and been replaced by someone wholly at ease in these humbler surroundings. She ate with a tin spoon, sharing a plate with two other women, unselfconscious, unaffected, happy. Reuben wondered who she really was.

After the dishes had been cleared away, Angelina explained that she wanted time alone with Mama Vijina.

'What about you, Reuben? What would you like to do?'

'I think I should call on the Hoopers, see how Doug Hooper is. Is it very far? Maybe I can call a cab.'

Angelina smiled.

'This isn't New York. Vijina doesn't have a telephone. Locadi will take you. It isn't far. Don't worry, you'll be perfectly safe. It isn't Harlem out there. Being white won't put you in any danger.'

The mention of danger made Reuben frown.

'I'm not worried about the street. What about here? Does Bellegarde know about this place?'

'Max knows everywhere. There's no point in trying to hide from him. Forget about him. There are other people to worry about. And this is as safe as anywhere in Port-au-Prince. Trust me.'

Even as she spoke the words, she remembered when she had last heard them. Did Reuben remember too? Better not to think.

He turned to go. Locadi was waiting by the door.

'Reuben?'

He turned back. Angelina stepped up to him and kissed him gently on the cheek, near his mouth.

'Be careful,' she said. 'Whatever you do, don't get separated from Locadi.'

She turned away. Mama Vijina was waiting for her in another room.

CHAPTER FORTY-EIGHT

New York

Sally glanced at Emeric, then crossed to the desk and took out a bottle of bourbon and a glass. She drained the bottle and tossed it into the waste basket. They were back in the glass tower, on a different floor, hugged by low clouds that left thin trails of condensation on the tinted windows. It was like being in paradise, to be so high without wings. Except that paradise was somewhere else, Sally did not know where. All she knew was that it was not here, that this was an anteroom of hell.

'You should have told him,' she said. She did not face Emeric, could not bring herself to face him. She looked through the window at the clouds, at the skyscraper lights reflecting off the droplets of water that made them.

'I told him a great deal,' Emeric said. 'We both did.' He was standing at a bookshelf, sorting through papers. 'More than he had a right to know, more than either of them was entitled to know.'

' "Had a right"? "Entitled"? Jesus, you don't understand, do you? Who gives people rights? Who entitles them? Reuben Abrams *deserves* to be told everything there is to know about this operation. You can give him that right.'

'And just what do you think he ought to know? Beyond what we've told him already, that is.'

She took a sip of bourbon, changed her mind, and drank it all in a single swallow. It took a while for her to reply.

'That twelve out of fourteen agents we had working as a surveillance unit in Haiti were massacred last week. That there's going to be a *coup d'état* there any day now. And that they are likely to get caught up in the fighting. Caught up, arrested, tortured, and put to very messy deaths.'

261

'That's not necessarily true. If all goes well . . .'

'Fuck you, Emeric! Just how much chance do you think there is of that?' She paused. 'Did you tell Reuben about Bellegarde?'

'Only that he is Angelina Hammel's brother. That he is chief of the security police.'

Sally turned sharply to face him.

'Is that all? Didn't you think to tell him who Bellegarde really is? Who he believes he is?'

'I didn't think it would help Abrams to know. I didn't think it was that important. I still don't.'

'What about her, what about the woman?'

'What about her?'

'You know damn well what I mean. Does she know?'

Emeric shrugged.

'I expect so. Yes. I spoke to her. I think she understood.'

'You think?'

Emeric put down a pile of papers.

'Sally, this whole thing happened so quickly. If we'd taken time to ask questions, put both of them through a proper debriefing, whatever, the whole business would have been over before they even got to Haiti.'

'So you just sent Reuben into that . . . mess . . . without a clue as to why he's really there, without any backup . . .'

'He's got backup.'

'What? A couple of frightened agents who are doing what they can to get the fuck out of there before somebody slices their throats?'

'I'm going to get more people in. I'm taking people out of Cuba and the Dominican Republic.'

'Who know next to nothing about the situation in Haiti.'

Emeric played with his papers. He looked nervous.

'Some of them have been there before. Look, Sally, I don't like this any more than you do. I'd prefer not to use Abrams like this. But I don't have any choice. And from the look of things he doesn't have much choice either.'

Sally looked down on the clouds. She thought of the city hidden below, of the streets, of the tunnels beneath the streets. She thought of Reuben kissing her, on a Sunday afternoon in August, long ago, or so it seemed. She thought that she could jump out onto the clouds and that they would buoy her up for ever.

And she knew it was all an illusion. Emeric was right. None of

them had a choice. They had what anyone else had: they had their
pick of illusions.

CHAPTER FORTY-NINE

Hooper was in bed in a cramped room behind the shop, surrounded by cases of books stamped 'Baha'i Publishing Trust, Wilmette, Illinois'. The room was stuffy, malodorous, dimly lit. Hooper was propped up against a pair of dirty pillows. Blood had soaked through the bandage on his jaw. He had been given a shot of something, morphine probably, and told to rest. A prayer book lay on a chair beside the bed. Next to it sat a half-eaten portion of rice and beans on a tin plate.

Reuben had brought a bottle of *clairin*, genuine Barbancourt, the very best. Hooper refused it. Reuben shrugged: he should have guessed they'd be teetotal. Locadi shrugged as well and slipped the bottle into her bag: it would make a suitable offering for the *loa*. Her gods were not so particular nor so mean-spirited.

'I guess I stepped out of line last night,' said Hooper between gritted teeth. He could scarcely move his jaw, was lucky it had not been broken.

'What you did was stupid,' said Reuben. 'But I admired you for it. You'll convert me yet.'

Hooper shook his head. His eyes seemed melancholy, focused on middle America.

'It wasn't the Baha'i thing to do. Law and order come before personal conscience. I was interfering with the rule of law. Maybe that policeman was rough, but this is his country. I'll pray for him, of course. I'll pray for him and the man he hit, both of them. But I was out of line.'

'It was the Christian thing to do,' said Reuben. 'Most people don't have the courage to step in like that. Maybe it would be better if more of us did.'

'You a Christian?'

Reuben wondered what he was supposed to answer. The truth was simplest.

'No, a Jew. What's your position on Jews?'

'Oh, we love all religions. God has revealed himself in many ways, to many people. But you Jews keep missing out. You rejected Christ, then Muhammad, and now Baha'u'llah.'

Reuben said nothing. He looked round the dingy, windowless room, at the dirty walls. It was stifling. Someone had hung a piece of Arabic calligraphy high up above the bed. It was the only new thing.

'Not much of a place, is it?' Hooper said.

Reuben shook his head.

'Jean will have it spick and span in a couple of days. She's a marvel. Wait and see.' He leaned across the bed and fumbled on the floor, coming back up again with a box in his hand. He laid it on the bed and reached inside, drawing out a Hershey bar.

'Here,' he said, holding it out to Locadi. An American with a candy bar, an impoverished child: the old, simple equation.

Locadi hesitated, then smiled and took the chocolate, ramming it in beside the *clairin* in her bag.

Reuben cleared his throat.

'Is there anything I can get you? Food? Medicine?'

Hooper shook his head, wincing as he pulled a suture.

'No, thanks. The friends are looking after us. We have everything we need.'

'If you find you do want something or if . . . you do have trouble on account of this business at the airport, let me know. Locadi can leave the address with your wife.'

'Thank you. The doctor says I can get up tomorrow. Maybe we'll come and visit you.'

'Yes,' said Reuben, wondering how Mama Vijina would take a visit from missionaries. 'Yes, that would be nice.'

He spoke to Jean Hooper on the way out. She was in the shop arranging books, along with two Haitians and a third man whom she introduced as Sirus Amirzadeh, an Iranian. Amirzadeh was a pharmacist, he had supplied the drugs for Hooper.

A refugee from the Islamic Revolution, he had lost a brother and a cousin back in Iran, both executed. The faith had started in Iran, was a persecuted minority there. Reuben asked him why he had come to Haiti. He gave the same answer as the Hoopers: 'To be a pioneer. *Muhajir*, we say in Persian. Someone who leaves home for the sake of God.' He was aged about thirty, slim, middle-class, intelligent. He spoke good English. Reuben would not have taken him for a missionary.

'I was taken through a slum this morning,' Reuben said. 'Maybe you've seen it, it's south of the city, on the way to Carrefour.'

'Yes, I've seen it. There are several slums in Port-au-Prince. Haiti has the worst shanty towns in the western hemisphere.'

'What does your faith say about that? Will your being here make any difference to them?'

Amirzadeh shook his head. He had large, soulful eyes, eyes without ambiguity. Reuben could not look at them.

'There is very little we can do. We are a poor religion, not like your American evangelists. Whenever we can, we put some money into development, education. This shop is part of an educational project.'

Jean Hooper broke in.

'Giving people bread isn't getting to the real problems, you know. What they need is a new society, a new structure. If you're living in a house that's falling down, you don't try to patch it up, you go out and build a new one. That's why we're here, Sirus and Doug and myself. We're laying the foundations for a new order. One day there'll be a Baha'i state here, eventually there'll be a Baha'i world state. Then you'll see. The whole world under a single faith. All mankind as one. Justice everywhere, no poverty, no starvation. You must learn to take the long view, Professor Phelps.'

Her eyes were shining. Like the Iranian's, they lacked ambiguity, they were vehicles for certainty. Her vision of a perfect world was the only rapture she possessed; it sustained her, it would let her walk through slums without flinching. Reuben said nothing. He wanted to ask how these people could plan to build a state and claim not to be involved in politics. But it was beyond him. He said nothing and left.

In a doorway facing the shop a man in sunglasses was watching them, not trying to conceal his presence. Locadi craned her neck and whispered in Reuben's ear, 'Sécurité'. He nodded and they passed on. The man did not follow. So Max was keeping an eye on the Hoopers.

Whether it was tiredness or being in unfamiliar surroundings or the annoyance he still felt at Jean Hooper's vision, Reuben let himself be careless. The man in the doorway was not the only watcher in the street. Other eyes followed him as he walked back with Locadi, gazing up like any sightseer at the pink and white towers of the great cathedral.

CHAPTER FIFTY

Macandal made contact on Saturday morning, not in person but through an intermediary. He used a child, a boy sent to deliver bottles of *orgeat* to Mama Vijina from a shop on the rue Borgella. There was to be a *vodoun* gathering that evening, at Vijina's *houngfor* on the outskirts of the city. The *orgeat*, sweet and sticky, along with bowls of flour and eggs, would form part of an offering to Damballah. With the bottles came a message addressed to Reuben as Professor Phelps, asking him to meet Macandal that night, at the *houngfor*. The message did not refer to a gun, but it did hint at Macandal's having something Reuben would find useful.

'Am I invited?' Reuben asked Angelina. They were sitting alone on the seafront, watching small boats unload their goods: coffee from Jacmel, *vétiver* from Ducis, sisal and rubber from St Marc. Large sacks moved from the wharfside to waiting carts. Men sweated, grinning or frowning under their heavy loads. There was plenty of work to do. But no-one was getting rich.

'To the *houngfor*? Of course. You're an anthropologist, a student of *vodoun*, it's natural that you should go.'

'I won't know what to do, I'll be out of place.'

Angelina grinned and shook her head. The sea breeze caught her hair and lifted it gently. Behind them, the city was dimmed by a faint haze of pollution. Dockers shouted, throwing heavy crates and sacks ashore.

'Don't worry,' she said. 'I'll be with you. There are no formalities. You won't be expected to do anything, just watch. You can do that, can't you?'

'What about you? Will you watch? Or take part?'

She shrugged.

'That depends.'

'Depends on what?' A seagull whirled past, white and mocking.

'On the *loa*. You cannot make them come. You can invite them, cajole them, even bribe them; but in the end they come on their own terms.'

'Will Max's man bother to follow us there?'

He was alluding to the man in shades who had tailed them all the way from Mama Vijina's down to the docks and who was still there, watching from a distance, partly hidden behind a derrick.

'Yes,' she answered. 'They aren't as stupid as all that. Don't underestimate Max or the people who work for him. They aren't being clumsy: they want you to see them. Be careful tonight when you meet this Macandal. It's a good place to meet, but don't think there won't be eyes on you.'

Reuben looked out to sea, past the pollution of the harbour to the simplicity of the blue horizon. Over two hundred years ago, something had come here from beyond the ocean, something for which men were still prepared to kill. Now boats arrived with a different cargo: white and soft, but just as deadly.

'Let's go back,' he said. 'I feel as if I'm on vacation here. We came to do a job: I want to take a proper look at Rick's notes.'

Angelina stood. She looked around and saw what Reuben saw: a polluted city on the edge of a blue sea, squalor at the foot of soaring mountains, corruption in paradise. But this was only the surface. If there was time, she would peel back the covers and show him what lay underneath. She would begin tonight.

They spent the afternoon in Mama Vijina's tiny front parlour, reading Rick's notebook. It was a large volume of over three hundred pages. Rick had kept laborious notes of all his researches, with cross-references, bibliographical details and the texts of especially important passages. Throughout the book he had pasted or stapled news cuttings, photocopies and letters. It was comprehensive and it was dynamite. The further Reuben read, the better he understood the Order's anxiety to lay hands on it. The notebook contained names, addresses, positions, details of criminal acts committed by Order members, surmises as to the real extent of their influence in American society. If half of what Rick had discovered was true, Sally and her fellow agents from the CSA were fishing in shark-infested waters.

An entire section of the notebook was devoted to material on the slave trade. It had been through his research into the movement of human cargoes from Africa to the New World that Hammel had first traced the origins and spread of the Seventh Order. His notebook was filled with photocopies and original documents related to his search, above all his quest for the ship that had brought the cult from Tali-Niangara to the shores of Haiti.

Slowly, out of ancient paper and faded ink, a world began to take shape for Reuben. A barbaric, incomprehensible world whose boundaries were chains and fetters, hooks and branding irons. As Angelina read to him, translating the dry accounts and stiff letters of long-dead traders and sea-captains into the living accents of her voice, phantoms took on flesh.

Young men sold for a piece of Guingamp cotton or an *ancre* of spirits, women made captive for a handful of *rassades* or a *toque* of cowrie shells, children snatched from their parents for a cocked hat or a dash of cotton. Black bodies crammed like books on a shelf into the holds of tiny, airless ships. The long wait off glittering African coasts for the ships to be fully slaved, the wasted bodies tossed overboard, the smell of vinegar on sundrenched decks, the suicides, the 'bloody flux', scurvy, the land receding, the open sea, the long journey into slavery.

Above all else, it was the imagined sounds that made Reuben's flesh creep in the silence of Mama Vijina's house: the roaring of surf, the creaking of timbers, the riveting of irons, the rattling of chains, the cracking of sisal whips, the groans of the sick and the despairing, the wind in tattered sails, the sizzling of tallowed flesh beneath the brand, the snapping of brittle bones.

They found what they were looking for late that afternoon. Towards the back of the notebook, Rick had made a long entry in red ink under the heading: 'Haiti – Items to be checked in Archives.' The note consisted of a list of eighteenth-century newspapers published in St Domingue/Haiti: the official gazette, *Les Affiches Américaines*; the *Journal Général de Saint-Domingue*, *La Gazette du Jour*, the *Journal de Port-au-Prince*, *L'Aviseur du Sud* and *La Sentinelle du Peuple*. In the margin Rick had placed several exclamation marks. And he had underlined the entire entry twice.

By each title, he had written a series of dates ranging from May to September 1775. Underneath, in a series of circles, he had jotted down several names, each with a question mark: Nairac? Maniable? Castaing? Le Jeune?

The previous page of the notebook had contained an entry dated a few months earlier, immediately prior to Rick's departure for Africa. If he had been planning on an investigation in the archives at Port-au-Prince, he had not been able to carry it out. Reuben and Angelina would go to the archives first thing in the morning.

While they were reading, it had grown late. There was a quiet knock on the door and Locadi entered.

'It will soon be time to leave,' she said. 'The gods will be waiting at the *péristyle*.'

CHAPTER FIFTY-ONE

In darkness, night begins. The air had grown thick with drumbeats. They were calling the night, urging it to take possession. Those who feared the darkness barred their doors and windows. Others watched and listened, remembering.

The night was warm, but Reuben shivered as he stepped into the car, a small Peugeot he had hired that morning. Angelina climbed into the driver's seat, while four of Mama Vijina's friends crammed themselves impossibly into the rear. Even with the doors closed, they could hear the drums, hard, insistent, at the edges of the night.

They drove through startled, ugly streets, past cramped and huddled buildings, silences, fears, beggars in doorways, tattered flags, shutters that winked briefly and slammed shut as they passed. Angelina headed straight down to the rue du Quai, then north towards the airport. They passed the ro-ro terminal on their left, then Bowen airfield on the right, and headed out into the plain. The city flickered, stuttered, and finally faded away entirely. The darkness entered them. No-one spoke. They were already half-divine.

The road took them down avenues of mango trees, ripe fruit hanging at the ends of long green stems. Soon the trees gave way to dark fields of sugar cane, still and silent in the unmoving night. Here and there, houses appeared in their headlights, whitewashed like tombs, hunched beneath the shade of giant palms.

A side road took them down to the *péristyle*, the central building where most of the night's activities would take place. People had already gathered in large numbers. Some had arrived on foot, others by *camionette*, several by bicycle, a few by car. The benches were packed with men, women and children, dressed in their finest clothes, but behaving more as if they were at a picnic than a religious service. Some were smoking, some were drinking from bottles of *kola-champagne*, a few were sipping *clairin*.

At the centre of the *péristyle* rose a tall pole, a tree trunk trimmed and set upright in a circular concrete base. It was down this tree that the *loa* would descend, entering the lower world from the realm of the spirits. The base had been decorated with lively paintings: a Haitian flag, a black goat, a serpent, several crosses, a human skull. On it stood candles in iron holders, several bottles of rum and sundry offerings.

The Hoopers were there, near the door leading into the *bagui*, the inner sanctuary. Locadi had asked them and they had come ahead in a *camionette* with Mama Vijina. They looked awkward and out of place, most of all because they were trying so hard to act natural and be nice to everybody. Doug Hooper's cheek was no longer bandaged, but for two inches it was severely marked by a line of black sutures, surrounded by the yellow and purple of bruised flesh. Jean had put on her best frock, but beside the vivid colours of those worn by the women around her, it seemed tame and drab. Doug caught sight of Reuben as he and Angelina entered, smiling and waving as though relieved to see another white face.

They found seats near the entrance. Angelina was different tonight, her hair, her skin, her eyes had changed. She wore a bright red scarf and a matching dress. In the light of the flaming torches planted round the *péristyle*, she seemed to take fire. Men noticed her, some casting unequivocal glances in her direction. Several women caught sight of her and smiled, a few came across to hug and kiss her, reminding her of when they had last met. Reuben felt excluded. He looked round the *péristyle*, wondering which of the participants was Macandal. Maybe he had not yet arrived.

A heavy drum began to beat, the *ségond*, hunting for a rhythm, running, catching, halting for breath, starting up again. Then, tacking round it, the staccato flourishes of the *kata*, sharp and nervous. And finally the deep throbbing of the largest drum, like a rumbling from a deep pit. People shuffled in their seats, awaiting the start of the ceremony, but no-one sat up straight or adopted a pious expression. Someone laughed, a couple argued, a child cried out. People still came and went, some carrying plates of hot *grillot* or bottles of warm *kola* they had bought at a little stand outside.

Suddenly, the drums stopped. A door at the rear of the *péristyle* opened wide and Mama Vijina appeared, accompanied by half a dozen *hounsis* carrying flags and a man dressed in white with a red scarf tied round his neck.

Mama Vijina proceeded to the *poteau-mitan* and began to pour libations of rum and other spirits all around its base. Reuben felt a shiver of unfamiliarity pass along his spine. This was not the affable, simple woman in whose house he had spent the past two days. Her features, her bearing, her stature – all had changed. She was the room and the night, the music, the darkness, the flaming torches; all eyes were focused on her, she took them and drew them into herself, ready to discharge them when she became a steed for the gods to ride.

The *hounsis* formed a semicircle and began to sing, clapping their hands softly for the rhythm:

> *Legba! soleil te lève, Legba,*
> *Ouvri barrié pou mon, Legba*
> *Ouvri barrié pou toute moune you*
> *Mait' passé toute moune moin Bondye.*

Her libations completed, Mama Vijina started to greet her visitors. Those well known to her she would take by the hand, leading them out onto the floor before turning them in a single pirouette as a mark of honour. The Hoopers she ignored.

She came towards Reuben and Angelina, not a large, fat woman any longer, but a priestess privy to mysteries. To Reuben she merely nodded, in recognition of his presence and the fact that he was her guest; but Angelina she took by the hand and turned three times on the dusty floor, her eyes fixed on Angelina's, her head nodding again and again in approval or encouragement. Angelina seemed flustered and sat down in some confusion. Reuben noticed people looking at her.

The ceremony bent the night to shape. Mama Vijina stood near the *poteau-mitan*, setting a rhythm for the *'zepaules*, the first dance, purifying the air, purifying the bodies of those present for the coming theophany. All round the *péristyle*, people clapped and stamped their feet. The drums acquired a voice, rising, falling, speaking aloud. Mama Vijina began to sing, a song for Erzulie, a song for Sin Jak Majè, a song for Damballah-wèdo, bringing them down, drawing them in. The drums went out among the crowd, tearing away both thin and heavy veils from eyes and faces, revealing other eyes, other faces underneath.

The gods entered her one by one. She knew their personalities, their likes and dislikes, their voices and their gestures. The *hounsis* brought out the clothing and accoutrements for each in turn: Sin Jak's sword, his rum and Florida Water; Gèdè's hat and dark glasses; Erzulie's gold-edged veil of blue. And she put them on and danced, possessed, entranced. And as he watched, Reuben understood what he had seen that first day, when he had puzzled at the contradictions in Mama Vijina's face. At her side, the *hounsis* began to tremble as the *loa* entered them, twisting, jerking, staggering.

And now the mood was changing and the gods were moving to the edges of the crowd. Reuben looked round as a woman near him started to tremble, then stood up, swaying from side to side. She saluted Mama Vijina, who turned her in a triple pirouette, then continued dancing. A *hounsi* produced a live white chicken from somewhere and began to dance, holding the bird by its legs, swinging it round and round her head, wings flapping wildly, head twisting from side to side in a futile bid for freedom. Feathers tore loose and fluttered to the ground, the *hounsi* rose and fell, the chicken's struggles grew weaker and weaker. And suddenly she took its head in her hand and twisted, tearing the head away, scattering blood over her white dress. Wings jerked convulsively, feathers fell like snow, the young girl danced. It was Locadi.

Someone touched Reuben on the shoulder, then a voice whispered in his ear, 'Follow me.' He looked round in time to see a man walking away from him, someone dressed in a white T-shirt and jeans. The T-shirt bore a slogan printed in black: *I Ran the World*. Reuben turned to Angelina to say he had to leave, but she did not respond. Her eyes had glazed over and she was breathing heavily, sliding deeper and deeper into trance.

'Are you all right, Angelina?' Reuben bent over her, worried. He took her hands in his, trying to get her attention. A woman sitting next to Angelina frowned and pulled his hands away, shaking her head.

Throughout the *péristyle* men and women were entering various levels of trance, some still seated, others rising and dancing or acting out the parts of the gods who were riding them. Reuben reasoned that Angelina could come to no harm. These people knew what to do. And he had business to attend to.

The man in the T-shirt had gone. Reuben stood and went in the direction he had taken, towards the entrance. There was no-one in a white T-shirt near the door. He stepped outside. It took half a minute for his eyes to adjust to the darkness. He could see no-one. Behind him, the sound of drumming and singing seemed suddenly remote. He could hear frogs croaking. Above him, stars riddled a black sky, more stars than he had ever seen.

He walked away from the *péristyle*. In the darkness he could make out only shadows, trees and bushes, *médiciniers*, *mapous* and sharp *sabliers*.

There was a rustling in the bushes to his left, then a shadow, moving away quickly, a man running. Reuben shouted out, but the man had gone. He thought of running after him, but knew it would be a waste of time in the darkness. Instead he hurried towards the bushes.

Barely visible in the starlight, something white lay on the ground. Reuben ran over and knelt down. The man in the T-shirt and jeans was lying there, moving spasmodically. There was a sound like a balloon deflating. Then a harsh bubbling. Then nothing. The limbs convulsed once and stopped moving. Reuben leaned across, trying to see the man's face. His head was framed in a spreading pool of blood. Someone had opened his throat with a thin blade. The blood glistened dully in the starlight. Somewhere drums were beating.

CHAPTER FIFTY-TWO

Quickly, Reuben frisked the body of the man he thought to be Macandal. There was something under his T-shirt, a hard object taped round the waist. Reuben used his pocket-knife to cut away the tape. The object was a gun, an automatic pistol – presumably the weapon Jensen had promised in New York. With it, taped to Macandal's back, were several magazines. The CSA kept its promises. At a price.

Reuben stood, fumbling with the magazines, trying to slip them into his jacket pockets. They were heavy, they would make the jacket hang suspiciously. He had to assume that someone might be looking. There was little point in trying to find the killer. And even less point in drawing attention to himself by alerting people to his discovery. Let someone else find him in the morning, next week, next month.

Taking the body under the armpits, Reuben pulled him back further into the bushes, where he would be better hidden. He scuffed over his own footprints, knowing that he was obscuring the killer's at the same time. He sensed that it did not matter.

He headed back towards the *péristyle*. With luck, no-one would have missed him, or at best they would have assumed he had answered a call of nature. The drums were beating faster now, the singing was growing hoarse. He wondered what was happening to Angelina.

Someone was standing by the entrance. As he drew nearer, Reuben saw that it was Hooper. The American was looking flushed.

'I thought I saw you come out,' Hooper said. 'Thought I'd do the same. It's a little hot and smoky in there. Guess I'm still not feeling like I should.'

Reuben still had the gun in his hand. He reached behind his back and slipped it into the waistband of his trousers. But something told him Hooper had noticed. He wondered if the missionary had seen anything else.

'I'd heard about this stuff before we came out. Doesn't make a lot of sense to me, though the folks in there seem happy enough. I can see it's going to be an uphill struggle to make any headway here. They're a bit like children, don't you think?'

'Didn't seem that way to me. Most of them looked pretty grown-up.'

'You think so?'

'It's their way, Hooper. They've been Catholics for three hundred years. It hasn't made more than a superficial impression. This is their religion, they want to keep it. I can understand. It ties you to your past. They don't want something new.'

'We'll see.'

Hooper shifted uneasily. There was a heady smell in the air, a fragrance too exotic for his suburban nostrils. After the fumes and incense of the *péristyle* he felt subverted.

Reuben moved to go back inside. He didn't want to be away too long in case his absence was noted. Hooper put a hand on his arm, drawing him back. He put his face up close to Reuben's.

'You know these people, Professor. What do you think? Can they be trusted?'

Reuben shrugged. Just what was Hooper's game? His bruised cheek looked hot and diseased in the light that escaped from the wattled enclosure behind them. Their conversation was half-drowned by the throbbing of drums and the pounding of dancing feet.

'As much as anybody, I suppose? Why?'

Hooper hesitated. He had bad breath. Reuben remembered the half-finished meal of rice and beans.

'Well, I'll tell you,' he said, like someone with a guilty secret. 'Something's wrong. I'm not sure what I should do. I went to see General Valris this morning. Dapper little guy, a mulatto. They say he's rich, owns a couple of plantations and some factories. Well, I went to see him to talk about the shop. You recall I told you he was the one who asked us to come here, made a lot of noises about having an English-language bookshop in Port-au-Prince. Only this morning he didn't seem to remember any of that.

'I had to wait two hours before I could get in to see him. Didn't seem to me that he was busy, though. I think it was done just to get me on edge. I thought maybe he'd heard something about . . . About what happened when we got here, out at the airport. But that wasn't it.'

Reuben thought he could guess what was coming. You didn't have to be too bright to see it.

'We talked a bit about the shop, but he seemed like he'd lost interest. Kept looking out the window, fiddling with a cigar, hardly listening. After a while he just went quiet. So I went quiet too, and we just sat there looking at one another. Then he leaned forward, his big cigar in his hand, like he was going to confide in me or something, and he said – will you believe this? – he said "Your people have a lot of money, don't they?" – though it didn't sound like a question to me.'

Reuben nodded. What else had Hooper expected? A kiss on his wounded cheek?

'I see. What did you tell him?'

Hooper pulled himself up, his eyes freshly filled with outrage.

'What the hell do you think I told him? I said we were a poor religion, we didn't have money like some big sects he might be thinking of.'

'Don't you?'

'No, sir, we don't. Most of our followers are what I suppose you'd call Third World people. We had money in Iran at one time, but that all finished after Khomeini came to power.'

'A lot of sects have money. The televangelists pull in millions. Even after what happened to Jim Bakker, they still bring in millions.'

'That's what Valris said. Hell, I told him we're not an operation like that.'

'You have a lot of temples and some pretty fancy buildings in Israel. I've seen photographs. Your set-up didn't look too poor to me.'

'Take my word for it, Professor, we don't have money to spare. Anyway, that isn't the point. Even if we had, it wouldn't be available for the purposes Valris had in mind.'

'Which were?'

'Come on, you know. He was going to feather his own nest. He'd dream up some project, some educational project to launder it all through, but it would end up in his own bank account. He's up to something, he needs cash badly. He . . . He more or less threatened that if I didn't persuade my people to come up with the cash, we'd be finished here. All of us, not just Jean and myself. Do you think he could do that, have us thrown out?'

Reuben nodded.

'I'm sure he could. You and your wife, no problem. You'd be out on the next plane, he'd only have to sign a piece of paper. With Haitians he might not even have to bother with the formalities. Can you get the money?'

Hooper shook his head. Beads of sweat had formed on his forehead. He was having difficulty holding down his anger.

'No, I'm not even going to try. All we can do is pray. Or maybe you know someone with influence, someone we could talk to. I'm told your friend Mrs Hammel is sister to the chief of police. Is that true?'

Reuben nodded.

'Yes,' he said, 'it's true. But I don't think Angelina has much influence with her brother.'

'One of the friends here tells me they're very close.'

'He must be mistaken.'

'Professor, we have a lot to offer this country, we can help in plenty of ways. But not with cash. Please ask Mrs Hammel to speak to her brother at least.'

'I'll do what I can.'

'Please do, Professor. We need to stick together. I need you, but you might need me. We can help one another.'

'I don't understand. I don't need help.'

Hooper looked sideways at Reuben. His battered face came close.

'Perhaps you do, Professor. We all need help. Keep in touch – you know where to find me.'

Reuben left Hooper standing in the doorway and went inside.

Angelina was in the centre, dancing with Mama Vijina, her hair uncovered, her dress pulled back from her shoulders, the tops of her breasts visible, sweat on her skin, her body swaying. The dance was a grinding parody of sexual union, the movements heavy and sensual. Angelina's hips undulated in time with the rhythm of the drums, now slow, now fast. Reuben felt roused. He wanted her, needed her. Her image thrust all other images out, her swaying form held him transfixed.

And then he looked down at his hands. They were covered in blood. He looked up quickly, but no-one was watching him. His eyes fell on Angelina once more, and this time he felt disgusted by her, repelled by her movements, by the contortions of her face.

Turning, he rushed out of the *péristyle*. Hooper was still at the entrance, watching him. Reuben ignored him and went on past, heading down the lane to where the Peugeot was parked. The key was still in the ignition where Angelina had left it. He got in and turned the key round hard. The engine started right away.

The only drumming he could hear was the pounding of blood in his own head.

CHAPTER FIFTY-THREE

The banging on the door woke him abruptly from a troubled sleep. Mama Vijina's maid had let him in the night before, an old woman by the name of Dieudonne. Actually, 'maid' sounded a little grand: she was some sort of relative, a cousin or aunt, who had come to Port-au-Prince five years ago from Les Cayes and taken up residence with Mama Vijina in return for help around the house. She was arthritic and seldom attended *vodoun* ceremonies now except for some small gatherings held in the house itself, when neighbours came to bring their problems to Mama Vijina.

He had not slept at first on his return from the *houngfor* at Bois Moustique. On the road back he had lost his way several times and worked himself into something of a state by the time he made it to Mama Vijina's door. In bed, he had tossed and turned, trying in vain to free his mind of the scenes he had left behind: darkness and the flames of torches, the tight skins of drums pulsating, doors opening between one world and the next, Mama Vijina changing, Angelina lost in a dream dark drummers wove.

The knocking came again, louder now. No-one had returned from the ceremony yet, and he wondered if they planned to remain there all day. Angelina had spoken of ceremonies that went on for days at a time, sometimes even weeks. She had not expected this one to last long, though. They had made plans to visit the National Archives that morning.

More pounding, the sound of footsteps and Dieudonne's voice shouting, telling whoever it was to hold on. For a panicky moment he wondered if something had happened at the *houngfor*, then he remembered that it had. He looked at his hands. They were clean: he had stopped somewhere on the way back, at a small stream or a ditch, he could not remember, and washed the blood away.

Someone knocked at his door. Dieudonne, saying something he

did not understand. He threw back the sheets and rolled out of bed. He was still wearing his trousers, but nothing else. A moment later the door burst open and two men crowded into the room. Reuben looked up. He recognized the sunglasses and the beige suit.

Bellegarde stood with his back to the room, staring through his window. There was nothing outside but an empty courtyard, bare brick, cracked flagstones. But if he closed his eyes the courtyard would fill with memories. Lights would flare and feet crack across the concrete, a voice – his voice, Loubert's voice, a thousand voices – would ring out, shots would be fired, silence would come. And he would open his eyes and the courtyard would be empty and ringed with weeds and stained with blood where the rains had not washed it away.

He turned and looked carefully at Reuben. Things were moving faster than he had anticipated. He walked to his desk and sat.

'Please, Professor Phelps. Sit down.'

There was a chair this time, a plain metal affair with a plastic seat. Reuben did as Bellegarde asked him.

'You did not like the hotel after all?'

'I'm sorry?'

'The Choucoune. You and Angelina only spent one night there. I've heard it's comfortable. Angelina likes her comfort. As you must know.'

'It's too expensive. Sabbaticals don't pay for themselves. And Mama Vijina is a valuable resource.'

'A resource?' Bellegarde's eyebrows lifted. 'Ah, I understand. For your research. Of course. How is that going, your . . . research?'

Reuben shrugged.

'As expected. I've made a little discovery since my arrival. Nothing major, but it may lead to more.' He hesitated. 'Major, why have you brought me here? I'm sure you're a busy man, that you don't have time for chitchat.'

'But I told you, Professor, how much I looked forward to our little chats. Had you forgotten?'

'No, I hadn't forgotten. Why have you asked me here today?'

In reply, Bellegarde pushed a sheet of paper across the desk. Reuben looked at it. It was a photograph, black and white, five by four, a man's head and shoulders.

'Yes?'

'Have you ever seen this man before, Professor?'

Reuben shook his head.

'You're quite sure? Take a close look.'

Reuben looked.

'No,' he answered. 'Never.'

'Perhaps we all look alike to you, could that be it?'

'Don't insult me. No, I haven't seen this man before. Not as I remember.'

'Perhaps your memory is deceiving you. You were seen speaking to him last night, at Bois Moustique.'

Fear drained Reuben's heart.

'That's not possible,' he murmured. 'I spoke to no-one.'

Bellegarde raised his eyebrows again.

'Oh? You spoke a few words to him, or he to you, my man is not sure which, then you followed him outside.'

Reuben hesitated.

'I went outside, yes. To get some fresh air. That's perfectly correct. And on my way back I spoke for a while with Doug Hooper, the American missionary who came here on the same flight. But I saw no-one else.'

Bellegarde reached out and took the photograph. He replaced it in a small buff file, put the file into his drawer.

'That's a pity, Professor. Yes, a pity.'

'Why?'

'Oh, you might have been of some help to us. The man whose photograph I showed you was found dead earlier this morning in some bushes less than a hundred metres from the *péristyle* at Bois Moustique. You're still sure you didn't see him?'

Reuben shook his head.

'Positive.'

'My informant thinks you had blood on your hands when you came back into the *péristyle*.'

Reuben's hands were on the desk, he had put them there when he looked at the photograph. He glanced down, thinking perhaps there were still traces of blood, that dried pieces might have lodged beneath his nails. But they were clean. He must have washed hard last night.

'Blood? That's absurd. The only blood I saw last night was chicken's blood.'

'You did not ask how the victim was killed. I find that a little curious, especially in someone like yourself, a man whose life is devoted to questions, little questions like that. Most people ask, "How did he die?", something of that nature.'

'I'd rather not know. I'd rather not know how he died.'

'His throat was cut. Someone cut it with a sharp blade. We haven't found the weapon yet.'

'But surely this has nothing to do with you, you aren't Homicide.'

Bellegarde scratched his chin. Reuben noticed that he wore a fine aftershave, something with cloves.

'You seem to know a lot about my job, Professor. It's for me to decide what comes within my province, what does not.' He paused, tapping his fingers lightly on the desk. 'The dead man may have been a victim of a robbery. There had been something taped to his waist. Drugs possibly. Or a gun. Something he did not want other people to see him carrying. Do you have a gun, Professor?'

With a lurch of fear, Reuben remembered that he had placed the pistol in a drawer in his room. What if they searched it? Could they use it to tie him to the killing? Should he admit to having the gun, pretend he'd brought it with him into the country? He wasn't even sure what type of weapon it was, there hadn't been time to look properly last night.

'No, of course not. Why would I have a gun?'

'Or drugs. Perhaps you use drugs. A lot of Americans use drugs.'

Reuben felt hot. There was no air conditioning, not even a fan.

'Are you planning to plant some drugs on me? Is that it? So you can have an excuse to arrest me?'

Bellegarde did not react.

'Why should I want to do that, Professor? I have enough trouble already, enough arrests to make, enough interrogations to carry out. You flatter yourself if you imagine I would go to such lengths. This is not a police state. Here you are free. We do not like to fill our prisons.'

'What about now? Am I free? Free to leave?'

'Of course. Perhaps later you would like to make time to give a statement. About your movements last night, that's all. It'll take ten minutes, a quarter of an hour. This afternoon, say.'

Reuben nodded. He wanted to get out. His head was pounding, he felt sick. He glanced sideways, to the corner, to the chair screwed to the floor. Bellegarde noticed his glance but said nothing.

Reuben stood. He felt unsteady. Breakfast would help. He had not eaten. Food would restore his balance.

'Tell me, Professor, how was Angelina last night?'

284

'Angelina?'

'Did she dance? Did you see her?'

'I think she . . . Yes, I think she danced.'

'Who was she this time? The snake Damballah? The ferocious Ogoun-feraille? Or sexy Erzulie?'

Reuben felt a knot tighten in his stomach.

'I wouldn't know,' he whispered.

'No? I imagined you'd seen her often before. But perhaps she's more restrained when you're around. Perhaps the *loa* do not favour her so well in your presence.'

'What are you implying?'

'Nothing, Professor. Absolutely nothing. I'm only her brother. You're her husband's friend. You must know so much more than I.'

Reuben said nothing. He turned and went out, slamming the door. It was even hotter in the corridor.

CHAPTER FIFTY-FOUR

The gun was gone. Reuben checked as soon as he got back, throwing open the drawer into which he had tossed it the night before. It was gone, and all the ammunition with it. He wondered if they would wait until that afternoon, or whether Max would send some of his boys round to pull him in right away.

Angelina and the others had still not returned. There was no telephone at the *houngfor*, of course, no way of getting in touch short of driving out there.

At the bedroom window he looked out. Someone was down there, lounging in a doorway opposite, watching the house. He had to think hard. Who had killed Macandal? Had it been done to implicate him, or had the timing been fortuitous, a mere trick of fate? The killer had not been a robber, of course, otherwise he would have found and taken the gun. Or had Reuben disturbed him doing just that? It was possible, but instinct told Reuben it was highly unlikely.

In the minute or two that had passed between Macandal's making contact and Reuben's following him outside, someone had attacked the Haitian and cut his throat. That suggested that somebody had not wanted Macandal and Reuben to meet, to talk. Which in turn suggested that Macandal had been onto something – or someone.

Reuben went downstairs and asked Dieudonne to make him something to eat. He wondered if the Hoopers were back yet. Someone had told Bellegarde about the gun, he couldn't have guessed from the tape alone, it could have been holding almost anything. Reuben was sure Hooper had seen the gun. Hooper needed to ingratiate himself with someone in authority, needed to badly. Badly enough to shop a fellow American? Probably. Law and order came first in Hooper's book. Turning in probable criminals wouldn't cause a man like Hooper many sleepless nights.

Dieudonne brought him a plate of boiled green bananas with two eggs and a cup of coffee. He finished it quickly, without relish. Yes, he thought, he should pay Hooper a visit, try to talk to him, maybe even tell him something about working for the government, appeal to his famous sense of loyalty.

He set off on foot, trying to remember the way he had gone with Locadi. Walking on his own, he felt exposed. He knew he was being followed, but there was nothing he could do about it. Kids waylaid him, little kids with bare feet trying to sell him things he did not want or to offer their services as guides. Their older brothers offered him women, drugs, boys. He wondered why the sight of a white face should turn some people's minds to thoughts of vice. The answer was simple, of course. Whites had money, and without ready money vice doesn't really stand much chance.

He turned a corner and saw the shop half a block away. Something was going on – people were gathered outside, there were bits and pieces of furniture on the street. Maybe business was booming already.

Jean Hooper was standing outside with a group of Haitians and the Iranian, Amirzadeh. The shop looked as though a bomb had hit it. The windows had been smashed, the books scattered and torn, the cabinets and other fittings torn from the walls and thrown into the street.

Jean looked round as Reuben approached. Her eyes were red and puffy. She was covered in dust. One sleeve of her Holly Hobby dress was torn. She looked at Reuben for a few moments, then turned and got back to work.

Doug Hooper came out of the shop.

'It happened while we were away last night,' he said. 'We got back late, there was some trouble up at the voodoo place. It was like this when we got back. It's Valris's work, of course. You remember what I told you.'

'Are you going to pay him?'

'Got no money to pay him with.'

'Maybe he'll make some other kind of deal.'

'What sort of deal?'

'I don't know. Try him.'

Hooper looked round. He bent down and picked up a handful of pamphlets. On their covers were smiling faces, people of many races united in the cause of world peace. Someone had trampled on them, ground his heel into the faces.

'Maybe I will,' Hooper said.

'There's no point your opening this place again if you don't.'

'No, I suppose not. But first we'll pray about it. You'd be surprised what doors can open when you pray.'

Reuben turned to go, then remembered why he had come.

'You said there was trouble out at Bois Moustique. What sort of trouble?'

'Bois Moustique? Oh, you mean the voodoo temple. Seems some guy got himself murdered last night. Kinda spooky. I mean, you read about voodoo and ritual murders, and there you have somebody getting his throat cut. They found him in some bushes this morning. We spent the night there, couldn't get away. Looks like we'll have to buy ourselves a motor car. Anyway, the police came out, questioned most everybody. Of course, nobody had anything. They took your friend, the priestess, into custody. Your friend Mrs Hammel's OK, though. She stayed behind to clear things up, but she said she'd be back soon.'

'You tell them anything about me, about our conversation?'

Hooper looked flustered.

'You're not telling me you had something to do with what happened, are you?'

'No, but I think somebody told the police I had a gun. I think you saw me with one last night. Maybe you mentioned it to them.'

'Well, maybe I did. I'm sorry if that caused you any trouble. But I had to be honest. I had to tell them what I'd seen. I saw you go out, then come back in carrying a gun.'

'You tell them anything else?'

Hooper shook his head violently.

'Listen, Hooper, I have business here in Haiti, business that has nothing to do with you. I don't want you poking your nose in. If it's any reassurance, it's legitimate business.' He indicated the shop, the broken glass with his chin. 'Maybe this has taught you something. You can't trust anybody here, not unless you know them. Maybe not even then. Stick to what you know. Sell books, make converts, but let me get on with what I came here to do. Do you understand?'

Hooper nodded. He was red-faced, a little embarrassed, a little angry. Reuben suspected he had a temper. Well, he knew he had, he'd seen it at the airport. He wondered what Hooper would do about the raid on his shop. Pray? Confront Valris head on?

'I have to go,' said Reuben. 'If there's something I can do, I'll do it, but I can't make any promises.' He paused. 'I still think you should consider leaving.'

Hooper said nothing. Reuben shook hands with Amirzadeh and spoke briefly to Jean Hooper. She looked worried. As though she knew something nobody else knew. Reuben turned and walked away. His heel crunched hard on a sliver of broken glass, a piece of the Hoopers' shattered dream. He remembered bright shards of photographs littering his kitchen floor, memories like confetti, dreams like garbage. Looking round, he saw the tiny knot of people milling about the shop. Doug Hooper was watching him walk away. He looked like a man in a dream who sees everything around him disintegrating but finds to his horror that he cannot wake up.

Reuben understood exactly how he felt.

CHAPTER FIFTY-FIVE

Angelina returned just after noon with Mama Vijina and Locadi. The police had held the *mambo* for a while, but in the end they had found no charges to press. She was popular, her arrest would serve no useful purpose. Angelina was quiet and withdrawn, as though her exertions of the previous night had exhausted her, not physically but in spirit. The sexuality she had displayed in the dance was wholly absent now. It was as though she had slipped on her virgin's mask again.

After a brief rest, she went with Reuben to the police station in Pétionville, where he made a statement to a monosyllabic sergeant in a silent room on the ground floor. Outside, he told her about Macandal.

From Pétionville they went to the central post office in the Place d'Italie. With his contact murdered and his gun snatched, Reuben felt vulnerable. He put a call through to Sally. It was against instructions, but he needed to speak to someone. Sally was terse. He thought she sounded worried. She promised to make contact again. This time there would be no slip-ups. When? asked Reuben. Soon, she said. Very soon. Reuben hung up.

It was a short walk from the post office to the archives, at the rear of the Episcopalian cathedral. The building in which the archives were stored had suffered from neglect for many years. That any books or papers survived in it at all was a minor miracle. The door was locked when they arrived, but persistent questions led to the director's house a street away.

The director was a wizened little man with a palsied arm and loose-fitting dentures. His name was Minot, and he had been in charge of the archives for as long as anyone remembered. The government paid him a miserly stipend that had not altered in decades, and from here and there he scraped up enough funds to keep the little institution going. Nobody really cared. Here, history lay in the blood. The printed books and manuscript papers of the seventeenth and eighteenth centuries were the work of colonists: what did such things matter to the descendants of slaves?

Minot found the journals listed in Rick's notebook. They were all there, but several had survived in extremely poor condition. The director remembered a letter from Rick that he had received earlier that year, enquiring about several items, including the newspapers and journals.

Heaped together, the papers did not amount to very much. They were all weekly or monthly publications, none running to more than a dozen pages. But the print was dense, the language archaic and the references frequently obscure. They were hampered most of all by Reuben's lack of anything more than basic French. He did his best, scanning items in bold type for one of the names mentioned in the notebook. Three hours after they started, he was still trying.

It was Angelina who struck lucky. Her attention was drawn by the wording of a leading text, and the very first line of the article confirmed that her instinct had been correct. The piece ran to several columns in the *Supplément aux Affiches Américaines* for 30 July 1775. It was headed *'Mystère maritime près du Cap'* – 'Maritime Mystery near Cap Français':

'Gaston Maniable, capitaine des Cinq Cousines, *négrier fraîchement arrivé de Nantes en passant par la Côte Guinéenne, a maintenant présenté un rapport sur son voyage aux fonctionnaires du port du Cap, rapport qui contient le récit suivant . . .'*

' "Captain Gaston Maniable, master of the *Cinq Cousines*, a slaving vessel newly arrived from Nantes by way of the Guinea Coast, has now submitted a report of his journey to the harbour officials at Le Cap, in which the following account is included. We reproduce the captain's story here by reason of its extreme curiosity and as a salutary warning to those inclined to treat too indulgently negro slaves still fresh from barbarism and not yet submitted to the yoke of civilization." '

Shorn of its flourishes and digressions, Maniable's account made engrossing reading. Engrossing and disturbing.

'Mon brick, les Cinq Cousines, *bateau de 150 tonneaux équipé en mars dernier par les armateurs d'Havelooze de Nantes, a quitté Ouidah sur la Côte Guinéenne le 5 mai, après y être resté ancré trois bons mois, dans l'attente d'un contingent complet de noirs de l'intérieur de pays . . .'*

' "My ship, the *Cinq Cousines*, a brig of 150 tons fitted last March by the slaving house d'Havelooze of Nantes, left Ouidah on the Guinea Coast on the fifth of May, having lain at anchor there a good three months, awaiting a full consignment of blacks from the interior.

' "The crew consisted of six *officiers mariniers*: myself, a second captain, M. Nairac, a lieutenant, an ensign, a pilot and a surgeon; three *officiers non-mariniers*: a master, a bosun and a carpenter; seven *matelots*: five novices and two ship's-boys. All the events herein described were witnessed by some or all of these, above all by myself and the staff and petty officers, all reliable men with whom I have sailed before. Their personal testimonies have been appended to my own report.

' "From Africa, we made good headway by the westward currents to within not many miles of the Ascension Islands, at which point we turned north for the Antilles, keeping well clear of the Brazil coast out of dread of Portuguese pirates. It was our hope to make a rapid passage before the hurricane season should begin, our destination being St Domingue, for since the last war only English ships lie at Martinique and our other possessions.

' "In the middle part of July, we entered the Caribbean, and on the twentieth were near our destination, in the coastal waters a day's journey west of Le Cap.

' "At midday on the 20th, we took a reading on the sun, finding ourselves a little north of latitude 18°, with a tall landmass far away on the starboard beam that we took to be the island of Navassa. Ahead of us lay another ship, a small vessel, seemingly in the same current, yet making little headway. There was a strong wind out of the SE, forcing us to tack westwards, falling behind the strange ship. By nightfall, we were fast upon her, but she had no lights, wherefore we deemed it prudent to hold back until morning.

' "At first light, we saw her to be an English snow and thought it wise to demonstrate our peaceful intentions. Even then we thought it strange that neither the main topgallant nor the fore topsail had been fully rigged. I was brought up on deck to see for myself, reckoning that perhaps there had been an outbreak of fever on board or a rebellion of slaves and that they might be in need of help.

' "Using my glass, I thought it curious that no-one was on deck, nor was any lookout stationed. The snow's name was written clearly on her stern, the *Hallifax*, out of Liverpool. I had heard of her at Cabinda, and of her master, Captain Briggs. A good ship that had completed the triangle ten times or more." '

'The triangle?' Reuben interrupted.

'He means the full slaving journey: England to Africa, Africa to the West Indies, then back to England.'

'I see. Go on.'

' "We lowered our ebb anchor and set down the yawl with six men on board: M. Castaing, the ensign, with the bosun and the pilot rowing, and three *matelots*, all armed for fear there had been a rebellion and there were slaves still below decks. They boarded the *Hallifax* by means of a Jacob's ladder at the stern and set about to search the ship.

' "Half an hour later all returned, having been through the *Hallifax* from top to bottom and found no-one, alive or dead. I myself boarded the yawl and returned with them to the snow. We found all intact, as though both crew and slaves had been spirited away and might at any time return. There was still ample food in the hold and water for a month in the kegs. The log was on the captain's table, which I took, though I saw it was incomplete.

' "We attached a cable from the *Hallifax* to ourselves with the intention of towing it in to Cap Français, for we thought it must be worth much to its owners, being wholly sound and in every way seaworthy. I left three men on board her, to keep her rigged and steered. The wind had changed, blowing now out of the SW, giving us an easy passage towards St Domingue.

' "It was in the early hours of the following morning, the 22nd, that there came the first hurricane of the season. Seeing it was not possible to sail both ships, I brought off my men and slipped the cable. We made the Windward Passage without difficulty and came into port on the 23rd, safe though much battered. Of the fate of the *Hallifax* I know no more than this, save that I think it certain she sank without hands on the morning of the storm." '

Angelina finished reading. The paper lay on the table in front of them, a piece of history crumbling to dust. Now that they had a date, it was not difficult to identify references to the mystery of the *Hallifax* in other journals. There had been some sort of enquiry at Le Cap, copies of Maniable's report had been despatched to the authorities in Paris, they had communicated with their counterparts in England. The *Hallifax*, its crew and its cargo of slaves had been given up as lost.

'It was the *Hallifax*, wasn't it?' asked Angelina.

'I'm not sure,' said Reuben. 'Maniable's account doesn't square with what you've told me. The position, the direction the ship was moving in, the absence of any signs of a rebellion. We know there was an uprising, that the crew and some of the slaves were massacred. Nothing fits.'

'But the report has three of the names we were looking for. Maniable himself, his second-in-command, Nairac, and Castaing, the ensign.'

'Yes, there is that. But it may all mean something else.'

'Perhaps we're overlooking something. The answer may not be in these papers but elsewhere.'

Reuben thought hard. If what they were looking for had been available in public documents like these, surely it would have been unearthed and acted on well before now. There had to be other documents.

They found the director cleaning his teeth in a tiny office at the rear of the building. He slipped the teeth back into his mouth, smiled and said he would be more than happy to assist. Wheezing, he accompanied them back to their table. It was growing late, and the lights had already been switched on, but Minot was in no hurry. Researchers came so seldom to see his treasures.

When he finished reading, he sat immobile for a long time, his withered arm askew across the table top. Then, all at once, he gave a little smile.

'Nairac,' he whispered. 'Of course. Nairac. Please wait here, I will be back.'

He was gone a long time. When he returned he was covered in dust and cobwebs. In the crook of his good arm, he carried a tin box. He set it down ceremoniously on the table top and wiped a layer of dust from the lid. On a faded brown label they could just make out the name 'Nairac', written in a crabbed eighteenth-century hand.

Inside were bundles of papers – deeds, bills of lading, letters. Minot and Angelina started to read through everything while Reuben watched pessimistically. It was a wild goose chase, nothing more.

The letter was right at the bottom of the tin, as though it had been hidden there. Angelina knew it was what they had been looking for because of the signature: Gaston Maniable.

It was a piece of paper folded in three, with bits of broken sealing wax clinging to one side and an indecipherable address somewhere in France on one flap.

'It's dated 26 January 1776, and directed to an address in Cap Français,' said Angelina. 'It starts, "My Dear Nairac, your Letter finds me in bodily health at home with my beloved Wife and Children, but yet in deepening distress of Spirit. I am not like to embark on a fresh Voyage this Year, and have thought that I may not set to sea again in the Years that remain to me. You must do as you reckon needful of yourself and Madame Nairac. Those Matters whereof you know give me no quarter. I have not known a peaceful night since then, though I pray incessantly for it. My dear Wife knows nothing, though my condition gives her grave distress. I cannot tell her, for fear it would so taint her Life as to make it unliveable.

' "Our Secret must go to the grave with us. We have sworn an Oath and must stick by it. If any knew the Truth of what we saw on board the *Hallifax*, it would mean the end of all our work and more besides. No ships would sail again for Africa, no slaves would know a moment's safety in the Antilles. But more than that, for as you know, it would cause universal perturbation of mind.

' "I have a favour yet to ask of you, if you will do it. In my Journal, I have stuck by the story we concocted with the crew, as is set down in my official report of the Voyage. But the ship's Log had the true entry for the position of the *Hallifax*, on the Formigas Bank at longitude 75° 52' and latitude 18° 27', where we sank her and all that was aboard her, at 14 fathoms, as you will not need reminding. I have changed that entry to show her further North, nearer the Windward Passage, at 74° 54' and 19° 21'.

' "I have also altered the Daily Record, that it may seem we met the *Hallifax* and took her under tow on the eve of the storm that took us on the 22nd. If any should question my entries, will you stand by me and say I made some errors, being taken of a slight fever? It is unlikely any will ask, but M. Gradis, newly appointed by my employers to supervise the Books of Ships, has a reputation for the assiduous checking of Logs.

' "If you should be in Nantes again, you must visit us. Poor Doctor Le Jeune is at Sea once more, having taken ship on the *Cygogne* out of Le Havre, but I fear he is not the man you knew. He cannot erase from his mind the sight of the Savage seated at his dreadful Feast. And those other Matters of which you know.

We did right to send him to the bottom of the Sea; but he will not lie at rest there. None of them lie at rest.

' "Arnaud sends greetings, as does Castaing. All are firm in their oath. May God go with you. And may you find the peace that eludes me." '

CHAPTER FIFTY-SIX

They passed in a flurry of sunlight and spindrift into the central waters of the Gonâve Channel. The sea-swell deepened perceptibly, tossing their little boat ridiculously through the waves, like a child's toy. From a distance, the water had appeared seamless, an unchannelled expanse of expensive blue silk shot with gold. Close up, it was broken and choppy, raked by petulant currents and heavy tides. A thin black oil slick, the castoff of a gravel scow just in from Jérémie, lay glistening lazily in the hot sun, casting a net of rainbows miraculously across their path. When Reuben glanced back, it was black and inert, a dull, flat streak against uneasy waters.

On the sides of their boat, the name *Fanchette* could just be made out. Old paint, old lettering, an old romance: not even the current owner knew who Fanchette had been. It was a forty-foot Bertram offshore motorboat that had seen better days. The wooden hull was patched, the decks unpolished, the portholes in need of cleaning. Only an experienced eye would have seen that the *Fanchette* was, in fact, a lot more seaworthy than some of those shining fibreglass cruisers that spend their weekends off the coast of Florida.

The *Fanchette*'s skipper was Sven Lindström, a fifty-year-old Swede who had arrived in Port-au-Prince for two weeks in 1969 and never left. He had grown accustomed to sun and sea, cheap rum, and people who did not go into a terminal sulk for six months every year. Each Christmas he swore that it would be his last in Haiti, that he would go home to his wife and children in Norrköping, that he would celebrate the coming *jul* and the long, dark days after it in their company. If Lindström had a singularity that set him apart from other men, it was that he really thought they would still be there waiting.

As the Haitian tourist trade had declined, so too had Lindström. For years, he had made a reasonable living out of rich Americans and sun-starved Scandinavians who came to fish and snorkel off the fabled coast of Hispaniola. Now, he fished mainly for himself, and what he couldn't sell he ate or fed to Sam, the ship's cat. Sam was a half-starved, one-eyed tabby with worms, a foul temper and sharp claws. He was about two hundred years old, regularly sick, and predisposed to violent diarrhoea in the rare event of his drinking milk. Lindström had been given him ten years earlier by an American tourist called Samuel Harris Latimer III, who had found the cat scrounging for scraps on the docks at Les Cayes.

Sam hadn't been the only thing found scrounging on the quay. Two years earlier, Lindström himself had picked up a waif, an orphan he had discovered sleeping on board his rowing boat one morning. The boy had not known his precise age, nor his name, nor where he had come from. Lindström had called him August — without an 'e' — in honour of Strindberg ('*Streend-berry*' he pronounced the name emphatically) and made him his ship's-boy. August was about twelve or thirteen, illiterate, unwashable, surly, and utterly devoted to Lindström. Man and boy enjoyed a curious symbiosis, a deep sympathy of one waif for another.

Angelina had known the Swede in the old days, before either Sam or August, and pinned her hopes on his still being around. If anyone could find the wreck of the *Hallifax*, he could.

There wouldn't be much left, that was the trouble. Back in Sweden, they could haul ships out of the murky depths after centuries and all but refloat them. Here shipworms called teredos could riddle a wreck in five years, destroy it in twenty. The warm waters of the south are not kind to wood. Timbers rot, the best ships fall apart, the tides and currents scatter what remains across the ocean bed. They would be lucky if they found so much as a nail.

Reuben had learned to dive on three successive holidays at Eilat on the Red Sea, starting when he was fourteen. Since then he had dived only a few times, always in safe waters.

He still remembered striking out to sea on his first visit to Eilat and staring across copper waves towards Aqaba, white and trembling on the coast of Jordan. So very near, so very far. He had dived, and all at once geography and history had both been wiped away: pink coral crept in all directions, fish swam past invisible lines of border and nation. Ever since, he had felt a sense of panic in open waters, a fear that he might drown and dissolve in waves that were more and less than water.

Devorah's death had introduced a harsh new element into his fear of deep water. The thought of what might lie ahead chilled him to the bone. The drowned do not lie at peace. Maniable had known it; and Reuben knew it too.

They carried an air compressor to keep their tanks filled, but Lindström had insisted on taking extra tanks as well: he'd known the compressor to break down in the middle of an expedition, forcing a return to port. With only two divers, and one of those fairly inexperienced, there would be a severe limit on the amount of time they could spend underwater, especially if they had to go down to any great depth.

But first they had to find a wreck or something that might have been a wreck. Lindström did not have the most sophisticated equipment, but he'd managed to cadge a proton magnetometer off a Haitian friend who still hunted for wrecks from time to time in the hope that one of them would yield up more than barnacles and interesting coral shapes. Once upon a time, pirates and treasure galleons had sailed these shores. A man could find a fortune in pieces of eight if only he knew where to look.

They were well past the Île de la Gonâve now, open sea to starboard, the padded coast of the long southern peninsula vivid on their port side, its green flanks punctuated by the flashing light on Grande Cayemite Island. Beyond the light, they could make out the higher peaks of the La Hotte Mountains, dark blue against a clear sky. Over the land, banks of white cumulus were stacked like dreams.

August was below stacking and filling air tanks. Angelina had gone up front. Sam was perched on top of the cabin, washing his paws and dreaming of coloured fish in coral lagoons. Lindström was at the wheel, Reuben beside him watching the radar.

If they kept to a steady fifteen knots, it would take about fifteen hours to reach the Formigas Bank, over two hundred miles away. Maniable had been precise about the spot where the *Hallifax* had been sunk, but Lindström had warned them not to put too much faith in his figures.

'What you got to understand is navigationals. Now is easy, now you got radio time signals, now you got Loran, now you got Vecta RDFs. Is easy, no? What they had then was bugger all. Quadrant, log line, half-minute glass, made plenty mistakes. Could be a minute out, could be ten minutes, could be more. *Jag vet inte*. Then is the weather.'

'The what?'

'Weather. Winds, stormings, this fucking hurricane Maniable is talking about. Tide, currents. Is always moving underneath, is always some frenzy. Round the Formigas you always got a heavy swell, strong breezes. A big storm can move some wrecks half a mile maybe. How many storms we got round here? Gales a lot. Hurricane maybe once, twice a year. Two hundred years, could be anywhere by now. Might not be on the bank, might have been shoved off the cliff, gone to the bottom, where we never find it.'

'What you're saying is you think we're wasting our time.'

Lindström pushed back his old peaked cap and scratched his head. He looked parched and leathery, like an Iron-Age prince dredged out of a Scandinavian bog. His fair hair had been bleached entirely white long ago.

'*Ne-e-e-j*, I don't say that. Not wasting. Could take time, is all. Could take years, I don't mind. You got enough money, we be big friends in our old age.'

Reuben sighed and looked at the sea. Maybe Lindström wasn't such a good idea after all. The Swede had nothing better to do than sail around all day soaking up the sun while pretending to look for a wreck that might not even be there. He could keep himself in *clairin* and fried chicken for months at this rate. He could keep Sam in lobster thermidor. The one good thing was that they didn't have years. They didn't have months. They didn't even have weeks.

Angelina was standing in the prow, staring out to sea. The gaudy waters entranced her, the sunlight on them in spasms, blatant, gilding an immensity of green-capped darknesses.

'*Vot you got to onderstond is navigationals*,' said Reuben in a heavy accent, mocking Lindström. The Swedish chef from the Muppets.

Angelina laughed and turned.

'Navigationals?'

'*Ond vedder. Stormings, fooking hurricanes.*'

She smiled and returned her gaze to the sea.

'His Creole's not much better,' she said.

'Can we trust him? He could be onto a good thing, sailing us around in circles out here for the next six months.'

'We aren't helpless,' she said. 'We can check his readings. I know how to use a magnetometer. My brother used to take me in his boat. When I was about fifteen.'

'Who, Max?'

She nodded.

'We never found anything; no wrecks, I mean. But there were some small discoveries. A cannon, an anchor, bits of chain. The sea round here is littered with objects, if you know where to look.'

'But no sunken treasure.'

'Oh, yes. We didn't find any, but it's out there, plenty of it. Spanish galleons, English buccaneers, French slavers returning home with booty from the colonies. It's there all right.'

'But we aren't looking for treasure, are we?'

She shook her head slowly.

He looked at her, unable to connect this calmness with the possession of two nights ago.

As though she read his mind, she half-turned. Her eyes were sad.

'You still disapprove, don't you?' she said. 'Of what you saw at Bois Moustique.'

'I . . . don't know. Most of it I didn't understand.'

'You left when you saw me dancing. They told me afterwards.'

'Macandal . . .'

'It had nothing to do with that. You still disapprove. You think I'm an addict, a slut, God knows what.'

'It seemed . . .'

'You thought it was an orgy, didn't you? That we'd be copulating in some sort of jungle frenzy, all our inhibitions torn away.'

'I'd heard . . .'

'You'd heard about voodoo, about sacrificing the two-legged goat, about scenes of sexual abandon, black bodies writhing in the throes of lust.' She paused and watched the long waves strike the bow. 'You're full of shit.'

'Angelina, you're putting words into my mouth.'

'What, then? What did you think? You didn't stay to watch, did you?'

'You were . . . You and Mama Vijina . . . Like a couple making love.'

'It aroused you, is that it? You'd have preferred it if you'd been on the floor with me. Listen, Reuben, you've got a lot to learn. That wasn't an orgy, it was a religious ceremony. If anybody gets out of line, goes too far, tries to take their clothes off, whatever . . . if they do that, the *laplace* takes them out of the *péristyle* till they cool down. The gods do strange things. They take our bodies, they borrow our emotions, they ride us like horses. Sometimes it's very dark inside, sometimes your whole life is dark, and then the *loa* come and light you up, you shine, there are stars and suns and forks of lightning all through your body. I can't explain, I can only tell you how I feel.'

She paused. The sea moved beneath her, aghast with its own energy.

'Sometimes there's anger, sometimes happiness, other times you feel you want to strut about and smoke a big cigar and laugh in people's faces. That's Sin Jak. And sometimes lust. There's nothing wrong in that, it's how people feel sometimes when they're being honest. Nothing happens, there's a morality. It's just . . . In the dance, feelings come to the surface, things you bury. You don't have to approve, I don't ask for your approval. But I'd like us to be friends. I'd like you to trust me.'

The boat was dipping and rising heavily now, the sea was all around them, the shore was slipping away, they were surrounded by water. Reuben looked over the side. It would be so easy to vanish here, to drop over the edge and into the waves, let the sea solve everything.

'I was brought up to deny all that,' said Angelina. 'We are civilized, French, as good as white, there was more France than Africa in our blood. When I was fifteen, I used to sit in a narrow room painted with white lilies reading Huysmans and Rimbaud and Gérard de Nerval. Can you imagine that, the pretentiousness of that? On pale evenings in summer, when the sun came down close to the sea and the boats lay scattered in the bay like fantasies, I would stand on my balcony, reciting poetry until the darkness silenced me. *Je suis le ténébreux – le veuf – l'inconsolé, Le prince d'Aquitaine à la tour abolie . . .*'

She paused and watched the water turn to spray.

'I was a spoilt, pretentious child,' she whispered. 'Without lust. I had such a darkness inside me, such a fierce darkness.'

'What happened?'

'I learned to dance. I went with Max once to watch our savage neighbours, to feel superior, to feel the power of my darkness against their light. And instead I lost myself, I became a puppet for the *mystères*. Lust came later.'

'With Richard?'

She looked at him quickly, then away again.

'Oh, yes,' she whispered, 'Richard.' She pronounced the name as though it were French, *Ree-shar*, in a mocking, testing tone.

'Richard came and touched me.' She hesitated. 'But I didn't feel any lust. He touched me here . . .' Her hand grazed her breasts, tenderly. 'And here . . .' Her hand moved lightly between her legs. Tears lay on her cheeks, or was it sea spray? 'But I didn't feel any lust. You don't have lust, your civilization has abolished it. Even my father, even he abolished it.'

'Your father?'

'You didn't know? Didn't I tell you?' But she was mocking him now, she knew she had not told him. 'My father touched me long before Rick, he was the first, the forerunner. But there was no lust, no fire. His hands were cold, he was an old man, he was civilized even in that.'

And Reuben heard her, saw her hands move, saw the sea spray on her cheeks, in her eyes; but in his folly, in his Jewishness, in his preoccupation with what was wholesome, in his dream of a different angst, more speakable, less private, in his darkness without lust, he did not believe her. With Devorah, it had never been like that.

Behind them, a voice called out.

'Is time for your trick at the wheel, Professor!'

And Angelina turned and wiped her eyes and smiled at her foolishness.

CHAPTER FIFTY-SEVEN

The Formigas Bank is really the top of an underwater mountain, thirty-four miles off the north-east tip of Jamaica. On average, it lies between four and eight fathoms deep, somewhere from twenty-four to forty-eight feet. At its edges, it drops away sharply into deeper waters, as much as three and a half thousand feet at one spot. Less than ten miles out and the depth grows to over seven and a half thousand. The bank is a reverse L-shape, with a leg thirteen miles long and an average of four miles wide, at whose southern end is a foot ten miles in length. It lies under more than fifty square miles of ocean. It is tiny when compared with the Pedro and some other banks; but you could sink a fleet of small ships on it and have trouble finding them again.

After three days, Reuben was beginning to think Lindström might be right: even if the *Hallifax* had gone down here, it must have slipped off the edge long ago. Using a combination of magnetometer and Wesmar scanning sonar, the *Fanchette* swept back and forwards along the bank, surveying the sea bed along a grid roughly marked out by Lindström. Each strip they covered was two hundred yards wide and thirteen miles long, and it took them about an hour to go from one end to the next. They were now almost finished with their first sweep, maybe their only sweep of the bank. So far, they had dived three times, all short descents. They had found two discarded oil drums, a propeller, a pirate's hoard of tin cans and a modern wreck already listed on the charts. Reuben had learned more about diving in those brief expeditions with Lindström than at any time before. But the fear had not left him.

The sonar showed the sea bed in a 360 degree circle round the *Fanchette*. It was more useful than a simple CRT depth sounder, which only showed what was happening immediately underneath the hull. It could locate a wreck, but not if it was as old and broken up as the one they were looking for. With luck it might show up an irregularity that would turn out to be a cannon or a scattering of ballast stones. But its main use was to prevent them running into unexpected obstructions. These were not well-charted waters.

Their chief hope lay in the magnetometer, a device designed to give a reading for any ferrous metal object on or near the sea bed. Even wooden ships carried plenty of metal: cannons, chains, gratings, swords and, of course, bullion. The latter was highly unlikely in the case of a slaver, but there would be chains and manacles in abundance.

Every so often, Lindström would set his autopilot to steer down one side of a square course, then come back to help either Reuben or Angelina make sense of the magnetometer and sonar. August sat up in the prow smoking or staring at the sea, moving only from time to time to prepare cups of coffee or meals. Sam prowled the deck or lay on the engine housing, gazing wistfully at the occasional passing seabird.

After the first day, nobody talked very much. The world in which they moved was silent to the core. If they looked hard, they could make out the peaks of the Blue Mountains to the south-west, but most of the time they were out of sight of land. There were no lights. They saw no other ships. In the nights, when they anchored, they would watch the last flecks of the setting sun turn to darkness, and it seemed as though they had slipped off the face of the earth.

'I'm sorry,' said Angelina. It was past noon. They had just eaten and were holding fast on the sea anchor for a while. 'I was unfair. You have no reason to make allowances for my hang-ups. I'm still spoilt and pretentious. You must think I'm a child.'

Reuben shook his head.

'I never know what to believe about you, that's all. You confuse me.'

'Believe anything and everything. I confuse myself. It's not your confusion I mind, it's your disapproval.'

'I can't help that,' he said. 'It's something I was brought up with, something I need to help me do my job. Most of the people I deal with are scum. Husbands who kill their wives, wives who kill their husbands, children who stab their parents to death, parents who batter their children's heads against bloody walls. I have to disapprove. I can't afford pity or understanding, an emotion like that. It would kill me.'

305

She did not answer at once. The sea was silent. It had no pity, no emotion. It killed at random, with or without reason.

'I'm sorry for you,' she said.

'Yes,' he answered. 'You can afford to be.' But in spite of his denials, he knew he was full of pity and racked with doubt, and that pity and doubt were killing him. He wanted to love her, to cancel all his doubts in a consuming trust, to turn pity into something resolute and kind. No-one had ever shown him how to do it.

Lindström raised the anchor and restarted the engine. They moved on. The sea stretched out in front of them like a death. It was altogether meaningless, it held no fascination, yet they were in awe of it, knowing it could turn on them at any moment and take them into its presence for ever. It was like death, like any death.

Two hours later, they completed the last leg of the grid. The Formigas Bank had defied them, turned them away empty-handed. Lindström turned off the engine and lowered the sea anchor.

'Looks like they missed the bank,' he said.

Reuben nodded. Maybe it hadn't been such a great idea.

'We could make another sweep. You can miss easy, this equipment not so fucking fantastic, you know.'

Reuben shook his head.

'This was just a shot in the dark anyway. Even if we'd found the wreck, there's no saying it would have meant a thing. I think we've been wasting our time. Let's go home.'

Lindström nodded, then turned.

'Of course, is one possibility,' he said. 'Maniable could have got mixed up. Mistook the position. Could be the *Hallifax* sank on the Grappler.'

'The what?'

'Grappler Bank. Here, let me show you.'

They descended to Lindström's smelly little cabin. At the rear, a small table was spread with charts and a sleeping cat. On top was the British Hydrographic Office chart of Jamaica and the Pedro Bank, first printed in 1866, with corrections up to 1973. The HMS *Vidal* had taken soundings round Jamaica between 1954 and 1957, the HMS *Fox* and HMS *Fawn* had done the Pedro Bank area in 1970.

Between Jamaica and the Formigas lay a smaller bank, the

Grappler. It lay exactly five miles south-west of the bottom end of the Formigas. Lindström made a quick measurement.

'Five miles long,' he said. 'Two wide. Deeper than the Formigas. About fourteen fathoms. Eighty feet. Deeper in some parts. We can do in eight hours. What you think?'

What was there to think? They had come this far, they might as well finish the job. They could be back in Port-au-Prince tomorrow night.

It was 3.47 exactly on the following afternoon when the magnetometer went wild. The sonar showed uneven patches immediately beneath the area it had just passed over. Lindström stopped the engines and ordered August to drop the light anchor.

Reuben was already dressed in trunks. He talced himself quickly and Angelina helped him slip on his black neoprene suit. Over it he pulled on the buoyancy compensator jacket that held his second-stage regulator and octopus, depth and pressure gauges, and compass. Lindström fitted Reuben's aluminium tank into the straps on the BC jacket while he adjusted his weights and fins.

'Well? Any good?' Reuben asked.

Lindström gave a Nordic shrug.

'Perhaps.'

'Anything on the sonar?'

Lindström went across to the instrument and looked closely at it for about half a minute. Interpretation was everything. Finally he pursed his lips. '*Jasâ.*' Slowly, he came back to the rail.

'Could be,' he said. 'Looks like ballast stones maybe. Wait for me.'

Reuben spat into his mask, smeared it, dipped it into the water, and slipped it on. He felt tense. His heart was beating more than it should. With an effort, he controlled his breathing. He had a full tank, but he had no wish to waste air. He picked up his Pulse 6 metal detector. Beside him, Angelina strapped on Lindström's tank.

It was time. Reuben stepped onto the diving platform attached to the *Fanchette*'s stern. Angelina bent forward and kissed his cheek.

'Good luck,' she said.

He slipped the mouthpiece of the second stage into his mouth and took a couple of experimental breaths. The system was working. Wordless, he toppled backwards into surging waves. The world vanished. In a terrible silence, in a singing of waters, he sank down into a world without wind or air or voices.

He was alone in silent waters, among green shadows speared by shafts of light, in a liquid caress that took him from all sides and dragged him down. A trail of bubbles joined him to the surface, vanishing upwards like a string of pearls. The sea was warm and full of light. His depth gauge read fifty feet and he had not reached the bottom yet. The bright eyes of fish stared at him, incurious and dumb. Somewhere above him, Lindström splashed into the sea. Light came slipping down from the surface, vibrating, strangely intensified. All around him, hastening, afraid, he sensed the shadows of drowning men.

Without warning, he found himself swimming among tall, waving fronds, sea-whips filled with sudden, darting fish. The sea bed here was lumpy and uneven, rising and dipping without apparent reason. As he topped a sudden rise, the floor flattened out abruptly. Strewn across it, like the beads of a broken necklace, lay hundreds upon hundreds of little spheres. Lindström had been right, they had located a trove of ballast stones. The deep currents had played marbles with them until they had settled, finding their own lodgements in the ocean floor, acquiring crusts of coral and weed. A moment later, the Swede swam past him and picked one up, cradling it in one hand while he gave a thumb-to-forefinger sign with the other.

They swam on. Half a minute later, Lindström made the second discovery. It must have been what triggered the magnetometer reading, a vast entanglement of corroded chains, scarcely recognizable at first. Nothing seemed real or constant in the parched underwater light.

The chains had been welded into a solid mass, or rather a series of discrete masses. Some sections had, however, been strung out more than others, their rusted links unmistakable. There were fetters at their ends, the gyves and manacles of a slaving vessel. In one, by some horrid accident, what looked like the bones of a human hand and arm were still enfettered.

For the next twenty minutes, they swam back and forth across the sea floor, crisscrossing one another's path, using their underwater metal detectors, seeking for something, anything that might identify the wreck. Reuben found an astrolabe and something that might have been a chamberpot, Lindström picked up a long, rusted bayonet. There were several other clumps of metal that would have to be thoroughly scraped and cleaned before their identity could be guessed. They put them in bags carried at their sides.

Reuben's air was already low when he spotted it. He was not at all sure what it was at first, just that it was made of metal and large. With Lindström's help, he managed to work it loose from a mass of sediment, breaking pieces away with his diving knife. Reuben decided to take it up with him for a closer look. He pulled the toggle on his BC jacket and it inflated in seconds, giving him extra buoyancy. Keeping a tight grip on his find, he rose with it through rays of streaming light. It seemed heavy and reluctant to return to the surface.

Almost unrecognizable beneath a crust of barnacles and coral, the narrow barrel of a small ship's cannon lay on the deck. Acting on Lindström's instructions, Angelina started work on it, carefully dislodging the calcified sediment that encased it. It took over an hour before anything came to light, but when it did it was worth it. Around the firing hole the armourer had cast a coat of arms and beneath that two names and a date: *Hallifax*, Liverpool, 1751.

CHAPTER FIFTY-EIGHT

'Who gave the fucking cat milk?' Lindström strode into the cabin in a fury. 'Is cat shit everywhere. Is fucking horrible.'

Angelina put a hand to her mouth and rolled her eyes. She confessed that she had been trying to ingratiate herself with Sam. The cat had three hates in life: children, women and policemen in uniform. He had given Angelina filthy looks ever since they set off. She had found a tin of powdered milk in the little galley and made up a saucerful. Surely, she had thought, powdered milk won't do any harm. Wrong.

'The last thing we need on a boat this size is a cat with squits,' Lindström thundered.

'It's all right,' said Angelina, standing. 'I'll clean it up.'

'Is everywhere. Is a lot of cleaning.'

Angelina grinned sheepishly and went on deck. Sam was standing in the prow looking aggrieved. The light was starting to fade from the sky. The surface of the sea was red with blood, or so it seemed. Slanting rays from the setting sun had laid a film of bright crimson across it. The water seemed glassy, ill at ease. Angelina waved at the cat. He looked away.

Lindström sat down beside Reuben.

'We have a problem,' he said.

'Cat diarrhoea?' Reuben smiled.

Lindström shook his head. He was not smiling.

'No, not like that. A real problem. Could be serious.'

'Well?'

'Is the radio. Is out of order.'

'What do you mean?'

'What you fucking think I mean? Is not working. Is kaput. We got to go back.'

'Can't you fix it?'

Lindström shook his head.

'Is something broken. Is an old radio, I can't get no spare parts. Not in Port-au-Fucking-Prince.'

'How badly do we need it?' As far as Reuben could tell, they'd hardly used it so far.

The Swede shrugged his broad shoulders.

'For navigationals, I don't need. But for weather, for warnings, that is important.'

'You think the weather's going to change? It looks fine to me.'

Lindström shook his head.

'No, is changing. Is still the storm season. Could be rough by tomorrow. Maybe very rough. I am nervous not knowing how much is getting worse.'

'Can't we sail to Jamaica? It's only . . . what? Thirty-odd miles.'

'*Ja*, we can do that. But in Jamaica they start asking questions. They get crazy about drugs. "What you do-yin, mon," they say. "Why you come all this way from Haiti?" Then they put you in jail.'

Reuben sighed and reached for a can of beer. It was a local Haitian brew called Prestige, scarcely worth drinking, but he was hot after the long spell underwater.

'I'd like to finish here,' he said. 'This was the hard part. I don't want to leave now we've actually found the wreck.'

'*Ja*, I understand, but you got to remember this is only a small boat. You want more, you got to hire somebody else. We can only go down a few more times. Look at the dive tables. And we is running out of fuel.'

'I'd still like to go down again. One more day, then we can leave. We can go down tonight. How about that?'

Lindström frowned, then shrugged.

'OK, we go down again. Tonight, maybe tomorrow morning.'

Reuben nodded. It didn't look as though he had much choice. If only he knew what he was looking for.

The long beam stabbed through the darkness like a rolled-up paper tube. Reuben let his breath out in a hiss of expanding bubbles. He was in a tunnel again, trapped on all sides by impenetrable night. Breathing hard, he closed his eyes, but that was worse: he could see white flapping shapes crawling sightlessly towards him down soft, sunless slopes. He opened his eyes and blinked as the light swayed ahead of him, scattering fish, revealing secret chambers in the coralled wilderness. Slowly, reason returned.

The worst thing was keeping one's bearings. At times, there was no up or down, no forwards or backwards, no left or right. He and Lindström were both attached to the *Fanchette* by lines like long umbilical cords, but even these could get tangled, lost in the shadows. The boat itself was brightly lit, but it was not always visible. He swam in a profound loneliness, through a silence filled with the sounds of his own mortality: the frightened beating of his heart, the coming and going of air through his lungs.

And then the shadows stopped and the water trembled, breaking his light into a million pieces. Reuben blinked and without thinking rubbed his mask. He looked again, holding his breath until it hurt. Slowly, he breathed out again, filling the world with broken bubbles. Like a ghost crammed into shadows it has come to detest, or the victim of a terrible accident nailed into a misshapen coffin, the remains of the *Hallifax* lay trapped in a low gully.

There was little left of her. The spars and rigging had been ripped away, the masts had disappeared, all of the prow and most of the upper and main decks had gone, and what remained of the hull had been broken up and scattered mercilessly. Long, flowing weeds covered the exposed beams. Sponges grew where there had once been portholes. Creatures with long legs and popping eyes crawled in and out of gaping apertures.

Reuben swam closer. Even in his neoprene suit, he was shivering. He didn't want to be here. What had Maniable found on board the *Hallifax* that had made him sink her and run? What had come from Africa, hidden beneath her hatches? What was still lying on the sea bed, waiting for someone to come after all these years?

The afterdeck had been the least damaged area. Reuben guessed that Maniable and his men had holed the ship near the bows, that she had gone down prow first, shifting her ballast as she went, scattering the stones, chains and other loose objects from that region, then running forward until she finally broke up here, half a mile in front. Time and the sea had taken care of the rest.

He knew he should wait for Lindström to find him, but in spite of his fear he felt an impatience, a burning curiosity to explore what was left of the ship. Just below him, he saw what must have been the wheel, several of its spokes broken, lying flat against the remains of the afterdeck. Near it, weeds fringed a large, rectangular hole. Reuben shone his light inside. It had been a doorway leading to after cabins where the ship's officers and captain had had their quarters. He tied his line to a rotten beam and prepared to go inside.

With his tank and other equipment, Reuben was almost too awkward to pass through the little opening, but with some manoeuvring he managed it. He knew he was being careless going down without Lindström. Diving without a buddy is reckless. If something happened, the Swede might never find him in time. Reuben checked his air gauge. There was enough left for another twenty minutes. That didn't give him long to search.

The staircase had rotted away long ago. A metal rail remained, pointing downwards at a sharp angle. Reuben followed it feet first. Moments later he touched bottom. He swung the light around. Through a second opening lay a large empty space, and for a moment he thought he had entered the open sea again. Then he noticed portholes. Swimming inside, he noticed that most of the contents of the cabin had been thrown forward onto the bulkhead through which he had entered. By some miracle, a lantern still hung, rusted and barnacled, from the ceiling.

There was a second door in the opposite bulkhead. Reuben swam gently towards it, leaving a trail of bubbles through the abandoned chamber. Even before the crushing and bending it had undergone, this had been a tiny ship. The officers would have slept and eaten here, cramped together in bad weather, stewing in the heat of summer, wasting with fevers, shivering with agues. Below them, in much worse conditions, the rest of the crew would have sweated and coughed their way through the long passage to Africa, the West Indies and back. Deeper still, in the bowels of the *Hallifax*, the slaves had been squashed together, manacled by wrist and ankle.

Reuben flicked his fins and headed for the second opening. He guessed this led into the captain's cabin. The light fumbled its way ahead of him into the gap. He followed, straining to make sense of a jumble of beams and debris. Small fish swam past him, unperturbed. Something scuttled into its hole. On a pile of debris slammed against the near bulkhead, he saw what was left of a human skull. Then another. Then an armbone. A ribcage. Bones as white as the underbelly of a shark. Eye sockets. Teeth.

What exactly had Maniable and the others found? A scene like the one in Angelina's apartment back in Brooklyn? Body piled upon body, limb upon limb? No wonder he had sunk the *Hallifax*. But why had he not spoken of it to a soul? Why had he sworn his crew to secrecy? What else had he found?

Prominent among the debris was something that looked very like a box. Reuben picked and scrabbled his way to it. It was a large metal chest, heavily encrusted and dented in places, but otherwise intact. He remembered what Angelina had told him: 'They broke the great circle in two and took one half on board the longboat, to remain with them in exile. The other half was left on board the ship in the great chest, together with the gold *nkisi* and the books of the gods . . .' He tried to prise the lid open, but it was sealed tightly by two centuries of encrustations.

He looked at his air gauge. Time was running out. There was no way he could manhandle the chest out alone. He would have to come back for it with Lindström. Turning a somersault in the confined space, he headed for the door. Through the officers' cabin, back up the stairs, his heart racing, his skin still crawling.

On top again, he untied his line. Where the hell was Lindström? The Swede had gone off fifteen minutes earlier to cover a different sector. Reuben scanned the darkness. He was nowhere to be seen. Perhaps he had already gone back up. Reuben decided to follow him.

Just then he saw a flicker of light, just to the left, towards where the prow had been. Going higher, he saw it more clearly. Lindström must have found the ship as well. Reuben waved his own lamp back and forwards. Lindström did not signal in reply. Reuben waved again, swimming closer. Still no response.

Reuben hurried now. Lindström might be absorbed in something, his back to him. Or something might be wrong. The sea bed here was littered with rubbish from the wreck. Lindström's light was only yards away now. Reuben could see a string of air bubbles rising through it. He swung his own lamp towards it.

On the bed lay the *Hallifax*'s sheet anchor, the largest of the three it had carried. Underneath it Lindström was pinned to the floor by his legs. The anchor must have been propped up against something, then dislodged somehow by the Swede.

Reuben swam right up to him. Lindström was breathing but barely conscious. Reuben bent down and put his shoulder against the anchor. It would not move. He guessed it weighed at least a ton. He scrabbled underneath in the hope of being able to dig Lindström out. The floor at this spot was solid. Raising Lindström's head, Reuben managed to take a squint at the air gauge on his tank. Different divers use up air at different rates. Lindström's gauge said he had five minutes' worth of compressed air left.

CHAPTER FIFTY-NINE

Reuben did not stop even to consider swapping tanks. His own were almost exhausted, and Lindström might be seconds away from death. He could be that close himself. Hurriedly, he tied the end of his line round the anchor. Without pausing, he kicked hard and pushed upwards at top speed, breathing fast but evenly to keep his pressure balanced.

On the surface, he ripped out his mouthpiece and pulled the mask onto his forehead. Inches away in the darkness, the *Fanchette* was bobbing against her anchor, her lights like something from another world. Reuben shouted loudly and moments later Angelina appeared at the gunwale, followed by August.

'You were down a long time, Reuben. Sven warned you about taking risks. Where is he anyway?'

Reuben pulled himself up the ladder and was helped over the side. Gasping for breath, he spoke quickly. The air felt tense, hard to breathe.

'No time . . . to explain . . . Need new tanks . . . Get one . . . for me . . . One for Sven . . . Hurry.'

Angelina guessed what was happening right away. She hurried off, shouting rapidly in Creole at August, explaining what was needed. In seconds they reappeared, each carrying a scuba tank. August helped Reuben unstrap his, then pulled the fresh tank into place. Reuben took the second tank and fitted his octopus – his alternate air source – to the valve.

'I'll be back up,' he said. 'Sven may be hurt. Get some first-aid stuff ready, make up a bed in the cabin.'

He did not bother with the dive platform. Jumping straight in over the side, he floundered for a moment, keeping tight hold of the second tank, then found the line he had attached to the anchor. Without it, finding the *Hallifax* in time would have been a hopeless task. As it was, the descent seemed to Reuben an eternity. More than five minutes had gone by, he knew that, but he was afraid even to glance at his wristwatch to see just how many. Lindström's only hope was that whoever had filled the tanks had erred on the side of generosity for once. It wasn't much to hang your life on.

Down he sank, twenty feet, thirty, forty, fifty, in slow motion, a dull ringing in his ears, the pressure growing gently. The light vanished more rapidly this time, the darkness felt even more complete; not only visible, but tangible. He could feel it creeping inside him, filling him, making him part of its world.

Suddenly, he caught sight of Lindström's light below him, like a beacon in the darkness. A beacon or . . . a corpse candle? He shone his lamp down, swinging the beam until he found the anchor and the man trapped underneath. A thin trail of bubbles trickled up from Lindström's mouth. The tank was on its last legs.

Reuben set the replacement tank down by Lindström's head. The Swede was still conscious enough to know what was happening and to help. At a signal from Reuben, he held his breath. Reuben pulled out his old mouthpiece and as quickly replaced it with the fresh one. Lindström sucked the air in greedily, knowing he could afford to breathe deeply again. He lifted a hand and grabbed Reuben briefly by the wrist, squeezing hard.

Reuben helped the Swede slip out of the BC jacket that held his empty tanks. Without them, Lindström was able to lie back at an easier angle. Reuben found a couple of large sponges growing nearby, cut them from their beds, and slipped them under his friend's head to serve as a pillow. Having done what little he could to make the other man comfortable, he turned his attention to the anchor.

It was large and it was heavy. What was worse, it seemed to have settled firmly. Reuben tried to rock it from several positions, but it was like trying to move a boulder. To shift it, he would need a winch. The nearest thing on board the *Fanchette* was a crowbar.

Lindström was held by the upper legs and abdomen. A quick check reassured Reuben that, even if there were broken bones, the Swede was losing very little blood from flesh wounds. A severe cut, something involving veins or arteries, would have caused him to bleed to death long before Reuben could bring help.

Lindström's only hope lay in their getting assistance of some kind in Jamaica. It would take them two and a half hours to get there, maybe an hour or two to buy or hire a winch or get another boat, two and a half to return. From five to seven hours.

They had about ten hours' worth of air left on board, assuming Lindström used it up at his usual slow rate. At least he would be still. The mathematics were inescapable. There was no way Reuben or anyone else could stay down here with Lindström, using up precious air at double the rate. He would have to leave all the tanks here, within reach of the trapped man, abandoning him where he lay to wait for their return. That was bad, and it couldn't be helped, but it wasn't the worst. If Lindström passed out and was unable to make the changeovers from tank to tank as time passed, he would drown anyway. Just like Devorah. Reuben shut his eyes to block out the images: a white hand floundering above tiny waves, ripples in cold water, an uninhabited darkness. He opened his eyes again to see Lindström staring at him.

Reuben had a small plastic slate and china glass pencil. Quickly, he scribbled a mesage.

'Pain?'

Lindström nodded.

Reuben rubbed out the first message and wrote a second.

'Not bleeding much. Not bleed to death.'

Lindström nodded again. He understood. Reuben rubbed and wrote.

'Can't lift anchor. Need machinery. Will bring tanks down. Must stay awake. Understand?'

Lindström nodded.

'Set alarm and keep resetting. Understand?'

He understood.

'Will get winch in Jamaica. Straight back. Not long.' He paused. There was just room for a few more words.

'No other way. Don't worry.'

He put the pencil away, bitterly aware of the meaninglessness of what he had just said. Lindström had every reason to worry. The Swede reached out and pulled him back, holding out a hand for the slate and pencil. Reuben passed them to him.

'Better kill me now. Don't want wait so long. Don't want stay down here alone. Afraid.'

Reuben had a diving knife strapped to his leg, a short Dacor Hi-Tech knife with a sharp blade. He could put Lindström out of his misery as he asked, spare him hours of physical and mental agony, waiting for help to arrive, watching the air dwindle in each tank, tank after tank, until he reached the last and there were only minutes left.

He shook his head.

Lindström scribbled frantically.

'Watch out for Sam,' he wrote. 'Is fucking stupid cat. Is getting old. Look after him. Promise.'

Reuben nodded.

'I promise,' he said, knowing Lindström could not hear him. Lindström rubbed the slate and wrote again.

'The boy, August. Need education. Do what you can.'

Reuben made an 'O' signal with his thumb and forefinger. Lindström let the slate drop to the sea bed. There was nothing more to say. Neither man said goodbye.

The darkness was rich, purple and menacing. It was humid at first, the air stifling. Then a breeze set in from the south. Half an hour later, it had moved to the west. By the time they saw Folly Point lighthouse to the east of Port Antonio, it had changed direction twice more. The sea had started to steepen, and they were pitching with increasing violence.

'I don't like this, Reuben,' murmured Angelina. They were the first words she had spoken since leaving the Grappler Bank. August was steering, she and Reuben were watching the radar and sonar screens. 'I wish to God Sven had mentioned the radio earlier. We might have been able to do something. This is still hurricane weather, we could be in for trouble.'

Back on the Grappler, they had left one of the *Fanchette*'s orange life-rings. A bright light flashed on top of it, designed to be visible to a search party. Now it bobbed about heavily, lashed by the growing winds. A line went from it to the sea bed, directly to the anchor beneath which Lindström lay trapped. He slipped in and out of consciousness, dreaming of firelight in Norrköping and waking to the dark sea all around him. The pain in his thighs was almost unbearable. All sense of feeling had left his knees and lower legs. He was already on his third tank of air, alternating between his first- and second-stage regulators. Beside him he could see the other bottles lying where Reuben had left them, precise reminders of the short span remaining to him.

Reuben glanced up from his screen.

'How long before it gets too bad to sail in?'

Angelina shrugged.

'I'm not a sailor. You'll have to ask someone when we dock at Port Antonio. But from general experience with storms, I wouldn't say very long.'

There was a long silence.

'We can't leave him there,' Reuben said at last. 'I promised I'd come back. He wouldn't be there if it wasn't for me.'

Angelina said nothing. Ahead of them, the Folly Point light appeared, then vanished, swept from view by a steep swell.

It took them almost another hour to make it to port. Entering the harbour in heavy seas through almost total darkness was a nightmare. They passed Folly Point on their port side and Navy Island almost invisible to starboard. There were two harbours on the chart, West Harbour and East Harbour, and Reuben did not know which to choose. In the end, he settled for East Harbour because it looked more central to the town. They passed Fort George and the high hill of the peninsula below it.

They anchored a little further in, staying in deep water. August stayed on board while Reuben and Angelina took the dinghy ashore, weaving their way in past wildly bobbing banana boats. It had started to rain, thick, stinging rain that scudded across the waves like metal shot.

There was no-one on the dock and no-one in any of the offices around it. The entire harbour area was deserted. They headed for the nearest lights. The rain had soaked them thoroughly by now and was busy trying to work its way deeper in, beneath their skin. Three hours had already gone.

Up on Harbour Street, a reddish light was coming from a small bar, its doors and windows closed tightly against the storm. The front was gaudily painted with flowers. A single illuminated sign hung over the door, advertising Red Stripe beer above the name of the bar: Goat's Horn Club. Reuben smilingly recognized it as the name of a cannabis variety. He pushed the door open. A blast of reggae music thundered into the night. Reuben pushed his way in, closely followed by Angelina. The door slammed behind them.

In one corner, a battered jukebox was hammering out hard rhythms by a local reggae band. '*Babylon gonna fall tonight. And all its children, black and white.*' A small group of men, some sporting dreadlocks, stood around it, cans of beer in their hands. From the ceiling hung strings of old single records by Jimmy Cliff, Toots and the Maytals, and old Skatalites discs from the sixties. There was a narrow bar, stocked mostly with Red Stripe and Dragon Stout. A few tables and chairs made up the rest of the furniture. On one wall, posters of Bob Marley and Yellowman added the only colour to the smoke-filled room.

The record stopped. In the silence, all eyes were on the newcomers. A low mutter was followed by laughter round the jukebox. The men were mostly young and well-built, with tight trousers and shirts. There were two women at the bar, hookers on a night when nobody much wanted to be hooked. Behind the bar stood an older woman, cleaning glasses. At a table sat two banana-boat loaders nursing glasses of white rum and *ganja*. One eyed Angelina up and down very thoroughly.

'We need help,' said Reuben.

Somebody pushed a button on the jukebox and another record fell onto the turntable.

'I said we need help. We have a man trapped out on the Grappler Bank. We need a winch. Do any of you know where we can find one?'

Most of his words were drowned by the loud music coming from the jukebox. The young men turned their backs and moved in time to the music. The loaders stared into their rums. The hookers stared at one another.

Angelina swore out loud and walked across to where the jukebox stood. It was plugged into a socket halfway up the wall against which it leaned. Without pausing, Angelina grabbed the plug and yanked it free of the socket. The music lurched and groaned to a halt. One of the men in dreadlocks made a grab for Angelina's arm. She gave him a look that froze him in his tracks.

'The man said we need help,' she stated. 'We've just come in off the Grappler Bank. We have to go back to rescue a man on the sea bed. We don't have time to fuck about. So, who do we see?'

There was a prolonged silence. Then one of the loaders spoke.

'No-bo-dy gonna go to sea tonight. You man is dead. Leave him be, lady. It go-yin be a bad night.'

'How bad?'

The loader shook his head.

'Bad, lady. Very bad. An' it gonna get a lot worse.' He paused and looked at her, straight. His eyes were red and his lips were wet with rum. 'Don' you listen to de ra-di-o? Dere a hurricane on its way. It comin' here to-night.'

320

CHAPTER SIXTY

Outside, the storm was growing in intensity, gathering strength and anger by the minute. While his companions watched, no longer laughing, the loader took Reuben and Angelina to the door and pointed through driving rain to their right, at a row of little lights. They were, he said, the windows of a shipping office on Bridge Street. Someone there might be able to help them, could at least tell them more about the hurricane.

Half-running, half-pushed by swirling gusts of wind, lashed all the way by squalling rain, they stumbled towards the lights. Nearby, there was a crash as something heavy fell to the ground. The concrete beneath their feet was treacherous, coated with oil and sluiced by a constant stream of angry water. They ran blind and deaf through the maelstrom, holding hands like children, as much for comfort as for balance.

The 'shipping office' was a low wooden hut connected by a single wire to the nearest telephone pole. Reuben tried the door. It was locked. He could feel the seconds slipping through his fingers, the minutes scurrying out of reach. He started pounding on the thin wooden panels. There was no answer. He lifted his hand and hammered again. And again.

'Hey, mon, what all dis knocking for, mon? Can't you see I busy?' Reuben hammered again furiously. The door was flung open.

In the entrance, haloed by yellow light, stood a little man of about fifty in shirt and trousers.

'Can't you see I workin', mon? I got bus'ness to do. What you want, knocking like dat?'

Reuben didn't waste time with explanations. He pushed past the man, bringing half the rain in Jamaica into the hut with him. Angelina followed, bringing the other half.

'Hey, mon, who ya t'ink you are, comin' in here jus' like that? You waan' some shelta, you go look somewhere else.'

The man's outrage, Reuben saw at once, probably had less to do with the rainwater they were spilling across his floor than with the presence in one corner of a pretty-looking girl with wide eyes and a wider bosom. She was seated at a flimsy wooden desk in front of a typewriter, but from the look of her blouse she hadn't been there long.

Reuben twisted round.

'Please, listen,' he said. He dragged a wallet from inside his sailing jacket and pulled out a wad of dollars. With the police making searches and his gun already stolen, he had not liked the idea of leaving so much cash lying round Mama Vijina's.

'You can have this,' he said. 'You can have whatever you like. All we want is your help.'

The man looked hard at the money, then at Reuben. Next, he looked at Angelina, and finally at the money again.

'You better sit,' he said.

It took a minute to explain. When Reuben finished, the man frowned.

'Listen to me, mon,' he said. 'Not even Jesus Christ, not even Jah walkin' on de waaters tonight, you understand what I sayin' to you? Is a hurricane comin' dis way, and it is comin' faast.'

'How soon?'

Carefully, the man explained. The hurricane had first been spotted forming in the Caribbean south of the Dominican Republic two days earlier. It had been travelling steadily westwards since then, picking up strength as it moved, at about ten miles an hour. The centre was expected to pass just south of Jamaica, between the island and the Pedro Cays. Northern Jamaica and the waters to Haiti and well beyond could expect gusts of over one hundred miles an hour. Expected time of arrival, between three and four hours from now.

Reuben turned to Angelina.

'What do you think?' he said. 'Would we have any chance at all?'

She took her time before answering.

'No, not much,' she said. 'Even on land, a hurricane is devastating. At sea, it's like nothing you've ever seen. But it is possible to survive. If you don't hit a reef or you aren't driven onto rocks, if your pumps are in order and you don't take on more water than your boat can handle, yes, maybe you can get through. Lindström could do it. He could sail that boat through anything. But you, me, August . . .'

'If we don't go, he'll die.'

'I know. But he may die anyway. We may succeed in rescuing him just to put him through hell before he drowns with us.'

'I'm going to take that risk. You stay here with August. There's no point in all of us getting killed.'

'Like hell. You can't handle that boat on your own. And you certainly can't dive and watch the *Fanchette* at the same time. August can stay here. I'm coming with you.'

Reuben opened his mouth to argue, then thought better of it. He turned to the owner of the hut, who was watching them with disbelief.

'You want to earn this money?'

'I not comin' in no boat, mon. Not if you give me a million dollars.'

'I'm not asking you to come with us. I want you to take me somewhere I can get hold of a winch. I need to haul that anchor up.'

The Jamaican raised his eyebrows.

'A winch? Tonight? You *mus'* be crazy.'

'I'll hire it, buy it, or steal it. Time's running out. You must know someone near here.'

The man thought hard.

'Does 'im have to be a winch?' he asked at last.

'I don't know. What else do you suggest?'

'What about a jack, mon? A big trolley jack jus' what you need. Have dat anchor off him in a flash.'

Reuben nodded.

'I should have thought of that. Where can we get one?'

The man gave a big grin and started for the door.

'C'mon, I show you.'

A curtain of water blotted out the lights of Port Antonio as though they had never existed. The lighthouse gave a final flicker and vanished into the night behind them. All around them the darkness was absolute, like no other darkness Reuben had ever known. It was alive with rain and wind and the deep, hollow thrashing and groaning of the sea.

Reuben realized that their chances of finding Lindström again were extremely slim. It would take all the skill and luck they possessed just to find the Grappler Bank again. If they did not get blown hopelessly off course, if the light was still attached to the life-ring, if the life-ring had not been torn already from the sea bed, they might just make it there in the end. A lot of ifs. And no room for error.

They had been unable to force August ashore. Neither threats nor cajoling had succeeded in undermining the boy's absolute devotion to Lindström, whom he called '*le Capitain*'. He sat now at the rear of the small deckhouse, cradling Sam in his arms, shivering, fighting his fear of the giant waves that pounded the boat.

Lindström, parsimonious when it came to paintwork or polish or fancy equipment he knew he would never need, had spent what money he had once earned on one or two items of real value. One of these was a top-of-the-range Aqua Meter compass, the sort that would stay rock steady in all but the very worst conditions. In such high seas, it would be impossible to sail straight back to the spot where they had left Lindström. As the wind shifted and turned, they would have to change course to avoid being overwhelmed by side-on waves. Their course would be erratic. They would be lucky if they got within twenty miles of their target.

The little boat ploughed through a steep swell that rose at times like a metal wall above her or opened to reveal a long drop down which she plunged like a roller coaster out of control. That they made progress at all was astonishing. The journey back to the Grappler would take much longer than originally calculated.

They had taken on extra fuel at Port Antonio, along with a trolley jack from a garage on Red Hassell Lane run by a man called Winston, a friend of the shipping clerk. Apart from payment for the fuel and jack, no money had passed hands. Once people had realized that Reuben and Angelina really did plan to sail back out to the bank in the hope of rescuing a friend, they had done everything in their power to help. Winston's family had come to the dock with them. The shipping clerk, whose name was Byron, had found a couple of fishermen to help carry the jack and fuel out to the *Fanchette*. Food had been pressed into their hands. There had been promises of prayers in the parish church. No-one had known where to find a two-way radio in time.

Now, all that was gone. They were alone where nobody could help them. Confined to the deckhouse like prisoners, they held on tight. They had all been sick several times, until all that was left was a dry retching that left them weak and trembling. Each time the boat ran to the crest of a swell, they waited for the lurching madness of the dive to follow. Each time it dived, they thought it would go on, straight down into the depths. Speech was useless. Wind and rain and waves tore words to shreds the moment they were spoken.

Reuben looked at the chronometer. 02.11.03. Lindström had four hours' oxygen left. They'd been at sea again for two hours now. Fighting against a wind that seemed to come from more than one direction at once, it would take at least another three to reach their destination. They held tight and watched as wall after wall of water came crashing down across their prow.

It seemed to go on for ever. Wind like slaps from a giant's hand, rain like a second ocean, swollen waves like houses, night like eternity, no light, no moon, no stars, no silence, a dry sickness in the pit of the stomach, nausea in the bowels, fear of drowning, fear of crushing, fear of the dark, a headache pounding like a hammer behind aching eyes, a shaking in the hands and arms, mere inches of thickened glass between them and the extremities of hell.

In the end, it was almost five hours after setting out from Port Antonio that they saw the light, a flicker of white far off, broad on the port bow. A moment later, it was hidden by tall seas. All three crowded to the narrow window, straining for the least hint of the light's return. Sam stayed where he was, riding out the storm. Minutes passed like hours. There was nothing but sea, nothing but the darkness of the storm behind it.

Suddenly, a heavy swell lifted them above the surrounding waters and they saw it, the white light of the buoy on the southern edge of the bank. If the life-ring was still in place, it would be about a mile and a half north-west of here. All they had to do was get to it. Lindström had about an hour of air left in his tanks.

At that moment, the wind sank briefly, as though taking breath. Reuben got a rough bearing. Angelina looked up from the sonar screen and nodded encouragingly. They were over the bank.

Twenty minutes later, they saw it: a red light shut in by unimaginable darknesses. The question was, how close could they get to it? Too far away, and Reuben would not be able to relocate the wreck in time. They changed course, heading for the spot they thought the light had last been. When they saw it again, ten minutes later, it was just as far away and abaft the port beam. Ten minutes more and it had shifted to starboard. It was still a mile away, maybe more. Given time and patience, they could make it. Now, they had neither.

Reuben changed into his neoprene suit and strapped on the remaining tank. He looked at Angelina. It was time.

The door opened onto madness. Reuben braced himself and stepped out, dragging the jack with him. The wind tore at him, threatening to hurl him bodily across the rail. Angelina came behind. They staggered to the gunwale, using a line to steady them against the blasts. Underfoot, water ran in a perpetual stream, tearing at their legs, pulling them down. Angelina grabbed a stanchion and attached a second line to it, one made up of several lengths tied tightly together. If it should snap or come loose, Reuben would have little hope of ever making it back to the boat.

Tying the line to his belt, she leaned forward and kissed him briefly on the lips. They tasted of salt. Everything tasted of salt. She wanted to hold him, but she dared not let go of the stanchion.

'Good luck,' she shouted, her words torn away before they reached him. He nodded, seated himself on the gunwale, flipped backwards, and was gone. She looked out at the spot where he had hit the water, but there was nothing, not even a ripple.

CHAPTER SIXTY-ONE

He felt himself sinking fast, wholly at the mercy of vast forces over which he had no control. Within seconds, the roaring of the storm had become a memory, but even here beneath the surface he was buffeted and tossed like a cork.

As he neared the bottom, the turbulence subsided, but the sea was still in a state of constant movement. He could feel himself lifted and dropped by a deep, nauseating surge that passed back and forwards through the water. There was a thud as he let the jack crash to the sea bed. Lifting it again, he used his spare octopus to inflate his BC jacket. Now he had enough buoyancy to lift the jack and swim with it on a strap around his neck.

Before diving, he had taken a rough bearing on the light, and now, using the compass on his combo gauge, he began to swim in its approximate direction. In spite of his buoyancy, the jack weighed him down, made his motions awkward. He propelled himself mainly with his flippers, head down, legs at full stretch, kicking, struggling in the dark interior of the ocean, flattened bubbles tight and bursting as they struggled upwards away from him, back towards the terrible surface and the storm.

He switched on his lamp. Beneath him, the ragged sea bed stretched away indifferently. Heavy fish mumbled past, their eerie fins dazzling, mouths opening and closing, watchful, sad. Several feet away, the grey flank of a lonely barracuda shark glided past. Reuben kept swimming, praying there were no makos nearby.

He saw the light long after he had given up hope, a faint white blur to his left, dim but unmistakable, the long-life glow-worm he had attached to the anchor before leaving Lindström. Twisting abruptly, he kicked hard, feeling renewed strength run through his veins. He might still make it after all.

The beam of his lamp caught the anchor, then Lindström lying where Reuben had left him. No air bubbles flickered upwards. There was no sign of life.

Reuben knelt down beside his friend. He was too late after all. Looking more closely, he saw that the Swede had not died because he had run out of air. He must have taken his own life, tearing the air tube away from his mask.

And then he looked even more closely. The tube had not been torn away. It had been sliced cleanly in two. Reuben looked down for Lindström's knife. It was not there. Scrabbling through mud and silt, he looked for it everywhere, but he could not find it. And then he looked at Lindström's ankle, where it protruded from the anchor. His diving knife was still in its sheath. Not only that, but Lindström could never have reached it from where he lay.

Lindström had not taken his own life. Someone else had done it for him.

CHAPTER SIXTY-TWO

Reuben unfastened the strap and dropped the jack to the sea bed. With a quick jerk, he pulled on the toggle that deflated his buoyancy jacket. It would be a waste of time now to move the anchor. He would leave the old sailor down here with the *Hallifax*, down in his element with the fish and the other anonymous dead. A sea burial; he would have wanted nothing less.

Relieved of his burden, he thought at once of why Lindström's killers had come here in the first place. He would have to look, of course, have to be sure. They had not killed Lindström for sport. He had been no threat to them – but perhaps he had seen something, somebody . . .

Someone had followed the *Fanchette* from Port-au-Prince, that was obvious, staying out of sight until they knew or guessed that they had found the wreck. They must have watched the *Fanchette* leave nine hours ago, sailed to the spot where she had been anchored, and found the life-ring. The rest had followed naturally.

Leaving his line tied to the anchor, Reuben swam freely through the surge back to the wreck. Nothing had changed. Here, things only changed in decades, in centuries. He slipped in through the quarterdeck entrance, then slowly down the narrow pit where the stairs had been, along the officers' cabin, into the room of bones.

The chest was gone, as he had thought it would be. The bones had been disturbed, other objects tossed aside, some, for all Reuben knew, taken along with the chest. They must have known what they were looking for. Angelina had known about the chest, and Reuben did not believe the Seventh Order was not aware of it too.

The killers would be heading back to Port-au-Prince by now, caught like the *Fanchette* in the grip of the hurricane. By tomorrow, the chest could be at the bottom of the sea again, more deeply submerged than ever, beyond human reach for good. Apart from the gold objects from Tali-Niangara, what had it contained? Treasure from Europe? Gold and jewels, rings and earrings, strings of rich white pearls, a lacquered portrait of a long-dead paramour? The usual relics of the damned?

Reuben swam back through the sea-eaten wreck, dejected, lonely, a man of sin, guilt heavy upon him like the air he carried on his back, weighing him down even while it kept him alive. Had his father and mother died for this, a handful of trinkets from the Gold Coast, a rusted locket, a lock of lover's hair? In a corner of the officers' cabin, a moray eel stirred its long, flexible body. Reuben kicked upwards and emerged into the emptiness of the deep and the green sea.

Boarding the *Fanchette* proved the most dangerous part of the entire operation. The boat had been circling, keeping as near as possible to the life-ring. He had swum to it underwater, guided by its lights. But to get aboard, he had to come to the surface, and conditions on the surface had deteriorated rapidly.

After reinflating his BC jacket, he let the now redundant tank and its array of tubes and valves drop to the bottom. He could breathe well enough through the snorkel attached to his mask. The problem was getting on board a bucking motorboat in thirty- and forty-foot seas before his strength gave out and he followed his tank to the sea bed.

Time and again, he was grabbed by giant waves and slammed hard against the side of the boat. He was bruised and tiring now, the deep exhaustion of days taking its toll at last. His hands slipped as he struggled to grab the ladder Angelina had lowered over the side. He lost track of the number of times he made the attempt, the number of times his bleeding fingers found a purchase only to be torn away again, leaving him floundering in steep waters yards from the yawing craft.

He was weakening fast, every effort draining him, making the next gargantuan. The next attempt or the one after would be his last. Desperately, he dragged himself through a torment of waves, kicking and flailing for safety. Just as he reached for the ladder, a wave more powerful than the rest threw him forward against the side of the boat, knocking the snorkel from his teeth. Fighting for breath, he saw the *Fanchette* pulling away from him. He was beaten down, tossing, swallowing water, choking, drowning.

Suddenly, something landed in the water five or six feet away.

Angelina had seen him at last and rushed on deck, risking her life in order to throw the second life-ring on a line to him. The ring righted itself, popping its tiny light to guide him. He paddled for it, fighting against a sucking undertow that sought to pull him under. And he had it, hard and perfect as a gem against his fingers, tearing skin from his knuckles. He had it and he was not letting go.

She pulled him in, sitting on the deck, feet braced against the gunwale, while August got a line round her and lashed it fast to a stanchion. Reuben made it to the side, got his hands round the first rung of the ladder, and started to haul himself up.

No-one said a word as he staggered on board and crawled to the deckhouse. He was alone, and that was all they needed to know. They followed him, slamming the door against the storm, watched as he collapsed helpless in front of the steering column. The deck lurched and lurched again, then the whole world heaved.

He was on his knees, vomiting salt water, his guts churning, his throat burning. A dry retching came, then coughing until he thought he would die. He looked up and saw Angelina and August staring at him, and he tried to say he was sorry, but nothing came but the thick, angry coughing, then he looked again and Sven was there, his white hair floating in the moving currents, then he was caught by the undertow and sucked down, down into dark and soundless depths where everything began again.

CHAPTER SIXTY-THREE

Washington DC
Sunday, 18 October
9.30 A.M.

Washington had never looked so unwelcoming. The storms had passed, leaving the land exhausted and the sky desolate. The Potomac was still muddy and swollen with heavy rainwater sluiced down from the Alleghenys. Sally rubbed mist from her windscreen; the city tumbled past. She had forgotten how lonely it could be here.

It was time to make a move. The CSA could not handle the Seventh Order on its own any longer. They had called a meeting of selected intelligence personnel, people they knew they could trust. Everyone had been invited on a strictly one-to-one basis: no-one knew the others would be present.

The conference was to be held at the home of Sutherland Cresswell, the CSA's Washington-based director. Sutherland had been fully briefed about the Order from the start, but on the basis of recent events had reached the decision to ask for help from other agencies.

Choosing whom to tell had not been easy. No-one knew precisely how far Forbes/Smith and his bosses had infiltrated the intelligence network and other government departments. They had the names of twenty-eight individuals known to have been recruited to the Order or placed by it in positions of influence. Another fifty-three names had been filed as suspected members. Eleven people were known to be under the Order's direct influence; Cresswell was fairly sure that Forbes held sensitive files on numerous other individuals whose sexual, financial or political indiscretions laid them open to pressure.

In the end, the CSA had drawn up a shortlist of people known personally to Cresswell, Sally and the New York team. The shortlist had been closely scrutinized by each one in turn, then run through a computer to eliminate anyone with more than formal connections to any known or suspected Order members, whether inside or outside the agencies. The list they were left with consisted of only five names: Mike Fordham, a senior official in the CIA's Directorate of Intelligence; Joel Garrison, secretary to the National Intelligence Council; Grace Sala from the National Security Agency; Chris Markopoulos, with the CIA's Directorate of Operations; and Kevin McNamara from the FBI.

The meeting had been made to look as informal as possible. Sutherland Cresswell lived in a large house outside the city, on the road to Annapolis. He had suggested a Sunday because it would help guarantee full attendance and encourage the invitees – and anyone else – to think this was no more than a weekend get-together. A barbeque was planned for lunch, provided the weather held up. Cresswell's wife and children would be there. Mike Fordham and Hastings Donovan were both bringing their children, who were about the same age as Cresswell's. Joel Garrison and Kevin McNamara were bringing their wives.

Sally was among the last to arrive. The drive was full of cars. At the doorway, Sutherland was waiting to greet his guests. The house was set back from the road among red and gold trees, at the centre of a thickening carpet of fallen leaves. Every so often, a figure would slip out from behind a tree, blow on his hands or mutter discreetly into a handset, and vanish again. Security was tight.

The cries of children at play could be heard from the back garden. Smoke spiralled from a low brick chimney. There was a bonfire somewhere near; as Sally stepped out of the car, the smell of burning leaves brought back to her memories of her childhood in New Hampshire. She did not notice the sunlight flash momentarily on a pair of high-powered binoculars on a ridge above the house.

The cosiness ceased the moment she got inside. Sutherland had arranged for them to meet in his den, a large, book-lined room on the second floor. Most of the people in the room were strangers to Sally and, for that matter, to one another. The little CSA group had huddled together in one corner. There was very little conversation.

Cresswell had had the entire house swept for bugs earlier that morning, using the team now guarding the grounds. They had all been hand picked by Sutherland himself. He had gone through the house with them to ensure that nothing was missed.

The last to arrive were the McNamaras. Kevin followed Cresswell into the study, puzzled – like everyone else except the CSA contingent – to find so many others there. Cresswell was silent and grim-faced. Outside, the voices of children wrenched the fall air, counterpoints to the words already passing through his brain. Perhaps it was appropriate, he thought. What else was it all about?

He went to the front of the room and took up a position facing his small audience. Never before in his career had he felt so nervous. In the next hour or so, decisions would be made that would have a profound effect on his own country and several other states. It was certain that, as a result of what this small group decided, lives would be lost or ruined. He felt a terrible responsibility. And a terrible fear.

'Ladies, gentlemen,' he began. 'I must apologize for practising this small deception on you and bringing you all here under false pretences. You will have guessed by now that I had special reasons for inviting you here today and in this manner. Most of you do not, I think, know one another by sight, although in some cases you may have heard each other's names. So, first of all, I'd like you to introduce yourselves one at a time.'

When the introductions were over, Cresswell took the floor again.

'In a few moments,' he said, 'CSA's New York Regional Director, Miss Sally Peale, will explain to you the reasons for this meeting. I want you to listen very carefully to what she has to say. Everything she will tell you has been checked and double-checked by myself and a handful of highly dependable operatives at CSA head-quarters here in Washington. I believe Miss Peale's information to be substantially correct. I also believe her conclusions to be extremely reliable. Please do not jump to hasty judgements. Let her finish what she has to say. After that, you may ask any questions you wish.' He paused and looked round. 'Sally . . .'

She spoke for over an hour, taking her audience from outright scepticism all the way to dismayed belief. She had facts, documents, photographs, sources, all at her fingertips. Using overhead transparencies prepared on her Apple IIcx, she showed them figures, maps, lines of communication, dates. But her words and images were merely a gloss on what lay beneath, like pancake make-up on the face of a corpse. In the narrow room, lit by a quiet sun, the laughter of children rippling in autumn-scented air, an ancient evil struggled to life.

'About a year ago,' Sally said, 'we set up a small surveillance unit in Haiti. We had a total of fourteen operatives, mostly locals and second-generation Haitian-Americans from Brooklyn and Miami. Three weeks ago, twelve of those operatives were killed in a series of separate, coordinated attacks in Port-au-Prince, Cap-Haïtien, and one or two smaller towns. One of the Americans managed to get out alive. The fourteenth man, a Haitian known to us as Macandal, was murdered nine days ago at a voodoo ceremony outside Port-au-Prince.

'The survivor was a man called Felix Simon. He managed to get to Miami and was able to make contact with us shortly afterwards. Unfortunately, he was badly hurt in the attack, and is currently in hospital, otherwise I would have had him here today to tell you what he knows. I spoke to him two days ago, however, and I was able to form a rough picture of what seems to be happening there at the moment.'

She paused and sipped water from a glass on the table in front of her. The tension in the room was tightening. Even the sounds of the children outside seemed muted.

'As most of you already know, the situation in Haiti has been more than usually unstable since General Cicéron came to power. Opposition groups have been formed in all the major towns. Money has been coming in from Cuba. Given time, we estimate that a full-scale revolution could put Haiti firmly into the communist camp. Now, some of you may disagree with that analysis. Unfortunately, that makes no difference to what is about to happen.

'The fact is that the Seventh Order thinks there will be a communist revolution if nothing is done to prevent it. Rather than wait for Cicéron to be overthrown and for their own plans to be set back indefinitely, they have decided to take pre-emptive action. They have a candidate for the presidency, the current Minister of Defence, General Louis Valris.

'We have . . .' This was the hard part. 'We have two people working for us in Port-au-Prince at the moment, neither a trained operative. One is a New York City police lieutenant, the other a Haitian woman whose brother is head of Cicéron's internal security service.

'Lieutenant Abrams and Angelina Hammel were sent to Haiti as . . . bait.' Sally closed her eyes. She saw dark fish with serrated teeth swimming through tumbling waters. She could not tell them everything, that had been agreed.

'We think the fish may have bitten. Yesterday, President Cicéron declared a curfew. There are reports of troops on the streets in several cities. The main airports have been closed. And we have lost all contact with our two agents. We believe Warren Forbes is also now in Haiti. I am personally certain that he is merely waiting for orders to act. We have to act quickly, and we have to act decisively. That is why you have been brought here today.'

Sally sat down. She felt drained. Her hands were shaking. The eyes of the entire room were fixed on her. She looked at her watch. It had been time for lunch ten minutes ago. She wondered why Sutherland's wife hadn't phoned through to the den to say things were ready. Sutherland had asked her to do so to avoid the morning session dragging on. It was vital that everyone be fresh and ready for the most gruelling part of the day, the afternoon discussion.

Sutherland looked at his watch too. He had an odd feeling that something was not quite right. Carefully, he looked round the room. Nothing seemed out of place. Sally got to her feet again to clarify one or two points that demanded immediate attention. Sutherland could feel the small hairs rise on the back of his neck. What was it? Why did he feel on edge?

Sally sat down. Emeric Jensen offered some comments. Someone else asked a question. Sutherland Cresswell did not hear what was asked, he was too busy listening, too busy clearing his mind. And suddenly it clicked into place. It was not a sound, but an absence of sound, a silence that had drawn his attention. The children had been playing outside, running back and forwards, shouting, laughing. At some point those sounds had stopped.

Had his wife brought them in to get ready for lunch? Sutherland listened hard. There was no sound of either children or adults downstairs. He knew the house, he and his family had lived there for fifteen years, he knew its sounds.

Without saying anything, he stood and walked to the side window of the study, the one looking out on the patio and garden. He looked down.

Something happened to time. It stood still, raced fast, stood still again. He listened to his heart beating, and between each beat entire lifetimes passed. He heard voices behind him, but he did not understand what they were saying.

'I said, are you all right, Sutherland?' Sally took a step towards him. He did not seem to hear her. What was he looking at? Why were his hands clenched together so hard? She drew alongside him. He had gone as white as paper. She followed his gaze, through the window and down to the garden.

'Oh sweet Jesus!'

The children were lying on the lawn, scattered where the gas had felled them, some face down, others face up. Suzie Cresswell was there, the one in a pink sweater. Sally recognized Donovan's twin girls, Ellen and Linda. A couple of adults were among the children.

A man dressed in black clothes and wearing a black gas mask was picking his way between the still figures. He carried a gun with a silencer in his hand, and one by one he was despatching his victims with single shots in the back of the neck. Each body jerked in turn and lay still.

Sally turned and grabbed her jacket, slung across the back of a chair. Faces were turned to her, uncomprehending. Some people were on their feet already. She pulled out her communications handset and pressed the transmit button.

'Gary! Robert! Are you down there? Can you hear me?' She was trying to raise the security team they had left on duty outside the house. She knew them all by name. 'Pete! Come in, anybody! Answer me, for God's sake!'

There was a sound of footsteps in the corridor outside the study.

The last thing she heard, the last thing any of them heard was a loud crash as the door exploded inwards. The last thing she saw was a man dressed in black and carrying a heavy sub-machine gun.

CHAPTER SIXTY-FOUR

Port-au-Prince lay battered and bruised in uncertain sunlight, guarded from the rear by towering, wasted hills. The sea thrust itself against the shore like a salt-tipped tongue probing a rotten cavity. Calm waters after angry seas, light after darkness, silence after rage, putrefaction after death. Only the sea moved, turgid, covered with oil and seaweed, flotsam of every description, a ragged, dirty thing.

The *Fanchette* limped towards the harbour, riding low in the water. A bird swooped out of the clear blue sky, white-winged and raucous, grazing the deckhouse as it passed. The little boat had taken on water and her pumps had started to seize up. Reuben, Angelina and August stood on deck, wordless and numb, watching the sea part in front of them. They had ridden out the storm all the first night and through much of the following day, sleeping and waking intermittently, their dreams white and naked, possessed by the hurricane.

Angelina had woken screaming on three occasions, with no-one to comfort her. August had sat staring out at the sea for a long time, until he too fell into a raging sleep. Reuben swam through bitter darknesses and was possessed by gods he neither knew nor loved. His parents did not visit him there, nor Devorah, nor Lindström, nor Danny, none of the dead. But he saw the living, he saw Sally and Forbes and Max Bellegarde dancing a strange dance, and Doug Hooper, bloody and heroic and grey-skinned, turning in their midst, a necklace of burning pamphlets strung around his neck.

'Where will you go, August?' Angelina had not wanted to put the question until now. 'What will you do?'

The boy shrugged. Without Lindström, he had nowhere to go, no means of making a living, no future. Angelina looked at his ragged clothes and dirty bare feet. What was he? Twelve, thirteen?

A piece of flotsam like the rubber tyres and empty bottles that choked Port-au-Prince harbour. A ship's-boy without a master or a ship. The *Fanchette*, she had little doubt, would be sold to pay off Lindström's debts. Not a gourde would be left.

'I think you should come with us,' she said.

The boy shrugged again. He held the old tabby in his arms, stroking the salt-stained fur with an automatic motion.

'Sam can come, too,' she said. But for how long? This was no longer her home, they would never get permission to take August into the United States. Perhaps Mama Vijina could help.

August nodded. He knew better than to reject the generosity of the rich. In his eyes, Reuben and Angelina were fabulously wealthy. He had learned how to take what little he could get from life with apparent grace. But he still resented it, still wished for the freedom to throw it all back in someone's face again.

They anchored off the little jetty just north of Fort Ste Claire and paddled ashore in the dinghy, leaving their equipment behind. The harbour was strangely deserted, as though the storm had sapped everyone's will, tempting them to stay off work for the day. There was a tension in the morning air that had not been there when they left, an uneasiness not wholly the work of the hurricane.

The Peugeot was waiting for them where they had left it. Everywhere there were puddles of water from the storm. Driving back to Mama Vijina's, they saw further signs of devastation on every side. The wind had torn across the island, ripping up trees, tearing down fences, snatching chickens from their pens and grackles from their nests, mincing, shredding, pummelling, wrecking without pity or shame. The tangled streets were filled with debris that had been carried miles before being deposited here: twisted pots and pans, broken calabash bowls, coconuts, spades, candles, a broken crucifix. Everywhere, windows had burst under the terrible pressure of the wind, strewing shards of broken glass in all directions. Reuben thought of the Hoopers, of the destruction of their shop. They had had their hurricane in advance. He wondered what had become of them.

Mama Vijina was waiting for them. Someone had seen the boat come in and passed the word on. The electricity had been cut, the telephones were out, but Port-au-Prince functioned after its own fashion, according to different rules. They were not dependent on telephones or newspapers to spread the word. If you wanted the real news, you didn't tune in to the radio, you listened to the bush telegraph.

They ate a little, pretending an appetite they did not feel. Someone talked of love in smooth, evasive terms: love of the *mystères*, love of the ocean, love of death. From their chairs, they could smell hibiscus and oleander, almond and bougainvillea, dark smells, labile and singular, resurrected from the storm. They talked of nothing. Mama Vijina watched the boy, knowing how little he could hope for. Someone else talked of solitude. There was a tinkling of spoons on plates, a brightness of knives, the scent of resurrection. In the street outside, men and women put their lives back together carefully, as they had done many times before. There was talk of penitence.

No progress had been made on the killing of Macandal. The police had identified him as a man of thirty-four named Otard Le Sauveur, a griffon from Les Cayes, a clerk with the Ministry of Culture, no criminal record. He left a woman – a *femme caille* – in Port-au-Prince, by whom he had three children, and another – a *femme placée* – in Carrefour. His killer was being sought. There were no clues.

When her friends left, the women who talked of love and solitude, Mama Vijina brought Reuben and Angelina close and told them disturbing news. The political situation was tense and deteriorating, there was talk of a crackdown on political opponents, of a curfew, of blood running in the streets. The long-promised elections would not now be held, people were urged to unite in loyalty to their chief and protector, President Cicéron, troublemakers would be shot on sight. Rumours abounded, graffiti had appeared on walls last night, fear lay on the city like a gloved hand. Love and solitude. The only ways out.

Shortly after breakfast, August disappeared. Sam remained behind, mewing discontentedly, refusing food. Locadi came in, wearing a flowered dress, and took him away, scratching, bewildered. Angelina gave her Lindström's hat, brought from the *Fanchette*, to put beside him, but Locadi refused it, saying it would not comfort him, that cats are not dogs after all.

They went upstairs after that, to sleep. Angelina lay awake for a long time, watching light diffused through the blue shutters, its patterns shifting lazily on the floor. If she closed her eyes, the room seemed to pitch and yaw, and she would be forced to open them again in order to focus on something hard and unmoving. When sleep did come at last, her dreams were filled with the smell of crushed vanilla and the bittersweet taste of French chocolate.

It was long past noon when she woke. The room was dark, but filled with tiny points of light. The sun made dappled shapes on the naked wooden floor, soft yet intense, like butter melting on a chafing dish. She had been awakened by a sound, and for a long moment she felt fear constrict her, pulling at her heart and throat.

There was a shadow at the foot of the bed, still, not moving. With a start, she realized it was Reuben. He was standing silently, watching her. A long arrow of sunlight fell slantwise across his chest. He did not move at all. And every moment he grew to be less shadow and more flesh, as her eyes regained their accustomed wholeness of sight.

'I couldn't sleep,' he said finally. 'The bed kept moving, everything kept moving.'

'I know,' she said, her voice languid with sleep.

'You were sleeping,' he told her. 'I watched you.'

'How long?'

'I don't know.' He paused. 'A long time.'

In the street outside, a woman's voice sang a love song, slow and poignant, before night fell. There would be a curfew, tanks would lumber past, the song would fade.

'I was dreaming about my father,' she said.

'Was that true?' he asked. 'What you told me before, about . . .' He could not complete the sentence. The thought appalled him.

She did not answer. True or untrue, she dreamed of vanilla-scented hands, of an old man's beard grazing her cheek.

Reuben came closer and sat on the edge of the bed. She had taken off her clothes, she was naked beneath a thin sheet, she was filled with remnants of uneasy sleep. All awkwardness had fallen away from them, the storm had torn down the barriers between them, they had been dead, they were undergoing a resurrection. Or another death.

She sat up in the bed, and the sheet fell away, leaving her breasts and shoulders bare, a terrible vulnerability. He leaned forward and touched her cheek and neck, brushing her tired skin with long, naked fingers. She sighed and turned to him, feeling sleep turn to arousal, death to resurrection. He bent down and kissed her shoulder, running his lips and tongue along the line of the bone. She had not washed, she still carried the sea on her body. Her skin tasted of salt, not the salt of the body, but a deep ocean salt.

341

He slid onto the bed alongside her, feeling her arms slip round his neck, pulling him to her.

'This is the dance as well,' she said.

'I don't understand.'

'Let me teach you,' she whispered.

The sheet fell away and she was naked beneath him. Somewhere a drum began to beat. In the street, the love song rose and fell like the sea.

CHAPTER SIXTY-FIVE

It took a long time for the smoke to clear. The street had filled with ash and cinders, the gutters ran thick with blackened water, people stood in little clumps chatting and watching. There had been some difficulty in getting the engine near enough, and even then the water pressure had proved unsatisfactory. Neighbours had helped with buckets, but little had been salvaged, the fire had been too fierce. There had been damage to the houses on either side as well. They might have to be demolished.

A thin breeze lifted some of the ashes into the morning air. They were light, as light as gossamer, they floated in the slightest current. Close up, it was possible to make out thin white ghosts traced over them, the shades of printed words. On the ground, indifferent feet trampled them to dust.

They had heard of the Hoopers' disaster soon after waking. Locadi had come in distressed, saying there had been a fire in the rue des Casernes, the American bookshop had been burned to the ground.

Without waiting for breakfast, they had hurried round to see what they could do. Ever since their arrival, Reuben had felt a strange sense of responsibility for the missionaries. And he was still uneasy about Doug; it was not a real fear that the American could do him harm, more a foreboding, a sense that Hooper's inner misery of spirit, his search for certainty of purpose might lead him into trouble.

The Hoopers were physically unhurt, but dazzled by the enormity of what had happened, the gross disenchantment of their loss. Everything had gone, even the small things, clothing, toothpaste, Hershey bars. Reuben found them huddled together in the ash-filled street staring numbly at the twisted ruin of their enterprise, as though engaged in a silent prayer that had the power to undo the viciousness of fire.

Haltingly, Jean explained how they had returned to the shop late the night before, after a meeting of some sort, a 'Feast' she called it, though it sounded a sober enough occasion, coffee, biscuits, interminable prayers. They had fallen asleep, Doug with the aid of painkillers as usual, and gone on sleeping until well after three, when they had been roused from paradisiacal dreams by shouting voices and crackling flames. Running outside, Doug had noticed an unmistakable smell of paraffin. It had been sprinkled liberally throughout the shop.

Doug drew himself close to Reuben. His hair was wild, he had not shaved since his beating, his eyes looked shocked and drugged.

'This is Valris's doing, just like before,' he hissed. 'He tried again yesterday, he gave me an ultimatum. I had to turn him down. Now this happens. But he'll pay, I'll see he pays.'

Jean Hooper grabbed her husband tightly by the arm.

'That's enough of such talk, Douglas Hooper. If this was anyone's doing, it was God's. He wants to test us, to prove we're worthy. The Assembly will help. We'll go to the Assembly.'

But Doug pulled away. He was not to be appeased, not even by the spectre of virtuous sacrifice.

'We're wiped out, Jean. Don't you understand that? God would test us, but He wouldn't wipe us out. What would be the point of that? Valris's to blame, Valris and his thugs. But I'll teach him a lesson, a good, old-fashioned American lesson that he won't forget.'

Reuben drew Hooper aside.

'Take your wife's advice, Mr Hooper,' he said. 'Don't let Valris drag you into something you'll regret. This isn't Indiana. The man who ordered this can have you jailed or shot or thrown into the sea, no questions asked. Something's going on, or haven't you noticed? They say there'll be a curfew tonight. There have been arrests. Beatings. Two people have died in custody. You're naked here, you have no-one to look after your interests. Forget Valris, forget Haiti. Cut your losses now, before it's too late. You may not get another chance.'

Hooper did not answer. He was unreachable.

Reuben sighed and turned to Jean Hooper.

'Where will you stay?'

She pointed to a group of half a dozen men and women standing near the shop.

'The friends will take care of us,' she whispered. 'They're our family now.'

'Go there now,' Reuben said. 'But be on the first flight out of Port-au-Prince.'

She fixed him with her persistent gaze.

'Thanks for your concern, Professor, but we came here for a reason and we'll stay until God tells us otherwise. Don't worry about us; worry about yourself.'

August was waiting for them when they got back to Mama Vijina's. Locadi had prepared a meal of fried chicken in Creole sauce, red beans, aubergine and rice. He was eating as though he had fasted for a month. Angelina thought he looked tired. No, more than that. Crushed. He looked fifty, not twelve or thirteen. Or was it just that she had not noticed it before?

They joined him, piling food high on their plates, realizing that they too were hungry. The previous evening had been spent with Mama Vijina, talking, switching between the government-owned Tele-National and the two channels of the nominally independent Tele-Haïti, listening to Radio-Cacique, interpreting the conflicting reports coming in from the city and the countryside. Reuben had gone to the post office to telephone Sally again, only to be turned away. All communication with the outside world had been suspended.

The Dessalines Battalion, the country's largest, had been confined to barracks and placed on round-the-clock alert. The Presidential Guard had been doubled. All military leave had been cancelled. General Nord Laguerre, the army's Commander-in-Chief, had been called to the Palais National for a lengthy consultation with the president and General Valris. There had been arrests in Port-au-Prince, Cap-Haïtien, Port-de-Paix, Jérémie, Les Cayes and Jacmel. Max had spoken on the radio, cautioning restraint, hinting darkly of worse deeds to come.

They had gone to bed early, made love again, and stayed awake talking into the small hours. Through the open window of Angelina's room, the moon had painted everything with magic. Slowly, they had opened themselves to one another, offering the broken pieces of their individual lives for scrutiny. This morning it all seemed unreal and far away, the caresses, the intimacies, the long, perfect silences. The taste of ashes filled their mouths.

August did not talk much at first. No-one asked where he had been or what he had been up to. Angelina watched him eating, the hurried, anxious motions of a scavenger brought up to fend for himself. Lindström had done little to civilize him. As he grew full at last he started to slow down. Finally, he laid his spoon aside.

'I found them,' he said. 'The ones what done it.' His mouth was smeared with sauce. Angelina reached across and wiped it with her handkerchief. He did not shy away.

'The ones who did what?' she asked.

'The ones what killed the Captain.'

She looked round at Reuben and told him what the boy had just told her.

'Ask him how he knows.'

She asked. He shuffled a little, then launched into his story.

'It weren't easy,' he said. 'I had to ask lots of people. Down the docks. I did all the jetties, the ro-ro terminal, container dock, all the way down near as far as the navy yard. It's a mess down there. Fuckin' storm's done the whole place up. Anyway, I asked who else come in after the hurricane, apart from us. See, whoever killed the Captain couldn't have got back in once the storm started. They'd have been maybe halfway back here when it got bad, maybe not as far as that. Either they'd've heaved to and taken their chances, or they'd've put down a storm anchor like what we did. Once things settled down, they'd've come in ahead of us.'

'You don't know they came back here, to Port-au-Prince.'

'They followed us out there, didn't they? After that hurricane, they wouldn't fuck about, they'd get straight back. An' there was three boats what got in before us. I got their names. There was a coaster what got stuck comin' down from Santiago. You can rule him out. There was a fishing boat called the *Ti Coyo*. Engine packed up. They knows them down the docks. I've seen them going out myself. They're all right.

'But the third one, that's the one. The *Quinquin*. Forty-footer, same as the *Fanchette*. Come in day before yesterday. No engine trouble or nothin', just got stuck, they said. Skipper's a man called Gro Moso. Had three passengers with him. Nobody knew them.'

'What were they like, these passengers?'

'Two blacks and a *blanc*. The white shouldn't be hard to find. He has a scar. A long scar on his right cheek.'

CHAPTER SIXTY-SIX

The knocking woke them just after midnight. Reuben rolled out of bed half-asleep, reacting automatically. There was a second round of knocks, heavier this time. He slipped on his trousers, opened the drawer by the bed, and drew out his new gun. August had obtained it from a man who owned a hardware stall at the Iron Market. It was an old Czech CZ75, a locked-breech, double-action auto that had needed extensive cleaning and oiling before it would even take a magazine. It wasn't much of a gun to trust your life to, but it had been the only gun in Port-au-Prince that afternoon. The knocking came again, more insistent than ever. There was a sound of footsteps heading for the door.

Angelina was bolt upright in bed.

'It's not the police,' she whispered.

'How do you know?'

'They wouldn't bother knocking. They'd smash the door down. If it was a mistake, too bad.'

'Who, then?'

She shrugged.

'Smith?'

'Same thing. Why give us a warning?'

Apart from buying the gun, they had spent the afternoon looking for Smith, speaking with August's contacts up and down the waterfront. There'd been no firm leads, only sideways glances, nervous coughs.

Someone knocked on the bedroom door.

'Who is it?' Angelina asked.

'Vijina. You've got to come quick.'

Reuben went to the door and opened it. Mama Vijina was standing in an old cotton dress. She looked empty, more desolate than tired.

'It's the American woman,' she said. 'She's with a man I don't know. Looks like she's in trouble. I don't understand what she's saying.'

Angelina told Reuben what Mama Vijina had said. She wrapped a sheet round her and slipped out of bed.

'Go down,' she said. 'I won't be long.'

Jean Hooper was in the tiny front room, nervously watching shadows gather round a collection of oleographs and figurines – Mama Vijina sometimes used the room as a *bagui* and as a place to meet people from the neighbourhood when they came for advice. She was sitting on the chair normally reserved for Mama Vijina herself, a large, ornate chair upholstered in cheap red velvet. Beside her stood Amirzadeh. He looked pale. In the doorway, Locadi stood quietly, keeping a sleepy eye on their visitors.

The missionary looked terrible, even worse than she had done that morning after the fire. She had been crying, and the little make-up she wore had run, staining her face. Everything about her was tense: her hands, her jaw, her neck, her eyes. When Reuben entered the room, she stood up at once, then sat down again, as though pushed.

'You shouldn't be here,' Reuben said. 'You took a terrible risk coming out tonight. They're shooting people on sight. Don't you know there's a curfew?'

He didn't know why he was so abrupt with her. Something in her manner made him want to be harsh. He wanted to shake her bodily, shake sense into her. Or was it just a reaction to his own fear of a few minutes ago?

She didn't answer at once, apart from a couple of gulps that sounded like a reply strangled at birth. For a moment she closed her eyes. Her lips moved in their old recourse. Reuben felt as though he could hit her: she had put everyone at risk, coming here as though her prayers rendered her invisible. And the Iranian, he should have known better, he had lived here long enough.

She looked up at Reuben. There was nothing in her eyes. No appeal, no apology, no anger, no rebuke.

'Doug's been arrested,' she said. 'They're holding him in jail; God knows what they're doing to him.'

Reuben looked from the woman to Amirzadeh. The Iranian held a short amber rosary in one hand, moving each bead deliberately through his long, tense fingers. The beads clicked gently together as they turned. Reuben looked at Jean Hooper again.

'How do you know this?' Reuben asked. 'There's a curfew. Your husband shouldn't even be out of the house.'

'I had a telephone call,' said Amirzadeh. 'Someone told me Doug had been arrested by the security police. He is being held at Pétionville.'

'Did they tell you what he's being charged with?'

Amirzadeh looked at Jean Hooper.

'May I tell him?'

'It's all right,' she said. 'I'll tell him myself.' She hesitated nevertheless. Speech had not touched her eyes. Her eyes were empty. Wherever she had gone, it was deep inside. 'Professor Phelps, Doug killed . . . he killed . . . that man . . .'

Reuben's heart skipped a beat. At that moment, Angelina entered the room. Locadi left to make coffee.

'What man?'

'That general, the one who was supposed to help us. The traitor in our midst, the Judas – Valris. They say Doug killed Valris.' She was growing distressed now, her eyes bulging with tears. What did she mean, 'the traitor in our midst'? Had the phrase some meaning other than the obvious? She was crippled in speech tonight, her tongue stumbled, spilling words. Angelina went across to comfort her, but she shook her off.

'You've got to find him, got to get him out, got to . . . got to . . .' Her voice was rising. The words came out in little jerks, fragments thrown out without meaning or purpose. Her manner was disquieting. She remained down inside herself, insulated from everything, warm and comfortable, in some sort of communion with her God, while her voice rose and her body shook as though they were things wholly independent of her. 'Got to . . . got to . . . got . . .'

Reuben turned to Amirzadeh. The Iranian seemed fairly casual, as though this sort of thing happened to him every day, as though grief and torment were a business like any other. The beads moved precisely through his fingers.

'Is it true?' Reuben asked. 'Did Doug kill Valris?'

Amirzadeh shrugged, an Oriental gesture, the equivocal, nuanced mannerism of a *bāzārī* merchant feigning a lack of interest in a potential customer.

'*Hīch namīdānam*. I don't know,' he said. He spoke in careful

English, in the fluted accents of north Tehran. 'That is what they told me. I think they are telling the truth. Why should they lie? There is no reason for them to lie.'

'Were you there? Did you see Doug when he left?'

Amirzadeh shook his head. His face was well-formed, an exquisite beauty, a carved solemnity, like Darius conquering.

'I only arrived half an hour ago. After the phone call.'

'And here? Why did you bring her here?'

The Iranian hesitated. Nearby, Jean Hooper smiled and frowned alternately, without reason, as though her conscience both rebuked and comforted her.

'I told her your friend Mrs Hammel is the sister of Bellegarde. I thought she might be able to help. Or you, you are an American. Maybe he will listen to you.'

'You could have come alone. There was no need to risk her life taking her out in the curfew.'

Amirzadeh shrugged again, remote, indifferent.

'She is safe now. But I think we have to do something.'

Reuben turned to speak to Jean again. She was staring at him, as though wondering who he was and what she was doing here. But she seemed more in control of herself, as though a crisis had passed and the next was still a little distance away.

'Mrs Hooper, do you think there's any truth in this story?' Reuben asked. 'I know your husband was hot-tempered, but surely . . .'

Reuben realized as he asked the question why the story sounded so hard to believe. He had not treated Doug Hooper as an adult. Hooper didn't drink, didn't smoke, didn't swear, maybe didn't have sex. Some religious people are children in adults' clothing. But it looked as though Doug Hooper had just grown up.

'He's been threatening something since last night. You heard him this morning. Threats, terrible threats. He has no forgiveness. He has no love any more: not for me, not for God. The fire was the last straw. I think it could be true.'

'They say he had a gun,' Amirzadeh said.

'What sort of gun?'

The Iranian shrugged.

'They did not say. A pistol of some sort, perhaps.'

Reuben looked at Jean Hooper.

'Do you know anything about a gun?'

She shook her head.

'No. Doug never had a gun back home. And he wouldn't have known where to get one here.' She looked at Angelina. 'Please, Mrs Hammel, you've got to do something. You've got to speak to your brother. The Faith will be finished here, finished. We've got to get him out of jail, make them forget this ever happened.'

It was all she cared about, the reputation of her faith. She didn't give a damn for Doug, nor for his intended victim. Reuben did not care whether the entire Baha'i mission got kicked out of Haiti; but Hooper's escapade could turn nasty.

'Mrs Hooper,' Reuben said, 'there's nothing any of us can do tonight. There's a curfew on. There are trigger-happy soldiers out on the streets looking for targets. It won't help the situation any if Angelina or I get shot.'

'I can help you,' said Amirzadeh. 'I can get you through the checkpoints.'

Reuben shook his head.

'Far too risky,' he said. 'They're shooting on sight.'

Amirzadeh made a gesture unfamiliar to Reuben, the Iranian equivalent of a quick headshake, a rapid, upward tilt of the head accompanied by a click of the tongue.

'They will make an exception, you will see. I am a pharmacist. Even in a curfew, people need drugs. Someone may be sick, someone else may be dying. I have a special pass. My car is painted with a red cross. There is a blue light for the roof. Believe me, you will be safe. I have done this many times. Curfews are nothing new in Haiti.'

'Please,' pleaded Jean Hooper. 'Please go with him, Professor. You and Mrs Hammel are our only hope. If you leave it till the morning, Doug could be dead. They say he tried to kill a government minister during a curfew.'

Reuben turned to Angelina. Jean Hooper had shown a bit of realism for a change.

'What do you think? Will Max listen to you?'

She shrugged.

'I don't know. But I can talk to him. If Mr Amirzadeh can get us to Pétionville safely, I'm willing to speak with Max. If Max is willing to speak with me.'

'Very well,' said Reuben. 'We'll risk it.'

CHAPTER SIXTY-SEVEN

In a curfew, silence mutates. Insensibly, it takes on different forms, different modalities. It drifts, it collects in doorways, it creeps in through unshuttered windows, open keyholes, unguarded fanlights. Sometimes it is tense, like the moments before a bomb explodes, or a gun fires, or a child dies. Sometimes it is seductive, like the quiet between a man and a woman before they make love. Or sad, as though a little time had passed and they were about to quarrel.

So many silences, so many moods, so many shields to keep the vociferous world at bay.

Reuben felt them tighten round him now, all the silences, skintight, perfect, mantles for his fear. They were halfway to Pétionville. Amirzadeh had stopped the car and switched the engine off, letting the silences flood inside. They had already passed through two checkpoints, at each of which the Iranian had flashed his papers. He explained that Dr Phelps had been summoned from the Adventist Hospital at Diquini, just south of the city, to treat General Valris at his Pétionville home. The soldiers had heard of the attempted assassination, but had no information on the state of the general's health. Rather than be.the cause of a potentially fatal delay, they waved Amirzadeh's Volvo estate through at once.

The roadblocks were serious affairs. At one, a light tank had been parked, its engine purring resonantly, ready to respond at once in the event of an all-out alert. Near it had stood a Fiat 55-13 armoured bus. Amirzadeh had whispered to Reuben that it was full of soldiers or riot police equipped to deal with any outbreak of civil disorder. Reuben got the impression that the Iranian approved. Disorder of any kind was anathema to him, as it was to the Hoopers.

They had entered the heart of Pétionville. On their right began a series of villas built on bluffs overlooking the road on one side, the city on the other. The Volvo's headlights picked out long gravelled driveways lined with red hibiscus. The flowers shimmered like blood, as though the darkness was bleeding. Huge white moths danced in the light, fluttering like pieces of silver, their powdered wings dizzy and confused. Angelina held tight to Reuben's hand in the rear of the car.

The square was filled with police and military vehicles. A steady throbbing came from the engines of two Panhard AML H60–7 armoured cars parked outside the Choucoune. There were no guests to revel there tonight. Nervous-looking soldiers, most of them little more than children, stood beside a personnel carrier, smoking or staring into the darkness. There were lights in none of the buildings except the police headquarters. Floodlights bathed the entrance in stark white light. Guards were posted at the door.

Amirzadeh showed his pass, but his story held no water here. Angelina came out and talked at length in Creole with one of the guards. Reuben watched her from the car. His hands were sticky with sweat. He wondered how they had ever allowed Amirzadeh to persuade them into thinking they could pull this off.

But Angelina was Max's sister in more than name. In New York, she was no-one, just a professor's wife, a failed painter, half-white, half-black, a creature of the in-betweens. Here, she had the confidence of family and class, the assuredness of someone who knew just how things worked. The guard disappeared inside with alacrity and came out less than five minutes later. Angelina and Reuben were to go inside. Amirzadeh was to wait in the car.

Max was waiting for them, not in his office, but in a large room on the ground floor. The walls of the room were covered with maps and bulletin boards. There was a large table bearing a map of Port-au-Prince on which roadblocks and guardposts were indicated by small models. As they entered, Max was busy shouting instructions down a telephone. He did not look up until he had finished speaking. Someone handed him a despatch. He glanced at it, nodded and threw it on his desk.

'Good evening, Angelina, Professor. I have been expecting you. You have come to see your friend Mr Douglas Hooper. Poor Mr Hooper, you will find him the worse for wear. He has been foolish, your Mr Hooper. No, not foolish – stupid. Extremely stupid.'

'Is it true he killed someone?' Angelina asked. 'A government minister?'

Bellegarde nodded. A soldier came in and handed him a heavy sealed envelope. He signed for it and put it to one side.

'I must apologize,' he said. 'As you can see, we are extremely busy here tonight.' He paused briefly, as though trying to remember what they had just been talking about. 'Yes,' he said, 'it is true. He shot General Valris. Somehow, Hooper managed to get into the general's house. Valris's bodyguard picked him up after the shooting. They beat him rather badly, I'm afraid, but the officer in charge had the wit to stop them short of killing him. He knew I would be interested in a white man, an American, who had carried out an assassination here in Haiti. And I am interested. Very interested.'

Reuben leaned forward across the desk.

'But surely you realize this was not a political act, that Hooper cannot have meant anything sinister by it. Valris had done those things to make life hard for Hooper. You must have heard. He wrecked his shop, then burned it down. Hooper's a fool as you say, he overreacted. But you must know that he's politically naïve.'

'Yes,' Max replied, 'I know all about that. But I cannot concern myself with motives or with who is and who is not naïve. We are in the middle of a political crisis, or haven't you noticed, Professor? I must go by what I see. A citizen of a country with which Haiti does not possess diplomatic relations, an American with a loaded gun enters the grounds of a house belonging to the Minister of Defence and shoots him. Surely you can see that that is serious. Or are you naïve as well, Professor?'

Angelina interrupted.

'Max, you said yourself that what Hooper did was stupid. Do you honestly think that if there was anything more to it that the CIA would use a man like that?'

'Who said anything about the CIA?'

'That's what was in your mind, wasn't it?'

Bellegarde shrugged.

'Not necessarily,' he said. He fell silent. His eyes alighted on the envelope. He opened it, glanced through its contents and pushed it away again.

'I'd like to see him,' said Reuben. 'Talk to him. Where are you holding him?'

'Hooper?'

'Hooper, of course.'

'He's here, where did you expect? I'm not sure that I want you to see him or speak with him.'

'I'd like to hear what he has to say.'

'Of course, that would be natural.' Max turned to Angelina. 'What do you think? Should we let them talk?'

Angelina nodded.

'Yes,' she said. 'If there are questions later, if Hooper dies, then Professor Phelps can testify he saw him alive while in your custody. I'd like to see him too.'

Bellegarde shook his head.

'No, little sister. I'd like to speak with you myself. You can stay here. I'll send one of my men with the professor. He may see Mr Hooper if he wishes.'

Bellegarde called a man lounging near the door. It was the man in the beige suit, the one called Loubert. He sauntered across and smiled at Reuben. Bellegarde snapped out instructions.

'Come with me,' Loubert said. Reuben went with him to the door. Angelina watched him go. Max watched him go. Angelina said nothing. Max said nothing.

CHAPTER SIXTY-EIGHT

The cell into which Hooper had been thrown was one of seven on the ground floor. The doors seemed flimsy and the bars on the window exaggeratedly thin; but Reuben guessed that nobody in here would be healthy enough to attempt breaking out. A stench of stale urine and human faeces hung on the unmoving air. Reuben gagged as he entered the cell.

A weak yellow bulb gave enough illumination to send half-formed shadows scurrying into the corners of the narrow cell. The ceiling was thick with spiders' webs. There were traces of dried blood on the walls. On the floor lay a low pallet bed, and on the bed Reuben could make out a dim figure covered by a thin blanket.

Valris's soldiers had not killed Doug Hooper, it was true. But that was more or less a technicality. It took no more than a glance for Reuben to tell that, even if Hooper did recover, his life would scarcely be worth living. The bed and blanket were caked in blood.

Hooper was semiconscious. He stirred as Reuben sat on the edge of the bed. There were no Hershey bars here, no photographs of saints. Hooper tried to move his arms in a vain attempt to fend off the blows he thought were about to descend. Both arms had been broken in several places. One hand had been repeatedly crushed beneath someone's boot.

'It's all right, Doug, it's me, Myron Phelps. I've come to help you. I'm going to try to get you out of here.'

Hooper rolled his head towards Reuben. The wound on his cheek had been reopened and enlarged. Both eyes were closed, puffy and bruised. His lips were thick and smeared with blood. He opened his mouth to speak, revealing bleeding gums; most of his teeth had been smashed out with a rifle butt. Reuben winced as he noticed that his left ear had been sliced partly off.

Reuben felt a huge anger swell in him. He turned and shouted at Loubert.

'Why the fuck haven't you taken him to hospital? He needs treatment! What are you people, savages?'

Loubert pretended not to understand. He leaned against the door and cleaned his fingernails. Even here he wore his shades.

'Phelps . . .' whispered Hooper in a broken voice. 'Who . . . I don't . . . remember . . .'

'It doesn't matter. I'm going to get you out, take you to hospital. I won't let them keep you here.'

'No-one . . . speaks English,' Hooper wheezed. He tried to move to a more comfortable position, but the resulting pain almost caused him to black out. Reuben suspected that he must have several broken ribs. He was afraid to touch him.

'Please,' he said. 'Try not to move. I'll tell Bellegarde you've got to be given morphine and put in a proper bed. Amirzadeh's outside. He has drugs in his car.'

'Co . . . closer . . .' whispered Hooper. Reuben bent down. 'No . . . gun . . . Never . . . had . . . gun . . . Wanted . . . to . . . talk . . . Valris . . . Not . . . kill . . . Please . . . believe me . . .'

'I believe you,' said Reuben. 'I believe you.' He reached out a hand uncertainly and touched Hooper gently on the side of the neck, where he seemed to be without bruises. Tears were leaking through the blackened lids of Hooper's eyes. Reuben took a paper tissue from his pocket and wiped them away. Where was Hooper's God now? he wondered. Where was anybody's God?

There was a sound at the door. Reuben turned. Max Bellegarde was standing in the doorway watching. Loubert moved aside to let his superior enter. Max seemed altered, strange, his affability, however false, now stripped away.

'What has Mr Hooper been telling you, Lieutenant Abrams? What sweetnesses has he been whispering to you?'

Reuben stood. For a moment he did not register that Bellegarde had used his real name. Had the major known from the beginning? Or had Angelina just told him?

'He tells me he had no gun,' Reuben said. 'He says he went to speak to Valris, that's all. I believe him.'

Bellegarde snapped his fingers. A uniformed policeman stepped out of the shadows behind and handed him something. The major held it up towards the light. It was a gun in a plastic bag, a Browning Hi-Power.

'I see you recognize it, Lieutenant. It is the gun found in Mr Hooper's possession when he was arrested. It has his fingerprints.' Bellegarde paused. 'It also has yours.'

'That's a lie,' exclaimed Reuben. 'Hooper never saw that gun. Your men took it from my room. You planted it on him, planted his fingerprints.'

'So you do admit that it is your gun, Lieutenant. Well, let us see if Mr Hooper remembers it too.'

Bellegarde took three long strides across the cell. He ignored Reuben, standing near the edge of Hooper's bed. Without warning, Bellegarde grabbed a clump of the missionary's hair in his right hand and pulled him to a half-sitting position. Reuben made to go for the major, but there was a click behind him and he stepped back again.

'Don't be a fool, Lieutenant,' Bellegarde said. 'Captain Loubert doesn't care if he shoots you or not, it's all the same to him.'

Max held Hooper's head a foot or so away from his own face. He dropped the gun on the bed and held his free hand close to Hooper's mouth.

'Such a mess,' he said. 'You need those teeth attended to.'

Deftly, Bellegarde inserted long fingers between Hooper's ravaged gums. The American cried out as Max took a broken tooth between thumb and forefinger and rocked it back and forwards. The tooth finally came free of the gum, spilling fresh blood over Hooper's chin and chest. Bellegarde repeated the manoeuvre with a second tooth. Hooper lost consciousness.

Max looked round. He seemed almost disappointed that his victim had slipped away from him.

'We have plenty of time, Lieutenant. There is no rush. My wife and children are safe asleep at home. I am not expected back while the crisis continues.

'Now, tell me if I am correct or not. You obtained this gun from a US government agency known as the CSA, an agency to which you are temporarily attached. You then gave the gun to Mr Hooper here, who is also an American government agent. Hooper proceeded to carry out his mission, namely to shoot and kill General Louis Valris, the Haitian Minister of Defence. Unfortunately for him and for you, but luckily for the Haitian people, Hooper was arrested by the general's bodyguard after completing his mission. That is substantially correct, is it not?'

Reuben said nothing. What was the point?

'You have nothing to say? Too bad. Mr Hooper goes before a firing squad later tonight. A confession might have gained him some time. No matter, I have absolutely no interest in Mr Hooper. It is you who interest me now, Lieutenant. You and the people you work for.'

The major stood. He glanced round the cell as though seeing it for the first time. His head almost touched the spiders' webs. Black shapes moved across the ceiling on dreadful legs.

'Very well,' Max said. 'I think it is time to leave Mr Hooper to his fate. There are more important matters to be discussed.'

He stopped and came close to Reuben, very close.

'We have a long journey ahead of us tonight. I will have to ask you to be patient, very patient.'

They left Hooper lying on the bed, like a piece of wreckage on the ocean floor. The blankets had fallen from him, divesting him of his last protection. Was he dreaming? Reuben wondered. And did he dream of paradise or hell?

Bellegarde led Reuben to the front of the station, out into the crowded square. Amirzadeh's car had gone. There was crackling from a radio set nearby, and a clash of gears as an armoured truck lumbered past the Choucoune. Angelina was nowhere to be seen. A large black Mercedes drew alongside. Loubert was at the wheel.

'Where's Angelina?' Reuben asked. 'If we're going somewhere, I'd like her to come with us.'

'Angelina?' Bellegarde repeated. 'You must be mistaken. I know no-one of that name.'

Max opened the door and motioned Reuben inside. For a moment, Reuben stared at him as though about to strike him. He looked round. Was Angelina there, in the shadows watching? Or downstairs in a cell like the one they had just left? He bowed his head and got into the car. Max got in beside him and closed the door softly. No-one said a word as Loubert drove off into the waiting night.

CHAPTER SIXTY-NINE

There was no wind, no rain – nothing but a blank sky and the night empty above a barren countryside. They drove through all manner of silences: the silence of curfew, and the silence of empty fields, the silence of night and the silence before dawn. No-one stopped them, no-one questioned their coming or their going: Bellegarde had telephoned ahead to each roadblock in turn. It was as if the country lay in his hand, perfectly, like an apple fallen from a high tree. An apple whose centre was already rotten.

They headed north out of Port-au-Prince, following the road that led past Bois Moustique. After Bon Repos, the road twisted north-west, skirting the coast towards St Marc. In the back of the car, lapped by silences, Reuben slept and woke several times; each time when he awoke he saw Max Bellegarde sitting in the same position, wide awake, his hands on his lap, staring at his own reflection in the window.

The night was full of soldiers. They sat in doorways smoking lonely cigarettes, or leaned against mournful barricades blowing on their fingers for warmth. Once, there was a sound of gunfire, hesitant and far away, drifting across the night through vast plantations of green sugar cane. They passed through St Marc without stopping. The town was deserted, as though a sudden pestilence had ravaged its inhabitants. It was a place of closed shutters and locked doors.

Dawn appeared, sullen and menacing, high in the east above the Black Mountains. In a haze of imperfect morning light, they passed ghost-like through a desert world: flat beds of mud stretched endlessly in every direction, pocked by the tangled wickerwork of dark mangrove thickets; huge salt pans lay stark and crystalline in the ragged sunlight, pools of blue and green and sickly yellow. The world seemed vast and uninhabited. There was no warmth in anything.

They passed through the slums of Gonaïves and headed east into the Chaîne de Balence mountains. Reuben rubbed his eyes and watched uncomprehendingly, lost beyond all hope. He knew where they were going. He had guessed the name of their destination.

Petite-Rivière stood dreaming in a dark and twisted valley ringed by hills. They came upon it abruptly, on a tight road arched by vines. Reuben knew it at once; even from the distance he could sense the taintedness that clung to it, an ancient corruption, time sensed as distance. The hillsides all around were charred and desolate. Stunted plants and gaunt, unnatural trees were all that remained of the old plantation. It was as though a sorcerer, bitter and defeated, had laid waste all about him with a single, poisonous spell.

Stone had fallen from stone, rooftile from rooftile, rafter from rafter, beam from beam. Neither time nor nature had been gentle with Petite-Rivière. Old walls stood bowed beneath the weight of long, clinging vines. Spiders wove webs in the spaces where doors and windows had once stood. How long, Reuben wondered, had things been like this? When did Angelina say she and Rick had visited the house? Twelve years ago? Could it have fallen into such ruin in so short a time? It must already have been well on its way by then.

The Mercedes bumped and slithered along a track that was little more than a groove through thick vegetation. The sun had gained in strength, filling the little valley with humid warmth. Between the trees, pale butterflies sparkled in strips of sunlight, moments of dreaming in the midst of rank reality. They drew up near what had been the entrance to the main house. There had been lawns and peacocks here once. Now weeds grew as high as a man's waist.

'Come with me, Lieutenant,' Bellegarde said, laying a soft hand on Reuben's arm. He had still not explained how he came to know Reuben's true identity, nor had Reuben asked him to.

They stepped out of the car onto an expanse of overgrown weeds and jagged thorns. A rough pathway had been hacked to the entrance, in which a door of sorts still stood. Bellegarde led the way. Reuben came next, followed by Loubert, not visibly tired by his long spell at the wheel.

Petite-Rivière was, if anything, more decayed inside than out. It looked as though no-one had set foot there in decades. Reuben could see no sign of habitation, no evidence of the family Angelina said had been in residence twelve years earlier. The staircase directly ahead had rotted and collapsed in the centre, eaten away by termites and damp. Where the plaster was still intact, the walls were sheeted in a layer of green mould, broken here and there by patches of naked stone.

Bellegarde seemed to know his way. He led Reuben along the passage, past the ruined staircase, to a gaping doorway beyond which lay a huge, unfurnished room. Reuben picked his way gingerly across a floor of cracked and broken stones. The original windows had been bricked up, but in places shafts of purple sunlight stabbed through gaping holes in the ceiling. Glancing up, Reuben saw traces of fine mouldings and elegant cornices, their detail lost for ever to the ravages of damp.

They passed into a smaller room, very dark and cold. Loubert pushed Reuben inside. At the far end, Bellegarde stood waiting by an open door. As Reuben approached, the major held something out towards him.

'Here,' he said, 'you'll need this.'

It was a battered hurricane lamp. Loubert came forward with a box of matches and struck one to light Reuben's lamp. Max lit one for himself and handed a third to Loubert.

'There's no electricity here, Lieutenant. Not even gas. But this is better than nothing. Whatever you do, don't lose it.'

Reuben could now see that the open door by which Max had been standing led directly to a flight of steep stone steps. Max did not falter. Holding his lamp high, he set off down the stairwell. Moments later, the light from his lamp had been swallowed by darkness. Reuben hesitated. Loubert came up behind and pushed him in the back. He stepped through the doorway.

The steps went down at an acute angle, spiralling tightly about a narrow central pillar. Bellegarde's feet could be heard below, ringing on the cold stone. Using his right hand to follow the wall of the narrow shaft, Reuben held the lamp in his left, shining its yellow light on the steps immediately in front. They were badly worn in the centre, the mark of generations.

Reuben already had a premonition of what he would find at the bottom. This must have been Bourjolly's first experiment in excavating chambers under the earth. Reuben wondered what he had accomplished here, assisted as he must have been by long-accumulated wealth and the strong backs of African slaves. He was not prepared for the sight that met him as he turned the last bend and stepped from the stairwell.

CHAPTER SEVENTY

A vast field of stone trembled in front of him, its broad flagstones lit by flickering torches. Above it, a low roof of stone stretched in every direction. Some distance in front, the open expanse gave way to a forest of iron-banded pillars crisscrossed by narrow-vaulted arches. It was as though Reuben had stepped into the heart of a dark cathedral, a hollow place without sunlight. The torches became mere sparks in the further reaches, and beyond the narrow radius of their unsteady light lay doubled and trebled darknesses without number.

Bellegarde was waiting outside the opening, lamp in hand, a shadow in a shadowland.

'They knew they could never return to Tali-Niangara,' he said, 'so they built another city here, a city beneath the earth, where they could speak freely with their gods. There were already caves here, underground passages that had been used by Bourjolly's ancestors as wine cellars. He spent a fortune widening and expanding them, throughout the years before the revolution. Afterwards, his followers continued the work, digging, repairing, building. There are tunnels that stretch for miles. There are natural caves so huge no-one has seen them from end to end.'

Reuben shivered. Why had Bellegarde brought him here? The major sighed and looked curiously at Reuben.

'Time to go,' he said. 'Time to meet old friends.'

He set off across the stone field without waiting. Loubert pushed Reuben between the shoulder blades.

At regular intervals, they saw small huts of stone. Something in the style of their construction reminded Reuben of photographs he had seen of the façades of ancient Egyptian tombs and palaces, though much debased. They came before long to the first of the great pillars, thick piers of stone carved in intricate patterns. Here again, Reuben was reminded of Egypt: the carvings showed tall figures bearing staffs, and beneath their feet clumps of reeds and lotus flowers. Bellegarde strode on ahead, glancing to neither left nor right.

They came after that to an open space like a city square, devoid of pillars or huts. Reuben could hear sounds like a susurration of muffled voices, low and faint. He glanced round, but whichever way he looked he saw only empty space. And then he looked down.

He was standing on a circular slab, a stone slab pierced with nineteen holes the size of coins. Everywhere he looked, the floor was made up of the slabs, identical to those he had seen in Brooklyn. The sound was coming from beneath the ground, through the holes.

Bellegarde halted and looked back. He saw Reuben staring at the ground.

'That interests you, does it?' he asked. 'That sound.'

As though prompted by his voice, there was a noise very like barking. It stopped and was followed by the sound of a human voice sobbing.

'They can hear us,' Bellegarde said. 'They hear our voices and they try to answer us. Don't be afraid, Lieutenant. They can't hurt you. They are long past hurting.'

'What is it?' Reuben demanded. The sounds were growing in volume now. Every time someone spoke, it seemed to act as a cue for renewed effort on the part of whatever was kept beneath the slabs. There were dozens, hundreds of slabs, all pierced with holes. 'What is making those noises?' he cried. And a sound rose up near him that was very like a human voice, muttering what sounded almost like words.

'The pets of the gods,' said Bellegarde. 'In Tali-Niangara, the children who were sent as tribute to the gods were placed in deep pits like these. Every few days, food would be brought for them, and water. They lived full lives, though much restricted. The youngest of them forgot the world outside and grew to adulthood knowing nothing but the pits. Those who displeased the gods were brought to join them. It was harder for them: they could not forget the life they had led before. The pits were always full. When one died, another would be found to take its place.'

Reuben stood frozen to the spot with horror. The gibberings and murmurings all around him were coming from the mouths of human beings. With a shudder, he remembered the pitiful remains he and Danny had found in the pit they had opened in Brooklyn. He heard a scraping sound beneath his feet, and a scampering, and he wondered what Danny had seen in the tunnel.

They moved on quickly across the pitted floor while the chattering rose and fell around them. Bellegarde and Loubert seemed wholly unaffected by the dreadful sounds, but Reuben could bear them no longer and ran with his hands clasped over his ears.

They came to a dark tunnel, very like the passage that had led to Bourjolly's library in Brooklyn. Bellegarde entered, motioning to Reuben to follow. The tunnel wound through solid rock for about five hundred yards before ending at a heavy wooden door. Bellegarde knocked and a muffled voice from inside answered. Grasping a stout iron handle, he pushed the door open and stepped through. Reuben followed, then Loubert, who closed the door behind him.

It was as if a genie, summoned up out of a brazen lamp, had transported wholesale to Petite-Rivière Bourjolly's Brooklyn library. The same books lined the same wood-panelled walls, the same portraits stared fiercely out of identical frames, the same great globe sat in the centre of the floor, and on the floor itself the great pentacle lay waiting for the touch of a sorcerer's hand.

At a desk littered with papers, withered fingers still clutching the pages of an open book, Bourjolly sat unmoving, still clothed in the garments in which he had died.

Only one thing was different. On the wall above the desk hung a large painting. It had not been in the library in Brooklyn. The style was realistic, but modern. It showed the scene from the engraving in the book Bourjolly had been reading, the scene of the resurrection. The open graves, the corrupted bodies rising, the horror on the faces of the risen dead. The painting showed two major differences from the original: here, the dead were black, not white. And the things that licked and sucked their flesh had come up out of deep pits, pits identical to those Reuben had passed only minutes ago. On the lower edge of the frame, a title could be read: *La Nuit des Septièmes Ténèbres – The Night of the Seventh Darkness*.

'Please don't worry, Lieutenant. What you see is not an hallucination.'

The voice came from the back of the room. A figure detached

itself from a clutch of ill-formed shadows and stepped into the centre. Reuben felt the hairs on the back of his neck rise. Smith.

Reuben tensed. He felt the barrel of a gun pressed against his temple; Loubert was taking no chances. Smith reached out one hand casually and lifted a strand of Bourjolly's decayed white locks, letting the hair run through his fingers almost playfully.

'It was an achievement, don't you think, to get him all this way intact.' He dropped the lifeless hair and waved a hand at each of the walls in turn. 'All of it dismantled, packed and shipped here in a matter of days. Then reassembled in his own private chamber, as though it had been waiting for his return all these years.'

'Why have I been brought here?' Reuben demanded. 'You've got what you want. I'm no further use to you.'

Smith smiled.

'Please sit down, Lieutenant. We know one another by now, there is no need to stand on ceremony.'

Loubert took Reuben's elbow and steered him to a chair. Smith took a second chair facing him. Bellegarde and Loubert stood at a distance, watching.

Smith reached down and lifted a large leather briefcase onto his lap. From it he took two large, buff-coloured envelopes. Leaning back in the chair, he smiled again. It was not a warm smile, more a baring of teeth, like a beast of prey moving in for the kill of a lifetime.

'I understand you like photographs,' he said. 'The art of observation and distortion. Or perhaps that is the nature of all art. Science too, if we are to be honest. But photography has a particular poignancy. It allows us to hold a moment for ever. A person, a place. Like an insect caught in amber. A painting is many moments, but a photograph is truly instantaneous. That smile, that frown, that injudicious look in the eye, that declaration of love or hate.'

Smith hesitated, then drew a bundle of photographs from one of the envelopes.

'Photographs have an affinity with death,' he said. 'When we are dead, we go on living in them, smiling, frowning, looking sadly at the photographer we love or hate, at our own image in the unyielding lens.'

He held up a photograph, near enough for Reuben to see, a photograph of Sally Peale. Then, without a word, he let it flutter to the floor. He raised a second photograph. This also showed Sally, but not as Reuben remembered her: riddled with bullets, spattered with blood, a look of surprise on her unmoving face. Then a close-up. Still Smith did not speak.

Reuben watched as he took photograph after photograph from the pile, first the living, then the dead: Sutherland Cresswell, his wife and children, Emeric Jensen, Hastings Donovan and his children, everyone who had been at the meeting in Washington. Smith told Reuben the identities of those he did not recognize. Then another batch of photographs.

Danny smiling, Danny on a slab; Reuben's father in an old photograph, young, newly arrived in America, Reuben's father, unrecognizable, bloody; Reuben's mother alive, Reuben's mother dead; Rick Hammel in academic robes, Rick Hammel where Reuben had first seen him, a newly discovered murder victim; Sven Lindström in a fall of sunshine, Sven Lindström underwater as Reuben last remembered him; and, last of all, Devorah at their wedding, followed by a photograph of Devorah's grave.

Smith let the portraits fall to the floor, a cemetery of stiff, shiny paper. Reuben recollected the dismembered photographs he had found in his own apartment, the ones Angelina had ripped to shreds, his own gallery of the living and the dead.

'I hope you are watching, Lieutenant,' Smith whispered. 'This is not an art lesson. I want you to remember all these faces.'

He gathered the photographs together, straightened their edges and returned them to the envelope. He paused and smiled. From the second envelope he drew out a single photograph and laid it on Reuben's knee.

Davita sitting on a chair, staring red-eyed into the camera. Beside her sat Smith, expressionless. Reuben made to lunge for Smith, but Loubert was there as before, his gun barrel hard against Reuben's neck.

'Don't worry,' Smith said. 'She is perfectly safe. No-one has harmed her. No-one need harm her. Assuming you make the right choice, that is. Otherwise . . .' He took another photograph from the second envelope. Reuben could not at first make out what it showed. Then he realized, and his blood went cold. A square of perfect blackness, broken only by a pattern of white dots, nineteen dots arranged in concentric circles, like a constellation of tiny stars. For a long time Reuben sat and stared at the darkness in the photograph. He knew the pit had been prepared, not for him, but for Davita.

'Why?' he asked. 'Why me? Why Davita?'

Smith shrugged.

'Why not? Life does not give us many reasons. It is enough for me that you are here and that I have a use for you. If you help me, your daughter will spend the rest of her life in the sunshine. It is entirely up to you.'

'What do you want me to do?' asked Reuben. There was nothing in his voice, not even hate, not even contempt. Nothing.

'I want you to kill someone,' Smith said.

Reuben held his breath. He felt a terrible pain in his head and the beginnings of nausea. 'Who?' he asked. 'Who do I have to kill?'

'The president,' answered Forbes. 'The president of Haiti.'

CHAPTER SEVENTY-ONE

She is sitting in a shaft of sunlight. It is oblique, it falls through the tinted glass of a high window, it is warm and trembling, alive with swimming motes of dust, and it lies perfectly against her skin like vanilla-scented ice cream.

Her father used to buy her ice cream years and years and years ago. Max was seventeen when he found them, Angelina eating ice cream, desperate, trembling, eyes half-closed, her father's hand halfway up her soft yellow skirt.

They had come for her father the next day, the men in cotton uniforms, the men with guns and eyes like lead. She knew Max had told, and she thought he had told them about that, about what her father had done with her, that they had taken him away for that. But later, much later she had learned the truth. What he had really told them. And why. It was not until Rick spelled it out for her that she understood how Max had built his own career on that simple betrayal of their father. Out of rage. And outrage. And malice. And greed. And jealousy.

The sunlight was real. Oblique and tinted and very real. Max had sent her to his house, high in the hills at Kenscoff. She was waiting for him to return. She was afraid.

Jealousy. More than anything it had been jealousy. Max had wanted her for himself. Somehow she thought she had always known that, always wished a little that it might be so. Max was powerful now. He would be more powerful yet. His betrayal had borne fruit.

She held something on her lap. A golden circle, a flat disc of beaten and incised gold, carefully repaired. The tiny staples that held it together were scarcely visible. It was as if it had never been broken. She ran a finger over it, again and again, savouring its hardness, its preciousness, its power. The light danced across its surface adoringly.

Il y avait une fois . . . Once upon a time there was . . . She smiled. Once upon a time there was a city in a forest. She smiled again. The old fairy story, the one her father had told her before Max had him taken away. It was her only comfort now. The smile left her face. Something dreadful was going to happen.

Tali-Niangara was a memory, a ruin in the heart of a vast and uncharted rainforest. The bones of its kings had long ago crumbled to dust in their ivory caskets. But the symbol of their power had been resurrected from the sea bed. The gods were waiting to be reborn.

Angelina held the disc up to the light. She remembered the story of Aladdin and his wonderful lamp, the genie that could be conjured up from its depths, the magic that the merest rubbing could unleash. There was no need for magic now. Let others believe in magic, in ancient gods. With her circle of gold, she knew she could accomplish all that and more.

She looked up. The clock said half past four. Max was coming home.

CHAPTER SEVENTY-TWO

The cathedral stank. Beneath layers of crusted wax and incense, traces of an older, thicker scent lingered like rotting flesh hidden by the uncorrupted skin of some long-dead saint. The church was not ancient; its oldest sections dated only from the late-nineteenth century, but it had acquired a patina of age. Something older than its indifferent icons, older than its painted windows, older than Christianity itself, something primeval clung to its stones. High up in one of the twin towers, a lonely bell rang out, tolling for the dead, a steady, doleful note repeated into an empty sky.

Below, the diminutive figures of priests and their assistants scurried about in the transept, setting the stage for the rites to come. The open coffin was already set up on a trestle, draped in the Haitian flag, nestling in a bower of red and white flowers.

The priests had gone to General Valris that morning at the cathedral gate, asperging his remains to the chanting of *Si iniquitate* and the refrain of *De profundis*. They had preceded him into the church, while choirboys sang *Exultabunt Domine*. Reuben had watched, hidden and alone, as they set the coffin before the high altar and lit candles all around.

Doug Hooper had been buried at night in an unmarked grave. Jean Hooper had been bundled on board the first flight to leave Haiti since the lifting of the curfew. The State Department had released a statement denying Hooper's involvement in a US plot against President Cicéron and condemning the execution. No-one had paid any attention. Today's funeral was to be a set piece, the focus of the nation's grief. Or at least a proclamation of victory. The curfew had been ended, the threat of a coup was over. So it seemed.

Forty feet above the floor of the chair-filled nave, Reuben huddled against the wall of the clerestory, nursing a migraine like a sentinel against sleep. He had been there since the previous night, smuggled in through a side entrance by two of Valris's favourites. The night had passed slowly, haunted by the little, meaningless sounds of the empty church and the faint susurration of his own breath. His only companion had been a small red light burning in the sanctuary. With dawn even that had faded.

He supposed he could escape, but what would be the point? Where could he run to? If he was not there at noon to shoot President Cicéron, Smith would set his terrible machine in motion. Reuben did not for a moment doubt his ability to carry out the threat.

It had not taken Reuben long to work out what Smith and Bellegarde wanted. They had set him up along with Hooper to provide proof of a CIA plot against Cicéron. Hooper's presence in the country had been purely fortuitous, but his disagreement with Valris had played into their hands. Today, Reuben would kill the president. Within minutes, he would be found and taken, dead or alive, probably the former.

His link to the Valris assassination would be established, his connection with the CSA made public. A US plot unmasked and announced to the world press. No doubt other plotters would be discovered. And arrested. And shot. In a matter of days, Smith and Bellegarde would watch power fall into their waiting hands like a heavy, ripe mango dropping from a tree.

Reuben had already assembled and checked his weapon, an H & K PSG1 semi-automatic sniper's rifle. The assassination was to look well planned and properly equipped. The PSG1 had a free-floating barrel with adjustable stock, it had been fitted with a 6 × 42 Hensoldt Wetzler scope adjustable from 100 to 600 metres, and it rested on a well-balanced tripod attached to the gun's fore-end. The fact that he had never used one before, that he was not in any sense a trained assassin would not, of course, matter in the least. He would not shoot to miss. Smith had spelled out the consequences of such a ploy. And its pointlessness. The pit was purely for psychological impact: they could shoot Davita just as easily.

He glanced at his watch. The funeral was due to begin in fifteen minutes. Already, the first mourners had begun to trickle in. The dignitaries would arrive late, of course, the president last of all. Reuben closed his eyes against a stab of pain, then settled back against the wall.

When the time came, he would be hidden behind a high stone balcony, one of several running all along the clerestory. He had been positioned almost halfway back along the nave, giving him a good angle towards the sanctuary, at the foot of whose steps the coffin had been placed. At some point in the ceremony, the president would place flowers on the casket, then ascend the pulpit to address the congregation and the press. That would be Reuben's cue, his signal to strike.

The cathedral was filling now. Candles had been lit, incense was being wafted through the aisles, a shaft of light entered through a window in the west transept, falling with almost theatrical perfection across the bank of flowers dying about the dead general.

The first arrivals were the nobodies: civil servants, local merchants, representatives of Haiti's dwindling foreign community, friends of the family. Next came the close relatives, some sobbing, others curiously silent. And at last it was the turn of the dignitaries. First, those of minor rank: the director of the Banque Nationale, the president of the Haitian Chamber of Commerce, the chief of police, the rector of the University of Haiti, several judges, lawyers, newspaper editors.

Finally, the *crème de la crème*: two generals, the commandant of the Presidential Guard, the admiral-in-chief of Haiti's tiny navy, representatives of the remaining diplomatic corps, the papal nuncio, members of the country's leading families, cabinet ministers.

There was a pause in the procession. People took their seats. Reuben felt sweat break out on his brow. He felt sick. Sick from pain and sick from apprehension. He was not an assassin, but shoot or not he would be a cause of death today. He wanted to stand and cry out, but that would only be a signal for Davita's death.

The bishop of Port-au-Prince entered. A voice announced the arrival of the president. The congregation rose to its feet with a scuffling sound and muffled coughing. Cicéron walked slowly down the centre aisle, flanked by guards in ceremonial uniforms. He was dressed in black and wore a black velvet armband. Reuben stared through a tracery of stone, eager to see the man he had to kill.

Behind Cicéron, wearing a dress uniform that suggested a major upgrading of his rank, walked Max Bellegarde. He too wore an armband of black velvet. He was not alone. By his side walked, not his wife, not his mother, but his sister Angelina, dressed all in black, in mourning, as Reuben had first seen her.

The bell stopped in mid-swing, as though frozen. Gently, the echoes of its last note vibrated and died away into the thin air. On the streets, all traffic had been stopped since eight o'clock. Silence swooped on the capital like a bird of prey, portentous and heavy-winged.

Inside the cathedral, a tiny, tinkling bell rang out, clear and precise against a sound of suppressed sobbing. Not everyone was here for show or veneration. The priests in their funeral attire began the Requiem Mass, their faces all solemnity, wreathed in clouds of incense.

She sat in the front row beside her brother, among the generals and the diplomats. He could tell that she was uneasy. Every few moments, her head would turn, now this way, now that. Was she looking for him, did she know he was still alive? He saw Max bend and whisper in her ear. He felt ice run through his veins. What was he to do? No-one had prepared him for this.

The Mass droned on, familiar cadences in an unfamiliar tongue, the mysteries of death spread out in a mixture of French and Latin. It was not the first Requiem Mass Reuben had attended. Every year since enrolling at police college he had gone to at least two funerals of fellow officers killed in the line of duty. A high proportion were Irish, Italians, Poles. He knew the funeral Mass almost better than the Kaddish. Surprised, he realized he was crying silently, crying because he had not recited the Kaddish for his father or mother. He had no brothers, it had been his duty. And if Davita died?

He leaned back and waited, his eyes fixed on the Mass below. The voices rose and fell, the figures of the celebrants moved among incense to unworldly rhythms, like participants in someone else's dream. Black faces, black hands, black voices, trapped in the gestures of a foreign creed. There should have been dancing, Reuben thought, there should have been drums. God should not be so remote, his son so ethereal, their visitations so parsimonious and so trite.

But at last there was an end. The bishop completed the rites of the *Absolutio*, the celebrants dispersed. A hush fell on the cathedral, an expectancy. At the altar, physically unaltered, Valris's body lay inert in its flower-heavy coffin, a mute testimony to the harshness of the world outside.

Reuben saw Cicéron stand and make his way alone to the altar steps. The president seemed tired, a small, unloved man with sad eyes. He faced the congregation silently for what seemed a long time. Someone coughed. Someone else cleared his throat. Cicéron began to speak, simple words in Creole, a eulogy for a man he had not loved. Reuben could not understand a word. It made no difference.

Reuben aimed for Cicéron's head, a millimetre above the nose. He was at an angle, but it hardly mattered: at this range one good shot would be fatal. It was easy to do. He thought of Danny, of his own father, of his mother, of Devorah, of all his dead and nearly dead. He thought of Davita. He thought of a dark pit. Softly, he closed his eyes and muttered the first words of the Kaddish, 'May His great name be magnified and hallowed in the world which He created according to His will.' He opened his eyes and aimed again. What was Cicéron to him? He put the rifle down. It was impossible. He was not a killer.

A second later, a loud shot rang out.

CHAPTER SEVENTY-THREE

The shot was followed by a silence so complete, so intense it was as though the world had been stopped dead in its tracks. Then pandemonium broke out, stifled at first, rapidly growing in volume and inarticulateness. Reuben looked down into the body of the cathedral. Cicéron was down, sprawled across the steps like a broken doll. He did not move. No-one went near him. Reuben had no doubt he was dead.

The president had been accompanied to the church by a circle of bodyguards. Everywhere, men in soft suits and uniforms were brandishing guns, their eyes roving the crowd, looking everywhere for the source of the killing shot.

The shot had come from the clerestory opposite. Reuben stood and looked across. The assassin was plainly visible, a dark face behind a gleam of burnished metal. Loubert. He lowered the rifle, turned and gazed across the empty space at Reuben. Their eyes met. Loubert raised his rifle and aimed at Reuben. He pulled the trigger. Nothing happened. His gun had jammed.

Reuben did not hesitate. He picked up his rifle and put it to his shoulder. Without aiming, without deliberating, he fired, three quick shots, iron among stone. One hit the opposite balcony, the others took their mark. Loubert lurched away from the edge, dropping his rifle into space. It fell to the nave with a clatter.

By now, most of the congregation had tumbled out into the street, leaving the president's bodyguard and several dignitaries huddled together in the transept. Some of the security men were trying to hustle the remaining dignitaries away from what was obviously the target area. There was a clatter of feet on the stone stairs leading to the clerestory on both sides of the nave. Reuben threw his rifle away and stood up. He put his hands on his head. They might not shoot if they thought him harmless.

Max appeared at the top of the steps alone, unarmed. He had known what to expect.

'It's all right, Lieutenant,' Max said. 'You'll be safe with me.'

Reuben stepped out of the shadows. He could smell incense. The sound of shooting still echoed in his ears.

'What's happening?' he asked. 'You're all too quick for me. You move from one death to the next like children sampling sweets.'

'I'm president now,' Max said. 'I'm in control. You're safe with me. Come downstairs. Angelina's waiting for you.'

'Is she all right?'

Max glanced at him curiously.

'Why shouldn't she be? Angelina has always been all right with me.' Reuben wondered what he meant.

They went down, Max leading the way, Reuben's abandoned rifle in one hand, Reuben following like a lamb. He had begun to understand. The stairs led down to the transept. Light fell at his feet, thick, like syrup. Ahead of him, the coffin stood like a misplaced carnival float, grotesque and redundant.

The crowd had thinned. Down the steps leading to the opposite clerestory, two security officers were manhandling the body of the president's killer. A third man carried his rifle. He brought the rifle to Max, who exchanged it for the one he had taken from Reuben.

Angelina was standing near the president's body. Correction, the ex-president's body. Max was president now.

Beside Angelina stood a tall man dressed in a sober three-piece suit. Smith. Or Warren Forbes. His name scarcely mattered. Smith's hair was carefully brushed and he wore a tiny silver ring on the forefinger of his right hand.

'Why, Angelina?' Reuben asked.

She said nothing. She seemed as though in a state of shock. Or indifference. There was something in her hand. A large disc, a disc of gold. It seemed both familiar and unfamiliar.

Angelina stepped towards Max. She held out the circle, the ancient token of the kings of Tali-Niangara. With this, Max would be more than a mere president. He would found a dynasty. He took it from her and held it up to the light. The metal glistened, gold more ancient than the pomp of Christ. He looked round the cathedral, like a conqueror in a foreign temple.

'It belongs to Max,' she said. 'One of the priests who came to Haiti on the *Hallifax* was the son of the king. He was our ancestor.

Max is the ruler by right. The king has returned. Tonight is the Night of the Seventh Darkness.'

And all at once Reuben knew who had painted the canvas he had seen in the small room beneath Petite-Rivière. 'Back in Haiti, I painted every day.' What else had she painted?

Angelina smiled a soft smile, unlike any Reuben had ever seen her smile before. *When I am king, dilly dilly, you shall be queen* . . . Then, quite without awkwardness, she turned and transferred the smile to Reuben. He regarded her impassively. He had loved her, he still wanted her. Max was her brother, he couldn't be jealous of her brother.

She came to him, poised, silent, smiling. Came to him and put her arms round him, hard, pressing her body to his, her lips to his cheek.

'Quickly,' she whispered. 'In the pocket of my jacket. The left pocket. Hurry!'

He stroked her back, then brought his hand round to the pocket of the light coat she wore over her mourning dress. She held him tighter. His hand fastened round the handle of a small pistol.

'Hurry, Reuben.' Her breath was hot against his ear, her tone urgent.

He looked over her shoulder. Smith was standing only yards away, watching, suspecting nothing. Reuben pulled the gun from Angelina's pocket, raised it and fired twice. Both bullets struck the tall man in the chest. He howled with unexpected pain. Reuben thought of his father and fired twice again. She held him while he fired, held him tight against her. Smith stumbled, his shirt stained with blood. Reuben remembered his mother and fired once more. No-one tried to interfere. No-one came for him. Smith pitched forward, his bloody chest in tatters. On the floor, he cried out with rage. He crawled forward. Reuben fired again, aiming at his head. The bullet struck the nape of his neck. Angelina held him, whispering, 'Enough, Reuben, enough.'

He tasted nothing. No sweetness. No honey. All a deception, then: revenge was nothing. She took the gun from him. It was a small automatic. It had been fully loaded with seven bullets. He had fired six. She held him and kissed him hard on the lips, then pulled away again.

She put the gun to his head.

'I love you, Reuben,' she said. 'More than my father, more than Max. You understand, don't you?'

'No,' he said. He said it to everyone, but most of all to her, most of all to Danny, most of all to his parents, most of all to himself. 'No,' he said. It was all he had left to say.

She bent forward again and kissed him very hard, the hardest kiss in all the world. As she did so, she squeezed the trigger. It was harder than the kiss. Her eyes were open. Wide open and utterly, utterly blank.